BOARD STIFF

BOARD STIFF

XANTH NOVEL #38

BY

PIERS ANTHONY

BOARD STIFF
Copyright © 2013 Piers Anthony

Print ISBN: 978-1-62467-085-5
eISBN: 978-1-62467-086-2

Published by Premier Digital Publishing
www.premierdigitalpublishing.com
Follow us on Twitter @PDigitalPub
Follow us on Facebook: Premier Digital Publishing

CONTENTS

CHAPTER 1:
BOARD

She looked at her reflection in the water of the shallow well. Luxuriant midnight black hair to her breathtakingly slender waist, matching dark eyes in a lovely face. A torso coming yea-close to absolute perfection. She was man's desire. That was part of the problem.

Well, on with it. "Oh, Wishing Well, they say you will grant any wish, provided you like the offering given for it. But that if you don't like the offering, you may still grant the wish, but not in a way the wisher wants. So the wisher is sorry she ever bothered you. So it's a gamble, because no one really knows what you like."

She paused, but of course there was no answer. The surface of the water remained mirror-smooth. But it did seem to be listening.

"They also say that the correct way to approach you is to introduce yourself, explain your situation, make your wish, and then drop the offering into the water. That the wish will be granted instantly, and that's it; if you don't like the way it is done, you're still stuck with it. You don't do un-wishes."

There was a faint ripple. Was that interest?

"I was named Irrelevant Kandy, because—well, I don't exactly know why. But I think I was named in part after the irrelephant, which is a large white or pink animal with a very long nose that is incapable of making any difference no matter how hard it tries. My name is a curse, because everyone ignored me, thinking I was irrelevant, when I'm actually a very pretty girl, as you can see. So I tried going by my initial instead. That made me I Kandy. Then everyone looked at me. In fact they looked too much; their eyes wandered to places that, well, made me blush. Wherever I go, now, those Wandering Eyes pursue me. I almost feel them peering down inside my halter and up under my skirt, trying to pull off my clothing. They don't care about me at all, just how I look, or how certain parts of me look, and their cynosure makes me feel dirty there. This is no good either."

She paused again. Now there was a stronger ripple, almost in the shape of an eye. The well was definitely looking. She hoped it was orienting on her face.

"So I'm caught between two extremes: irrelevance, or getting eyed. Maybe that's my talent; I'm not aware of any other. This ruins my social life. I'm actually a smart girl who would make any man an excellent wife. But no man sees that. No man is interested in my mind or personality, just my whatevers. So here is my wish: I'm board stiff. I want Adventure, Excitement, and Romance."

Now the ripples made her reflection shimmer. She definitely had the wishing well's attention.

"I searched all over for a suitable offering," she continued. "It occurred to me that how *you* look is governed by the sand on your bottom. It is frankly sort of dull. So I found a pretty colored stone that should add interest. Here it is: my offering, and I hope you like it."

She brought out the stone, which was like a faceted blue diamond, sparkling all over. She dropped it into the well.

Something happened. A sudden whirlwind surrounded her, lifting her up and ripping off her clothing. She was changing, somehow. Then she fell flat on the ground.

Literally. She had been transformed into a flat, stiff board with two knotholes for eyes.

Belatedly she realized her mistake: she had said she was "board stiff" when she meant "bored stiff." It was a mental typo, done in the tension of the moment. The well evidently had not appreciated her offering, and had punished her by making her bored a punnishly literal board.

She was doomed. She tried to cry, but all that happened was a small oozing of sap from her knot eyes.

She wasn't sure how long she lay there, feeling justifiably sorry for herself. Never in her wildest dreams had she anticipated becoming a stiff board. It was not the slightest bit feminine. What was to become of her? Would someone gather her for firewood? Oh, the horror!

Then another person approached the wishing well. Kandy's knot-eyes extended to either side of the board, and she could see very well despite lying flat on the ground. She could also hear the footfalls despite having no ears she knew of. It was a handsome young man with short curly blond hair, a bit of a blond beard, and a muscular body. Exactly the kind she might have liked to flirt with, assuming his eyes stayed in his face.

The man's foot just missed stepping on her. *Watch it!* she thought. *If you were a woman I'd see right up under your dress to your panties and you'd never live it down.* But of course he wasn't a woman, and his jeans showed nothing; her attempt at sarcastic humor fell flat as the board she was. It was probably just as well that she was unable to utter it.

He came to stand by the well, gazing down into the water. "Hi there," he said, and paused as if expecting a reply. When there was none, he continued. "My name is Ease, because it is my talent to make hard things easy. I can do just about any simple thing without much sweat. That's the problem: I crave a challenge that will give me personal satisfaction, and I haven't found it. I even went to the Good Magician to find a challenge, but he had no answer for me, and I never paid with any service. But I know better than to wish for that outright; I need to be more specific, or you'll give me something that's technically correct but actually messes me up. Such as changing my talent to the ability to absorb magic from something, then play it back, or emulating animalistic ability so I could fight like an animal, or the talent of always taking the shortest distance between two points; I'd just foul those up. So I have thought of three things that might help, any one of which might bring me satisfaction: the perfect weapon, the perfect adventure, the perfect woman. Give me one of those, your choice, and I'll use it to get satisfaction."

Now that was interesting. Recognizing his own limitations, he was letting the well decide which wish to grant, while offering it fairly general directions. Maybe there was a bit of originality in him. She liked that.

"Actually they don't even have to be perfect," he continued. "I'd settle for just about any pretty girl who liked me and would support me loyally, or any adventure that was exciting and interesting, or even a cutless or cutmore, you know, a sword that cuts women less or others more."

He paused, probably contemplating the ripples on the water in the well. "What I have to offer is a lesser thing, but maybe you'll like it. It's this old worn-out dagger my grandpa gave me. The blade's dull, the handle's falling

3

apart; if it got used in a fight it would lose. But here's the thing: Grandpa's spirit infuses it. He had a lot of experience, back when the world was young. He can't talk to me now, but maybe he could talk to you, if you read his mind. He must have a hundred great old stories he could tell you so you wouldn't be bored. That's really my offering: entertainment. Here's the knife." He set the old dagger on the surface of the water and let it go.

That, too, was interesting. He was offering something for the well's intellectual side, rather than its physical side. She liked that too.

Nothing happened. After a while Ease sighed. "Don't like it, eh? I'm sorry. I thought you would. I'll take it back." He reached into the water. "Oops, you're deeper than you look. I can't reach it. Well, I'll leave it. Thanks for nothing."

She sympathized with his frustration. The well had accepted his gift without granting his wish. That was too bad, because it really was a thoughtful gift.

He turned away from the well. Then he saw the board. "What's this?" He bent down to pick it up, grasping Kandy about her ankles. "A board. Good hard wood, nice heft. Must've fallen off a wagon. Might make a halfway decent club." He swung her experimentally, so that the air swished by her face. "Okay, I'll take it; might as well leave here with something."

He wanted to use her as a club? Kandy was outraged. *Why don't you club your own fat head, yokel?"* she demanded silently.

Ease walked on, talking to himself. "I really thought the stupid well would grant my wish. I even made it easy, with the three choices. But all I got was this dumb board."

Kandy was outraged anew. *Dumb board?! I'm a transformed woman, you idiot! As far as you're concerned, the perfect woman: in your grasp and completely silent.* But her joke wasn't funny, even to her.

Then she suffered a blinding revelation. She *was* his perfect woman! The well had taken his dagger and given him her. But he didn't know it. Wasn't that just like a man!

Then she suffered a follow-up thought. If the well had granted Ease's wish in such a way that the man didn't know it, what about Kandy herself? She had asked for Adventure, Excitement, and Romance. Was she about to get it, while in the form of a board? What irony!

Yet this was one way she could be involved in things without those dread Wandering Eyes constantly goosing her. So maybe there just might be the hint of a suggestion of a reason for her present state. She could get to know Ease pretty well by being his club, without him being distracted by her appearance. It was possibly the only way she could associate closely with him or any man without being eye candy.

Except for one thing, one humongously huge thing: she was a board. Even if he realized her true nature, what good would it do him, or her? A man couldn't love a board.

Dispirited, she drifted off to sleep. What else was there to do?

She woke when it was evening. Ease was using her to whack down some dry grass to make a bed. He must have walked, and eaten and located a place to sleep in the field. Why hadn't he simply gone home?

Irritated by this minor mystery, she tried something pointless: she threw her thought at him. *WHY?*

"Because they'd laugh at me back home," he answered. "I said I was going off to seek the perfect weapon, adventure, or woman, and they said well, return when you succeed, knowing that any such thing was well beyond my talent of making things easy. If I return with nothing but this stupid board, they'll laugh their rear ends off."

Kandy was amazed. He had heard her! And responded. But he didn't know it was her, or even that it was the board. He must have thought it was his own rhetorical question. Still, that was progress. Could she tell him her nature? She was dubious. Even if she got through to him, and he realized that she was a woman, what then? He still couldn't *do* anything with her, other than use her to club things, which wasn't very romantic. It would be an exercise in frustration for both of them. She had to throw off the transformation spell before identifying herself.

Still, she was curious, so she tried again. *WHAT NOW?*

"I have no idea," Ease said. "If the Good Magician couldn't help me, and the Wishing Well couldn't help me, maybe I'm helpless."

Kandy was not satisfied with that. *TRY THE GOOD MAGICIAN AGAIN.*

"Why should I do that?"

WITH A DIFFERENT QUESTION.

Ease paused, considering. "I think I'm getting smarter. If at first I don't succeed, try try again. Or whatever."

Good enough. *SO DO IT.*

"Now I shall hie me off to see the Good Magician, first thing in the morning," he decided. "I know he charges a year's service or equivalent for an Answer, but since the wishing well failed me, what else is there? So I'll just go ask him how I can achieve personal satisfaction, and that will be that. If he fails me again, I've lost nothing."

Kandy doubted it. She knew about Good Magician Humfrey, the century-old-and-not-counting Magician of Information, notorious for his terminal grumpiness. Truth be told, he wasn't much better than the wishing well for giving satisfactory Answers. There was no telling what Ease would find himself involved in. But as he said, what else was there?

Ease completed his nest making, which because of his talent had been an easy chore, and lay down in his clothing, holding the board firmly in one hand. She knew why: if a hungry monster came during the night, Ease wanted to be able to bash it on the snout without having to cast about for his weapon.

The man closed his eyes, and in two and a half moments was asleep.

And Kandy reverted to woman form. There she was, nude, with the man's hand clamped on her left ankle. The spell was gone!

"Oh!" she exclaimed, gratified.

The sound woke Ease. But as his eyes opened, Kandy was the board.

Seeing nothing, Ease shut his eyes again and reverted to sleep. And Kandy womanformed again.

Now she worked it out: the spell abated only while she was in contact with a sleeping person. When by herself she had been a board, and with Ease awake ditto. When he slept, holding her, she was herself. What torture!

Or was it? He could not grope her or mistreat her or even look at her bare form while asleep. She was safe from the things she had detested. She had wanted a man to get to know her other qualities before orienting on her body. She just hadn't figured it would happen while she was a board bashing monsters on the snout.

She explored her situation. Because he held her ankle, she was extended halfway over his head. In fact had she remained a woman when he woke, he would have been staring into her pantyless whatever. That would not do.

She folded over to put one hand on his hand at her ankle. She could lift it away, and slide down so that they were face to face. But she would have to make sure they never lost contact.

She drew his hand slowly off her ankle, then held it in hers while she slid down. Now where was she to put it? On her slender leg? On her full thigh? On her plush bottom? Her soft chest? None of these would do. Finally she put it on her back, as if he were dancing with her. That was about the only safe place.

Now what? She was lying next to him, facing him. In fact their faces were close together. Suppose they were to kiss?

Why not? She slowly put her lips to his mouth and kissed him. His breath caught and his hand on her back stiffened, but then he relaxed. She had not awakened him, fortunately.

But that seemed to be the limit. She could touch him, she could kiss him, but anything further might wake him, and then she'd be a board again.

Kandy made a small sigh of frustration. The kiss had been fun; she could get to like Ease if she tried. Then she got an idea as a bulb flashed over her head. She would talk to him.

"Hello, Ease," she murmured. "I am Kandy, your dream woman. I came to the wishing well to make a wish, but got transformed into a board instead. I hope you aren't bored with me, hee-hee. Maybe someday I will be able to join you in my natural form and fulfill your wildest dreams. Meanwhile I will be your weapon."

But what was the point? He was asleep. This was dull. So she closed her eyes and tried to sleep herself. And failed; it seemed that while he slept, she could not. Maybe it was something about the spell, that allowed her to sleep only when she was in board form. She had to be board, or bored.

So she lay awake, irritated by the situation. Why hadn't the well had the courtesy to let her sleep while reverted?

Then she heard something. It was a faint rustling, as of a mouse in the grass. It came closer. Then she heard another sound, as of something breathing. A serpent! Slithering toward its prey.

"Ease!" she said. "Wake!"

But this time her voice did not awaken him. He was too soundly asleep. Bleep!

So she bit him on the ear.

"Ow!" he exclaimed, waking.

Kandy was the board again, with his hand on her middle. She could say nothing.

Then Ease heard the breathing. He leaped up, sliding his hand down to her ankle. Good thing she was not flesh while he did that!

The serpent came into sight in the moonlight. It was enormous, big enough to swallow a man. Ease reacted immediately. He swung the board at the snake's snout, just as the head shot forward, fangs bared.

Kandy realized that the board was going to miss the snout and strike the neck. That was no good; the serpent would slither on by and bite the man's arm. She reacted before she even worked it out mentally, adjusting her course so that she was on target. She smacked into the snout with a satisfying impact.

Surprised, the serpent whipped back. Then, seeing its prey on guard and effectively armed, it slithered rapidly away.

"Good thing I happened to wake in time," Ease said. "I forgot I wasn't on an enchanted path. If it hadn't been for that itch in my ear, it would have had me."

He didn't know. Yet how else could it be? He would never believe that a board had nipped his ear.

Still, now she understood why she had to be awake. To keep watch when he was not alert. It did make sense. She had to be satisfied with that.

In due course Ease settled down again. He slept and she womaned. She moved his hand to her back, kissed him, and settled down to listen for the rest of the night. This was not the relationship she would have chosen, but it would do for now.

In the morning Ease woke and went about his morning routine. Kandy was embarrassed to see him catching up on natural functions, but chided herself for her attitude. How else could he survive, without taking care of his body? She herself seemed to have no natural functions while under the spell; she merely existed, like a nymph. There might be some catching up to do at such time as the spell concluded.

Meanwhile she was concluding that she definitely liked Ease. He was a typical somewhat ignorant man, but he did have some manly virtues, like courage. He had not hesitated to bash the serpent. So if she was his perfect woman, he just might be her acceptable man.

Then Ease set out for the Good Magician's Castle. That was another thing: he had taken her advice. Of course he didn't know it wasn't his own thought, but still, she liked this aspect of their relationship. He found an enchanted path and followed it, whistling. There was a network of enchanted paths leading to the important destinations. Travelers on them were safe from molestation by monsters, and shelters were provided. Kandy had on occasion walked an enchanted path herself, appreciating the safety it offered.

At noon Ease came to such a shelter. There was a neat cabin, a pond, and a grove of trees growing shoes, clothes, pillows, and food.

There were also other travelers. A red-haired girl arrived from the opposite direction as Ease approached the cabin. "Hello, handsome human," she said brightly.

Kandy suffered a spot siege of pointless jealousy. She did not want Ease associating with amenable young women.

"Hello, pretty girl," he answered. "I am Ease, with a talent of making things easy, on my way to see the Good Magician to find a challenge."

"I am Cherry Centaur."

Ease paused. "You don't look like a centaur."

She laughed. "I am in human form at the moment. It's more convenient when traveling among humans."

"You can change back and forth?"

"Not exactly."

"Am I missing something?"

"Something," she agreed. "My complete form is a centaur. But I can separate into my components: a red-haired girl, and a red mare. Sometimes we prefer to have some alone time. She's more mature than I am, at age fifteen, because mares grow faster than girls. So I go among humans and she ranges the wilderness, running with horses." She paused, blushing delicately. "I'm not sure what she does with stallions, but she seems to like it."

"I can tell you," Ease said. "She—"

STOP! Kandy thought, interrupting him. *SHE'S UNDERAGE*.

Oops, the dread Adult Conspiracy that relentlessly bound all adults to keep interesting things from children. He had to change course without alarming her. "...probably races them, something she can't do with you, because you're too slow."

"That must be it," Cherry agreed. "She does like to run. Sometimes I ride on her back, before we merge."

"I'm tired," Ease said. "I think I'll take a nap before moving on."

"Maybe I will too," Cherry said. "There's room for two on the bed."

"Oh. All right."

UNDERAGE. He was a man and she was a pretty girl; he needed reminding. The fact that Kandy was jealous was irrelevant, wasn't it?

"Of course," he muttered subvocally, not completely pleased by what he thought was his conscience. He lay down and closed his eyes.

Cherry lay down beside him. After a moment she spoke softly. "But if you should happen to want to—"

This time Kandy directed the thought to her. *WHAT PART OF UNDERAGE DO YOU NOT UNDERSTAND?*

"Oh, fudge, I'm developing a conscience," Cherry muttered. "Just when I thought I might find out what the Adult Conspiracy is all about."

So she was not entirely innocent, at least in intention. Kandy knew girls could be like that, because she herself had chafed at the Conspiracy, before she got there and came to understand its rationale. Sometimes children needed to be protected from their innocence, lest they get into more trouble than they knew. But they didn't like hearing that from adults.

Ease slept. Kandy transformed. She made her maneuver to get his hand on her bare back instead of her ankle. Then she realized that for the first time it was happening in the presence of another person. She could talk to Cherry, tell her about the spell. Then when Ease woke, Cherry could tell him. Then he would know. "Cherry!" she said.

The girl was still awake, but not paying attention. She was staring at the ceiling, still frustrated by her conscience.

"Cherry Centaur," Kandy repeated.

Still no response.

Annoyed, Kandy projected a thought. **HERE.**

Startled, the girl looked at Ease. "Funny. I thought someone spoke to me. But there's only him asleep holding that stupid board."

Kandy realized with a feeling verging on horror that the girl could not see or hear her. She saw only the board.

Then she remembered that she had already concluded that it was better that Ease not know, because she would still be a board, unable to do anything with him. In her excitement she had forgotten that. She needed to break the spell before she told him about it. Now she knew that the spell protected her from accidental exposure, in much the manner the Adult Conspiracy protected children from dealing with storks prematurely.

At least she had discovered that she could project her thoughts to others too, even if those others did not realize the source of those thoughts. That could be useful, limited as it was.

There was the sound of hooves pounding the ground. Cherry sat up. "That's Red!"

Ease woke. "Who?"

Kandy was the board again, as it seemed she had always been, in appearance.

"Red. My better half. She must be tired of running alone and is coming to merge."

"Merge," he agreed, as if thinking of something else.

Cherry got to her feet. "I must go to her." She walked out of the cabin, removing her clothing as she went.

Ease followed, carrying the board. He was evidently curious about the girl and the mare. So was Kandy.

There was a fine red horse. The color suffused every part of her: head, mane, tail, hooves, and hide. She was a fine looking animal.

"I missed you, Red," Cherry said, running to hug the horse. Only it wasn't exactly a hug; the two overlapped, sinking into each other. In a moment they were a single red-maned red-haired centaur. Her body was that of the mare, her upper torso and head that of the girl. She was bare-breasted, as all centaurs were. They had different conventions about clothing.

The centaur turned to Ease. "Thank you for sparing my innocent half," she said. "She sometimes gets impulsive." Her face was similar, but her manner quite different, so that she hardly seemed the same.

"I understand," Ease said, stooping to pick up the girl's shed clothing. He handed it to the centaur, who packed it away in a saddlebag that seemed to appear from nowhere. "I have a dream girl of my own. She keeps me in line."

Oh? He was aware of Kandy after all?

"Dream girl?" the centaur inquired politely.

"She comes only when I'm sleeping. Maybe she's a forest nymph, or a demoness. She warned me that Cherry was underage."

He had been awake when Kandy did that. Maybe he misremembered.

"She is," the centaur agreed. "For a human."

Did the centaur know how to summon storks? Kandy had heard that centaurs didn't use storks, but had some other mechanism, cutting out the middleman as it were. Regardless, it seemed that Cherry had not retained any such knowledge. She had truly been innocent, and now Ease was getting the credit for leaving her that way.

"Farewell." The centaur turned and galloped away, her red tresses flying behind her. She was a beautiful creature in every part.

"That was an interesting experience," Ease said to himself. "Too bad I didn't meet an of-age girl."

Kandy suffered another instant siege of jealousy. She had been with him throughout, and she was of age. Bleep that spell!

"Let's see what there is to eat, before I move on." He walked to the nearest pie tree, but all it had at the moment was pot pies and the pots weren't ripe enough to be edible. He went to the pond and saw a round gray object growing underwater. "A navel orange!" he exclaimed, pleased. He reached down and brought it out. "The merfolk won't mind if I eat one of these." He brought it to his face and tried to take a bite, but its hide was metallic; he couldn't get his teeth into it. "Bleep!"

I CAN HANDLE THAT, Kandy thought.

"Maybe if I bash it with my board," he said.

He set the fruit on a stump, then whammed it with the board. Kandy saw the key seam and oriented to score exactly on it. This had to be done just right, or the fruit would be squashed instead of opened. She scored; the fruit split apart, revealing several ship-shaped orange sections. Now it was edible.

Ease popped a wedge into his mouth. It was soft and juicy. "I'm glad I thought of doing this."

I thought of it, you numskull," Kandy thought. But what was the use?

He finished the orange. "I'm still hungry."

Well, he was a healthy young man. But there just didn't seem to be any other food at the moment.

"I smell something," he said. "Tarts!"

Kandy looked. There at the edge of the forest was a girl with a raised bed. Smoke was rising from it. It was a fire bed, probably left behind by a fireman and still smoldering. She was baking something on it. Tarts. Indeed, she looked like a tart, with a dress that was cut too low above and too high below, so that too much of her overstuffed body showed.

"That's for me," Ease said.

The stupid man! The tart was off the enchanted path, which meant she was probably not what she seemed, bad as that was. *Don't go there.*

But she had forgotten to put it into **bold** CAPPED *italics*, and he didn't hear. He was already forging off the path, lured by the display.

"Well, honey, what can I do for you?" the tart inquired, smiling with too many teeth.

"I'm hungry! How about some tarts?"

"Well of course!" She lifted a steaming tart from the hotbed and handed it to him. "Here is a really sweet one. A sweet tart."

Don't eat that! But again she forgot to enhance her thought.

"Sweetheart," Ease agreed amiably. He took the tart and bit into it. "Oh, say! I want to kiss you!"

Now Kandy got a good whiff of the tart. She recognized the smell.

SPIT IT OUT!! IT'S SPIKED WITH LOVE POTION!

This time he heard her. He spat out the biteful.

But the woman tart was already in motion. She was leaping forward, her fangs coming into sight. She was a troll!

SWING THE BAT!

Ease swung, somewhat clumsily. That was all right; Kandy guided it to the proper target. ***WHAM!!*** It connected with the tart's bottom with a foul-smelling smack, knocking some of her flesh out of the top of the dress on the other side. It wasn't nearly as appealing when thus exposed. She stumbled, missing Ease's face, which she had been about to bite off. Her teeth clacked together empty, showering sparks.

Ease, not being entirely dull, dodged around the troll and ran back to the enchanted path and safety. "I'm sure glad I caught on in time!"

He had caught on? What was the use?

The troll, realizing that the prey had slipped the net, retrenched. She tucked her flesh back into her dress and folded her fangs out of sight. "But you didn't finish your tart, honey!" she called.

Ease opened his mouth. He wanted to argue with the troll? There was nothing to be gained by that, as she was probably smarter than he was. He would also need a bully-proof vest that would bounce things back on the perpetrator to withstand her attacks. *DON'T ANSWER! JUST WALK AWAY.*

"I guess that's best," he agreed. "Don't stoop to her level. Depart with dignity." He started walking.

"Go bleep yourself!" the troll screamed after him. "You'd never have escaped if it wasn't for that bleeping enchanted board! But you probably wouldn't have tasted very good anyway."

"Enchanted board?" Ease lifted the board to look at it. "Maybe that explains some things. When I swing with this, I always connect. I never was much with a weapon before. When I wished for the perfect weapon I was thinking of maybe a magic sword that always scored, making me expert. But you know, with this board, I get the job done. I found it right there at the wishing well. So maybe I did get my wish. This is the perfect club."

That wasn't the half of it, but Kandy decided to be gratified that at least he was now giving her some credit.

"And I wished for the perfect woman," he continued. "And you know, maybe that's who comes to me in my sleep. My dream girl. Maybe the well gave me another wish, just not the way I expected it."

His perfect woman. She was certainly that. So he was two for two. Would he make the connection between the two?

"So I guess all I need now is the perfect adventure," he concluded.

So much for that. Yet if the well had granted two of Ease's wishes and maybe was working on the third, what about hers? She had wished for Adventure, Excitement, and Romance. As a Board she was certainly in a sort of adventure, and there was some excitement as she saved Ease from his follies, and a weird kind of romance as she lay with him at night, unable to do anything that amounted to anything. So maybe it was happening, but as yet was incomplete. Maybe it would become whole once all the parts of it were accomplished.

Maybe Ease's wish and her own were linked, and had to be fulfilled together. So all she had to do was see that he did what he was supposed to do. Encourage him, goose him when he hesitated, correct him when he went wrong, bail him out when she had to. It was a role she was already playing. A role any women played with any man, could the men but know it.

So be it, for whatever it was worth. He wanted adventure?

GO FOR IT.

"I think I'll go for it," Ease decided. "Onward to the Good Magician's Castle."

Just so. Kandy went to sleep.

CHAPTER 2:
CHALLENGE

When she woke, Ease was standing before the Good Magician's castle. He must have made good time, because it was still mid-afternoon. It was picturesque, with tall turrets surrounded by a moat, surrounded in turn by assorted terrain. There was a winding path leading to the drawbridge across the moat.

"I don't know," he muttered. "This looks complicated. I know a person's natural magic doesn't work at the Good Magician's Castle, so it won't be easy. It wasn't before. I'm not used to that. Maybe it was a bad idea to come here."

For pity's sake! *GET YOUR DONKEY IN GEAR!* she thought imperatively. *MOVE!*

Ease stepped forward, thinking he had been prompted by his own impulse. His donkey was in gear.

Immediately he was at the foot of a small hill. There was a sign saying BOOT HILL. It was hardly necessary, because the hill was populated by walking boots. Not by people, just boots. Kandy realized that the original wearers of the boots must be buried in the hill. She had heard that legendary gunfighters of Mundania favored such a place, maybe because it facilitated some expression of their restless spirits.

The path led over the hill, so Ease stepped smartly out. And was immediately blocked by a tall pair of black boots. He stepped to one side, but the boots stepped with him. He stepped the other way, and so did they.

"Bleep!" he muttered. There were no children present, so he could have spoken an adult word, but the convention started to protect children had insidiously expanded until now it covered many adults as well, limiting their expressions. It occurred to Kandy that there might be a power motive there, as some folk tried to make other folk conform to their personal tastes. Where would it end? But that was incidental at the moment. This was obviously a Challenge, and Ease had to figure it out and get through it.

He did no such thing. "Get out of my way, leather-for-brains. I got business beyond." He strode forward. Evidently diplomacy was not his forte.

The boots did not yield. In fact one of them kicked Ease in the shin.

"Ow!" he yelled. Then, bridling, he drew his Board. "Try that again! I dare you!"

Kandy realized she was not fated to avoid this Challenge. She would have to get Ease though it, one way or another, despite his blunders.

The boot tried it again. This time the Board intercepted the one doing the kicking and knocked it for a loop. The loop was formed by its flying laces as it fell on its back, its tongue lolling.

But in half a moment the boot was back on its foot, as it were. It looked annoyed. It stomped the ground angrily, then came at Ease again. It lifted high, drew back, and started swinging forward in a roundhouse kick, its laces forming the outline of a round house.

Ease swung the Board. Kandy scored on the boot, this time knocking it up so that its inner lining dropped out like a baby boot. But meanwhile the other boot scored, catching Ease on the rear and boosting him off the hill. There might not be people wearing those boots, but they had good power.

Ease got up, rubbing his sore rear. "Why you bleeping waste of shoe polish!" he swore. "I'm going to pulverize you!"

But Kandy saw that other boots had gathered, and there was now a solid wall of them across the path. It would be impossible to clear them all out of the way without getting kicked into oblivion. This Challenge required some thought, and it was clear that Ease, being masculine, was not up to it.

How could they deal with these obnoxious boots? The people in them could not be reasoned with or clubbed into submission, because there were no people. They were empty headed, in fact headless.

Empty. That gave her a notion.

PUT YOUR FEET IN, she thought.

As usual he thought it was his own idea, and acted on it without question.

He lurched ahead, caught a boot by the laces, and thrust his foot in. He didn't even need to remove his shoe; the boot fit over it. Now his right foot was booted.

The boot struggled. It tried to jump away, but that only made the man's leg wobble. He pressed his foot down hard on the ground, pinning down the boot, and in about a moment and a third it gave up the struggle. It was captive.

GET THE OTHER!

Oh. Ease grabbed for the matching boot, but it jumped away. He pursued it. The other boots came at him, making ready to kick his butt. But he had the Board in his hand, and Kandy swung around pretty much on her own volition and knocked the other boots away.

It was a fair chase, but Ease could run faster with one boot and one shoe than the other boot could hop. He caught it and jammed his foot inside. The boot struggled only briefly before yielding. It was after all footwear, and could not deny its nature. Yet Kandy, perversely, wondered if it was like a woman being ravished. How did boots feel about having smelly feet thrust into them?

Fully booted, Ease stood. Now the other boots ignored him; he was two of them. He strode on over the hill and down the other side. As he went the boots faded; it seemed they could not leave Boot Hill. But he had passed the first Challenge.

Only to encounter a snow-white slope guarded by a huge white bear. By two white bears. They stood as if conjoined at the hip, blocking the way.

Ease raised the Board. The bears raised their big front paws. They could knock the Board out of the way before it could knock them. That was no good.

PAUSE. THINK.

Ease paused and thought. It wasn't that Kandy thought he would up with anything useful, but that this would give *her* time to think before he did something terminally foolish. She understood that often the details of a Challenge provided the key to its solution. Like the detail of the boots being empty, so they could be filled and thus governed. These bears weren't empty, but there must be something about them.

There was. One bear looked happy, the other sad. Other than that they looked like identical twins.

"Oh, bleep!" Ease said. "It's a pun."

What did he have against puns? They were ubiquitous.

"I hate puns," he continued as if in answer. "Once I stepped on one, and it squished and stuck to my shoe. I couldn't get the mess off. Another time I ate one by accident; I thought it was a bun. Then I got pundigestion, and started emitting puns, and nobody else could stand to be near me. It took days for the stink to get off me. I'd like to see every pun in Xanth abolished."

Maybe it was just as well that he hadn't realized that Boot Hill was a pun. But what was the pun here? Kandy didn't see anything funny about the twin bears.

"They're bi-polar bears," he said. "On an ice bar."

Kandy feared her wood would warp. How could she have missed that? One happy bear, one sad bear, opposite extremes.

Then she realized something else: he had been responding to her regular thoughts. She was starting to get through to him without shouting. That was good, maybe.

"So how do I get by this Challenge?" he asked rhetorically. "If I have to try to think of a pun, I'll retch."

Kandy's turn. What would nullify a punnish pair of bears? Could they be made to dance? Do a pole dance?

A bulb flashed. A bi-pole dancing bear. FETCH TWO POLES, she thought, in caps but not bold or italic.

"Poles," he echoed, looking around. Along the border between Boot Hill and the polar ice were some stakes, boundary markers, maybe so the bears and boots wouldn't argue about territories. He went and pulled up two stout ones. He brought them back to the bears and jammed them into the icy snow. "All yours," he said, backing off.

Sure enough, the bears were fascinated by the poles. Each took one pole and began to dance around it. They were indeed bi-polar dancing bears.

Ease quietly walked by them and on across the ice bar. The second Challenge had been navigated.

Then there was a zombie. "Oh, bleep!" Ease muttered. "It just gets worse. I can't stand zombies."

Kandy wasn't partial to them herself. But if this was the third Challenge, it had to be handled. Maybe they should talk to it, just in case they could make it go away.

"Um, hello," Ease said. "Can you understand me?"

"Ssure I understhand you," the zombie replied with a moderate slurring because of rotten teeth. "I'm undead, not stupid."

"So are you a Challenge?"

The zombie eyed him with its deteriorating eyeball. "You're sstupid yet alive. Of coursh I'm a Czallenge! I am shpending my year of Shervice thwarting other petitioners. Try to get by me and I'll shlime you with a shleazeball."

"Oh, yeah?" Ease pushed forward, leading with the board.

The zombie lifted one stringy arm. Its discolored fingers held what looked like a huge sludge of snot. It lofted the ball toward Ease.

Kandy smashed the ball with her face. SQUISH! Instead of flying cleanly into the sky the way a fair-minded ball would, it flattened and clung to the board. She had to peer through its greasy green goo. Yuck!

"Yeah," the zombie answered belatedly. Zombies were not notably quick minded; they had rotten brains.

Ease backed off as the zombie readied another sleazeball, knowing when caution was the better part of valor. He wiped the board off on the turf. That was a relief.

So how could they handle this disgusting opponent? Kandy looked around; she could do that without actually moving her eyes, because they were flat like a picture, gazing directly at whatever was in sight. She saw an eggplant growing to the side, with a number of fresh eggs. Could this be a way?

"I see an eggplant," Ease murmured. "I wonder."

Exactly.

He went to the eggplant. The eggs were oddly labeled with words like SPLORE, PLAIN, and CITED. What did it mean?

Kandy focused. These were likely to be puns, because the eggplant itself was a pun. What kind of an egg was a Splore? A Plain?

Ease groaned. "Egg Splore," he said. "Eggs Plain. Egg Cited. More punnishment."

Kandy groaned too, but it wasn't even a board squeak. Next question: how could pun eggs stop a zombie?

"I'm just going to throw them," Ease decided.

Well, why not? Kandy did not have a better idea at the moment.

Ease picked the Splore Egg and hurled it at the zombie. It struck a ragged shoulder and splatted messily. Immediately the zombie started looking around, checking everything nearby.

He was exploring, of course. His mangled pronunciation wasn't good enough to distinguish between spellings. But he still wasn't out of the way.

Ease tossed another egg, the Cited. It struck the zombie, who suddenly began dancing around, excited. But he still wasn't off the path.

Ease threw the Plain egg. It caught the zombie on the head. "I need to eggsplain ssomething," he said. "You can't egg me on off the path."

"Maybe I just haven't yet found the right egg," Ease said. He took one labeled Xactly and threw it.

"Eggzactly," the zombie said. "You'll never find the right egg. Not until you're eggzausted."

This wasn't working. It occurred to Kandy that the eggs were a distraction—an eggstraction?—placed there to confuse the issue. There had to be something else.

She looked around. There was a kind of garden with pretty flowers, but on closer eggsamination—stop that!—they turned out to be small flowery cars. They were arranged in maplike outlines the shape of nations. What were they?

Then her board really did warp. In-car-nations! Another eggregious pun. She had to stop this before she eggsploded.

Beyond the flower cars was a beehive. It looked to be in poor condition. So were the bees. They looked as if they would fall apart at any moment.

Then she caught on. They were Zom Bees! If anything should mess up a zombie, it should be bees of its own type. That had to bee the key.

All they needed to do was get the bees to attack the zombie. How could they arrange that?

"Zom Bees," Ease said, picking up her thought. "That's easy." He walked to the hive and swing the board. It struck so hard that the hive sailed through the air like a lead balloon and smacked into the zombie. He had, per his talent, found the easy way.

The bees were annoyed. In fact they were furious. They swarmed over the zombie and started stinging him.

His reaction was curious. Instead of exclaiming in pain, he burst into wild laughter. He rolled on the ground, laughing uncontrollably.

Kandy realized that Zombies were different from alive folk. What hurt a person might have the opposite effect on a zombie. So the stings were more like tickling. At any rate the zombie was out of commission. Ease walked right by it and through the setting. He was through the third Challenge, as much by luck as by skill.

And there before him was the drawbridge over the moat.

He walked boldly across it, jauntily swinging his board. There was a moat monster; it raised its toothy green head from the water, eyed him, and let him be. It knew he was entitled.

He marched up to the front gate. A woman with a baby stood there. "Hi, Wira!" he called. "It's me, Ease, again."

"So I see," she agreed. "We seldom see a querent a second time."

"Well, the Good Magician didn't help me before. Then I got this notion, how about asking him a different Question? Maybe this time he'll give me an Answer."

"He regretted letting you go, before," Wira said, guiding him into the castle. "Because after that there was a really tough mission, and he had to send a woman who almost wasn't up to it, because she lacked your magic." She paused.

It was a significant pause. There was something on her mind. Maybe he should inquire.

"I heard that pause," Ease said. "What's on your mind, Wira?"

"Two things. One about you, the other about me."

"About me?"

"Ease, the Good Magician has a mission in mind for you. But I remember from when you were here before. You don't much like puns."

"I sure don't. And there was half a slew of them out there today."

"Yes. I think maybe he was trying to turn you off so you wouldn't finish the Challenges. Because the mission involves puns."

"Oh, bleep!" Then, remembering the baby, he mended his language. "I mean, oh, no."

Wira smiled. "She doesn't understand language yet. No harm done. But you may want to pass up this mission."

But Kandy was curious. A mission involving puns? That could be wonderful or horrible, depending on the mood of the puns. She preferred to see it through.

"I prefer to see it through," Ease said bravely. "What's the other thing?"

"I really shouldn't bother you."

"Oh, come on, Wira. You were nice to me before. Maybe I can help."

"All right. It's that I can't decide what to name my baby. Normally men get boy babies and women get girl babies, and she's a girl, so she should have a W name, after me. But I'm not sure I want to be that conventional. That leaves me with no idea. I don't want to leave it too long, because a person is incomplete without a name. Do you have any idea? Maybe what is difficult for me will be easy for you."

Ease considered, flattered. "What's her talent?"

"She can summon lizards and tame them. Small ones, so far, but they may get bigger as she matures. I'm hoping she'll be a dragon tamer when she's grown."

"Then name her after her talent: Liz."

"That's it!" Wira said. "That's perfect! Thank you." She kissed him on the cheek.

"Always glad to be of service to a lady," Ease said gallantly.

Kandy had to admit that he had come through on that one. He had indeed done easily what had stymied Wira.

Now they came to the castle reception hall. "Mother MareAnn!" Wira exclaimed. "I have a name! Ease thought of it." Then, embarrassed, she remembered her role. "This is Ease, who was here once before. Ease, this is MareAnn, the Designated Wife of the month."

"Hello, Ease," MareAnn said. She was a pretty woman with a brown ponytail. "We haven't met before, because I was not here when you were. I am glad to meet you now." Then she turned to Wira. "A name?"

"Liz! After her talent."

"Perfect," MareAnn agreed. "Thank you for finding it, Ease."

Ease opened his mouth to say something modest. But Wira spoke instead. "Oops! I think Liz has to poop." She hurried off.

MareAnn smiled indulgently. "She's so pleased with that baby. For years she couldn't signal the stork for one, because she needed to help Humfrey. Now at last she and Hugo are parents, and they are happily unsettled." She shook her head, politely bemused. "New parenthood is as wonderful and challenging in its way as new love. I remember—" She broke off. "But I don't mean to bore you with reminiscences. The Good Magician is not able to see you at the moment, so there is time for you to eat and relax. We have a fine salad bar." She produced what looked like a soap bar. "Also boot rear."

Ease hesitated. ACCEPT, Kandy thought, realizing that he needed schooling on social manners. AND ASK HER TO REMINISCE.

So Ease, duly prompted, did the socially polite things, accepting the food and inquiring about the reminiscence.

"You're interested?" MareAnn asked, surprised.

Ease opened his mouth.

YES

"Yes."

"Or are you just being polite?"

Kandy hastily dictated a feasible answer, and Ease obligingly echoed it. "I don't know what I face when the Good Magician answers my Question and gives me some Mission to accomplish. There may be some insight you can offer."

"But I have no idea what Humfrey has in mind. I can't help you that way."

"I mean, your memories may do it. Not something that either you or I know about now, but they could provide me some perspective that will help."

She contemplated him thoughtfully. "Perhaps," she agreed.

Wira returned, bringing drinks. "I found some gin," she said. "This should be good." She presented a tray of glasses to Ease.

"Gin? Isn't that a Mundane drink?"

"There's a crude variant in Mundania, but this is better. There's Ca-jin, Mar-jin, Ora-gin, Ima-gin, and Gin-jer. We also have rum."

IMAGINE, Kandy thought. That seemed less likely to intoxicate him.

"Ima-gin," Ease agreed.

Wira gave him the glass. He sipped it, as Karen stopped him from gulping. With luck it would illuminate his mind.

"I will have the Deco-rum," MareAnn said, taking her glass.

"You were remembering new love," Ease said, prompted again.

"Ah, yes," MareAnn agreed. "Long ago, when I was young, which is longer ago than I care to say, I enjoyed my talent of summoning equines. That is, animals with some horse ancestry."

"You don't look old," Ease said, yet again prompted by Kandy's thought.

MareAnn laughed. "I am a hundred and eighty one years old."

Ease needed no prompting this time. "No way!"

"You forget, we Wives have access to youth elixir. Humfrey uses it to maintain himself at approximately one hundred. Women prefer a somewhat younger default, and Humfrey is satisfied to accede. So physically I am twenty nine and counting, but chronologically I am more than six times that."

"Oh. Of course." Still, both Ease and Kandy were set back by it.

"My favorite equines were the unicorns, and since I was young and genuinely innocent I had no trouble summoning them. Then I met Humfrey. At first I took him for a boy of twelve, but he was my age, fifteen. Then I thought he was a gnome, but he wasn't. He helped me, and we got to know each other, and I liked him. He liked me too, especially when I innocently kissed him. So that was my first love, and I think his too. But our relationship was not to be, at least not at that time."

Ease and Kandy were working this out together. "Unicorns—"

"Exactly. Folk who marry soon get un-innocent and summon storks. I knew I couldn't afford that, because I would lose my ability to be with unicorns. So though it broke my heart, I declined to marry him. He married Dara Demoness instead."

"But then how—?"

"How did I come to be his Designated Wife of the month?" she filled in. "That's a long story, so I'll condense it. In the course of his long life Humfrey lost several wives and associates to age or indifference, and when they died they wound up in Hell, I among them." She smiled. "It's not that we were evil, just that we weren't ready for Heaven. We had unfinished business on Earth. Then when Humfrey rescued us, suddenly there were six of us, but of course he couldn't remarry us all at once. So we arranged to alternate, month by month, and this is my month. Actually I'm his half wife."

"Half wife?"

"It was a very small ceremony. I had turned him down before, preserving my innocence. But Hell is hard on innocence, and I had already lost my unicorns, so now I married him. I was the only one who had not married him before, so my status was less, even though I was his first love. So I am now a half-wife of twenty four years. But my love is undiminished. I am a half wife but not a half woman. And I remember how it was, to love and yet be denied." She looked at Ease. "You have not yet experienced first love or denied love, but I think you soon will. Then you will understand."

"I have not," Ease agreed.

Wira had faded out. Now she returned. "Humfrey still is not ready to see Ease," she reported. "He will do it tomorrow morning."

"Then you will stay the night," MareAnn said. "Wira will show you to your room. I hope my reminiscence was not too boring."

Boring. That word electrified Kandy. Being bored stiff had been her undoing, and this might relate. The idea of unexpected love and denial also might relate. Both Kandy and Ease had wished for Romance, and it was seeming increasingly likely that they were destined for each other. If only she could stop being a board. NOT AT ALL.

"Not at all," Ease echoed.

Wira showed Ease to his room. "It was nice of you to listen to MareAnn," she said. "She's a nice person, but she does miss her unicorns."

There was food in the room. Ease ate, cleaned up, and changed to pajamas because Kandy insisted. Then he lay down and slept, still holding the board, which he had never relinquished.

And she reverted to her natural form. In half a moment she had moved his hand from her ankle to her back. "You did well today," she murmured.

The door opened. MareAnn entered. What was she doing here?

"Hello, Kandy," she said.

Kandy was amazed. "You can see me!"

"Yes. I suspected something was going on; Ease was too alert and sensitive for a typical man. Someone had to be prompting him. So I checked the Good Magician's archives and found a ghost-seeing spell."

Kandy moved the man's hand back to her ankle so she could sit up or stand. "I'm not a ghost!"

"Of course you aren't. But you are invisible in the manner of a ghost, and the spell enables me to see you. I'm sure you could make yourself visible and audible to a person if you chose, however. So I came to talk."

That was interesting. Kandy had assumed her nonentity was involuntary, but maybe she did have some control. "When you looked at us, pausing—that's when you suspected."

"Yes. And the man's responses thereafter were those of a woman rather than a man. But how did you come to be a board?"

"I made a wish at a wishing well, only I said board instead of bored. Thus I got aboard. But I confess it hasn't been boring."

"Despite not being able to do anything un-innocent with him, despite being bare, lovely, and in contact."

"Yes, I really relate to your frustration with Humfrey."

"I suspect that your situation is part of a larger destiny. But I actually came to beg a favor."

"A favor? I can't do anything."

"You can influence Ease. You have been doing a marvelous job with him."

"Well, yes, when I try. But that's strictly an immediate personal thing, mostly stopping him from making a fool of himself, and waking him when danger threatens."

"That is good. But you can do more."

"What more? Kissing him asleep isn't satisfying."

MareAnn smiled reminiscently. "I know. You may not like what I ask."

This was evidently not incidental. "What do you ask?"

"My talent is for summoning and taming equines, but I have sympathy for other animals too. A young female came here, seeking romance, as so many do. Humfrey invoked a spell to convert her to human form, and it is a most winsome one, but she remains no closer to her objective. I would like you to get Ease to take her on his quest. She can be useful as a bodyguard. Somewhere out there she may be able to find a human man who will properly appreciate her. She really deserves that; she's worthy."

MareAnn was being too cautious. "What's the catch?"

"She's a basilisk."

Kandy stared at her. "Their gaze is deadly!"

"So is their breath, and their very odor. That's why she has a problem. No one can get close to her and live."

"She would kill Ease!"

"No. It is her direct gaze that kills. She wears dark glasses to mask it. And her lethal odor has been converted to intoxicating perfume. A man could hold his breath."

"She's winsome in human form? Ease would be interested. He would hold his breath."

"Yes. Extremely. The conversion spell made her a virtually perfect human specimen."

"So why do you think I would want her with us? She's mischief, whether considered as a killer or a one-breath stand."

"I know this is difficult. Kandy, she needs a human friend. One who could caution her the way you caution Ease. Who would have some understanding of her situation. You could be that friend."

She was horrified. "To a basilisk?"

"Her origin is her curse, the way becoming a board is yours. But if she can navigate it, she has a chance to be happy, as you do."

Kandy realized that the woman was getting to her. She did understand the frustration of not being properly understood or appreciated. "One thing: could you give her some of that spell, so she could see and hear me?"

"I could mix it in with her perfume. But I repeat, you can make yourself apparent to others when you choose to, and after the initial effort, they will see you without trouble."

"Okay." Kandy hoped she was not making a disastrous mistake.

"Thank you. I will introduce her to Ease tomorrow, after you have seen Humfrey."

"I think I'd rather meet her first."

"If you wish. I can bring her here."

"Do that."

MareAnn departed, and Kandy stewed in her own pondering. A basilisk! One of the most deadly creatures known. She had to be her friend? And suppose Ease did decide to hold his breath? How could Kandy ever constrain her jealousy?

MareAnn returned with what looked like a nymph: a supremely endowed young woman without clothing. Her heavy dark glasses only added to her appeal. Kandy's jealousy magnified.

"Kandy, this is Astrid Basilisk-Cockatrice," MareAnn said formally. "Astrid, this is Kandy, who is spelled to be a board when Ease is awake."

"I think I am pleased to meet you," Astrid said.

She had evidently not had a lot of experience with human beings. She would indeed need guidance. "You need clothing," Kandy said.

"But you are not clothed."

Touche. "I lost my clothes when I became a board. I normally am not visible. But you will be active by day. Unclothed you will freak out any man who sees you."

"I am not comfortable with clothing," Astrid said. "But I will accept your guidance. I will find clothing. What do you recommend?"

"Panties, bra, socks, shoes, dress. Donned in roughly that order."

"I will search out these things," MareAnn said, departing.

"I think you do not want me with you," Astrid said. "Nobody does."

This needed to be finessed. "MareAnn said you could be a bodyguard. I'm not sure how that would work. If your presence is lethal to monsters, isn't it similarly lethal to us?"

"It is not the sight of me that kills," Astrid said. "It is my direct gaze. As long as I mask it, you are safe. But should a monster come, I would remove my glasses and stare at it. Only at it. It would die. If less is needed, I can use only one eye to stun, or stand close, masked, and the monster would become intoxicated and be unable to attack. I should be able to protect you."

So it seemed. "As long as you remember who your friends are."

"If I had any friends, I would remember."

Ouch. "I am with Ease, here, whom you will formally meet tomorrow. He likes the look and feel of women. He may seek to—to be close to you."

"I would like that."

Ouch, again.

"I mean to kiss you and feel you and do things he shouldn't."

"That would be nice. I have no human experience, and would like some."

She had no romantic experience because every creature she got close to died. Kandy knew she had no right to be jealous of the girl's potential with Ease, but she was. She needed to handle this the way a sensible person would. "To summon the stork with you."

"The stork?"

And of course she had no knowledge of that human convention. "Men and women—they get together and arrange to send a signal to the stork, who then brings them a baby."

"A baby!" Astrid exclaimed. "A baby what?"

There was a question. "In your case, probably a crossbreed, half human, half basilisk. It might be awkward for you."

"I don't want a baby! At least not yet. I have to learn all about the human culture first, and find a man to keep. Then maybe we could send for a baby whatever."

Good enough. "So you will need to avoid signaling the stork."

"Yes! And kissing and feeling does that?"

"In some magic lands, yes. But here in Xanth it takes a little more. You should be safe if you just keep him out of your panties."

Astrid looked at the sleeping man. "I don't think he would fit in them."

"I mean you should try to keep him from doing anything with any part of you that is covered by them."

"Oh. That should be easy enough."

"That depends on the man." Kandy hoped she would not have to explain about aggressive men who did not seem to know the meaning of "no."

Astrid shook her head, bemused. "It is odd that storks require such obscure signaling. Why hide the mechanism in panties?"

"It's protected zone. Just looking at panties can freak a man out."

"Then how can he ever—?"

"When you really want to signal the stork, you take them off."

"Oh. Now I understand. I think. It's a good deal less subtle with basilisks."

Kandy did not inquire about that, but realized that basilisks probably did not gaze soulfully into each other's eyes. They probably just went at it.

MareAnn returned with an armful of clothing. In short order Astrid donned panties, bra, and socks. The dress was more complicated. MareAnn had brought three of them, so that the girl could choose what she preferred. One was pink with frills, another was blue with ribbons, and the third was metallic gray with flashing sequins. "Oh, how did that get in with the others?" MareAnn exclaimed. "That's not supposed to be here."

"That's the one!" Astrid said, delighted. "It's the color of snakeskin, with pretty scales."

"But it's dangerous," MareAnn protested. "It belongs in the hazardous artifact chamber along with the New Clear Bombs, Poise & Gas, and other dreadful magic. I'll put it there and fetch you a safe dress."

"No, no!" Astrid protested. "This is the one I want. It will make me feel comfortable in this alien body."

MareAnn looked at Kandy. "What do you say?" She plainly wanted a corroborating opinion.

But Kandy was curious. "Just what is it about this dress that makes it hazardous?"

"This outfit is called the Sequins of Events. The sequins are loosely attached and tend to fall off during activity. When one does, the dress is disturbed and loses its color, becoming translucent. When the sequin is replaced, it triggers its Event, which can be anything from an incidental encounter to a full-fledged adventure. All those in the vicinity of the dress are caught up in the Event, and can't escape it until it runs its course. That can be extremely inconvenient, even life-threatening. So this is not a dress to be trifled with. I will exchange it for a safer one."

But Astrid hugged the dress. "This is the one I want."

"I think she has decided," Kandy said. "She deserves to wear what makes her comfortable."

MareAnn glared at her. "But—"

"I speak as her friend," Kandy said.

And MareAnn had asked her to be the friend that Astrid needed. She could not argue this case. She folded, or rather unfolded the dress. "Just be careful. Very careful."

"I will," Astrid promised raptly as she donned the dress. Kandy had to admit that she looked exquisite in it; it fit her perfectly. Then she donned slippers and was complete.

"So be it," MareAnn said grimly. "It is time for us to go. Ease is about to wake."

"Wake?" Astrid asked.

"I become a board," Kandy explained. "I can see and hear and send my thoughts, but I can't move or speak on my own."

"Oh, you're enchanted too!" Astrid came to hug her, briefly. "You truly understand. Thank you for being my friend."

"You're welcome," Kandy said, discovering that she meant it. Astrid was a nice girl despite her origin. Despite her perfume, that made Kandy feel dizzy.

Then Ease woke. Kandy was a board again.

"Oh!" Astrid said, taken aback. Fortunately the man was not facing her, and did not see her.

I'M STILL HERE, Kandy projected.

"Still here," Astrid agreed.

Ease rolled over and went back to sleep. Kandy reverted to woman form. "He doesn't know," she said. "And I think it best not to tell him. He must find out for himself. That seems to be that nature of the enchantment."

"Yes, enchantments must be honored," Astrid agreed. "I will delay telling him my nature, too, when we meet tomorrow."

Then MareAnn ushered her out of the room and Kandy was alone.

Now it occurred to her that the real challenge of the Good Magician's Castle had not been Ease's struggling his way into it, but hers: to sincerely befriend the least lovable of creatures, a basilisk. Amazingly, she was doing it.

CHAPTER 3:
EVENT

Kandy spent the remainder of the night pondering her situation. Now not only was she a stiff board by day and a frustrated ghost by night, she had to be friends with a converted basilisk. But she had to admit it was adventure of a sort. Meanwhile, there was a certain satisfaction in being able to hug and kiss Ease without him trying to take over the relationship. If all men behaved that well she wouldn't have had any problem. He was handsome and naive, which were commendable qualities in a man, and she did like him. But she had to admit that the nights did get dull. Maybe a man's ideal woman was a tacit zombie, letting him do anything he wanted, but a woman's ideal man did have some initiative.

Initiative. Maybe she could at least simulate that. She took his hand and moved it to her bottom, stroking it. She felt his fingers quiver; on some level they knew what they were touching.

"Stop that," she murmured, while continuing the motion. "Stop it or I'll kiss you, you naughty man." When his hand didn't stop, she did kiss him. He reacted to that too, but not enough to wake. She could not afford to overdo it, lest he find himself stroking a board. But it was fun in its fashion.

In the morning Ease woke. Kandy promptly tuned out, not interested in overseeing his routine natural functions. But she overslept, because when she woke Ease was just entering the Good Magician's dark cramped den. Well, Ease evidently hadn't needed her; Wira or MareAnn must have guided him. That faintly annoyed her, ironically; she preferred to be in charge, even if she got no credit for it.

Good Magician Humfrey was a gnomish little man who looked to be a hundred years old, by no coincidence. He peered up from his giant open tome. "Who are you?"

Ease was taken aback. "I'm Ease. You're finally ready to see me."

"I saw you years ago, and sent you away, and later regretted it."

"Yes. Now I'm back."

Humfrey made a little shrug of impatience. "What do you want this time?"

"I want the perfect weapon, the perfect adventure, or the perfect woman: your choice." He had evidently forgotten that he had decided on personal satisfaction for his Question. Well, these would do.

Humfrey scowled. He did it well; he had the face for it. "I don't give people things, I provide Answers. What is your Question?"

For a moment Ease was at a loss, not having anticipated this distinction. So Kandy prompted him. HOW CAN I GET ANY OF THESE THINGS?

"How—"

"I heard," Humfrey said curtly.

Both Ease and Kandy were surprised. "You heard my thought?" Ease asked.

The Good Magician paused slightly, glancing at the board. Obviously he knew about Kandy, which wasn't surprising, considering that his wife knew. "In a manner. Here is my Answer: you already have all three of those things. You have merely to realize it."

Kandy felt her sap warming with pleasure. She knew she was the perfect weapon for Ease, because she guided his clumsy strikes to make them score. He must be in his perfect adventure, maybe still unfolding. And according to the Good Magician she was his perfect woman. She really appreciated that recognition.

Humfrey looked directly at her and nodded ever so slightly. Oh yes, he knew. And wasn't telling.

"But all I have is this board," Ease protested. "I don't even know where I'm going. And where is my perfect woman?"

"Your dream girl," Humfrey said.

"My dream girl," Ease repeated. "She *is* perfect. She has the most marvelous rear, and her kisses—" Then he realized he was speaking aloud. "What about her?"

"You will achieve her when you are worthy of her, and recognize her, and kiss her."

"I don't understand."

"Par for the course," Humfrey said. "That is why you will need Companions on your Quest. They may have some of the sense you lack." It seemed that diplomacy was not the Good Magician's strong point.

"Quest?"

"My assignment for you, in return for my Answer."

"But—"

STIFLE IT. Kandy knew that the Good Magician had given a Good Answer, and that argument was worse than pointless.

Humfrey nodded faintly again. Kandy was coming to understand why folk had so much trouble with his Answers: they simply didn't know enough to appreciate their relevance. Maybe it required the ordeal of a Quest to educate them enough to appreciate what they had.

"Now some necessary background," Humfrey said. Then he paused, looking annoyed. "Oh, bleep!"

"Bleep?" Kandy was curious too. This did not seem like the Good Magician she had heard about.

Humfrey sighed. "I must explain. I hate explaining, but this time I have to. Every so often, maybe once in a decade, I foul up. That interferes with my interaction with the Book of Answers here." He tapped the page. "When that happens, the Answer goes not into this book where it belongs, but into the Book of Lost Answers, where I have to look it up. It's a bleeping nuisance. But there's a problem."

A PROBLEM? Kandy couldn't help herself; she was womanishly curious.

"The Book of Lost Answers is itself fouled up, because of its nature. It is printed in the Elfabet, which only elves can properly handle. Things in its vicinity tend to spoil, such as food. The Wives don't like the smell. One of them may have hidden it because of that. That means that not only can I not look up information I'm missing, I suffer forgetfulness, because part of myself is written in it. So I can lose track of things, such as the current Querent."

"Querent?"

"You. The one who asks a Question, who queries. I should never have had to ask. Now my Answer will be necessarily incomplete, an aggravation. I am forced to speak vaguely."

He had been doing that for decades, Kandy thought.

"More than usual," the Good Magician said grumpily. "That lost book made me late for this interview. I simply have to move on without it, aggravating as it is."

"Well, give me what you have," Ease said, hardly grasping the problem. But Kandy did. It could be infuriating to lose something right when you needed it.

"Yes," Humfrey agreed, speaking to both Ease and Kandy with different meanings. "There is a virus extant that destroys puns, Stuck-Net. It may have been developed in one of the more conservative regions of Mundania by anonymous parties and covertly released. It has to be stopped. Your Quest is to find and release the antivirus so that the puns can be saved. I regret I am unable to provide specific directions to the location of the antivirus, but my general information establishes that you will find it eventually."

"Why? Who cares about puns? Nobody likes them. I'd be glad to see them all wiped out."

"Because Xanth is largely made of puns. Without them it would be a hollow, dreary place, like Mundania."

"Well, find somebody else to stop them. I'm not interested."

"You speak as if you think you have a choice."

"Well I *do* have a—"

STIFLE. YOU'RE STUCK IN THIS NET.

Ease did not understand his second thought, but there it was, cutting off his argument. "...duty to complete my Quest," he concluded lamely.

"Exactly." Humfrey closed his tired old eyes momentarily. "I can remember only one more thing, with the context gone. That is to Merge the Hair. That is what you must do when the time comes."

"What time?"

"You will have to be the judge of that."

"But I have no idea what this is about!"

"Perhaps in the course of your necessary travels you will develop an idea. The welfare of Xanth depends on it."

Ease opened his mouth.

STIFLE Kandy repeated.

The Good Magician's eyes returned to his book, dismissing him.

Downstairs MareAnn was waiting. "Ease, allow me to introduce a prospective Companion."

"I don't want a Companion," Ease said shortly.

"You will need her as a bodyguard."

"A woman as a bodyguard? Are you daft?"

MareAnn brought the person forward. "Her name is Astrid."

"I told you—" Then he got a good look. Astrid was absolutely lovely in the Sequins of Events dress. Her ratty hair had been brushed out into a flowing brown mane that curled down around her shoulders and bosom all the way to her nicely rounded posterior. Her face was a marvel of maiden symmetry, and her large dark glasses lent an aspect of alluring mystery. Her legs were marvelously sculptured down to her petitely slippered feet. She was a sight to take away any man's breath.

BREATHE! Kandy thought impatiently.

Ease gasped, restoring his breathing. "Uh, hello Astrid."

"It's so nice of you to have me along," Astrid said. "I really appreciate it."

"That's all right," Ease said. His objection to having a Companion had mysteriously faded out.

"But I need to warn you that her dress is special," MareAnn continued.

"I see that." His eyes were straining to take in the whole of it, especially where it moved with her breathing.

"The sequins must stay on. If one falls off, you must replace it immediately, or the dress will suffer a wardrobe malfunction. She can't see well enough through her glasses to do it herself."

"Replace immediately," he agreed, his lips trying to restrain the drool as he gazed at the small ripple where a current of air tugged the hem near her lovely knees.

Kandy fought to bridle her jealously. She couldn't afford it. It wasn't Astrid's fault that they had given her a drop dead beautiful body. Maybe that was because of her lethal nature.

"And you must leave her alone, apart from necessary cooperation. She is not for romance."

"Romance," he echoed raptly.

"I'm so glad you understand," MareAnn said.

Understand? He understood none of it. Kandy knew she had her work cut out for her.

"I have prepared backpacks with food and tools," MareAnn said. "You should be all right on the trail, especially considering Astrid's protection."

Ease finally recovered a bit of his common sense. "Where are we going?"

"Oh, didn't the Good Magician say?"

"All he said was I had to find the antidote. He didn't say where."

"Then I suppose you will have to look for it."

"The dress," Astrid said. "I have a feeling it knows and will get us there."

"You can talk to it? MareAnn asked.

"No. It's just a feeling."

"That dress," MareAnn said. "I wondered how it got in with the ordinary dresses. I wonder if Humfrey put it there? For you to find? Those sequins—"

"I don't know," Astrid said.

"Well, it's bound to take you somewhere. I just hope it's where you need to go."

Kandy hoped so too. She knew the dress was mischief. But as with men, it might be necessary to tolerate the mischief for the sake of the benefits they offered.

Soon they were on their way, wearing the backpacks, walking along the enchanted path with no immediate destination in mind.

They encountered a young woman walking toward them. "Hello," she said brightly. "My name's Penny. That's because I'm collecting thoughts. I will give you a penny for yours."

"I'm not much for thinking," Ease said.

"Here is a penny." She produced a shining copper coin.

Ease wanted the pretty penny. "Uh, I'm thinking that I have no idea where I'm going, but I hope it's interesting."

"Thank you." She gave him the penny, and turned to Astrid. "You?"

"I am thinking that you are the type of girl I wish I could be, but I can't."

"Why not, if you want to be? You're twice as pretty as I am."

"Because I am a basilisk in human form. My direct gaze would kill you."

"Oh. Thank you." Penny flipped her a penny and hurried on.

"Bleep," Astrid said. "Maybe I should avoid telling folk the truth."

"No, tell them," Ease advised. "I know the truth, and I think you're fascinating."

"I am forbidden fruit."

"That, too, I guess. But I'll try to be careful."

Kandy feared that it was in part the very deadliness of the basilisk that intrigued him. Forbidden fruit was generally the most tempting. This was bound to be mischief.

Sure enough, mischief soon found them. Astrid saw a pair of large animals grazing beside the path, and skipped ahead to look at them more closely. But her skipping caused the dress to flounce, and a sequin dropped off. Immediately the dress went translucent, revealing the outline of her fine torso complete with bra and panties.

Ease froze in place. The sight was not clear enough to freak him out completely, but it was a close call.

"Oh look!" Astrid said. "There are words on their sides. PROB and IMPROB. What do they mean?"

Kandy focused, knowing that Ease would not be up to it. The animals were male bovines, bulls, probably siblings. So the words plausibly named or defined them in some manner. Maybe it was a pun.

Then she got it. PROB-A-BULL and IMPROB-A-BULL!

"Proba-bull and Improba-bull," Ease said, relaying her thought though his mind was largely in stasis. He was still staring through her dress.

Astrid laughed deliciously. "Oh, that's so clever! Thank you for figuring it out."

"Welcome," he replied automatically.

"Oh, I could kiss you!" Astrid said, turning around so that her skirt flared. Her legs needed no enhancement, but nevertheless got it.

DON'T!! Kandy projected to her.

That jolted the basilisk girl back to reality. "But of course I won't. We must not be social."

A SEQUIN FELL OFF.

Astrid looked, and realized that she was not far from nude. "Oh, my! I didn't know!"

PUT IT BACK ON

That jogged Ease out of his trance. He went to pick up the sequin, then kneeled to fasten it back in the place it had been. There was a pin on the back of the sequin that needed to be poked through the material and fastened to its clasp. But he was mannishly clumsy, failing to get it right.

Then Kandy realized it wasn't just butterfingers. His position put him barely a hand-span in front of Astrid's vaguely visible panties, and their power was stronger at close range. He was also breathing her perfume.

CLOSE YOUR EYES. HOLD YOUR BREATH.

He obeyed. That helped. He was finally able to get the sequin fastened. The dress went opaque.

NOW BACK OFF. BREATHE. OPEN YOUR EYES.

He did so. In a generous moment he was able to stand. He took a deep breath, opened his eyes, and looked around. "Wow!"

For half an instant Kandy thought he was expressing appreciation for the restored dress. Then she realized it was more.

They were no longer on the enchanted path. They were in a clearing in a forest near a hillside cave. There was a horrendous aroma.

"I recognize that smell," Astrid said. "Invisible giant."

Whose body odor was said to be like that of a hundred fat men sweating in unison. Indeed, this was every bit as bad. Invisible giants didn't wash much.

Uh-oh. Kandy remembered stories about a place where an invisible giant herded stray travelers into a cave. It was best not to go there.

"I don't like this," Ease said. Then a bulb flashed over his head. "The sequin! When one gets put back on, it triggers an Event. This must be an Event."

"It must be," Astrid agreed. "We had better depart before the giant comes."

There was a not-distant-enough yell. "**A-OOO-GAH!**" followed by the sound of splintering trees. Kandy saw a swath of trees depress as if being stepped on by a giant foot. As if? That was the giant!

RUN!

They got the message. Ease and Astrid took hands and ran away from the crunch.

Crash! Another invisible foot crushed a swath of trees ahead of them. The giant, taking a giant step—what else?—had cut them off.

"The cave!" Ease said. "He can't get in there, or crush the rock. I think."

Kandy remembered more. DON'T GO THERE! THAT'S COM PEWTER'S CAVE!

"Who is Com Pewter?" Astrid asked.

Any reply Ease might have made was drowned out by a third crushing footstep, this one perilously close.

Ease and Astrid dived into the cave.

Kandy knew that now they were in for it.

"Com Pewter is a nasty machine," Ease belatedly answered. "He doesn't much like people, and seeks to use them for nefarious purposes."

"Machine?"

"He's not exactly alive. He's made of Pewter and stuff."

"Pewter?"

"Well, I'm not sure exactly what pewter is. Some kind of metal."

ALLOY OF TIN AND LEAD Kandy thought.

"Tin and lead," Ease said. "And maybe other stuff. Anyway, he's dangerous to be around."

"He is?" Astrid was evidently intrigued, suspecting a fellow traveler.

"Maybe. The giant's gone. Let's get out of here."

They turned and stepped toward the cave exit.

Printed words appeared across the air before them. TRAVELERS GO TO CENTRAL ANNEX.

The two people turned around and marched into the mountain.

Bleep, Kandy thought. Pewter had become aware of them.

"Why are we going the wrong way?" Astrid asked.

"Because Pewter controls reality in his vicinity," Ease said. "He types it out, and we do it, whatever it is."

"Maybe we should tell him no."

She had much to learn about some aspects of Xanth.

They came to a central lighted chamber. There was a bank of metal boxes surmounted by a glassy screen. On the screen was printed WELCOME TRAVELERS.

"Are you Com Pewter?" Astrid asked. "We don't feel welcome. We were driven in here by a smelly invisible giant and then couldn't get out. That's not nice."

WHO ARE YOU?

"We don't have to tell you that," Astrid said.

TRAVELERS TELL ALL

"I am Ease," Ease said. "My companion is Astrid. We're on a Quest for the Good Magician."

THAT DOES NOT MATTER. NOW YOU ARE MY SERVANTS.

"We're not—" Astrid started.

GIRL IS SILENT

Astrid shut up. She was learning.

YOU LOOK LIKE HEALTHY YOUNG SPECIMENS. MAYBE I WILL USE YOU TO START A BREEDING COLONY TO RUN MY ERRANDS.

That would be a disaster, Kandy thought. But how were they to escape the power of this evil machine?

Maybe she could arrange it. Pewter didn't know about Kandy. She could prompt Ease to do things Pewter didn't expect, such as escaping. START WALKING OUT.

Ease started walking out.

STOP WALKING OUT

Ease stopped.

RESUME WALKING

He started walking again.

WHAT IS OPPOSING ME? Pewter demanded.

Ease continued walking, as that order had not been countered.

REVEAL YOURSELF

Oops. Kandy didn't want that. I'M AN INDEPENDENT CUSS.

"I'm an independent cuss," Ease said, still walking.

STOP WALKING. TURN AROUND. RETURN TO ME.

Ease did these things, and stood before the nasty machine.

Then Kandy got an idea. BASH COM PEWTER WITH YOUR BOARD.

Ease bashed the screen before Pewter could understand and counter his attack. His aim, with Kandy's guidance, was true. Glass shattered.

But Kandy knew that the monitor was not the whole of Pewter. He had been blinded, not destroyed.

"Get out of here!" Ease said, prompted by Kandy's urging.

They scrambled for the exit tunnel. In no more than three moments they were back in the forest.

But the giant was still there. An enormous invisible hand blocked them off. SO YOU DEFY ME, he said.

Oh, no! That was Com Pewter talking.

But now Astrid, evidently not used to being bossed around, talked back. "You have no right to hold us. We're on a Quest. Now get out of our way or I will be forced to hurt you."

OH YEAH?

"Final warning. Retreat."

HO HO HO! The hand moved forward; Kandy could tell by the swishing of the breeze around it as it moved. Also by the smell.

Astrid removed her dark glasses and gazed up into the region of the sky where the giant's face might be.

OOOMPH! There was an enormous thud as the giant fell back, evidently landing on his rump, in the process squashing a fair section of terrain.

Now Kandy realized what had happened. Com Pewter might be animating the invisible giant, and talking through his mouth. But the giant was a living creature. The basilisk's death gaze had struck him.

Astrid put her glasses back on. "I warned you."

There was a stirring as the giant leaned forward. "So you did. What manner of creature are you? A gorgon?"

So the giant wasn't dead. Maybe it had been too big for the death-gaze to do more than stun, or maybe its invisibility had diluted the effect. It might have been a glancing blow. But there had been an effect, because now a faint outline of a giant man was showing. It was the man, rather than the machine, now speaking.

"A basilisk," Astrid said. "Astrid Basilisk-Cockatrice, or ABC for short. Transformed to human form for the purpose of this Quest. Now will you leave us alone?"

"I will be glad to," the giant said. "But it is with my master Pewter you must deal."

"Why do you serve a machine?" Astrid asked. She seemed more assertive, now that she had unveiled herself, as it were.

"There are benefits," the giant said. "During off hours I get to play games on the Outernet and exchange messages with girls who don't know my nature."

"I appreciate the point," Astrid agreed. "I think I might enjoy flirting with boys who don't know my nature."

Now Ease came to life. "You're a basilisk!"

"I'm sorry you found out so soon. I believe you found my form interesting, before you knew."

"It's still interesting," Ease said. "Especially when that dress turns translucent."

"It does that?" the giant asked, interested. Evidently he could see well enough, even if he couldn't be seen, and he appreciated the sights.

"It's complicated," Astrid said. "But the essence is that when a sequin falls off, the dress becomes un-opaque and my, um, legs show. It also triggers an Event, because these are Sequins of Events. This is an Event."

"A visit to Com Pewter," the giant agreed.

"Yes," Ease said. "We aren't looking for trouble. We didn't realize how the sequin would take effect."

"I suggest you go back in the cave and talk with Pewter," the giant said. "Now that he knows your nature, he will treat you with more respect."

"It's actually Ease's Quest," Astrid said.

"And surely a worthy one," the giant said. "If I may ask, what is it?"

"Something is destroying puns," Ease said. "I have to find the cure so puns won't be eliminated from Xanth. Even though I'd rather let them all be wiped out."

"I appreciate your mixed emotions," the giant said. "The only thing worse than one pun is two puns. But you can't simply walk away from Pewter. He defines reality in his vicinity, and this is part of his territory."

"Well, I'm walking away," Ease said.

"Lotsa luck," the giant murmured.

Ease started walking. Right back into the cave.

So it was like that. Astrid shook her head, bemused, and followed. Kandy was coming to like her as she saw her sensible reactions.

Back in the central nexus the monitor had been repaired. HOW DID YOU BASH ME?

"With my trusty board," Ease said, brandishing it. "And if you don't let us go, I'll do it again."

STUPID MAN IS UNABLE TO STRIKE.

Ease stood still, unable to move.

But Com Pewter still didn't know about Kandy. STRIKE! she ordered.

Ease struck. But before the board could connect, a man stepped in from the shadow and caught it in his hand. Where had he come from? He seemed to be an android, a somewhat mechanical man, with visible links at his elbows and knees.

In fact he *was* an android. Because he was holding her board, Kandy was able to tell something about him. There was no person there, just the automaton. A machine animated by Pewter. It was just standing there, protecting the monitor.

WHAT POWER IS BYPASSING MY CONTROL?

Now Ease had to answer. "I don't know."

The screen oriented on Astrid.

WHAT DO YOU KNOW OF THIS?

That put the basilisk on the spot. Astrid knew about Kandy.

"The board has a will of its own," Astrid said.

That was true, as far as it went. Would Pewter be satisfied?

The screen addressed Ease. WHAT IS YOUR QUEST?

Pewter was satisfied. Kandy was relieved. She appreciated Astrid's simplification, preserving Kandy's secret, such as it was.

"I have to save the puns," Ease said.

WHAT PUNS?

"All puns. A virus is destroying them."

A VIRUS! The screen looked shocked.

Then Kandy realized that Com Pewter himself was a pun. Their Quest should really interest him. Was that good or bad?

YOU MUST COMPLETE THIS QUEST

"Well, actually I'm not partial to puns—"

MAN REALIZES HE LOVES PUNS

"Then again, they do pretty much define Xanth, so we'd better keep them."

YOUR MISSION IS INADEQUATE. AN IGNORANT MAN AND A BASILISK IN HUMAN FORM WILL NOT ACCOMPLISH MUCH. YOU NEED HELP.

"We need help," Ease agreed

SO I WILL JOIN YOUR PARTY.

Ease looked at the screen. "How? You can't walk or talk."

The android moved. "In my android format," he said. His blank screen face animated, becoming a smiley-face. "I will park my cave data for the duration."

"I don't know—"

"Man changes mind," Pewter said.

"Why we didn't think of this before," Ease concluded.

Kandy wasn't sure about this either, but preferred to stay out of it lest Pewter catch on to her nature and change her mind too.

So it was up to Astrid to make the objections. "The Good Magician set up this Quest. If you take it over, it may mess it up so that we fail."

Pewter considered, his smiley face becoming thoughtful. "The Good Magician is grouchy, but he generally knows what he is doing. So I will join the Quest as a Companion, assisting without interfering."

"How can you do that?"

"I have installed my fatherboard in the android host so that my essence is here."

"Fatherboard?"

"My girlfriend Com Passion has a motherboard; I have a fatherboard, of course."

"Point made. But what I meant was, how can you accompany us without constantly interfering? It's your nature."

"The same way you do: by following the protagonist's lead and helping to guarantee his safety."

"Guarantee his safety? How can you do that in a way I can't?"

"Myriad ways, Basilisk. When a threat comes you can stare it into submission. That's limited. I can change reality in the vicinity so that the threat abates without even becoming threatening. That's far less limited."

Astrid nodded. "Excellent point. But it would be better if you assumed a better human likeness."

If Pewter was annoyed, he didn't show it. "How so?"

"For one thing, you should coordinate your screen mouth with your speech, so it is not obvious that you are not actually talking with your mouth."

"Excellent point," Pewter said, his face mouth now moving with his speech.

"And you should mask or change your visible joint bolts."

"Bolts disappear," Pewter said, and they did. He looked significantly more human.

"And—" Astrid hesitated.

"What, Basilisk?"

"You should stop calling me that. It is true; I am a basilisk in human garb.

But it is better to conceal my nature from strangers, or I will be less effective as a bodyguard. So you should refer to me as Astrid, and look at me as if I were a real woman."

"I will do that," Pewter said. "Actually your form is impressively human, not that I care about that sort of thing."

"And I will treat you as if you are a real man, not that I have the slightest interest. But there is one more thing."

"What thing?"

"You will have to stop changing reality against our will. Ease and I need to function as ourselves. You should change reality only when we ask you to."

"Astrid changes mind," Pewter said. Her expression changed.

Kandy had to act. She prompted Ease.

"Nuh-uh," Ease said. "None of that."

"Cancel," Pewter muttered. Astrid's expression reverted to its prior setting. "Got it. Use my power only when necessary or requested."

Kandy realized that this was actually working out. But there was more. She prompted Ease."

"Something else," Ease said. "You're a pun, Com Pewter. Where we're going, puns are in danger. You need to protect yourself from the virus."

"I hate viruses," Pewter agreed. "But I can't counter it without knowing its type. So I will build an invisible firewall around us all."

"We don't want to burn!" Ease protested.

"Figurative, simpleton. It means a barrier that viruses can't get through. It won't eliminate the viruses, but it will prevent them from reaching us. That will ensure my survival when we encounter the pun-killing virus."

Ease evidently didn't know what the term "simpleton" meant, so didn't argue. "Do it, cartoon face." Or did he? He was picking up more of her thoughts, and in effect she was upgrading his intellect. Something she probably couldn't have done if she had retained her real form.

The android fetched papers filled with obscure printed 0 and 1 symbols, placed them in a circle around the three of them (Kandy of course didn't count), and spoke a fiery spell. The papers burst into flame that rose up in a circular wall around them, then merged above them. They were in a blazing hemisphere of light. This was of course the firewall.

Pewter snapped his fingers, and the light faded.

"But it's gone," Astrid said.

"It remains," Pewter said. "I merely rendered it invisible. Regular folk won't be aware of it at all. It affects only viruses."

"What about below ground?"

Pewter considered. "That might be regarded as a trapdoor. The pun virus shouldn't be able to get through there."

Kandy wondered, but let it be. Pewter surely had some expertise in viruses.

"Good enough," Ease agreed. "Let's be on our way."

"Where are we going?" Astrid asked.

"Wherever it was we were going before we got sidetracked here," Ease said.

Astrid didn't argue the case. Neither did Kandy. Where they were going was largely random.

They walked back out of the cave. "Hey, Giant!" Pewter called. "We're leaving the cave in your charge. Try not to step on it."

"What about web cams?" the Giant called from far above. Evidently he had recovered form Astrid's stare.

"Watch them all you want. Just don't let anyone intrude in the cave."

Kandy wondered what a web cam was, but wouldn't have asked even if she had been able to do so directly. She suspected it had something to do with sneak peaks at young women. The giant was male, after all.

They started walking away from the cave. Then a sequin on Astrid's dress snagged on a section of brush and dropped to the ground. Her dress turned translucent.

"Really impressively human," Pewter said. "I think I am coming to appreciate the power of panties."

Astrid looked down. "Oops."

"But why has your dress faded?" Pewter asked.

"These are Sequins of Events," she explained. "Each time one falls off, my wardrobe malfunctions, and when we put it back on, we suffer a new Event. That's how we came to your cave. It was an Event. Now we're in for another."

"That is interesting magic. The action of the sequins may not be random, since one brought you to me. We should consider this?"

"I need to get that sequin back on my dress before Ease's eyeballs glaze."

The android glanced at Ease. "Point taken. But plunging into an unknown Event without preparation is dangerous. What other aspects of your Quest should I know about so that I can act sensibly?"

He did have a point. MAYBE WE SHOULD TELL PEWTER ABOUT ME, Kandy thought to Astrid. PRIVATELY.

Astrid nodded. "Come here," she told Pewter.

Pewter approached her. She whispered in his ear. Ease paid no attention;

his eyes were locked on Astrid's vaguely visible panties. He had not quite freaked out, but was getting there.

Then Pewter nodded. "Ease sleeps," he said.

Ease lay down where he was, beside the sequin, and closed his eyes. In less than a moment, hardly more than an instant, he was asleep. Kandy reverted to her ghost form.

"Pewter, I need your guarantee of silence on what I am about to show you," Astrid said.

"You have already shown me enough," Pewter said. "I repeat: I appreciate its perfection, but it is not the sort of thing I crave to handle."

"Not my body. Something else."

"Is it relevant to the quest?"

"Yes."

"Then I will keep your secret."

"Good enough. Look at Ease's board."

"I don't like that board. It whacked my monitor."

"Look more carefully."

The android did. Kandy focused on becoming visible. "That's odd. It's not exactly a board. It's a—a transformed woman."

"Hello, Pewter," Kandy said. "I'm sorry I had to bash your monitor."

"And she talks," Pewter said.

"I am Irrelevant Kandy. I made a wish, but was transformed into a board," Kandy said. "I return to my own form when my companion sleeps. Until I can escape this curse, I prefer to remain anonymous. I can direct the blows the board strikes so that they score, and I can project my thoughts when I try. I am Astrid's friend. I try to guide Ease when he needs it."

"That accounts for his occasional intelligence," Pewter agreed. "I might be able to nullify the spell on you, if you prefer. However that nullification would remain in force only when you are in my vicinity."

"Yes. For now it seems best for me to remain a board. But we thought it wise for you to know my nature, in case things become complicated in the course of the Quest."

"It is wise," Pewter agreed. "I will act with your best interests in mind, as part of the quest."

"Thank you."

The android glanced down at Ease. "Ease wakes."

Ease woke. His eyes saw the translucent dress and started to go vague again.

"Now I think we can replace the sequin," Astrid said.

"Of course." Pewter picked up the sequin and fastened it to her dress, not suffering any of the distraction Ease had.

The dress immediately went opaque, and the scene changed.

CHAPTER 4:

ISLANDS

"The events are definitely relevant," Pewter said. "I feel the strong magic of both Sequin and Dress, locked in so that I can't change its reality even on a spot basis. But I do know that we must fathom the relevance of each Event to our Quest before moving on to the next. The relevance of the prior Event was in adding me to the Quest."

"That's good to know," Astrid said. "Now please let go."

Pewter dropped the section of dress he had been holding to replace the sequin. His fascination had been with the dress rather than her form, in contrast to Ease's attention. "So let's see what we have here."

They looked around. They were on an island, one of several. It was pretty, with a sandy beach, pleasant foliage, handsome trees, and a tall tower.

"Help!" It was the voice of an innocent maiden in distress.

They looked. There was a maiden in a turret atop the tower. She was waving a hankie and calling to them.

"A damsel in distress!" Ease said, interested.

"We're not here to rescue damsels," Pewter said.

"How do you know?" Astrid asked.

That set Pewter back. "This is not my home environment. I do not know. I had better Goggle it."

"Do what?" Astrid asked.

"Tune in to the OuterNet Search Engine, Goggle. It has many answers."

"Ask it where the anti-virus solution is," Ease said.

"It doesn't answer that kind of question; it's too serious. It's Goggle, not Giggle. Goggle is for superficial questions."

"Hilarious," Astrid said, clearly not amused.

"Give me a moment to connect." Pewter froze in place. Exactly one moment later he unfroze. "Goggle says damsels in distress should be promptly eyed and rescued."

"We might almost have come up with that answer ourselves," Astrid said sourly. "But you say this is relevant to our Quest?"

"I don't know. Only that this Event is relevant. Rescuing a damsel may or may not relate."

"Help! Please!" the maiden called.

Astrid sighed, echoing Kandy's sentiment. Neither of them were enthused about adding more pretty maidens to their party. "So we'll rescue her and send her on her way."

They walked toward the tower. It was a good ten times the height of a man; obviously the maiden could not just jump to the ground. The round wall of the tower was featureless; it was not possible to climb it.

"Hello, Distressed Damsel," Ease called. "Who are you and what do you want?"

"Hello, Handsome Man!" she answered. "I am Tiara and I want to be rescued from this elevated dungeon. I would be most grateful."

She surely would. That was the problem. But how could they turn her down?

Astrid glanced at the board, obviously sharing the sentiment.

"Perhaps she knows something useful," Pewter said. "We had better get on with it."

"How?" Ease asked. "I can make things easy, but I have to know what I'm doing. I have no idea about this."

"Fortunately I do," Pewter said. "There is obviously an access so that her captor can bring her food, water, and remove wastes. There will be a tight spiral stairway inside the tower. We will access it."

"But there's no door!"

"No visible door," Pewter said. "Masking illusion is the simplest of spells; I can undo it without vacating the firewall." He went to the featureless base of the tower. "Illusion vacates."

The featureless wall dissipated, revealing rough stone with a door inset.

Pewter did know that he was doing.

"But it's locked," Ease said.

"Lock unlocks."

There was a click as the lock unlocked. Then the door swung open to reveal the tight spiral stairway.

Kandy was really coming to appreciate Pewter's ability to spot change local reality.

"Well, let's go," Ease said. Then he had a cautionary notion. "But suppose there are scorpions or things on the stairs?"

"I will go first," Astrid said. "I will reason with any dangerous creatures that may lurk." She touched her dark glasses meaningfully.

Kandy was also coming to appreciate the basilisk's qualities.

Astrid entered the tower first, and started up the staircase. Ease followed, and Pewter was third.

"But it's dark," Ease said.

"Dark stones glow," Pewter said, and suddenly there was comfortable light. They could see the steps clearly.

In barely more than a moment Astrid was on a coil of the spiral above Ease. Her marvelous legs under her dress showed plainly in the glow, all the way up to her glossy gray panties.

Ease started to glance up.

EYES FRONT!

His eyes returned to the steps immediately ahead. Kandy had just saved him from a terminal freakout. He really did need her guidance.

"Good job," Pewter murmured. He knew what she had done. He might not be subject to panty freaks himself, but he knew that regular men were.

They proceeded up the stairway to the top. There was another locked door. "Door unlocks," Pewter said, and it was so.

Astrid opened it and stepped out onto the turret. "Hello, Tiara," she said. "I am Astrid, part of your rescue party."

The girl, thrilled, hugged her. Kandy saw the sequins jiggle, but fortunately none fell off.

Ease was next to arrive. "I am Ease, your rescuer."

"Thank you so much, Ease!" Tiara hugged him too, to his obvious enjoyment.

"And I am Pewter, completing the party," Pewter said. "No need to hug me."

They were in a small but neat round chamber with a bunk bed, table, chair, storage box, and windows. They sat on the bed while Tiara took the chair. She was indeed a pretty girl, with nice features in a nice print dress, large blue eyes, a cherry mouth, poised, except for one thing: her fair hair was wild. It looked as if it had a completely unruly will of its own that no brush or comb could conquer.

"So how come you're locked up here?" Ease asked. "You a captive elf or something?

Tiara laughed. She had a pleasant laugh, too. "No nothing like that! I'm a normal girl. My sisters bring me food every day, and I have a virtual reality illusion game to keep me occupied."

"A game?" Ease asked.

"Yes. It is marvelously inventive and fun. But it is about rescuing a maiden in a tower. That gets old fast."

"Because you are a maiden in a tower," Astrid said.

"Exactly. I don't want to play the game, I want to get rescued myself."

"We can rescue you," Pewter said. "But we are cautious. We need to know why you are confined. Is there some horrendous spell that will destroy Xanth if you are freed?"

"No, of course not. It's more personal. It's because I don't fit in."

"Maybe you had better tell us the full story," Astrid said.

"Oh, I wouldn't want to bore you with such a tedious narrative."

"Bore us," Pewter said.

Tiara immediately complied. "I have many sisters, each with her special nature. There's Apopto sis, who can program the death of cells. Ba sis, who always gets to the fundamental aspect of an issue. Cri sis, who handles difficult situations. Ellip sis who saves words that others omit. Gene sis who can make almost anything from almost nothing. Neme sis, who makes a bad enemy. Sta sis, who can make anything stop. They're all very talented, and they all have very neat hair." At this point Tiara choked up.

Kandy began to get a glimmer. The Good Magician had told Ease to "merge the hair." Could this be the hair? How could it be merged?

"Hair," Astrid prompted.

"And I don't!" Tiara wailed. "My unruly hair is simply awful! I can't do a thing with it. I am an embarrassment to them all. So they gave me this awful sarcastic name and put me away so as to be out of sight. But I hate being alone. I am a friendly person. I wish I could find and be with someone who doesn't care about neat hair."

Kandy found herself warming to this distraught young woman. If only she knew how much worse things could be than having bad hair! Such as becoming a board, or being a basilisk. But the problem really wasn't with her, it was with her narrow-minded sisters who wanted her to conform in appearance, when she couldn't. Just letting her out would not suffice; her sisters would simply put her back in the tower.

HAVE PEWTER FIX IT she thought to Ease. Maybe that would qualify as merging.

"Maybe Pewter can fix it," he echoed. He never questioned the origin of his thoughts, maybe assuming that anything halfway smart must be his own.

"Let me see," Pewter said. He approached Tiara and touched her wild hair.

Immediately it settled down, becoming neatly brushed and coiffed. "Check that," he said.

Tiara went to her mirror on the wall. "Oh!" she exclaimed, delighted. "It's perfect! Now I can rejoin my sisters."

"Unfortunately there's a catch," Pewter said. "My talent is to change reality in my immediate vicinity, but the effect won't last when I depart. This is merely an exploratory demonstration; we have not yet solved your problem."

"Oh!" she wailed, crushed.

COMFORT HER Kandy thought to Astrid. BRIEFLY. Because too long a hold would intoxicate her.

Astrid embraced Tiara reassuringly. Kandy was sure this was an new and unfamiliar role for the basilisk, but surely one it was worthwhile for her to learn.

In a scant two moments Tiara, reassured, stepped away, looking slightly dizzy. "At least you showed me that you understand. You don't seem to be repulsed by my hair."

"Your hair has flair," Astrid said. "Personality. Your sisters are wrong to insist that it conform. They should accept you for your other features, such as your magic talent."

"But I don't have a talent!" Tiara wailed anew.

"Everyone has a talent," Ease said.

"I never found mine. The only thing that distinguishes me is my awful hair."

Hair that was supposed to be somehow merged?

"I wonder," Pewter said thoughtfully. "If you truly can't control it, there must be magic there, if only a curse."

"It just wants to fly off my head," Tiara said. "Even when I put a hat on it, it won't stay. I even tried tying it own with a scarf knotted under my chin, but that only made me feel light-headed. Nothing works."

"This is interesting. Perhaps we can find out the exact nature of this curse." Pewter touched her hair again. "Hair reverts to normal."

Immediately the hair threatened to sail off her head in a tangled cloud. "Oh, it's back!" Tiara wailed. She was good at wailing, having had much practice.

Pewter picked up a dish from Tiara's little counter. He held it over her head, then let go. The dish did not fall; it hovered there half a moment before starting to slide of to the side. "Anti-gravity," Pewter said, catching it. "That is special magic."

"I don't understand."

"Your hair floats because it resists the magic of gravity. When you tie it down, it tries to make your head float, so you feel light headed. Your hair is your magic talent. I wonder what the limit is?"

"I don't want it to float! I want it to behave, so I can be a regular person."

"You are unhappy because you are trying to suppress your magic," Astrid said. "Instead you should encourage it."

"That's easy for you to say. You have neat hair."

"I have no hair at all!" Astrid snapped. "I'm a basilisk." Then she caught herself, too late.

"A what?" Tiara asked.

"Oh, bleep! I shouldn't have said that. But it's out. I am a transformed basilisk, given human form and language so I can seek friendship and happiness that I can't in my natural form. It's just that I think you should appreciate what you have, instead of bewailing it."

"A basilisk! But your stare didn't kill me."

"Note the dark glasses," Astrid said. "Also, I try not to look at others too much. I am lethal, whatever my form."

"If I had known, I would have been terrified of you," Tiara said. "But you comforted me."

"I am a person," Astrid said. "A deadly person, but I mean well by this group, and by you too. You have no need to fear me."

"Now that I know you, I don't fear you," Tiara said. "And you're right: my bad hair is nothing compared to your situation."

"About that hair," Pewter said. "It may be your blessing, not your curse."

"No more than Astrid's death glare is her blessing."

"She helps ensure the safety of our party. Your hair may be similarly useful."
"How?"

"For one thing, it might enable you to float or fly, if you gave it full rein."

"I don't see how." But she was obviously intrigued.

Astrid found a toehold and stepped into the dialogue. "Repeat after me: 'I love my hair. I want it to prosper. More power to it.'"

Bemused, Tiara repeated the words. Her hair flared out twice as far, reaching toward the ceiling. It was almost pulling her up with it.

"That's it," Astrid said. "Now wrap it around your head, under your chin."

Double bemused, Tiara did so. And the hair drew on her head so hard that she was pulled up onto tiptoes.

"More," Astrid said.

"I love my hair," Tiara said.

And for a faction of a moment her feet left the floor. She wasn't jumping, she was being pulled upward.

"More."

"I want it to prosper. More power to it."

Now her feet left the floor entirely. She floated slowly up to the ceiling.

"So you can fly," Astrid said. "That may be only the beginning. If you stretch out your hair so that you can sit on it, it may lift your body more comfortably."

Tiara descended back to the floor. "What does it mean?"

"It means that you can escape this tower by yourself. Just train your hair, sit on it, and coast down to the ground. You can be free."

"Oh, I wouldn't dare!"

"You're afraid your hair might weaken and drop you to your death?"

"Or that my sisters would not approve."

The girl lacked confidence, for sufficient reason. Kandy prompted Ease, who was hardly loath. "Come with us for a while. We're looking for something significant that may be on one of these islands. You can show us around while you practice with your hair."

"That would be wonderful!" Tiara said. "You folk are accepting me as I am."

"We know the value of that," Astrid said.

They descended the long spiral stairway, Tiara preferring that to jumping out the window. But her feet were hardly touching the steps, either from lightness or delight.

Back on the ground, Pewter reverted the lock to locked. Let the sisters wonder how Tiara had escaped.

"I know all these islands," the girl said eagerly. She pointed. "That one's the Isle of Flies, populated by Mom and Pop Flies, Infield Flies, Time Flies, Fly Balls (uncouth as it is to refer to them), and Fruit Flies. You could catch some of those last ones; they are many kind of fruits, all quite ripe."

"I think we'll skip that island," Astrid said.

Kandy agreed. There was unlikely to be any hair to merge there, and she wasn't partial to flies anyway. Some of them bit.

"Next to it is the Isle of Bats," Tiara continued. "They're always playing baseball, cricket, and other games with bats."

"No," Astrid said.

"Then there's the Isle of Man. That's where men go who want to marry princesses, waiting for love-lorn ones to show up. I hear they don't even check their royal credentials, if a girl is pretty enough."

"Now that interests me," Astrid said. "I'm not a princess, but I am shapely."

Tiara looked at her. "If you promised not to kill them, many of those men might be interested."

"I will keep it in mind," Astrid said. "After the Quest is done."

"You're on a Quest? What is it?"

Astrid looked at Ease. "Is it all right to tell her?"

Ease had been covertly eying Tiara's body, evidently liking it. "Sure."

"We are on a Quest to find an elixir or something that will nullify the virus that is destroying puns."

"There's a virus destroying puns?" Tiara asked, shaken. "Most of my sisters are puns, and many of the creatures on these islands. It would be horrible if such a thing struck here."

"Horrible," Astrid agreed.

"But your sisters locked you in a tower," Ease said. "Wouldn't you be better off without them?"

"Oh, no, I don't want to lose my sisters," Tiara protested. "I want to fit in with them."

She was a nice girl, Kandy thought. That was perhaps her problem. But unless she found a permanent way to make her hair behave, her sisters would not welcome her. But how could they encourage riotously free hair to submit to taming? Wouldn't that in itself be a crime, considering that her hair was her magic?

Tiara returned to business. "Over there is the Isle of Conclusion. It's close enough to jump to, but folk who do aren't too popular, for some reason." She demonstrated by jumping to it. But she had not allowed for her newly-empowered hair, and sailed up over head height, doing an involuntary somersault in the air. She came down on her bottom, but fortunately her hair still lightened her, and the landing was not hard.

"Oh, I'm sorry," she said, getting up and brushing herself off. She looked at Ease. "Are you all right?"

"Oh, foo," Astrid muttered. "He's freaked out."

"Freaked out?"

"You must have spent some time in that tower," Astrid said.

"Yes, since I was a little girl. Why?"

"So you never learned about the power of panties. Which is all right; I only recently learned it myself. It's that when a man catches a glimpse of them, he freaks out. You flashed him when you jumped and tumbled."

"Oh, I'm so sorry! How can I fix it?"

"First, watch how you jump."

"I will."

"Then, snap your fingers."

Tiara snapped her fingers. Ease resumed animation, apparently unaware that he had been in stasis.

"And continue as if nothing happened," Astrid concluded.

"Something happened?" Ease asked.

"Tiara accidentally flashed you and you freaked out."

"I didn't know."

"And that's how it is," Astrid said to Tiara. "Go on with your tour."

"Gladly. I have spent years looking at all the islands from my turret, using my telescope. I have seen so much happening on them." She frowned prettily. "Though some of it was fogged out."

"Fogged out?" Ease asked.

"When a man and a woman came together, I see them hold each other and kiss, but then the fog surrounds them and I see nothing more. I really wonder what they do."

"How old are you?" Astrid asked.

"I will be eighteen tomorrow."

"That explains it. The Adult Conspiracy prevented you from seeing what you weren't supposed to. But tomorrow you will be able to see it."

"But I don't want to go back to the tower!"

"Maybe I could show you," Ease said.

Kandy gave him a mental kick in the groin.

"Or maybe not."

"But I'd really like to know!"

"Let's get on with the tour," Astrid said.

"Oh. Yes, of course. Over there is Key Board Island."

Kandy jumped at the mention of "board," though she realized it was not the same thing.

"What is there?" Pewter asked.

"It is full of keyboards and other useful interfaces," Tiara said. "But it is also overrun with mice. I would not want to go there, lest a mouse run up my leg."

"Maybe we can skip it," Pewter said with regret.

"Then there's Unicorn island," Tiara continued. "But they won't associate with anyone who's not a, um—"

"Virgin," Astrid said. She knew about it from Humfrey's half wife MareAnn.

"Yes, whatever that is." Tiara was evidently treading carefully here, hampered by her innocence. "The unicorns seldom cross to other islands. Sometimes young ones come from Love Spring Isle, but I've never been able to see what happens there."

TELL HER, Kandy thought to Ease. It occurred to her that Astrid was unlikely to know all the details either. STANDARD LORE.

"When creatures meet at a love spring, they summon the stork," Ease said. "Later the stork delivers a baby to them."

"But how do they—"

TOMORROW

"We'll tell you tomorrow," Ease said.

"Tomorrow," she agreed, not quite understanding the significance of her eighteenth birthday.

"Actually it's getting late in the day," Astrid said. "If we're not through with the Islands, we need to find a place to spend the night."

"We're not done," Pewter said. "We have not yet discovered the significance of this Event."

"And we haven't fixed Tiara's hair," Ease said.

Ease remained entirely too interested in Tiara for Kandy's taste. But she couldn't protest without confessing to herself that she was foolishly jealous.

"Tiara, do you know of an inn or other place where travelers on a Quest could safely stay the night?" Astrid asked.

"Why yes. There's a nice Inn on the Isle of Missed."

"The Isle of Mist? That sounds pleasant."

"No, it's the Isle of Missed. That's where women go who are looking for men. It's like the Isle of Man, only for women."

"The women who have been missed," Ease said. "That's really interesting."

Kandy had been afraid of that. She kept her mind shut.

"Yes, I have heard that Miss Q is there. She can't get anything right. And Miss Isle; she likes to throw things but her aim is very bad. She can't hit the broad side of a barn. Then there's Miss Shapen, who is not very pretty. And Miss Carry, who can't get the stork to deliver. And—"

"We get the picture," Astrid said. "It's only the inn we want."

Kandy was slightly comforted. It seemed there were reasons those women had been missed instead of misses-ed.

"This way," Tiara said. "It's on the other side of this island, beyond the Lethe stream. There's a boat." She started walking, light on her feet because of her uplifting hair.

"What stream?" Pewter asked alertly.

"Nobody can remember its real name. It's just a thin flow of water from somewhere to somewhere else. It's quite forgettable. No need to be concerned."

"On the contrary," Pewter said. "That streamlet is dangerous."

"Oh, have you been here before?"

"No. But Lethe water makes folk forget. We don't want to go anywhere near it."

"I don't remember anything bad associated with it." Then Tiara paused. "But if it makes folk forget—"

"Precisely. Avoid it."

"I will try to go around it. But I don't know the route well. It has been maybe ten years since I played there as a child."

"You didn't touch the water?" Astrid asked, alarmed.

"I don't remember. In fact I don't remember any of my childhood before that time." Tiara paused again. "Oh, my!"

It occurred to Kandy that there might have been more than just Tiara's hair to cause her sisters to lock her in the tower. It might have been for her own safety. At least until she got old enough to understand some of the more serious facts of life. Such as staying away from enchanted water of any kind.

They came to a field of flowering plants. "Oh, those are peas," Tiara said. "I do remember them. Try not to touch any."

"Why not?" Ease asked.

"They make you—oops!" For she had just brushed by a pea plant. She swayed uncertainly on her feet, looking foolish. "That must be a dip pea."

"Nonsense," Astrid said. "Peas should not make you foolish, they should make you—" Then she burst out laughing.

"And you touched a ha-pea," Tiara said.

Ease touched a plant, and suddenly made a loud twanging sound.

"And a harp-pea," Tiara said.

"Let's just plow through and be done with it," Pewter said. "There are too many for me to nullify."

They plowed through what turned out to be dip, nip, skip, slop, slur, snap, and others, judging by their reactions.

"I wonder if the Good Magician eats grum peas?" Astrid asked as they emerged from the field.

Kandy was almost tempted to hope that the pun virus passed here before they found the cure.

They came to a circular depression. It seemed to be a spring from which a streamlet of water flowed. They skirted it, but Astrid's dress flared out in a breeze and caught on a shrub. It pulled free in a quarter of a moment, but a sequin snagged. It ripped off and fell to the ground. It tumbled down the slope and splashed into the shallow spring.

"Oh, bleep!" Astrid swore as her dress became translucent.

"Your dress!" Tiara said, surprised.

"It happens when it loses a sequin," Astrid said. "I need to replace it. But there's a complication."

"I'll fetch the sequin," Tiara said, stepping carefully down toward the spring.

"Wait!" Pewter said. "That may be the source of the lethe stream!"

"I suppose it is," Tiara said. And paused again. "Oh, no!"

"We have a problem," Pewter said.

The others agreed. They sat on the bank gazing at the sequin.

"Here is the problem," Pewter said. "The sequin is just under the surface of the water. It will be easy to retrieve if this is ordinary water. But if it is lethe water, whoever touches it will forget what he's doing, and perhaps a lot more. This is a risk that should be avoided."

"It's my fault," Tiara said. "I shouldn't have led you here. I'll go fetch it, and if I forget, it's not much of a loss. You can go on with your Quest."

"This is reasonable," Pewter agreed.

"The bleep it is!" Astrid exploded. "I'm a basilisk, but even I know that's not the way to treat a girl who is helping us."

Good for her! Kandy was positively coming to like Astrid. Actually, Tiara was showing sterling qualities too.

"Pewter is a machine," Ease said. "He doesn't care."

"A machine?" Tiara asked.

"I guess we haven't clarified that," Pewter said. "I am Com Pewter, an electronic machine. I can change reality in my immediate vicinity."

"You are odder folk than I knew," Tiara said in wonder. "But I like you and want to help you. So—"

"Not that way," Astrid said firmly.

"I'll just fish it out with my board," Ease said.

Astrid opened her mouth to protest, but paused. Kandy knew why. She didn't want to blab the secret.

Kandy tried to formulate a mind-changing directive, but Ease acted with the assurance of a man to whom hard things could always be made easy. He leaned over the pool and swept the board down into it before Kandy could send her thought. The tip caught the sequin and heaved it out of the water to land on the bank.

Kandy discovered she was holding her wooden breath. Did she retain her memory? It seemed she did. At least she couldn't think of anything she had forgotten. So maybe it wasn't lethe water, or it didn't affect wood.

Astrid was looking stricken. "Are—is—is the board all right?" she asked.

"Nothing wrong with the board," Ease said. "Wood doesn't have memory anyway."

"Maybe not any more," Astrid murmured, pained.

"I made a spell," Pewter said. "Lethe nulled when touching board."

"What a relief!"

So that was it, Kandy thought. Any lethe water that touched her had been nullified into ordinary water so that it didn't affect her. Pewter might just have saved her memory, and thus her life. Too bad he hadn't thought of that before, instead of wasting time discussing how they were going to get the sequin out.

"Who cares?" Ease asked. "It's just a board."

Kandy bridled. But she reminded herself for the umpteenth time: he didn't know.

Astrid, who did know, reorganized. "I get foolishly attached to things. Forget it."

"So do I," Ease said, gazing fixedly at her dress. It remained translucent, and the outline of her panties showed.

"Outline fades," Pewter said. The panties faded out. This meant that now Astrid's bare-seeming bottom showed instead, but that was less magical. Indeed, Ease's attention faltered.

"Let's get that sequin back on," Ease said.

"Not yet," Pewter said. "For three reasons. First, the sequin will generate a new Event, and we don't want that this late in the day. Second, we want to find that inn and get a good night's rest. Third, we have not yet fathomed how Tiara's hair relates, so must settle that before we depart."

"I could use a good dinner and some shut-eye," Ease agreed.

"I can use a night's rest," Astrid said.

"And I need to study that hair more thoroughly," Pewter said.

"I just wish it would behave," Tiara said. "I can't even sleep well when it keeps trying to fly away."

"Hair behaves," Pewter said.

Immediately the hair relaxed, falling neatly into place.

"Oh, that's wonderful!" Tiara said. "Thank you, Pewter."

"That is only a temporary solution, as you know," Pewter said.

Ease's attention focused on her. "You know, with your hair like that, you aren't bad looking." It was a typically clumsy male observation. The girl was almost excruciatingly pretty.

"Thank you," she said, glancing at him speculatively.

Oh, foo, Kandy thought, disgusted. If he wasn't eying panties, he was eying faces. And those with the panties and faces were responding. While Kandy remained a board.

"I will carry the sequin," Pewter said, picking it up.

They moved on, Tiara leading the way, followed by Ease, then Astrid, then Pewter. That meant that Ease's attention was on Tiara. Kandy was pleased to observe that Astrid looked slightly uncomfortable with that. But if Astrid had led the way, the man would probably have freaked out even without her panties showing.

They passed a tree with hanging streamers of cloth. Astrid considered it. "I could tear off one of those and wrap it around outside my dress, so that it wouldn't be so distracting."

"Don't do that," Tiara said. "That's a tearable idea."

"A terrible idea? Why?"

"That, too."

"I don't understand." Neither did Ease, or Kandy.

"I know this tree. It grows tearable cloth that is terrible to wear, because it wraps around and tries to make a cocoon with the person inside."

"Let me try it," Ease said. "With my board." He poked the board at one of the sections of cloth, then twisted so that the cloth wrapped around the board, making a tricky maneuver easy. Then he twitched his wrist, and the cloth was ripped off the tree. Immediately it constricted tightly around the board, completely covering it.

"See? Tearing it is dangerous."

"Yeah. Now how do I get it off?" Because the cloth had indeed formed a firm cocoon and he didn't want to touch it lest it wrap around *him*.

"I'll do it," Astrid said. She put her face to the cloth and breathed on it. The cloth wrinkled and shriveled. Soon it dropped limply off.

Tiara was plainly impressed. "Maybe you could wear it, after all."

"No. It would take longer, but it wouldn't last. My body ambiance is not as intense as my breath or gaze, but it is there."

Still, Kandy thought, it was a clear demonstration of the basilisk's power.

They came to the shore. There was a small boat tied to a tree near the beach. Across a brief expanse of water was another island shrouded in mist: the Isle of Missed.

"We have a problem," Pewter said.

Ease saw it. "Four people. Boat for two."

"We girls will sit on your laps," Tiara said brightly.

Worse and worse. Pewter would not be affected, but Ease would be disgustingly delighted.

Which was exactly the case. Astrid sat on Pewter, Tiara said on Ease. Ease was clearly on the lowest rung of heaven. Fortunately the boat was self propelled, and the trip was short. In a brief time minus a few moments they were there.

The inn turned out to be very good. They had a nice dinner, then retired to a two room suite, the girls in one room, the men in the other. Kandy had to give Ease a hard mental jolt to persuade him to decide on that arrangement.

When Ease slept, Kandy transformed. She moved his hand from her ankle to her waist and sat up. "Thank you for saving me," she said to Pewter.

"It was necessary," Pewter said. "Without you, Ease would be ungovernable."

Oh. "That, too," she agreed.

"Tiara's hair will revert the moment she is out of my vicinity. She will not have a feasible reception by her sisters. We must find a solution, or take her with us."

"Do we have a solution?"

"No."

"What about merging the hair?"

"Aside from my ambiance keeping it tame, I am not aware of any relevance."

"Is it possible that later in the Quest that relevance would appear?"

"It is possible."

Kandy sighed. "Then I suppose we must take her with us. She does seem to be a good girl, even if she is too pretty for my taste." She looked around. "There's nothing here to interest me. Can you make me sleep?"

"No, your wakefulness at night is integral to the spell and I can't override it without unkind consequences."

"Unkind?"

"You might never wake again."

That was persuasive. "Can you conjure some diversion?"

"Do you play chess?"

"No."

A checkered board appeared with a number of carved figurines. "Learn."

Kandy learned. It turned out to be quite a game. Pewter set his playing level at the lowest tier, and when she got good enough to beat that, he reset it at the next tier up. By the time the night was done, she had reached the third tier and was thoroughly conversant with the moves and strategies. "I like this game," she concluded. "I think I will not be bored at night again." She smiled. "Not a bored board."

"You have a flair for it."

Then Ease woke. She reverted and the chessboard faded out.

"My dream woman plays chess," Ease remarked. "I don't know how I know, but I have this vision of her sitting up nude and moving the pieces."

"Your dreams are foolish," Pewter said.

"Why would she play chess when she was nude with you?" Astrid asked.

"Beats me," Ease admitted. "I wasn't watching the board anyway."

That was what he thought.

Pewter oriented on Tiara. "Your hair will revert to wildness the instant we depart."

"I know," Tiara said sadly. "I will be so sorry to see you go. But I know you must complete your quest."

"Come with us," Ease said.

"Oh, you wouldn't want an innocent girl like me along." Yet she was plainly tempted, and perhaps not entirely because of how it would help her hair.

"You are now of age to abate your innocence," Astrid said. "We would be glad to have you."

"Are you sure?" She was almost pathetic in her eagerness. Kandy knew why: they accepted her, regardless of her hair.

"Yes," Pewter said.

"Well, then, all right. Thank you." She tried to stifle a tear, unsuccessfully.

Just like that it was decided. They wrapped up whatever business they had and departed the nice inn. When they had a suitably private place, Pewter brought out the sequin and pinned it to Astrid's dress. And the scene changed.

CHAPTER 5:

VIRUS

They stood at the edge of a flowery meadow. People were coming from a
nearby village, including a man and a horse. He was not riding the horse, he
was walking beside it. He wore a hair shirt but seemed cheerful.

"Hello, friends!" the man called jovially. "Have you come to join the party?"

"Party?" Ease asked blankly.

"We are about to celebrate the Pun," the man said. "Let's introduce
ourselves. I am Mitch, the master of ceremonies. This is the mare of Punic
Curse, so called because there are more puns here than anywhere else. It was
considered a curse, until we got the bright idea to make something of it and
convert it to a blessing. But we don't want to change the name of the village.
So the mare authorized it and I am implementing it, and everybody is welcome
to a punderful time."

"Hello Mitch," Ease said, slightly uneasily. "Hello, mare. I am Ease, and
this is Astrid. And Pewter. And Tiara. We're on a Quest. So its just coincidence
that we landed here. I think."

"You think?"

"Well, we're trying to save the puns from the plague."

"Plague?"

"It evidently has not yet reached here. It's a virus that destroys puns. We are searching for an anti-virus to stop it."

"Surely you jest!" Mitch said. "Nothing can stop puns. We depend on that."

A glance circled around, starting with Ease, glancing off Astrid and Tiara, and landing on Pewter. The events were supposed to be relevant, so there should be a reason they were here. But the folk of Punic Curse were oblivious. There seemed to be no point in bothering them about something that, with luck, would never happen here.

"We hope you are correct," Pewter said. "We shall be glad to participate in your festivities, until we find whatever it is we are looking for here."

"Excellent!" Mitch moved on, organizing the party.

Many more villagers were gathering. Soon there was music, as they played huge ear-shaped drums, a trio of ugly bird-women played harps, and odd-shaped horns tooted. Kandy diverted herself by checking off the puns: ear drums, harp-Ps, insti-toots. Parrots played really dirty stringed instruments, (poll-lutes), violent-looking men rang bells, (reb-bells), reading from sheets hung on a line in front of them, (sheet music). Women pounded out rolls with rocks in their hands, (rock and roll). A man whose shirt identified him as Trom beat out the rhythm with a bone (Trom-bone). Another man identified as Nick whistled a tune, (Tune-Nick). Beside him an alien creature shaped like a gourd strummed on strings stretched across its belly, (ukul-alien). Several others were playing so hard they were sweating, a sweat-band. Others were blowing into their shoes, (shoe-horns). Nearby were a number of musical bars: soap, salad, sand, gold, candy. There were tuning forks, knives, spoons, plates, and glasses.

Before long the villagers were dancing, some decorated with buns, (abun-dance), cords, (ac-cord dance), while some seemed to ignore their partners (avoid-dance). A man in armor danced with several women (Dance Knight).

"Oh, let's do it!" Tiara said. "I haven't danced with a partner in so long, and never with an adult!"

"I don't know how to dance," Astrid protested.

"These days that doesn't matter," Tiara said. "You just get out there and bounce your body around. I'll show you." She tugged Astrid onto the dance floor and started jiggling her body.

Astrid just stood there uncertainly. Mitch glanced her way. Suddenly she began to jiggle too. Her body was well made for it, and in one and a half to two moments several men were heading her way.

"What did you do?" Pewter asked Mitch.

"I sent her an idea I got from Tiara," Mitch said. "That's my talent: to fetch and send ideas. Not big ones, and just one at a time, but sometimes it helps."

So it seemed. Now that she had gotten started, Astrid was really animating her body. Kandy hoped she didn't shake off any sequins.

Then two young women oriented on Ease and Pewter and dragged them into the dance too. The one opposite Ease had a nymph-like figure and seemed to be wearing little beside a bra and, well, her mid section seemed to be missing. She saw Ease staring without seeing, and explained: "Camouflage Panties. Don't worry; they are there." She caught his hand and put it on her hidden hip. "See?"

DON'T FREAK OUT! Kandy thought, catching him just in time. He couldn't see the panties, but it seemed that touching them was just about as effective.

In due course the music paused, and the dancers sought refresh-mints along with boot rear, Peace Tree Tea, and cakes in the shape of cups.

A male bovine wandered onto the field. "Scram, Bull!" someone yelled, and the creature hastily departed.

Overhead two terns flew. One doubled sharply back the way it had come: a U-tern. The other flew in a straight line, never swerving: a tern pike. Then several male sheep whose wool resembled open books charged across the field, trampling flowers and upsetting tables: ram pages.

"What is that?" Tiara asked.

Ease looked. It was a giant hand wearing a skirt, walking along on its fingers. A HAND MAIDEN Kandy thought to Ease.

"A hand maiden," he said.

"Oh, you're so smart!"

She was flattering him, and he was enjoying it. Kandy stifled her resentment yet again.

"It getting hot," Astrid said. "I'm going to the shade of that pine tree."

"Don't do that," Pewter warned. "It's a porcu-pine, with quills."

There was a scream from the edge of the field. "My blood hound just dissolved!" a woman cried.

Kandy had seen that hound, which looked as if it were constantly bleeding; it was a pun. They looked toward the woman, and there before her was a puddle of blood. The hound had indeed gone all the way.

"That could be mischief," Pewter murmured.

It was. The pun musical instruments were dissolving into gunk, as were the pun foods. So were some pun people. The malady was spreading slowly across the field, leaving putrid gunk behind.

"What is it?" Mitch asked, distraught.

"It is the plague," Pewter said. "The pun dissolving virus has arrived."

"We must stop it!"

"That is our Quest. But we have not yet found the antidote."

Mitch rushed off toward the disaster. "Move out! Move out!" he cried. "Get away from the carnage. It's a pun destroyer."

That was not the best thing to do. People screamed and panicked, knocking each other down as they tried to escape.

"Do something!" Astrid told Pewter. "I know you can."

"My firewall is operative only in my immediate vicinity," Pewter said. "But I will do what I can." Then his voice amplified enormously. "It affects only puns. If you're not a pun there is no danger. Hold your ground."

The people heard him and hesitated.

"Let the puns escape," Pewter continued loudly. "Help them escape."

Then the people knew what to do. They stopped stampeding and let the pun folk run unhampered. The virus advance was slow, and the people easily left it behind. But most of the puns were things that could not move on their own. They had to be carried, or they were doomed.

Mitch hastily organized a crew to pile stones, making a crude wall, in an attempt to stop the virus. But it surged over the wall unimpeded.

"Do something more," Astrid told Pewter.

"I need an idea. I'm a machine, not an original thinker."

"Mitch!" Astrid called. "Pewter needs an idea!"

"I'm busy at the moment," Mitch called back.

"To save the pun folk," Astrid clarified.

"Oh!" Mitch concentrated. "Fetching fetching....sending!"

"Got it!" Pewter said. "There's an old walled fort near the village. I will defend it with a firewall. But I need to get there before the virus does."

"I'll help," Tiara said. "Can you make my hair stronger?"

"Yes." Tiara's neat hairdo puffed apart and her hair radiated straight out from her head like a spiked helmet. The tug was strong; her feet started to leave the ground. She skipped across to Pewter and flung her arms about him. "Now run!"

Pewter ran, and Tiara ran with him, lifting him so that he was light on his feet. They made excellent time. Ease and Astrid followed, falling behind despite their best efforts. That hair really did make a difference!

They reached the village, ran through it, and came to the fort. It was dilapidated but sturdy, and fairly small, but there was a fair amount of space in the central court. "I can do this," Pewter said as they entered.

Tiara let go of him—and floated up over the fort. Quickly she reached up and wrapped a hank of her hair in her hand so that it no longer radiated. That cut down the flotation, and she sank slowly back to the ground.

Pewter climbed to the highest turret, which was barely a second story, and stood gazing around. He gestured. "Firewall is up," he announced. "Now get the puns inside."

Mitch had continued organizing, and had half a slew of pun people hurrying to the fort, accompanied by others carrying valued puns. One woman had a small potted pas-tree loaded with sweet breads; another carried a basket of acting rolls, with the rolls posturing grandly as if on stage. Another carried a basket of corn ears, many of them alertly listening, and yet another, musical beets playing a thumping melody. They all crowded into the little fort.

Sparks jumped as they crossed into it. "It's the firewall," Pewter explained. "It won't hurt you, it just needs to be sure there's none of the virus on you."

Soon the fort was crowded with people and puns. The last ones just in time; after them the fire rose high, sizzling, as the virus touched it.

They stood and gazed out the front gate and narrow windows of the fort as the crackling continued. The virus surrounded the fort, trying to get in, but the firewall blocked it. Every time the plague tried, the wall of fire burned it up. After a while it stopped trying, but they knew it was still lurking out there, just waiting for some avenue inside, or for a pun to try to leave the fort. They were prisoners.

"Oh, my hair!" Tiara wailed. Indeed, it was tugging every which way, completely unruly; people were noticing.

"Pewter's whole attention is taken up maintaining the firewall," Astrid said. "He can't pacify your hair without risking a break that could be disastrous."

"Of course. I'm not complaining." But she looked miserable.

"It's interesting hair," Mitch said. "And you really helped get Pewter here in time."

Tiara melted, appreciating the insight. "But you wouldn't want to be close to it."

"Why not? It's a challenge." He took a double handful of it and put his face in it. "Makes me feel light-headed."

Well, now, Kandy thought. Maybe Mitch and Tiara would get along.

"You shouldn't grab her hair like that," Ease said.

"You're right," Mitch said, embarrassed. "I got carried away, as it were. I was over-familiar. I apologize, Tiara."

"Oh, there's no need," she said.

"In fact I'd better make it a gourd-style apology."

"A what?"

Kandy knew what that was, but evidently Tiara didn't, having been isolated so long.

"Like this." Mitch took her carefully in his arms and gently kissed her. "Do you accept?"

Tiara was plainly stunned. "I don't know," she said uncertainly. "What has a kiss to do with it?"

"Then I must try again," Mitch said. He kissed her more emphatically. "Now do you accept?"

She gazed at him, amazed. "I don't—"

"So I must try again." This time he kissed her so thoroughly that little hearts flew out. "Do you accept now?"

Kandy prompted Ease. "Say yes," he called.

"Yes," Tiara said faintly. "But what—?"

"That was a gourd style apology," Mitch said. "They are never declined."

"I can see why," Tiara said dazedly.

"It is a social convention that originated in the dream realm of the gourd," Mitch said. "Then it got loose in the waking realm. Folk seem to like it."

"I wonder why," Tiara said, sitting down to recover.

"That's interesting," Astrid said. "I'd try it, but I doubt my partner would survive."

Then Mitch had to get back to business. "Folk, we'll have to organize for a siege. We need to know how much food we have here, for one thing."

The mare walked a little apart, and the villagers gathered around her, showing what they had salvaged. Kandy realized that though the mare might be a pun for mayor, she was doing the job. It would be a shame to let the virus get her.

Soon the report was in: there was one small pie tree in the fort, two tea peas, a spect rum, and an Apple tree, but that last grew app pills for magic mirrors rather than anything edible. So they would soon need more food, until they found a way to lift the siege.

"We'll make a party of non-puns to go out and scout for more food and drink," Mitch decided.

"That's me," Ease said.

"And me," Tiara said. She evidently liked the idea of going out with Mitch. Kandy realized that the gourd-style apology had profoundly affected her.

"And me," Astrid said.

The party of four (Kandy didn't count) went out into the stricken landscape. They felt the tingle as they passed through the firewall.

What they found was desolation. The pun folk had been dissolved and the regular folk had fled. All around were messy puddles where puns had been. One made Kandy wince, to the extent she was able: a large hand-shaped splotch of goo, the remnant of the hand maiden.

"We can dip water from the river," Mitch said. "We can pick fruits from non-pun fruit trees, and dig mundane vegetables from the ground. It won't be a fancy repast, but it can be done."

"Yes, of course," Tiara said. Kandy suspected she was likely to agree with anything Mitch said, and not because she feared another apology.

They got to work doing it, and reasonably soon had several bags of assorted things. They brought them back, passing through the firewall and presenting them to the mare.

But there was a problem. The fruits could be eaten, but there were not enough to feed all the refugees. The vegetables were corn and potatoes, that needed to be cooked. For that they needed fire, and no one knew how to make it without magic, and no one had fire-making magic.

"Anyone have an idea?" Mitch asked.

A villager raised his hand. "Got it," Mitch said. "Use the firewall."

They made a fireplace, filled it with bits of wood and dry moss, then Ease poked some paper into the firewall. There was a crackle and it caught fire. It was a pun, but puns were protected here, by definition. Ease touched it to the kindling, making what might have been a difficult task easy. Soon they had a nice little blaze and were able to roast the potatoes and cook the corn.

But when they passed these foods out, the people didn't like them. They were used to fresh pies from pie trees, while these were just individual things. No one knew how to cook. It was the same for the water: folk who had existed on boot rear and tsoda pop found plain water to be tasteless.

Mitch shook his head. "I fear we're in for a long siege."

A smoky blob formed beside the fire. "What is encountering here?"

"Oh, bleep!" Mitch swore. "I hope that's not what I fear it is."

Kandy hoped so too. She had heard of a pesky demoness who used inappropriate words. Who loved to seduce innocent men.

"What do you fear it is?" Ease asked.

"I don't understand," Tiara said. "Encountering?"

"Occurring, coming out, taking place, bechancing, materializing—" the voice said.

"Happening?"

"Whatever." Now the smoke formed into the semblance of a dusky shapely woman: the demoness.

"And it is," Mitch said, disgusted. "The notorious Demoness Metria."

"Thank you," the woman said. "I love being appreciated."

"I still don't understand," Tiara said.

The demoness eyed her. "Well, maybe if you tried brushing your hair out, your head would function better."

"I can't do a thing with my hair!"

"Don't let her bait you," Mitch said quickly. "Metria is always mischief. She seeks out anything interesting, and comes to mess it up. Just ignore her and she'll go away."

"Obese fortune," Metria said. "I'll digress exactly when I choose to."

"You'll what?" Tiara asked innocently.

"Exit, straggle, diverge, quit, leave—"

"Depart?"

"Whatever," Metria agreed irritably.

"If you know so many words, why can't you get the right one?"

"She has a speech impediment," Mitch said. "It dates from the time a sphinx stepped on her and scrambled her brains."

"A sphinx!" Tiara said, impressed. "It's a wonder she survived at all."

"It wasn't easy," Metria said. "I fractured into three partial identities: myself, D. Mentia who is a little crazy, and Woe Betide, who is an innocent child. We don't always get along."

"I would probably like the child," Tiara said. "I was locked up in a tower as a child, and I'm still getting used to the complicated outside realm."

Metria softened visibly, her sharp curves turning woolly. "Maybe so. But about your hair—"

"Its my magic. It is anti-gravitic. It wants to float away, maybe taking my head away with it. I can't control it, and it ruins my social life."

"All it needs is a cardiopulmonary exercise."

"A what?"

"A condit," Mitch said impatiently. "Stop reacting to her lapses. That's what she wants."

"What kind of a con?" Metria asked.

"Ference, template, gress, sole, troll, solate—" Mitch said.

"Ditioner?"

"Whatever," Mitch agreed irritably. "Now you've got me doing it."

Metria eyed him. "You'd really be annoyed if I stayed around."

Mitch opened his mouth, but stifled his retort, knowing that the demoness would just become more annoying.

"A conditioner?" Tiara asked.

"Like this." Metria dissolved into smoke, which swirled around Tiara's head. It infiltrated her hair, and faded out, leaving the hair perfectly coiffed.

A mirror appeared in Tiara's hand. "Look," it said.

Tiara looked. "Oh my! I'm beautiful!"

"That's me infusing your hair, holding it down," the mirror said. "Do you want me to go away?"

"No!" Tiara said, just before Mitch could say yes.

"Good enough." The mirror puffed into smoke and dissipated.

"Bleep," Mitch muttered, and moved away. But Kandy saw him glance back at Tiara, whose whole aspect was now a magnitude prettier. He was noticing.

"Actually it is a useful service, and it keeps her out of *our* hair," Ease said. "She strikes me as a pretty interesting creature."

"Oh, bleep," Astrid muttered. She was no more interested in having a sexy demoness along than Kandy was, for the same reason. But what could they do? Tiara obviously adored the hairdo.

"We have a problem," Mitch called from the periphery.

"We'd better check," Astrid said. She and Ease hurried to join the man.

"I think the firewall is weakening," Mitch said. "That was a Cough-Fee drink."

There was a mug on the ground, but it wasn't coughing, it was dissolving, an obvious victim of the virus.

Ease acted immediately. He swung the bat down to strike the mug, sending it hurtling out through the firewall and into the mess beyond. Kandy made sure the hit was strong and true.

"Thank you," Mitch said. "But we had better check on Pewter."

They did. "I am weakening," Pewter admitted. "The fort is larger than my home cave. I shall not be able to maintain the firewall much longer. I am also unable to do any reality-changing magic while maintaining the firewall, now that the virus siege is upon us. Such as enhancing Tiara's hair-flotation ability."

So it wasn't just Tiara's hair that had enabled her to float, Kandy realized. Pewter had been enhancing it.

"We shall have to move on soon," Astrid said. "Ultimately Pewter must protect himself, or the Quest is likely doomed."

"How can you do that, trapped here in the fort?" Mitch asked.

"We travel via my Sequins of Events," she explained.

"There's a pun, I think. What does it mean?"

"Each time a sequin falls off my dress, and we put it back, it triggers a whole new Event. That's how we came here, and how we'll move on. But we don't want to desert all these folk who have taken refuge here."

"I think we need an idea," Ease said.

"I will cast for one," Mitch said. He closed his eyes, concentrating. "Got one: take us with you."

"I don't know," Astrid said uncertainly. "The sequin affects only the immediate vicinity."

"We'll crowd close," Mitch said.

Pewter glanced at him. "Do it soon. I am fading."

"I need to make an announcement that will override the background noise and confusion," Mitch said.

Tiara joined them. "I heard that," her hair said. "I'll help."

"We don't need your help, demoness," Mitch snapped.

"Yes you do." The hair formed into a large cone. "Blow me; I'm a megaphone."

Mitch hesitated, then yielded with imperfect grace. He took the phone, put it to his mouth, and spoke. "Here ye! Hear ye!" his voice blasted out, wonderfully loud. "We have to get out of here. There is a way. Gather immediately around me."

The megaphone shaped back into Tiara's neat hairdo. "See? You needed me," the voice of the demoness said. Mitch didn't answer. It seemed that he liked Tiara but not the demoness, and having them so closely linked disturbed him.

Folk hesitated, but then the mare showed the way, trotting to the stair, climbing the steps, and joining them on the upper floor. The people followed. They did not know exactly what was going on, but they trusted the mare, and the mare trusted Mitch. Soon all of them were jammed tightly around Pewter, Ease, Astrid, and Tiara.

"You had better do it, Tiara," Astrid said. "You won't freak out."

"Freak out?" Mitch asked.

Tiara removed a sequin and held it. The dress went translucent, showing Astrid's phenomenal bra and panties. Mitch was silent; he had freaked out. So had several male villagers.

Tiara pinned the sequin back in place. The dress resumed its color. Ease, whom Kandy had prompted to close his eyes, snapped his fingers, waking the other men. All folk gazed around, surprised.

The scene had changed. Now they were in a large castle courtyard big enough to have enclosed the entire little fort.

Just in time. Pewter, strained to the breaking point, collapsed. So did the firewall. Fortunately no virus came to wipe out the puns.

"Well, now!" Two children, about two years old, were standing on a balcony overlooking the courtyard. One was a human boy in a boy suit. The other was a skeleton girl in a girl dress.

"I know of them," Mitch said, amazed. "Princess Dawn married a walking skeleton and the stork delivered two crossbreed children. This must be Caprice Castle!"

"Sure it is," the boy said. "I'm Piton. She's Data. Who are you?"

"I am Mitch, and these are my friends. We just escaped the pun plague. May we talk to your parents? We may have a problem."

"Problem?" Ease asked.

"They collect and put away puns at Caprice Castle."

"Oh-uh."

The children considered, then decided to approve this.

In a moment and a half a skeletal man and a beautiful woman appeared. "We are Picka Bone, master of Caprice Castle and Xanth's leading musician, and Princess Sorceress Dawn," the woman announced formally. "To what do we owe this unexpected visit? The children tell us there may be a problem."

"There are puns among us we don't want dispatched," Mitch said bluntly.

"May I touch you?"

Mitch was startled. "If you wish, Princess."

Dawn stepped forward and took his hand for a moment. "Oh, my."

"We really did not choose to come here, and do not wish to cause trouble," Mitch said. "We—"

Dawn silenced him with a smile. "Of course." She turned to the skeleton. "Dear, see that our guests are comfortable. We have much to discuss with a few members of this group."

Soon Mitch, Pewter, Ease, Astrid, and Tiara were seated on comfortable chairs in the castle living room facing Princess Dawn, while Picka Bone, ably assisted by the two children, saw to the comfort of the villagers. It seemed that the castle had plenty of everything needful, whether food, drink, or elbow room.

"My talent is to know everything about any living thing I touch," the Princess said. "I have now touched each of you, so there is no need for further introductions. Only Mitch is precisely what he seems: a man trying to help his village."

Oh? Did she know that Astrid was a basilisk? That Tiara's hair was a demoness? That Ease's board was an enchanted woman?

"Yes," Dawn said, looking directly at the board.

Kandy stifled any further thoughts she might have had.

"We had not known about the pun virus before," the Princess continued. "We presume the Good Magician was keeping it quiet so as not to incite panic. But your recent experience shows that the time for quietude is past. Something has to be done."

"But—" Mitch said.

"But we at Caprice are in the business of eliminating puns," Dawn said for him. "That does not mean we hate them or want to see them all gone. It is simply that puns have been spreading so widely that they are choking off normal things, like weeds, so need to be culled. We collect them and store them, and will release them again at such time as they are needed." She frowned, and the room seemed to darken. "Which may be sooner than we anticipated. This virus, in contrast, completely destroys them. That is quite another matter." She smiled, and the room brightened again. "Bluntly: we are on your side. We do not support punhibition, with secret speakeasies that get raided. We will continue collecting puns, but not to destroy them; to preserve them for the future. Meanwhile the virus needs to be stopped."

"This is a relief to hear, Princess," Pewter said.

She laughed, and the castle seemed to laugh with her. "Whatever would Xanth do without you and Com Passion?" she asked. "The shoe trees and humble pie plants? De-Ogre-Ants that repel ogres? No, Xanth is largely made of puns. We just don't want it to be overwhelmed by them."

"So the villagers of Punic Curse have nothing to fear from you?" Mitch asked.

"Nothing," Dawn agreed. "Indeed, we will care for them here until they can find a new location for your destroyed village. They have had a horrible experience."

"We thank you, Princess," Mitch said gratefully.

"Now the question is how can we address this menace of the virus? How can we best assist your Quest to discover the antidote?"

A despairing look passed among them and fell to the floor. None of them had any idea.

"I think we will set our pun collectors to searching for that antidote too,"

Dawn said. "While your Quest continues. Is there anything we can provide you that will facilitate your mission?"

"Just information," Ease said. "The Good Magician said to merge the hair. Do you have any idea what he meant?"

"Surely not the way the Demoness Metria has done with Tiara's hair," Dawn said. "He can't stand Metria. It must be some other person's hair." She glanced at Mitch. "That might be you. You should join the Quest."

"Me? I'm just the village master of ceremonies, assisting the mare." He grimaced. "That did not work out well today."

"No fault of yours. Your village just happened to be in the path of the invading virus. What is remarkable about you is not your talent so much as your hair. I've never seen hair on a man quite like it."

"It's nothing compared to Tiara's hair. Hers is fascinating, when not tied down by the demoness. I envy it."

"You do?" Tiara asked, pleased.

"What's so unusual about it?" Ease asked.

Dawn smiled. "Mitch, perhaps you should take off your shirt."

"What does that have to do with his hair?" Astrid asked.

Mitch shrugged. "If you say so." He drew up his hair shirt and pulled it off over his head. He let it drop. It did not fall; it hung there from his head.

"Your shirt is your hair!" Tiara exclaimed.

"It's so long and thick it gets in my way," Mitch said. "Sometimes folk mistake me for a woman. So I try to make it useful. Yours, in contrast, is magic. That's much better."

"I don't mistake you for a woman," Tiara said.

"The question is whose hair is to be merged, and how," Dawn said. "None of you know that, so I don't know it either. But the Good Magician, however grumpy and obscure he may seem, is always correct. It has to be relevant in some manner. It could be Tiara's hair, but it also could be Mitch's hair. Since we don't know, the sensible thing is for you to join the Quest, Mitch, so as to be there when it counts—if it turns out to be your hair."

"I might think of ways I'd like to merge with Tiara," Mitch said. "But I wasn't thinking of our hair." He started plaiting his hair back into the shirt. His fingers worked rapidly; it seemed he had done this many times before.

"Good thing, too," Tiara's hair said while Tiara blushed. She had not yet been educated about the secrets of the Adult Conspiracy, but she was evidently getting a notion. Kandy realized that having the demoness around was likely to hasten that education considerably.

"Well, think about it," Dawn said. "Now I must go to be sure our other guests are satisfied." She got up and departed.

"She's giving us a change to discuss it among ourselves," Astrid said. "There does seem to be a good chance that Mitch's hair relates. Maybe he should join us."

"If he does, I'll go!" Tiara's hair threatened.

"Is that a promise?" Mitch asked.

"Oh, manipulate!" Metria said, separating from the hair to float as a dark little cloud over Tiara's head.

"Oh, what?" Tiara asked.

"Circumvent, sidestep, avoid, cheat, hedge, chocolate—"

"Fudge?"

"Whatever," the demoness agreed crossly. "No it's not a promise. It was supposed to be a threat, had you had the wit to take it as such."

"If the members of the Quest want me, I'll join," Mitch said as he pulled his new shirt on over his head. When it settled into place it was hardly evident that it was made from his own hair. He was indeed making it useful.

"I want you!" Tiara said eagerly.

Mitch nodded. Her interest was sparking his interest.

"I second the motion," Astrid said. "You are a talented, useful person who well might help us accomplish our purpose."

"Well," Ease started. Then Kandy, concluding that she liked Mitch, prompted him. "I third it."

That left Pewter. "Mitch acted to get us here when I was failing. That will do for me."

"Very well, then," Mitch said. "I will join, and help in whatever way I can." He stroked Tiara's wild hair. "I hope you can keep the demoness out of your hair, however."

"Corpulent gamble!" Metria said, diving for the hair. In half a moment it was conventionally coiffed.

"Maybe that's the point of merging the hair," Astrid said. "To get rid of the demoness."

"I heard that!" the hair said.

The others laughed. They might not be able to get rid of Metria, but they could tease her.

"But we still need to find the virus antidote," Pewter reminded them.

"I have no idea how to do that," Mitch said.

"None of us do," Astrid said. "But if it does happen to be your hair to be merged, you'll surely do your part."

"I will do my best."

"I wonder," Tiara said. "Can you weave your hair into a blanket?"

"Oh, I do that all the time, at night. It's warm."

"For two?"

He looked at her. "If your hair joined it, they might even make a bouncy mattress."

"Yes," she whispered, blushing furiously.

"Oh, for bawling out deafeningly!" Metria said.

Princess Dawn returned. "The villagers are satisfied. Caprice Castle will drop them off at a safe place to make a new village. Will you be joining them, Mitch?"

"I fear I will not," Mitch said. "I am joining the Quest."

"Then you folk will want to stay the night, to rest, before you go to your next Event in the morning."

"That makes sense," Pewter said. "I am recovering, but could use more rest."

The others agreed. They were on the verge of relaxing when the two children, Piton and Data, appeared. "The virus is outside," Piton said.

"Oh, bleep!" Pewter swore. "I'm not ready for it."

"Do not be concerned," Dawn said. "Caprice is a traveling castle. It will simply move to a safe place before we let anyone out. You may relax."

Even Kandy felt relieved by that.

"I must go bid parting to the others and the mare," Mitch said.

"I'll go with you," Tiara said.

The two departed. "I wish I could find a man like that," Astrid said. "I mean one who could handle my fundamental nature as he handles hers."

"I'd be glad to hold my breath and handle you," Ease said. "Especially with your sequins off."

What he cared about was her bra and panties. He was a typical man, hardly able to see farther than the moment. Kandy was disgusted, yet also intrigued. She could make him handle her body, but it did neither of them much good.

"Thank you," Astrid said. "But you couldn't hold it long enough."

"And I couldn't gaze into your eyes," he agreed. Horribly true.

"Have we discussed recent developments with everyone?" Astrid asked.

There was two thirds of an awkward silence. Then Pewter said "Ease sleeps."

Ease lay down on the nearest bed and slept. Pewter might be in a weakened state, but this was incidental magic. Kandy animated. "Thank you."

"How do you feel about adding Mitch to the Quest?" Astrid asked her. "We shouldn't have voted without you."

"What choice did you have?" Kandy asked. "Actually I did vote. I prompted Ease. Mitch is taking Tiara's attention, and that makes one less pretty girl to take Ease's attention."

"How is that relevant?" Pewter asked.

Astrid laughed. "You would have to be a woman to understand that. Ease is destined for Kandy, somehow, somewhen."

"I don't even understand Com Passion," Pewter complained. That was his girlfriend, a rather nice machine with similar powers of persuasion.

Kandy laughed. "No male really understands any female. Let's play chess."

They played, explaining the game to Astrid, chatting incidentally. It was fun being friends. When Mitch and Tiara returned Ease woke, Kandy reverted, but the chessboard remained. Astrid took over in Kandy's place. It was too early to tell Mitch about Kandy.

But the larger question remained: the pun virus menace was growing. How could they find the antidote in time to save Xanth from the horror they had seen at Punic Curse?

CHAPTER 6:
CENTAUR

In the morning they bid parting to Princess Dawn, Picka Bone, and the children Piton and Data, who were in transition: his bottom half and her top half were skeletal, the rest fleshly. They evidently had fun with variants.

The members of the Quest drew in close, while the Bone family watched. Tiara removed a sequin from Astrid's dress. Kandy saw Picka's eye sockets flash with appreciation, and the children loved the change in the cloth. Then, before Ease or Mitch could freak out from the view beyond the translucency, Tiara put the sequin back on.

They were standing in a pleasant pavilion. Kandy suspected that the Bone family was surprised to discover them so suddenly gone, though they had known what was going to happen. Event transitions occurred instantly, with no special effects, somewhat the way Caprice Castle traveled.

A handsome red-haired, red hided centaur stepped up to meet them. "Hello, travelers," he said. "I am Chase Centaur, liaison, and this is the Centaur Isle receiving center. Please identify yourselves and explain the nature of your visit."

Well, the centaurs were nothing if not efficient. Kandy had never been here before, and she suspected that the same was true for the others.

INTRODUCE THEM Kandy prompted Ease.

"I am Ease, and these are Astrid Basilisk, Com Pewter, Tiara, and Mitch,"

Ease said. "We are on a Quest for the Good Magician to locate and invoke the anti-dote to nullify the anti-pun virus so that puns shall not perish from Xanth."

Centaurs were known to be a magnitude smarter than humans, and two magnitudes more rational, but Chase was evidently taken aback. "A Quest to salvage puns? Surely you jest."

"No," Astrid said. "Xanth is largely made of puns, and if they are abolished Xanth will be little better than drear Mundania. The puns must be saved."

"And you are a transformed basilisk? Why are you even associating with normal humans, let alone assisting them? Why are you shading your baleful gaze?"

"I am seeking a better life than killing other creatures," Astrid said evenly. "Also better companionship. I have friends here, whom I wish to help, not hurt, and I appreciate the threat to Xanth. Don't you?"

Chase evaded the question. "Nevertheless, we do not want your kind on Centaur Isle for any reason. Basilisks are dangerous. You must depart forthwith."

This could be mischief. The virus did not seem to be here yet. Could Pewter risk pausing the firewall and using his magic?

"Centaur changes mind," Pewter murmured.

Evidently so.

"However, considering—" Chase broke off, turning on Pewter. "Did you just practice magic on me? We centaurs detest magic on our persons. Kindly keep your unclean talent off me. You are out of your bailiwick, animate machine."

Kandy remembered: regular centaurs, as opposed to flying centaurs, regarded magic as unclean, somewhat like poop, and treated it as a necessary evil. They were quite open about natural functions, like pooping, but avoided personal magic. That was why the winged centaurs had been banished from their society: they had obvious magic.

"We are on a Quest," Pewter said. "As citizens of Xanth you are bound to assist us in whatever way you can, regardless of our membership in the human culture. You know that."

Chase ground his teeth with an audible crunching sound. "We do know that. We also understand the need to preserve at least some puns, abysmal as they may be. But we don't like it."

"So we understand each other," Pewter said evenly. "Will you help?"

"There are constraints. Even Quests must pay their way."

"Of course," Pewter said. "You are obliged to offer a fair and compatible deal." Pewter evidently knew all about Centaur conventions. It occurred to

Kandy that Pewter's contribution to the Quest might relate more to his intellect than his magic.

"We have an elder historian who may be able to offer insight. We also have a difficulty that your group might alleviate."

"Historical?" Mitch asked. "The pun virus menace is not in the past, it is now."

"Caution," Pewter said. "Centaurs have perspective beyond that of most humans. They don't much like puns, me included, but they understand them well enough. Their historian should have useful insights."

Chase nodded, marginally mollified. "True. Do you accede to the deal?"

"Now wait," Mitch protested. "We don't know what they want. It may be unreasonable."

"Caution again," Pewter said. "Centaurs do not practice unreason. The deal is fair."

"I've heard that," Tiara said, putting a hand on Mitch's arm. Mitch shut his mouth. The two had met only recently, but already she had power to pacify him.

"But regardless," Ease said, "we do need to know what is expected of us. What is difficult for a centaur might be impossible for us."

"Your point is well taken," Chase said. "Though we do not practice magic ourselves, we do avail ourselves of it on occasion. In this case we queried a human foreseer, who informed us that while no centaur could accomplish the task, and no individual human, the members of a Quest would be able to handle it. Further, that a Quest would arrive at the correct time. You would seem to be that Quest. So we wish to make a deal with you, assured that both parties will be satisfied."

Ease opened his mouth to protest that the task still had not been clarified, but Kandy stifled him. ACCEPT.

"We agree," Ease said, seeing the way of it.

"Then enjoy our hospitality while we contact key parties," Chase said, and galloped off.

Another centaur stepped forward. This was a buxom female with lustrous brown hair curling down around her shoulders. Both Mitch and Ease looked at her bare chest, not freaking out but considering it.

"I am Curvia Centaur," she said. "I will be your hostess for the duration. What refreshments would you like?"

Both Mitch and Ease made an effort to speak, but so much energy was going to their eyes that there was not enough left for their mouths.

"Thank you," Astrid said. "We will be glad to take your standard fare."

That turned out to be excellent. They dined on homemade blackberry pizza served with carrot wine.

"I have been locked in a tower most of my life," Tiara said. "I have heard of the centaurs but never interacted with them before. May I ask some questions?"

"Of course," Curvia said graciously.

"I have heard that you don't much like magic. But Xanth is a magic land, and there must have been some magic in the origin of your species. How do you handle it?"

"We indulge in some social denial," Curvia said candidly. "We know that we have both equine and human ancestry, but prefer to pretend that the human element is a fading relic. We also know that magic exists and is almost universal in Xanth, and we tolerate it in other species. We merely avoid it to the extent we can here on Centaur Isle. We arrange for inferior species to perform necessary magic, so that our hands may be free of it."

Kandy saw that the centaur was unconscious of her social slip. By inferior species she meant human beings.

"But if you don't use pie plants or beer-barrel trees, because they are magical, how do you get along?" Tiara asked.

"We do most things ourselves, the old fashioned way," Curvia explained. "We grow, harvest, thresh and grind grain, shape it into dough, and bake it in ovens into bread. The pastries you are eating now were made that way. The wine was made by juicing the carrots, fermenting the juice, and aging it properly. No magic at all. In fact Centaur Isle is a low magic zone, which is one reason humans and magical creatures tend to avoid it." She glanced at Astrid. "A few hours or days here won't hurt you, but you would not care to remain here permanently."

"Then how do you make deals with humans?" Mitch asked, getting interested in more than her bosom. "We use magic all the time."

"We trade services with them," Curvia said.

"But suppose one service is worth more than another? It would be hard to make a fair deal."

"We have a standard measure of service. A small one is a favor. Ten favors are a full service. So a person can accumulate enough services to cover what she might want in return. We keep accurate records, and there is no time limit. Those humans who choose to reside with us pay one to five services a week for fodder and stabling." She saw their expressions. "Sorry. Food and board. It works out. There is also free schooling for their children, the best in Xanth. Many prominent human families hire centaur tutors or send their children here for a few years."

"Suppose the children don't study hard?" Mitch asked.

"We give them regular tests. If they don't measure up, they are sent home. Their families don't like that. So most children do study hard, as they have to try to match even mediocre centaur levels. It is also a new kind of discipline for them to do things without magic. At first they hate it, but then they usually discover that the route to personal fulfillment is personal accomplishment, not depending on a crutch such as magic. That is perhaps the most worthwhile lessen they can learn: to be able to do anything without magic. Because sometimes, unexpectedly, it is necessary."

Kandy found this interesting. She had had to learn to make do not only without magic, but without her body. It provided her an entirely different perspective.

"I understand that in Mundania many children cheat," Pewter said. "All they want is a good grade, and they don't care how they get it."

"That is just one of the problems with Mundania," Curvia said. "They have many distorted values. We do not have grades as such, and if we did, there would still be no point in cheating, as they would be only an indication of the student's progress. What is the point of learning, if the learning itself is not valued? Any child who does not want to learn is free to go home; we will not waste our time with him."

"With him?" Mitch asked. "Girls don't cheat?"

"Girls generally want to get along. They do that by studying hard. Boys may have other agendas." She paused reflectively. "I tutored a boy once, and had to send him back, because his attention never got higher than my chest. I never had that problem with a girl."

Mitch took the hint and yanked his gaze free. AWAY! Kandy prompted Ease, and he reluctantly obeyed. She realized that the centaur did not care what they looked at, being without modesty of that kind, but did want reasonable attention paid to her words, not merely her form. This was actually a kind of school, as she acquainted them with centaur conventions.

Chase returned. "We have verified that the stork will arrive tomorrow morning. Our guests need to be there by then."

Tiara looked at Mitch, stricken. "The stork? But all we did was hold hands!"

Astrid seemed to be stifling a laugh, and Pewter seemed about to say something patronizingly informative. The poor girl!

Curvia handled it smoothly. "The stork is not for you, Tiara. It takes somewhat more than hands to generate the signal, and there is a nine month

83

delay in delivery. You were in a tower and oppressed by the human Adult Conspiracy so could not be expected to know."

"Oh," Tiara said, relieved. But she remained nervous.

"We have some traveling to do now," Curvia said. "I will carry you on my back, and as we go I will acquaint you with the content of the Conspiracy. You should find it interesting."

"Oh, I couldn't ride," Tiara protested. "I have no experience; I would fall off."

"By no means. I am an experienced mount. I have never yet dropped a rider."

"Not inadvertently," Chase said with half a smile.

"Amorous centaurs don't count."

Tiara looked blank, but the others got it. It was clear that Curvia could handle herself with males, who surely got notions the moment they saw her outline.

"Oh. Well, all right," Tiara said dubiously.

Curvia helped Tiara get on her back, where there was no saddle and no reins, but the woman looked comfortable the moment she got there. It seemed that experience counted for a lot.

"I thought centaurs didn't use storks," Mitch said.

"We don't," Chase said. "I will explain the situation as we travel. This way, please."

They followed him to what looked like a large baby pram. Very large. It seated four adults. The four of them exchanged a mottled glance, then got into it, duly fastening their seat belts.

Chase put his hands on the pram handles and propelled it forward at an alarming velocity. They moved onto a paved lane and fairly zoomed along through town, field and forest. Fortunately the canopy was strong, protecting them from the cutting wind, and they were in no danger of falling out.

Curvia trotted ahead of them, carrying Tiara, who remained poised as if she had always ridden equines. Probably there was magic there, though the centaurs would not admit it. The centaur was beautiful throughout, with flowing hair, mane, and tail. As they traveled they talked. Kandy saw the girl put her hands to her face, blushing; she was learning the details of the Adult Conspiracy, evidently a stiff dose for one who had had no prior inkling. Blushing was a signal of maturity; children were generally unable to learn anything warranting a blush.

"As I was saying," Chase said, "Centaurs don't use storks; they are strictly a human convention. We prefer to eliminate the middleman, as it were. But some few humans dwell among us, and they do employ storks. That complicates things, because Centaur Isle is a low magic zone and the storks can't readily handle it. So they don't make deliveries here." They could hear him clearly despite the wind; the pram was evidently designed so that the proprietor could converse with the occupants. It was obviously intended for humans, as centaurs would never fit in it.

"Then what happens if a resident human summons a stork?" Astrid asked.

"Normally the human goes to the Xanth mainland to meet the stork," Chase said. "Then she returns to the Isle with her baby. However, in some rare cases they are unable to do that. We are about to intercede in such a case."

"A woman can't leave Centaur Isle?" Astrid asked. "Why?"

"She came to the Isle because she suffers an allergy to magic. In fact her name is Allergy, for that reason. The low magic environment here enables her to function normally. But the moment she leaves it, her malady is back in full force. It seems to accumulate in her absence, and now is at a lethal level. She can not venture to the continent even for a moment."

"And the stork won't deliver here," Astrid said. "I see the problem. But I don't see how we can help."

"You will cross from the edge of the closest Key to the beach of the mainland, where you will meet the stork," Chase said. "You will carry the baby across to its mother. That will be your party's service to us."

"But couldn't a centaur do that, saving the complication of involving us?"

"It is a type of magic we prefer not to touch."

Because magic was obscene to the centaurs, Kandy reflected. The way certain natural functions were to humans: necessary but disgusting. They did not want to dirty their hands, even to this minimal extent. Storks were simply too magical for them.

"Storks do not normally give babies to anyone except the mother who signaled, for any reason," Pewter said. "I understand they are quite strict about that."

"That is another complication," Chase agreed. "Perhaps they make exceptions for Quest personnel."

Exceptions? Kandy had never heard of that. This task might be impossible to fulfill. In which case the centaurs would owe them no return service. Was that the idea? No, centaurs were notoriously fair minded.

They came to the shore, but the paved path crossed the water to another island, a smaller one. It seemed to be in the shape of a large key.

"We will be crossing several keys," Chase said, confirming it. "They are centaur territory also, though fewer of us choose to reside on them."

They crossed the key, and came to another, still smaller. Then Curvia slowed her trot to a walk. There was something ahead.

"Oh, bleep," Chase swore. Kandy suspected that he would have been more explicit but for the presence of humans. "The dirty birds are at it again."

"Dirty birds?" Mitch asked.

"Harpies. Every so often they seek to intrude on our demesnes and we have to warn them off."

"I can help," Astrid said.

"Not necessary, basilisk. Curvia will handle it." Chase brought the pram to a halt.

Curvia did. She walked up to the huge grotesque nest the harpies were making beside the path. "You are not welcome here, harpies," Curvia said. "This is centaur territory, as you surely know."

A harpy flew up and hovered, her wings greasy, her bare breasts smudged, her hair messy, her face ugly. Indeed, she was a dirty bird, one of three. "Forget it, horse-face," she screeched. "We're a crossbreed, same as you. You don't need all these islands. We're taking this one."

"You are not," Curvia said evenly. "Now depart before I drive you away."

All three harpies burst into screeching laughter. "You and what army, tail-for-brains? Go away before we bomb you with eggs."

"I tell you again," Curvia said. "Go in peace, lest I drive you away in war. You have no right to any of these keys; the winged monster covenant establishes that."

"You asked for it, hidebound." All three harpies flew up, holding eggs in their talons. "Bombs away!"

But before they could hurl the eggs, a bow appeared in the centaur's hands. Three arrows flew. Three harpies tumbled cursing to the ground, dropping their eggs. The eggs struck the sand, exploding with foul smoke and the stench of rotten garbage. Tiara, on Curvia's back, looked startled. The threat of the eggs had been more than messiness, and the efficiency of the lovely centaur was impressive.

"My tailfeather!" a harpy screeched, picking up a dislodged feather. The others were in similar state: all had lost feathers as the arrows grazed them.

"Those were warning shots," Curvia said evenly. "The next ones will be for effect. Don't make me soil my clean arrows on your wretched flesh. Depart!"

It was clear that this was no bluff. Curvia, like all centaurs, had hit exactly what she aimed for. It would have been easier to aim for the bosoms instead of the feathers. Kandy was sure Chase could have done it as readily as Curvia; it must have been her turn to deal with the nuisance.

The harpies considered briefly, then decided that retreat was the better part of valor. They lurched into the air and flew across the water, raggedly because of the missing feathers, cursing all the way. "Bleepity, bleepity, bleepity, bleepity bleep!" Plants at the shoreline wilted, and fish near the surface rolled over dead. They certainly had fowl mouths. Tiara was now conversant enough with some of the terms to blush, while Astrid nodded with covert admiration.

"Now we can help," Mitch said, jumping out of the pram. He ran to the nest and started hauling its dirty sticks to the water. In a moment the others joined him, dragging the nest to the water. They also recovered the three arrows, rinsed them in the sea, and gave them to Curvia, who smiled appreciatively.

"Thank you," Chase said gruffly as they returned to the pram. "We don't like to handle anything the dirty birds have touched, and they know it."

They resumed their journey, crossing a number of small keys. One of the larger ones had a sign identifying it as NoName Key. Kandy had heard of that one, as it was supposed to have an access to Mundania. That might be just a legend, however. After all, who would ever want to go to Mundania?

As evening approached they came to a village on the last key before the mainland. "You will night here," Chase said. "You will meet the human woman you are helping."

They drew up beside a stone house with a large stall, evidently a centaur residence. They were met by a human man and woman. "Oh, we're so glad to see you!" the woman said. "The centaurs promised, but still we were concerned. I am Allergy, and this is my husband Robert." She smiled at him. "We met on the job. He is Robert Ulysses Dunn, from Mundania. He died of old age there, thus losing his family, but managed to come here, and the centaurs gave him rejuvenating elixir in return for his applying his expertise for them. He's a fine cabinet maker and woodworker. He got so tired of folk constantly asking 'R U Dunn yet?' Nobody asks that here."

"Um, yes," Astrid said, introducing the others. Allergy was evidently talkative. The two centaurs moved on, seeking their own lodging.

Soon they were in a comfortable room, not a stall. "This is a way station," Allergy explained. "Centaur visitors stay here and the staff tends to them."

"The staff?" Astrid asked.

"We are part of a larger staff, but no one is visiting now, so we have it to ourselves."

It seemed that the only visitors who counted were centaurs. Humans were merely hired help.

"What is it that you do here," Astrid asked, "that the centaurs can't do themselves?"

"Robert makes cabinets they value, since they won't craft them magically, and he built the wooden framework for the wine cellar. I store the bottles, and bring them out at need, because the cellar is too tight for the centaurs to fit."

"Why don't they build the cellar big enough for centaurs to fit?" Tiara asked.

"Oh, that would not do! The one here is actually a beer cellar, for root beer. It's shielded against magic so that the root beer doesn't change into boot rear, which they detest. It's a pun, you see, and centaurs aren't keen on puns. They regard them as an inferior form of magic. So it is very tight and dark, and only I can fit conveniently in to handle the bottles."

"We understand you are allergic to magic," Astrid said.

"Yes I am. My life was awful before I came here; I just dragged along. But magic is largely suppressed here, and it's wonderful for me. Except—"

"The stork," Astrid said.

"Yes. We were really worried that the stork would not be able to deliver our baby. But now, with your help, it will be all right."

Astrid considered. "Maybe Tiara had better do it. You see, I am a transformed basilisk, and my ambiance would be bad for the baby." Yet she looked a little sad, and Kandy knew why: she would have liked to have held that baby to see what it was like, because she might never have one of her own. Because she might never be able to get a man close enough, long enough, and even if he did, what kind of a baby would it be? A person whose look could kill?

"I can do it," Tiara agreed gladly. "I just learned all about how babies are signaled for and delivered."

In due course they were shown to two nice rooms. "I'm sorry we don't have one for each of you," Allergy said.

"These are fine," Astrid said quickly.

Mitch and Tiara took one room, by mutual consent. Pewter, Ease, and Astrid took the other. Ease was soon asleep, and Kandy emerged. "There is surely a man for you somewhere," she said immediately to Astrid. "You have the body to attract any man you want, if only he could handle your nature."

"There's the rub," Astrid agreed sadly. "I would encourage Ease to hold his breath, or meet me in water, but I know he belongs to you."

"I'm a board!"

"You're a woman. You just need to be rid of that spell."

"We seem to have vaguely similar problems," Kandy said. "We can't safely touch a man in the way we might like to."

"Neither of you would be any problem to me," Pewter said.

"Because you're a machine," Kandy said. "Let's play chess."

They played, with Kandy and Astrid teaming up against Pewter, but it was obvious that he could defeat them both any time he chose to. They couldn't even distract him by flashing panties. They tried, with Kandy borrowing Astrid's for the experiment. That failure annoyed them more than they cared to say. It was fundamentally dis-empowering.

In the morning they rejoined Mitch and Tiara, both of whom looked annoyingly satisfied, and prepared for the rendezvous with the stork. They walked to the shore, which wasn't far from the house. The bright Gold Coast was a short distance across the water, with golden coins washing up in the tide. The centaur path did not continue there, because the centaurs did not want to encourage intruders. Allergy stood and gazed across, unable to go there.

There was a boat that seated six. Mitch and Ease got in and took paddles, though Ease's paddle was the board. Well, that gave Kandy a good taste of the water. Pewter took the prow. The two women sat in the center.

"There may be loan sharks," Robert warned them. "They frequent the Gold Coast. They'll take an arm and a leg if you let them, so be careful."

"I will handle the sharks," Astrid said grimly.

They started across. No sharks showed up, but something else did: a fast low scudding cloud. It quickly expanded, blowing a gust of wind at them that started sending them away from the main shore despite their frantic paddling. "Oh, beans!" Pewter said. "That's Fracto Cumulo Nimbus, the worst of clouds. He has found a parade to rain on, as it were. He is beyond my range to influence."

"I will see what I can do," Astrid said. She oriented on the cloud and removed her dark glasses.

In no more than three quarters of a moment the cloud paused, its edges flickering into steamy vapor, then scudded rapidly away. Fracto had gotten the message. Astrid put her glasses back on, satisfied. It was a reminder of just how deadly she could be, when she chose. Kandy was glad they were friends and not enemies.

They resumed progress toward the golden beach. Soon they got there, disembarked, and drew the boat up on the golden sand. Now all they needed was the stork.

And the stork arrived, flying in with its bundle hanging from its beak. It landed, folded its wings, and looked about.

"Your turn," Astrid murmured to Tiara.

"Oh. Yes." Tiara walked toward the stork.

The big bird eyed her. "This baby is not for you."

"Oh, I know," she said, blushing. She had really perfected her blush in the past day and night. "I am here on behalf of Allergy, who ordered this baby. I will carry it to her, because she can't come here herself."

"This is highly irregular," the stork said. "We deliver babies only to their mothers, not to intermediaries."

"But she's right there across the water," Tiara said. "She'll have it very soon. We have to do it this way, because—"

"I am not interested in excuses," the stork said. "Obviously there is a mixup here. I will take this baby back to the stork works." It spread its wings, about to take off.

This seemed to be another occasion for Pewter to take a risk. "Stork changes mind," he said. "Agrees to deliver to surrogate mother."

"But of course there are exceptions," the stork said.

It was coming clear why a Quest had been required to handle this matter. Their assorted talents were making it possible.

Tiara stepped up to take the bundle. She cradled it in her arms as the stork took off. "Oh, what a darling little boy! I wish I could keep—"

"No!" Astrid and Pewter said together.

"But of course I know better," Astrid said, smiling wistfully. Kandy realized that that was another pitfall of surrogate motherhood: the desire to keep the baby. The storks were wise to insist on the natural mother.

They got back into the boat. The baby looked at Astrid and cooed. Astrid melted visibly. Then, cautiously, she extended one hand. The baby grabbed a finger. That was all, but Astrid seemed to be in heaven. But soon she disengaged, uncertain how long it was safe for her to touch the baby. The breeze was blowing her perfume away, but that could change at any moment.

Kandy knew that Astrid would never be satisfied until she had a baby of her own. But how could that ever be accomplished?

They reached the key. Tiara got out carefully, and carried the baby to Allergy. Allergy took him and cuddled him. Then both women dissolved into tears. The men looked perplexed, but Kandy understood: they were recognizing the overwhelming value of this gift.

Chase and Curvia Centaur came forward. "The service has been accomplished," Chase said. "Now we will convey you to the historian."

It was sad to leave the happy couple so soon after meeting them, but this was the way of it. They had to go learn what they could about their mission.

"This time I will carry you," Curvia said to Ease.

"Me?" the man seemed about to freak out.

STRAIGHTEN OUT Kandy told him.

The man did, and soon was on the centaur's back, looking dazed. Meanwhile Tiara joined the others in the pram, sitting beside Astrid. They would have something to talk about; both had felt the power of the baby.

This time Chase led the way, pushing the pram, and Curvia followed. "Are you comfortable, Ease?" the centaur inquired, turning her fore-section around so that she could face him. In the process she brought her magnificent breasts into his sight, up close. He promptly freaked out.

And Kandy transformed, dangling by the man's side. She scrambled to get mounted ahead of him, his hand on her waist instead of her ankle.

"Hello, dream woman," Curvia said.

"You know of me?" Kandy asked, surprised.

"We centaurs don't practice magic, but we do recognize it when we encounter it. I suspected there was something about Ease, and confirmed it when his board touched me. Guessing the nature of the spell, I invoked its partial abatement."

"You freaked him out on purpose!"

"I confess it," the centaur agreed. "He will be secure enough for the duration. I wanted to meet you. Who are you, and how did you come to be enchanted in this manner?"

"I am Kandy. I went to a wishing well to wish for excitement, adventure, and romance, but instead got changed into a board. But actually I am getting the first two."

"And surely the third, in due course. I suspect the wishing well, trying to handle a complicated wish, found a devious way to grant the whole of it. You probably would not have been able to keep company with the man in your natural form. At least, not in the manner you prefer. Men encountering women of your proportions are not interested in getting to know their finer qualities."

True words! "But keeping company as a board is no joy! It's sheer frustration!"

"You are getting to know him well. When he is ready to know you similarly well, the spell may abate, completing your wish."

"So there may be reason for this frustration," Kandy said, seeing it.

"Spells are not smart. They operate within their parameters, which are not always convenient for those affected by them. But the spell will not abate until its purpose is accomplished."

"Unless he loses the board before that happens."

"There is that risk," Curvia agreed. "But normally a spell is framed so that it can't be nullified by accident. Something must make him want to keep the board close."

"He keeps me close," Kandy agreed. "His hand is always on my wooden ankle."

"Is he at all aware of your real nature?"

"On some level he is. He speaks of his dream girl, and has a vague awareness of what I am doing. But he thinks I'm a nymph visiting him in his sleep, fleeing when he wakes. He is frustrated by that."

"Then he is falling in love with you," Curvia said. "At such time as he realizes that you are with him all the time, the spell may fade."

"It shows no sign of fading," Kandy said.

"Conditions must not yet be right."

"When will they ever be right?"

"Transformation spells are fairly standard. I have studied them somewhat. Normally they are abated by a kiss."

"I have kissed him many times!"

The centaur shook her head. "Ah, but the transformee can't do it herself. It has to be done by the un-transformed one. Such as the prince kissing the sleeping maiden awake after centuries. Probably he needs to kiss you when he is awake."

"When I'm a board!"

"Yes. He must kiss the board. He may also have to declare his love for you. It varies with the spell."

"He loves the way I bash monsters. That's not exactly the same."

"It is not," the centaur agreed. "But perhaps the occasion will come. One never knows, with magic."

Then they passed a tree with hanging foliage. A branch brushed Ease's head, and he snapped out of his freak. Kandy was the board again. But her dialogue with Curvia had given her something to think about. Maybe there was a way out of this enchantment. All Ease had to do was kiss the board, maybe. Then she would do the rest.

They arrived at a centaur stall in a town. Kandy, her attention on her dialogue with Curvia, had not noticed the passage of time or geography. "This is the home of Cognition Centaur, our most learned historian," Curvia said. "If anyone can provide the information you require, he is the one."

An old centaur came out. "Ah, Curvia," he said. "It is surely too much to hope that you seek me with romance in mind."

"Too much," she agreed, smiling. "These are the humans we told you about. They have completed a service to us, and we hope you will be able to help them glean the information they need."

"And if I do, will you vouchsafe me a kiss?"

"Possibly."

He sighed. "The filly plays hard to get." He glanced at the people. "Come in, Ease, Mitch, Com Pewter, Astrid, Tiara and whomever else may be along." He turned and led the way into his substantial stall.

So he knew them. He had to have been given a complete briefing, and had the chance to do his homework. Again, Kandy saw how efficient the centaurs were. They might play little games of flirtation, but they knew exactly what was what.

The central room of the house was what appeared to be a comprehensive library. Cognition was obviously a scholar. They were made comfortable in chairs that must have been brought out for the occasion.

"Now if you will kindly frame your question, I will endeavor to address it," Cognition said.

"We must locate the antidote to the virus that is destroying the puns of Xanth," Pewter said promptly. "The Good Magician has suffered a lapse of memory, and was able to tell us only that to find it we must merge the hair. We do not know what that means."

The centaur looked at Tiara's hair, which was in its wild state, since Mitch seemed to like it that way. Then he looked at Mitch, in his hair shirt. "Presumably you have tried merging your hair without effect."

"We tried," Tiara said, blushing. "Our hair didn't merge, though something else did." Her blush became deeper.

"There are of course different types of merging," the centaur said. "So the presumption is that it is not your hair to which the fractional prophecy refers. It was proper to try the most convenient hair first, before going farther afield. We must consider what other hair there may be."

"Yes," Pewter agreed.

"I have done a bit of spot research on the key terms "pun," "virus," "hair" and "merge," and discovered an interesting and perhaps relevant legend. It seems that long ago in the human realm there was a rogue Magician who created a virus that melted puns."

"That's it!" Ease said.

"Perhaps," Cognition agreed. "He also created the relevant anti-virus as a matter of simple caution; it is not wise to start something you can't stop. He locked both safely away for future reference and moved on to other things. But it seems that subsequently the virus container corroded and leaked, releasing the virus. So the question becomes where was the anti virus stored, and how may it be found? This becomes complicated."

Kandy saw that the centaur scholar was taking his roundabout time, but was getting there. But what were the complications?

"It seems the Magician was courting a lovely Sorceress, who demanded as a token of his love and trust some supremely powerful secret. So he gave her the antidote as an engagement gift. That was effective, and the two were duly married and lived reasonably compatibly thereafter. The Sorceress placed the antidote elixir in a magic net in her luxurious hair."

"Hair!" Ease said.

"The virus did not escape in their lifetimes, and she never used the elixir," Cognition continued. "Now both of them have long since faded out, and the location of that elixir is unknown. They did have children, and grandchildren, who might know what happened to that precious packet. Find those descendants and inquire. They will surely cooperate once they know the importance of the elixir."

"You don't know where they are?" Ease asked.

"I regret I do not. I am a historian, and these folk were evidently not regarded as worthy of tracking, so they disappeared into the larger fabric of the human society. I am sure they exist, but my references do not clarify any further detail."

"What about the merging of hair?" Astrid asked alertly.

"I did discover some slight reference to that, or at least to the hair. It seems that the Sorceress had quite impressive hair, voluminous, glossy, and lovely. Those qualities were passed along to her children, any of whom could be recognized instantly by the appeal of her hair. I presume it carried through to the grandchildren, but there the record becomes obscure. There simply is no reference. I do not know what 'merging' in this connection might mean. It is not a term that is commonly applied to a person's hair. I can only conjecture that after the Sorceress faded out her hair might have been saved and plaited into cloth, in this manner merged. Or perhaps it needs to be so plaited, for your purpose. But this is speculation only, and should serve only as a corollary reference. Perhaps if you can find the descendants it will become clear." He smiled at Tiara. "I don't suppose you have Sorceress ancestry, my dear? You do have remarkable hair."

"Not that I know of," Tiara said. "And no one else in my family has hair like mine. My sisters' hair is all quite well groomed."

"I suspected as much. This, then, seems to be the limit of my usefulness to your party. I fear it will not suffice to evoke a kiss from Curvia."

Kandy realized that he had really wanted that kiss; academics did not get much access to lovely creatures. That gave her an idea. KISS HIM she sent to Astrid.

The basilisk girl was astonished. *But I'm a—*

A SURPASSINGLY BEAUTIFUL WOMAN, IN YOUR TRANSFORMED STATE. ASK HIM. WARN HIM.

Are you sure?

IT'S A REASONABLE GAMBLE. TRY IT.

Astrid took the plunge, trusting her friend's judgment. "Yet it provides useful direction for us," she said to the centaur. "Will you accept my kiss in lieu of Curvia's? You will have to hold your breath, lest you become intoxicated by my perfume."

Cognition contemplated her, surprised. "Because you are a basilisk," he said thoughtfully. "Yet your human form is fetching, assuming it is as represented."

Astrid glanced at Tiara. "Take off a sequin."

Tiara did, as Ease and Mitch turned away, having learned caution. The dress went translucent. Astrid stood there in her phenomenal near-nude glory.

"Oh, my, yes," the centaur agreed appreciatively. "I believe I will." He approached Astrid, picked her up by the elbows, and kissed her on the mouth. Then he set her down a bit unsteadily; he must have caught a sniff of her perfume. "That will certainly do."

"You're welcome," Astrid said, looking unsteady herself. Kandy realized it must be her first such kiss. Basilisks did not get many such opportunities. It had been a mutually rewarding experience. Kandy knew she had done right.

Then Tiara pinned the sequin back on, unbidden. The scene changed.

CHAPTER 7:

VOYAGE

"Attention, all personnel. This is Grey Murphy, your Captain, speaking."

Kandy looked around. A group of folk were gathered in what appeared to be the control room of a mundane spaceship. They were men, women, and centaurs, all with badges identifying them as crew members. The Quest people were all here, too.

"And you know," Captain Grey continued, handsome in his double-breasted woolen naval pea-coat. "Several years ago the centaurs launched a colonizing ship bound for Alpha Centauri, where they hoped to find a planet without magic or puns. They promised to report on their progress every year. At first they did, employing the Very Large Array of enhanced magic mirrors, and the settlement seemed to be progressing well. They were building many stalls in the expectation that more centaurs would soon be going there. Eventually they hoped that all centaurs would live at last totally free of egregious puns and obscene magic.

"But then they stopped communicating. The Array seemed to be in order, but we could evoke no answer from the colony. We have not heard from them in two years, and fear mischief. Hence this space mission, commissioned by my wife, King Ivy, and staffed with the very best personnel, including our three daughters, Princesses Melody, Harmony, and Rhythm, who comprise the Special Assault Team." He gestured to the three young women, who smiled fetchingly. They looked to be about eighteen, and Kandy knew they all were general-purpose Sorceresses whose power squared or cubed depending on how many of them acted in concert.

Grey paused, letting the significance sink in. Any mission that required the services of all three princesses was serious indeed. Kandy knew that one of them, Harmony, was destined to be King after Ivy, because she was the most sensible of the three. There had been clumsily squelched rumors of phenomenal naughtiness on their part, such as employing a temporary aging spell to violate the Adult Conspiracy, or tackling the notorious Ragna Roc bird, but they seemed to be shaping up to becoming reasonably responsible citizens.

"Now we do not know what is out there," Grey continued after a pause of approximately the right length. "Whatever might have prevented the centaurs from contacting us might also prevent us from returning home safely. So this may be a dangerous vision, going where no human has gone before, only centaurs. Whatever is a threat to centaurs may also be a threat to Xanth itself. Our mission is to discover what has happened, to search out and rescue survivors, and to return as quickly as possible to Xanth. Under no circumstances are we to attack. Is that understood?" Grey's gaze fixed sternly on the three princesses, who reluctantly nodded in unison.

"This is primarily an intelligence gathering mission. We are not a battle cruiser and we have none of the assets of one. While all of you have been chosen for your unique talents, to make this mission possible, you are also here because you believe in Xanth, and because you believe in and care about each other. We do mean to rescue the centaurs, but to do so without violence if at all possible. Nothing can stop us when we work together."

He paused, and when there was no response, spoke once more, briefly. "I am now turning the mission over to our First Officer." He nodded to Ease.

Oops! Kandy had assumed that the members of the Quest were more or less invisible spectators. Certainly they did not belong in this mission, about which they knew nothing. How could he be a First Officer?

But Ease handled it as if he belonged. "Thank you, Captain Murphy. I believe we stand ready to proceed." He turned to Astrid. "Chief Engineer, is the ship operational?"

Chief Engineer? What did Astrid know about engines? She wasn't even human!

Astrid smiled. "Most systems are now operational, Ease, but they are of course untested. We need to be far away from gravity wells such as from

97

planets or moons before we can warp away to interstellar space. That means maneuvering the main engines to about Jupiter's orbit. But first the engines have to be ignited. All I need now is your word."

Jupiter's orbit? This was sheer gibberish!

"Astrid, the word is given. Start 'em up!"

There was a keyboard before Astrid. She set her hands on it. "This is our second star-ship," she murmured. "Xanth only knows what would cause the first one to fail. Here's hoping." Her fingers touched the keys. "Raising rods from the heavy water in the nuclear fish'in pool. Power now at eighty percent. Ninety. Full power." Her index finger hovered over her panel. "Ready to dump the fish'in energy into the sunflower fusion plants. NOW!"

This was absolutely crazy! She had to be making it up.

Astrid stabbed her finger into the icon on her board. All the lights on the bridge went out, leaving everyone in darkness. They came back on seconds later, brighter than ever. There was a muffled roar from the bowels of the ship, and a deep shudder of power.

Astrid smacked her right fist into her left hand. "Yes!" she whispered to herself. Then, to the captain: "We now have self-sustaining fusion reaction! Main engines are yours, sir."

"Outstanding, Engineer," Grey shouted over the noise. "We are on our way."

The crew relaxed as the ship moved out. They had little to do while the ship forged through space. That gave the members of the quest a chance to get together.

"What have we gotten into?" Mitch asked. "I'm the Communications Officer, but I don't know anything about the mission apart from what the Captain just told us."

"And I'm the Refreshments Officer," Tiara said. "Have some hard tack." She proffered a plate of biscuits made in the shape of tacks.

"Pewter, what do you know about this?" Mitch asked.

"I am the ship AI," Pewter responded. "That is, Artificial Intelligence. I actually operate most of the systems, out of sight; the people merely give the commands. Ultimately I control the ship, and could, if I deemed it necessary, eliminate the people."

"You wouldn't!" Tiara said, horrified.

"Fortunately I am unlikely to deem it necessary."

That was not a completely reassuring answer.

"You have not answered my question," Mitch said. "What do you know about this? How can we be here, filling positions for which we are not qualified, accepted by folk who don't know us? What is going on?"

"It's a dream," Pewter said. "A gourd setting. Your bodies are lying comfortably on the ground while your minds are participating in this communal dream of a space mission. You are not actually in physical danger."

"You're a machine. How can you be in the dream?"

"I am in it because I choose to be. The realm of the gourd is marvelous and intricate, with many variants. I did not deem it appropriate to allow you mortals to flounder unsupervised."

"Each sequin setting has contributed something to our Quest," Astrid said. "Either a participant or an insight. What is the point of a dream?"

"That is what you will need to discover," Pewter said. "Your best course is to carry on until you learn the point of it."

"That actually does make sense," Mitch said. "So we might as well enjoy the ride."

"Some ride!" Astrid said, but she did seem mollified.

The three princesses approached them. They were attractive girls of Tiara's age, wearing little crowns. "I am Melody," the first said. She wore a green dress with matching hair and blue eyes. "I am the prettiest one."

"I am Harmony," the second continued. She wore a brown dress with matching hair and eyes. "I am the most sensible one."

"I am Rhythm," the third concluded. She wore a red dress with matching hair, and green eyes. "I am the naughtiest one."

Kandy found their candid introductions interesting, but she doubted that there was very much difference between the three in pretty, sensible, or naughty.

"No need to introduce yourselves," Melody said.

"We know who you are," Harmony added.

"And what you seek," Rhythm concluded.

"But we do wonder how you got added to this space mission," Melody said.

"And what your two fellow travelers are up to," Harmony continued.

"And how your hair relates," Rhythm concluded.

Fellow travelers? That meant they knew that Demoness Metria was along, and Kandy. What else did they know?

"It's my dress, with the Sequins of Events," Astrid explained. "When a sequin comes off, the dress turns translucent, and that distracts any local menfolk. When we put the sequin back on, it triggers an Event. This is an Event."

The princesses eyed Astrid. "It's a nice dress," Melody said.

"And a nicer body," Harmony added.

"And you're nice too," Rhythm finished.

"For a cockatrice," Astrid's hair said.

"For a what?" Melody asked.

"Mythical monster, bird-lizard, death-glare, poison breath—"

"Basilisk?" Harmony asked.

"Whatever," the hair agreed crossly.

"Hello, Metria!" Rhythm said.

"So what are you doing here?" Melody asked.

"I'm keeping Tiara's hair neat."

"And snooping on what does not concern you," Harmony said.

"That's my nature!"

"And perking up dull scenes like this one," Rhythm said.

"Of course. It's a dirty job, but somebody has to do it, lest we all perish of boredom. So can you bothersome Sorceresses figure out what hair has to do with the price of beans in Bohemia?"

The three circled a glance. "Not yet," Melody said.

"But we're working on it," Harmony added.

"And there must be a hint on this centaur mission," Rhythm concluded. "That's the way the Good Magician's Quests work."

Then the three moved on, ending the dialogue.

"That was actually interesting," Mitch said. "Too bad those pretty princesses are already taken."

Tiara's hair swelled up indignantly. "Too bad?" it demanded.

"Not that I have any interest," Mitch said quickly.

So Metria was now supporting Tiara the way Kandy supported Ease. That, too, was interesting.

"It is time," Captain Grey announced. "We are crossing the orbit of Jupiter. Officers and stations, report readiness for our first space warp."

"Space warp," Tiara's hair muttered, keeping the volume low enough so the Captain would not overhear. "Science fiction is polluting our fantasy. It's loathly."

"It's what?" Tiara asked.

"Distasteful, hideous, repulsive, revolting, loathsome, foul, yucky—"

"Disgusting?"

"Whatever," the hair agreed crossly. "Nothing's sacred any more."

"This is a dream," Mitch reminded the hair. "Anything goes, in a dream. It doesn't have to make sense or remain unpolluted."

"It's still a shame," the hair muttered.

"First Officer?" Grey asked.

"Ready," Ease said.

"Chief Engineer?"

"Similarity drive at your discretion," Astrid said. Privately she muttered "I have to say it. It's in the script."

"Navigator?"

A centaur spoke up. "Equations written and checked for one light year out."

"Thank you, Chet. Tactical?"

A female centaur answered. She was clothed in the centaur manner, which was to say, not. "The complex curves have been calculated, sir. One is a damped sine wave with larger amplitude on the left and right hand sides, but having no amplitude in the center. The space-time wave has been plotted."

"Thank you, Chem. Com Pewter, are you functional?"

"Yes," Pewter said shortly. He too had to follow the dream script, though he obviously didn't like it.

"Commence warp countdown."

"This is all pseudo-science gibberish," Tiara's hair muttered. "In real life, the Captain would just push a button and it would happen. No fuss, no muss, no discommode."

"Bother," Tiara said, cutting the routine short.

"That's what I said."

Meanwhile a large white dot appeared on the left of Captain Grey's viewing screen. It traversed the sine curve, bouncing up to the top of it, then to the bottom, slowly making its way to the center of the screen. Astrid tapped out some commands on her console. The sound of huge turbines started slowly and quietly, then gained in speed, loudness, and pitch. "Fusion plants dumping power into the warp flywheels," she reported. "Rotations now increasing to five hundred per minute...a thousand...five thousand...ten thousand and increasing."

"Just one button would do it," Tiara's hair muttered.

As the turbine sounds became deafening, Astrid's control panel began chirping in time with the dot's traversal of the sine waves on the display. "Fifteen seconds, Captain," Chem Centaur declared. "Com Pewter is locked on the space-time fabric."

"To be sure," Pewter agreed, annoyed about being locked.

"One lousy button."

"Twenty thousand rotations, Captain," Astrid reported.

"Ten seconds, Captain. Nine, eight, seven—"

"Get ON with it!" Tiara's hair snapped.

"Six seconds. Five...four...three...two..."

Captain Grey took a deep breath. His hands gripped the chair rests as he saw the dot almost at the center of the display.

"One," Astrid said.

"WARP!!!" Grey shouted the order.

"What utter crap!"

To the view of the outside observer, the ship slowly became transparent. Then it completely disappeared. Kandy knew this because one screen showed the external view. They were warping.

Inside the ship, the tactical display changed to show stars elongating into streaks, forming into a tunnel for the ship to zoom through, creating a shortcut across vast amounts of time and space.

The rescue mission to Alpha Centauri was on its way.

"Actually it is sort of impressive in its cliché fashion," Tiara's hair admitted.

The ship emerged from warp near Alpha Centauri. There was the centaur colony planet, lovely in the glow of the triple suns of the constellation. The technicians activated the large magic mirror set at maximum magnification and saw the centaurs happily going about their business. Some were cultivating mundane crops, while others were constructing highways suitable for galloping.

"Try the communication band," the Captain suggested.

Mitch was the Communications Officer. He twiddled with settings of his console. "Calling Alpha Colony. Calling Alpha Colony. This is Xanth ship Beta. Come in, Alpha."

To their surprise there was an answer. A centaur appeared on the screen. "Welcome, Beta! You are cleared for landing. Come on down!"

A perplexed look hovered in the vicinity. No contact for two years, then this sudden welcome? It was distinctly suspicious.

"We need to know somewhat more of your situation," Mitch said. "Why did you not answer our prior queries?"

"Oh, did we overlook them?" the centaur asked. "A clerical error, no doubt. We've been quite busy here doing important things, and it must have slipped our attention. Come down and we'll go through the records and discover the glitch. I'm sure it's nothing be concerned about."

Mitch opened his mouth, but hesitated. Something was definitely wrong.

Then the screen split. Another centaur appeared on the right side, a haggard creature with straggly hair and mane, sores on his body, and a general attitude of despondency. "Don't land!" he gasped. "Flee immediately! It's a trap!"

The centaur on the left glanced across. "Pay no attention to that creature on the other side. He's crazy, a known lunatic."

"They can't touch the ship while it remains in space," the bedraggled centaur said. "But once you land, they'll—"

There was no more. His whole screen had disappeared.

"As I was saying," the suave centaur said, "come on down. We'll have a grand party and catch up on recent events. You will love it here. You'll never leave."

Captain Grey made a chopping motion with his hand. The screen went blank. "It seems we have a situation," he said grimly. "Show of hands: which side seems more credible? The left or the right?"

All hands pointed to the right.

"So we are agreed," Grey said. "The centaur colonists are captive to some dark power. That is why they have not answered prior queries, and have responded only now that our ship is in range. Should we flee?"

"The bleep!" Ease said, then added "Sir."

"Point taken. We stay, of course," Grey said. "We will orbit the planet while we decide what to do. We will not act rashly, but we will act. We shall now dissolve into separate discussion groups to consider our best course of action." He turned away.

"Now this is interesting," Tiara's hair said. "Of course we know who is behind this."

"We do?" Mitch asked.

"Capital D Demoness Fornax. She hates Demon Xanth and is always messing him up if she can. Far out as this colony is, it's still in Xanth's territory, because Fornax is from a whole separate galaxy far far away."

"Fornax," Mitch said. "I'm not conversant with big D Demons. How does she fit into the hierarchy?"

"Well, that's complicated to explain."

"I'm curious too," Ease said. "If there's any likelihood that we shall have to deal with the Demoness, we'll need to know as much about her and the Demon framework as we can. Aren't Demons all-powerful?"

"Oh, yes. But that's not the whole story."

"Anyone else want this information?" the hair asked.

"Yes, demoness," Captain Grey said. "We are all interested."

Metria was so startled she floated right up out of Tiara's hair and coalesced into a cloud. Tiara's hair sprang immediately to wildness. Then the demoness formed into a luscious woman figure with tight clothing just shy of the minimum standard of decency. Half an instant before all male eyes glazed, her bikini expanded into more competent coverage. She was of course a tease. "If that's the way you feel," she said. "If I may borrow the mirror for this purpose."

"Borrow it," Grey said.

Metria drifted up to the mirror, which illuminated for her. "No mortal or lesser demon knows how many Demons there are, or whom they may be," she said. "But I have been around a while, a few centuries, and have picked up tidbits. There are about ten local Demons, and innumerable Dwarf Demons, which are below the Demons but above anything else. Each has its associated world and power. The Demon Xanth, for example, governs the Land of Xanth. In fact, all of the magic of the land of Xanth is the mere leakage of radiation from the skin of the Demon Xanth." The screen showed the outline of the peninsular Land of Xanth, with the word MAGIC.

"Similarly the Demon Earth associates with Mundania, and his magic of gravity suffuses that dreary realm." The globular planet Earth appeared on the screen, together with the word GRAVITY. "The Demoness Venus has her own planet as the weak force, though it is weak only compared to the power of other Demons. The Demon Jupiter has his own big planet and the strong force. The Demon Mars has electromagnetic force. Demoness Saturn has the power of dimension; anything measured in any way relates to her. The Demon Neptune relates to mass and energy, and the Demon Nemesis to dark matter. There are others, but you get the picture." Indeed, the screen was now full of planets and descriptive words.

"What about Fornax?" Mitch asked.

Metria flashed him with a brief fade-out of her clothing, showing her overstuffed bra and panties. That shut him up. "I was getting to her. She's from a whole other galaxy, a million or so light years away. Why she messes with us I don't think anyone knows. Her power is contra-terrene, CT (seetee), or anti-matter, the reverse of ours; it would take a scientist to explain it properly. Let's just say that any of us who might touch any of that would disappear in a horrendous flash of energy, unless special arrangements were made. She and Demon Xanth have had Demon run-ins. I think she had her eye on him and thought to seduce him, but he married a local mortal girl instead, and that annoyed her." Metria smiled grimly. "It is not wise to annoy any woman, but especially not a demoness, and totally not a Demoness. They say Hades has no fury like that of a woman scorned. That's an understatement. Hades is too tame a term; that region associates with the Dwarf Demon Pluto, and Princess Eve now helps him govern it. So if we are up against Fornax, and I think we are, that second centaur's advice is good: we need to get far, far away from here in a hurry hurry hurry, because she will have no mercy."

"Thank you for that summation, demoness," Captain Grey said. "Assuming that we are not going to flee, what is your advice?"

"Appeal to some other Demon to help. Nothing short of that will balk her."

"And if there is no Demon convenient?"

"Hide as long as you can, for what little that's worth."

"And there we have it," Grey said. "We shall need to come up with something very special to have even the slightest chance to save ourselves, let alone rescue any centaurs. Let's return to our pondering." He walked away.

"Metria, why have you elected to be so helpful?" Mitch asked.

"Because your Quest has gotten really interesting, and I want to see it move on to the following mysteries. You'll never get there on your own." Then the demoness dissolved into a ball of smoke, floated to Tiara's head, and infused her hair, which became absolutely neat again.

"Which leaves us in a picklement," Mitch said. "The Captain refuses to do the sensible thing and flee back to Xanth, so we are all doomed unless we figure out a way to stop a scorned Demoness."

"I wonder," Astrid said. "If the Demon Xanth married a mortal girl, there must be some appeal to mortality, even for Demons. I wonder what it is?"

"It's their souls," Pewter said. "Demons are souls of a sort, but don't have souls. Human souls are fresh and new and strong, and D/d demons are fascinated by them. Metria married a mortal man. But souls are also severely limiting for demons, so they are cautious."

"Souls," Astrid repeated. "Exactly who has them?"

"Human folk, or part human folk," Pewter said.

"I am an animal. So I don't have a soul?"

"That is correct. Neither do I, because I am a machine."

"Where in a person is the soul?"

"In the Soul-R-Plexus, of course, the center of the body."

"Is there any way for a non-human to acquire a soul?"

"Yes. Jumper Spider acquired one via his prolonged close and intimate association with several humans. But the easier way is simply to marry a human. Then you will get half his soul."

Astrid smiled sadly. "If only I could do that."

"Your body and personality are more than adequate to attract a man. You merely have to discover a way to be close to a man without killing him."

Astrid returned to the subject. "So is there any chance the Demoness Fornax would be romantically interested in a mortal man, such as Mitch or Ease?"

"No!" Tiara cried in emotional pain. Kandy understood exactly how she felt.

"There is a chance," Pewter agreed. "But so small as to be inconsequential."

"Still, that's better than outright doom. Maybe some other man aboard this ship."

"Grey Murphy is already married," Pewter said.

"Do Demons care about that?"

"Probably not," Pewter said. "That is, not about mortal marriages. Marriage to a Demon would be another matter."

"Someone needs to sacrifice himself," Grey said. "I will do it."

"Captain, you can't," Mitch said. "The mission needs you."

"Then I need a volunteer."

Oh, no! There was a protocol. Kandy saw it coming and couldn't prevent it.

"I volunteer," Ease said. "As First Officer the security of the ship is my prime concern. Beam me down. I will distract Fornax while you land on the opposite side of the planet, rescue the centaurs, and take off. Then you can beam me back up."

"That may be a considerable challenge," Grey said.

"My talent is to make things easy. I can do this."

"A Demoness is far beyond your talent."

"We'll come too," Princess Melody said.

"Hidden," Harmony agreed.

"As buttons," Rhythm concluded.

The three vanished. Ease's shiny jacket buttons expanded slightly.

"Very good, Ease," the Captain said gravely.

In no more than a moment and a half, Ease was in the beaming station and reforming on the ground below. He landed in a centaur paradise of open meadows and flowering trees. There was a localized rain shower, but a convenient paved walk circled around it so that no centaur needed to get wet. There were nicely kept stalls pleasantly spaced, stocked with all manner of foodstuffs and beverages, none of them remotely punnish. Healthy centaurs worked in the fields, harvesting fruits, vegetables, grains, and gathering stones to build stalls and rushes for plaiting into roofs.

"I'm not a centaur," Ease said. "But this seems idyllic."

"It's all illusion," the top button said. "In reality, this is a barren plain, with emaciated centaurs laboring in chains to break rocks."

"Because this is a mining operation, for rare earths," the second button continued.

"So the Demoness Fornax can make a better interface between her and normal matter, so she won't go up in smoke," the third button concluded.

Kandy concluded that she liked having the three princesses along. They were a useful source of information.

But Ease, being a typical male, believed mostly in what he saw. "I wouldn't mind living in a place like this. Especially if my dream girl was along."

"Well now," a dulcet voice said. "What a handsome man."

Ease turned. There was a lovely bare woman. She had luxurious midnight hair to her slender waist, dark eyes, and a cute face. Kandy was amazed: this was herself! Ease would have freaked out had she been wearing panties; as it was he was in an instant chronic daze. "Who are you?"

"Don't you recognize me? I am your dream girl." She did a slow pirouette that nudged him dangerously close to freak-out.

Kandy realized that Demoness had read his typically male mind, and picked up that memory. She had mixed feelings about that. She did look pretty impressive from this perspective. She was glad that he had picked up on her assets. But to have someone else steal them to impress him annoyed her.

"My dream girl!" he exclaimed, amazed. "But that's impossible! She comes to me only in my sleep."

That was only the half of it, Kandy thought. If only it could be her real body addressing him in this manner, instead of her remaining the board.

"That is true on Xanth," the woman said. "But this is Alpha. Different rules obtain."

"Different rules?" he asked blankly.

"I could not come to you openly in Xanth, because it is not my dominion. But Alpha is halfway neutral territory, at least for a while. Come to me in my own domain, and our love will be complete."

Then Kandy was sure. Fornax, faking a familiar form!

"Fornax!" Ease echoed.

"Of course. Now at last you know the identity of your dream girl."

That was a bare naked lie. Kandy was his dream girl. But she couldn't clarify that without giving away her presence to the Demoness, who must have been so sure of her power that she never checked the buttons or board. But what did she want with Ease?

"I don't get it," Ease said. "Exactly why couldn't you come to me outside your domain? What's yours?"

"Mine is Fornax Galaxy, of course. It consists of contraterrene matter, otherwise known as antimatter, CT for short. It is the exact opposite of terrene matter, with positrons instead of electrons, and—" She broke off, seeing his blank look, then tried again. "When terrene and contraterrene matters meet, they destroy each other in total conversion of mass to energy. This complicates social interaction. So I had to come to you in your sleep, so that we could interact without destroying each other. But here on neutral ground we can interact. Come love me at last, you handsome man."

CAUTION. Kandy hoped the Demoness would not pick up on her warning to Ease.

"You're a Demoness, but you want a mortal man?"

"A *handsome* mortal man. Let me show you how wonderful it can be." She approached him, lips pursed.

But he was understandably wary. "What do you really want?"

"Apart from your love? It would help if you signaled your ship that it's safe to land, so that everyone can enjoy this perfect place, as the centaurs do now. But right now let's forget all that and enjoy our love."

Ease was sorely tempted; Kandy could tell. But he also knew that a Demoness was unlikely to have a simple romantic interest in an ordinary lout like him. "I don't know."

Fornax sighed, in the process doing fetching things with her bosom. "Oh, I have been naughty to tease you so at night in Xanth. I should be punished. Spank me."

"Spank you?"

"Spank me," she repeated firmly, presenting her shapely bare bottom. "Then forgive me so we can make phenomenal love."

He lifted the board, clearly intrigued by more than punishment. "Well, if you insist."

"Oh, yes! Lay one on me, delightful man."

Ease swung the board tentatively. But Kandy enhanced its authority considerably, and she felt the magic of the three princesses magnifying the effect. The board accelerated savagely, striking the bare flesh with a flash like lightning and a clap like thunder. Smoke roiled out from the contact, and when it cleared there was a board-shaped scorch mark across the bottom.

Well, now! Kandy was thrilled to have delivered such a blow to her own seeming body. It served the Demoness right for her identity theft.

"Whoo!" Fornax exclaimed, pleased. "You'll make some lover!"

The Demoness liked it! That made Kandy wonder just what sort of a lover she was. Did she go for sado-masochism? That was interesting but scary. Ease could not afford to get involved with her.

Then Fornax returned to business. "But before we take it to the next level, signal your ship. It's wrong to deny your shipmates the pleasure of the planet."

DON'T SIGNAL Kandy thought. Because the ship would be vulnerable the moment it touched this enchanted world.

"I don't think I should do that," Ease said doubtfully.

"Pretty please with sugar on it? I'll even throw in information relating to your Quest: about the five maidens with the wonderful hair."

"Five maidens?"

"The Magician's grandchildren you're searching for. I will tell you where to find them, and how to invoke the merging spell."

"Oh, yes!" Ease agreed.

Then the woman's expression changed. "It's down! On the far side! While you distracted me. I will make you pay, traitor!" Her lovely features began to change alarmingly. Fangs sprouted, and claws, and dragon-like wings. Those were the nicer features.

"But isn't that what you wanted?" Ease asked. "For the ship to land?"

The Demoness considered for three fifths of a millisecond. "Yes! Now we'll deal with it." She reached out and hooked his arm with a talon.

Then they were on the far side of the planet. It looked hideous, with barren craters and lava flows. There was the ship, with the crew talking with haggard centaurs. It was obvious that the centaurs had not been well treated, and needed to be rescued.

"Gotcha!" Fornax cried. "You're in my power at last. I'll torture all of you until the ransom comes."

"Ransom?" Ease asked.

"A Demon Point. You wouldn't understand, lout."

Arnolde Centaur, the Magic Officer, gazed at her. "What is this? We merely came to rescue the centaur colonists. Who are you?"

"I am Demoness Fornax, mistress of this sorry planet, you doddering fool. I set this trap so that I could gain a point on the Demon Xanth, who has interfered with me too often. Now join the chained creatures, since you are now of their number."

"I think not," Arnolde said.

"Are you completely senile, you ancient gelding? Move or be moved."

"Don't aggravate her, Arnolde," one of the chained centaurs said. "She's merciless when provoked. We learned the hard way."

"She does not have the authority to do this," Arnolde said. "This is not her planet or her galaxy."

"Listen, you flea-bitten nag," Fornax said. "By the time any Demon of this galaxy catches on, I'll have the bunch of you in my home galaxy where they have no power. Then you had better hope that Xanth ransoms you back promptly, because you will not be enjoying your stay with me."

"I think not," Arnolde repeated.

Kandy almost had to admire the old fool's stance. He was not so old that he did not recognize the threat, yet he persisted.

"That does it," Fornax said. "I have lost my patience with your folly, cretin. Take that." She raised her claws. Lightning magic streamed from them to strike the old centaur. Kandy winced as well as her wood allowed.

The lighting surrounded Arnolde, illuminating him in silhouette. But he did not seem to be in pain. "Is that all you have, Demoness?" he asked.

The others were astonished. So was Fornax. "You can't be resisting my magic! You're an inferior mortal!"

"I am neither," Arnolde said. "Now try this." He gestured, and the lightning curled back on itself, reoriented, and shot back to surround Fornax, little bolts eagerly seeking her flesh.

"This is impossible!" she protested, fending it off with her claws. "You can't have Demon magic! Who are you?"

"I'm so glad you finally asked," the centaur said. Then he changed form, becoming a donkey-headed dragon. "I am Demon Xanth, and you are now in my power, Fornax. I have caught you messing with my creatures in my home galaxy, where my power is greater than yours."

Kandy and the others were awed. They were witnessing a Demon encounter! None of them had known that the Demon Xanth was hiding among them. His counter-trap had just worked, nabbing Fornax.

"Oh bleep!" Fornax swore. "Now I'll have to pay a Demon Point!"

"At least," Xanth said. "That will be negotiated by the Council of Demons, since there was no preliminary agreement on the terms of this encounter. Until then you will be remanded to your galaxy under supervised house arrest."

"What supervision?" she demanded. "The lout? I will corrupt him in seconds." She resumed the form of the dream girl, complete with the welt on her lovely backside. Kandy had to admit it was a very shapely welt.

"Not exactly," Xanth said. "Princesses?"

The three buttons on Ease's jacket expanded rapidly, becoming the three princesses, fully clothed.

"Yes, Demon Xanth, Melody said.

"We volunteer," Harmony added.

"We always wanted to see the CT galaxy," Rhythm concluded.

"These three Sorceresses are under my protection, to be treated as honored guests for the duration," Xanth said. "You will not soon be seducing or corrupting them, I think."

"She sure won't," Melody said grimly.

"We're not into dream girls," Harmony agreed disgustedly.

"But spanking her again might be fun," Rhythm concluded zestfully.

"Curses, foiled again," Fornax muttered darkly.

Then the Demoness and the three princesses disappeared. So did the donkey-headed dragon. Xanth had accomplished his purpose and moved on to other Demon business, such as negotiating Fornax's penalty.

"Well, now," Captain Grey said. "It seems we can rescue you centaurs after all. I admit it was uncertain going there for a bit."

"If you please, Captain," a centaur said. He was no longer in chains; they had vanished with the Demons. But he remained haggard. "We no longer need to be rescued. We prefer to remain here and make of this planet the paradise we had planned. It will be hard work, but we can do it."

"But it's a desolate wasteland!" Grey protested. "You're in no condition!"

"Exactly," the centaur replied. "But in time, with our attention, it will become a perfect centaur residence, and we shall be healthy again. We will enjoy the challenge, now that there is no malign Demon interference."

Grey was moved. "If that's the way you want it, you shall have it. We'll spend the night, then take off for home."

That was the way it was. The members of the Quest borrowed a vacant stall and settled down for the night. Soon Ease was asleep, and Kandy appeared, ready to compare notes with the others, play chess with Pewter, and maybe tease Ease a bit more as his elusive dream girl.

"What is that?" Astrid asked.

That was when Kandy discovered the formidable shapely welt across her backside. It seemed the Demoness had left her a parting gift. "That bleep!" she swore.

CHAPTER 8:

FORNAX

In the morning they had come to an agreement: they would not make the tedious space journey back to Xanth, but jump to the new Event from here. It did not seem to make a difference where they were when they evoked a sequin, so why wait?

Mitch approached Captain Grey to explain that they would be leaving. "But you're part of this mission!" Grey protested. "We can't strand you here with the centaurs!"

The three princesses approached them. "They have special magic, Father," Melody said. "They're on their own Quest."

"That's how they joined us," Harmony added. "They weren't part of this mission originally. They invoked a Sequin Event."

"And they can move on as readily," Rhythm concluded. "They won't be stranded here, and the original members they replaced will return to take their places with the mission."

Grey shook his head, bemused. "In that case, Daughters, I'll let them be." Then he did a double-take. "But aren't you three in Fornax, supervising the Demoness while she's under house arrest? What are you doing here?"

"We are there," Melody agreed.

"But also here," Harmony added. "To explain."

"We're ad-hoc illusions," Rhythm concluded.

Then the three princesses vanished.

Grey sighed. "I fear I'll never truly understand teenagers." He glanced at the Quest members. "I wish you the best in your next Event. I do appreciate your assistance here. If your Quest should ever take you to Castle Roogna, be sure to say hello. I'm sure King Ivy would love to hear your story."

"We will," Mitch said. "Thank you for a most interesting Event."

Then they returned to the stall, where Tiara removed a sequin from Astrid's dress, both men goggled at the resulting exposure and even Pewter seemed mildly interested, and replaced it.

They were in a pleasant suite of a grandiose stone house. There were five well-appointed bedrooms, each with its own bathroom complete with shower, toilet, basin, closets, and wall-sized mirrors, a living room with elegant pictures on the walls and couches that looked soft enough to bounce on, a kitchen with phenomenal stores of food and drink, and anything else anyone might have thought to imagine.

"Whose royal suite are we intruding on?" Tiara asked.

Then Ease spied a plaque by the door. WELCOME HONORED MEMBERS OF THE QUEST.

A glance fairly banged their faces as it careened around them. "We were expected!" Pewter said.

"But I thought the Events were random," Astrid said.

"Apparently not entirely," Pewter said.

"Where *are* we?" Ease asked.

That was the question of the hour.

"Let's explore," Tiara suggested. "Just to be sure we're not locked in a tower."

They went to a window and looked out. Beyond was cloud-studded open air. The ground was far, far below. "We *are* in a tower," Astrid said grimly.

"But what a tower!" Ease said. He went out the door, and the others followed. There was a grand hall extending until it curved out of sight.

"I will wait," Pewter said, remaining at the door to their suite.

They followed the hall past door after door, intersection after intersection, discovering bays and stairways without seeming end. Finally they came back to Pewter without turning around; they had completed a large circle. Pewter had known. It was just as well that he had stayed, because they could have missed their suite and gotten lost otherwise. As if they weren't already lost.

"Are we alone here?" Mitch asked.

"Maybe we have this floor," Tiara said. "We haven't checked the others."

So they descended to the floor below. It was much like the other, only with a different wall color.

"Shall we make another circuit?" Mitch asked.

"Why don't the two of you circle," Astrid suggested. "While Ease and I mark the place."

That seemed to make sense, so they did it. Astrid sat on the lower steps while Ease looked around the immediate vicinity, peering into rooms. "Empty," he reported as he returned. Then he froze in place.

"Ease!" Astrid said, alarmed. "Are you all right?"

Then Kandy caught on. PULL YOUR SKIRT DOWN she thought to the woman.

"Oh." Astrid's skirt had ridden up over her knees so that Ease had seen under it. "I'm still not quite used to clothing. Or to male's reactions to it."

THAT'S WHY I'M HERE. I'M YOUR FRIEND. Which made Kandy wonder: had she been transformed only to serve this purpose, guiding the basilisk in human conventions? No, there had to be more to it than that. She had to believe that.

Astrid covered her thighs, then snapped her fingers.

Ease resumed walking, unaware he had ever stopped. "Nothing there," he reported.

Astrid smiled, knowing that he meant the rooms. "So it seems that we have at least two floors to ourselves, and perhaps others. But this is curious. Why should there be so huge a tower, so well appointed, with no occupants? And how does it relate to our Quest? I am not making much sense of this."

Ease opened his mouth to answer, and paused, listening. There was a sound.

"Oh—Mitch and Tiara completing the circuit," Astrid said.

But then they saw the figures coming around the curve. Not two, but three. Three women. Wearing little crowns.

"The princesses!" Ease said. "What are they doing here?"

The three saw the two. "Ease!" Melody exclaimed.

"Astrid!" Harmony added.

"Why are you here?" Rhythm concluded.

"Oh, my!" Astrid said. "This must be Fornax Galaxy!"

"Of course it is," Melody said.

"We're here to watch the Demoness," Harmony added.

"For the Demon Xanth," Rhythm concluded.

"We're on our next Event," Ease said, covertly eying the three pretty girls.

Kandy was getting used to it, similarly covertly tuning into his mind, and even was beginning to appreciate their points as he did. It was simply the way men were hard wired. "We turned up in a huge suite upstairs."

"We were exploring," Astrid said. "Trying to make sense of it."

"The Demoness calls this her cottage by the sea," Melody said.

"Her incidental lodging," Harmony agreed.

"One of hundreds or thousands," Rhythm concluded.

"There's a sign, by our suite," Astrid said. "Welcoming us. So someone knew we were coming. That must be Fornax."

"Where did you use the sequin?" Melody asked.

"On the centaur planet?" Harmony added.

"Where Fornax's influence may remain strong?" Rhythm concluded.

"That's where," Ease agreed.

"But assuming she could hijack our Events," Astrid said, "Why would she want to? We're of no use to her."

"Maybe she's still interested in Ease," Melody said.

"Because he's handsome," Harmony agreed.

"And she's lonely," Rhythm concluded, smiling.

"But she called me a lout," Ease said. "Twice."

"She was angry," Melody said.

"Because her wicked plan had been foiled," Harmony added.

"And it was partly your fault," Rhythm concluded.

He was foolishly moved. "Do you really think so?"

"We're women," Melody said.

"We know how women think," Harmony agreed.

"Hell has no fury like that of a woman scorned," Rhythm concluded.

Kandy realized that they were teasing him, almost flirting. Were they lonely too? Or was there something else going on? They were princesses, and Sorceresses, with other interests. Yet at the moment they were on this somewhat lonely duty. Teasing a man might be harmless entertainment. For princesses or Demonesses.

"But of course your Quest-mates might not approve," Melody said.

"So you probably shouldn't discuss this with them," Harmony added.

"Keep it secret," Rhythm concluded.

"But Astrid already knows," Ease protested.

"I won't tell," Astrid said. She had evidently caught on to the game. She was not really human, and was still learning.

"We have to move on now," Melody said.

"To snoop on the Demoness," Harmony added.

"To make sure she's not violating her parole," Rhythm concluded.

"Glad to have met you," Ease said.

"It's been nice," Astrid agreed. She was learning the social conventions.

The princesses moved on, soon disappearing around the bend. Then Mitch and Tiara appeared, having completed the circuit. "Empty," he reported.

"Not quite," Astrid said. "We saw the three princesses. You just missed them."

"The princesses!" Tiara said. "But that means—"

"That we are in Fornax Galaxy," Astrid said.

"That explains a lot," Mitch said. "But also mystifies anew. Why would the sequin send us here?"

"There must be something we need to do or learn here," Astrid said. "Assuming the sequins are not entirely random."

They mounted the stairs and rejoined Pewter, who seemed to be playing with some sand from a potted plant. "We met the three princesses!" Ease announced.

"You too? They stopped by here while you were gone. We discussed sand."

"Sand?" Mitch asked.

"The presence of the princesses suggests that we are in the contra-terrene galaxy," Pewter said. "Sand could be quite useful in a CT realm."

"Sand?" Mitch repeated.

"Every grain of terrene sand would be like a bomb in a CT setting, because anything it touched would go up in total conversion of matter to energy. This is because terrene and contra-terrene are diametric opposites, positive and negative, canceling each other out. This castle is obviously terrene, so as to be safe for we terrene visitors, but outside must be deadly."

"Sand like a bomb," Mitch said, intrigued. "It might be smart to keep some of it on us." He took a handful. So did the others.

"It was actually the princesses' notion," Pewter said. "They are now carrying sand."

That was curious, Kandy thought; the princesses had not mentioned carrying sand or meeting Pewter, though they had evidently had a solid dialogue. But of course they could have stopped by to see him briefly.

"Something's piscatorial," Tiara's hair said.

"Something's what?" Ease asked.

"Funny, shady, suspect, questionable, suspicious—"

"Fishy?" Astrid asked.

"Whatever," the hair agreed crossly. "Why should the princesses visit with two of us downstairs, and one upstairs, and not the rest? Maybe they were fakes."

"I assure you the ones I encountered fifteen minutes ago were genuine," Pewter said.

"And the ones Ease and I met weren't?" Astrid asked.

"I can tell you why they avoided us," the hair said. "Because they knew I could tell a fake when I saw it. It takes a demon to recognize one."

"Exactly what are you saying?" Mitch asked.

"I'm saying that you could have been talking with the Demoness Fornax masquerading as the princesses."

"This is possible," Pewter said. "But what would be her motive? If this is her castle in her domain, she has no need to hide from anyone. Certainly not the princesses, who are here to watch her."

"Wrong, wire-brain. They are the very ones she would most want to hide things from, because they will report to Demon Xanth about any parole violations."

"But why emulate the princesses, then?" Mitch asked. "That's bound to attract their attention."

"That is curious," Astrid agreed. "We may be wading through murkier waters than we suspect." As a basilisk she was familiar with murky waters.

"Well, let's relax and prepare for the morrow," Mitch said. "The answers may come clear in due course."

The others were glad to agree. The mysteries here seemed to be too big to assimilate all at once.

They went into their fancy suite. Ease, being mannishly hungry, checked out the kitchen supplies. The women joined him, lest he spoil perfectly good food in his clumsy ignorance. Soon they settled down to a nice meal of bread and jam and boot rear.

Or was it? "There's no kick," Mitch complained.

"You're right," Ease said. "This is denatured. It's root beer."

"This food has been imported from Alpha Centauri," Pewter said. "Which makes sense, as there would be nothing we could safely eat here in the CT realm."

"Because it would destroy us in total conversion to energy," Mitch agreed, shuddering. "That's more kick than I care for."

"Fortunately we won't be here long," Astrid said. "Just until we complete or discover whatever it is that brought us here."

"Assuming the sequins have some purpose," Pewter said.

They finished their meal, then found themselves ready to relax. Kandy was suspicious; had the food been drugged? But what would be the point in that? So their unwinding was probably natural.

Mitch and Tiara took one room, not seeming to be bothered by the hidden presence of the demoness Metria; nice hair counted for a lot. Pewter settled down in another, hardly needing the company of the living folk. Astrid lay on a bed in another room for a nap. That left Ease, who was happy to take another bed in another room. Kandy tuned in on his idle thoughts, as she was increasingly able to do.

But as he lay there pondering this and that, such as whether a lovely Demoness really could be interested in a lout, there was a sound at the window. It was like sand. Kandy thought of sand in a new way now, because of the CT connection.

Ease got up and went to the window. There across the gulf of air was an attractive sunlit pavilion. And there within it, sunning herself, seemingly innocent of any awareness of her exposure, was the dream girl: Kandy's form, nude.

The nerve! The Demoness was doing it again. She was flashing Ease with the body. And Ease, the male fool, was eating it up. His eyes were close to glazing. Then the figure crossed her bare legs, proffering an all-too-perfect view, and Ease almost freaked out, prevented only because the angle was almost but not quite right to show a panty line. As if that close call was accidental. The Demoness knew exactly who was watching and what the effect on him was. She was playing him like a fish on a hook.

Then the sunlight shifted subtly to illuminate a path that led from the base of the castle to the pavilion. It wound through lovely colored foliage and statuary, surely concealed from ground level but clear enough from above. A person could readily walk that path to get from here to there.

Ease was already in motion, going out the door, down the stairs, and around to the exit to the path. The fool!

Kandy knew she had to do something, but what? Ease's mind had been preempted by the vision and was not subject to a HALT idea at the moment. Kandy realized that the Demoness must have pretended to be the three princesses to plant the notion of her own amenability in Ease's foolishly eager mind, setting him up for the seduction. Now she was doing it, luring him to her. It remained a mystery why, since he was not the guardian; the three princesses were that. Fornax couldn't want a mere dalliance; that was not the way a scheming woman's mind worked. She wanted something else. Whatever it was was unlikely to be good news for the rest of them.

Kandy tried to mentally signal Astrid, but she was asleep. Mitch and Tiara were locked in love, unreachable. Pewter was a machine, hard to reach unless attuned. The princesses seemed to be out of range. Meanwhile Ease was down to the ground floor and heading outside. He had made an easy job of getting on his foolish way, unfortunately.

Then she got a notion. METRIA! she called mentally. She was getting better at aiming at specific minds, but could she reach the demoness?

Do you mind? Metria answered. *This couple is in a most interesting embrace, and her hair is curling around his head and locking it in for a prolonged kiss while it seductively tickles his neck.*

And just who was facilitating that? Tiara's hair was anti-gravity, not prehensile. The demoness must really be enjoying her lascivious participation. But at least Kandy had reached her.

THIS IS IMPORTANT! EASE IS LEAVING THE CASTLE.

What do I care? Then the demoness did a mental double-take. *Who are you, anyway? There are no telepaths in this Quest.*

Oops. They had not told the demoness about Kandy. It seemed that now was the time. I AM KANDY, A WOMAN CHANGED INTO A BOARD. THE ONE THAT EASE CARRIES, ONLY HE DOESN'T KNOW IT'S ANYTHING MORE THAN A BOARD. IT'S A LONG STORY. BUT TRUST ME: I HAVE HIS WELFARE IN MIND. DEMONESS FORNAX IS LURING HIM TO A SEPARATE PAVILION, WHERE I DON'T KNOW WHAT WILL HAPPEN.

Oh bleep! That is important. She'll seduce him and corrupt him, and then he won't be much fun anymore for the rest of us. What do you want me to do?

Trust the demoness to have a selfish motive. WAKE THE OTHERS. LOCATE THE PRINCESSES. THIS COULD BE A VIOLATION OF FORNAX'S PAROLE, OR WHATEVER.

Whatever, the demoness agreed. *At any rate, interesting. You say you are a board? That's interesting too.*

And of course interest was what motivated Metria. She wanted to be where the most action was, of whatever nature, especially if it was violent or naughty. It might have been hard to pull her away from the lovemaking couple if a confrontation with a Demoness were not more exciting. If seduction was occurring, Metria wanted to be on hand to see every detail.

But Tiara's evocative hair is important too. I'll have to split.

Kandy took that to mean Metria had decided to let the loving couple be for a while. GET BUSY she thought impatiently.

Soon Astrid was awake and communicating. *I'm looking out the window,* she reported. *I see that path, and the sunning she-devil. We'll hurry down there, but I fear not in time.*

That was Kandy's concern too. DO YOUR BEST.

A female figure popped into view behind Ease. The man did not see her, but Kandy did. It wasn't Metria, though there were points of similarity, notably on her chest. Was it Fornax? But she was busy sunning herself, visible from the path. Could she be in two places at the same time? Well, she was a Demoness, and if she had emulated the three princesses, she could do this. But why would she bother? Her ploy was already working.

Well, maybe it was best to be direct. WHO ARE YOU?

"I am D Mentia, Metria's alter-ego," the figure said, not loudly enough to attract Ease's attention, but quite clear for Kandy. "We had to fission to be in two places at once. What's this about a board woman?"

D Mentia. A pun. And that split had been literal fissioning so Metria could continue with the couple. This was wasting precious time. WHAT DO YOU CARE?

"I care because though I have no speech impediment like my alter, I am a bit crazy, and this is the kind of craziness that intrigues me. If you want my help, cater to me to this extent."

No speech impediment? That seemed to be true. This was a slightly different creature. Kandy sighed inwardly. She had better oblige. So she sent the story of her wishing well wish and conversion in a single concentrated mental blast.

"Interesting indeed," Mentia agreed. "Let's see what I can do." She vanished.

Ease paused. There before him was a crazily luscious figure of a woman with a dress whose decolletage plunged toward unknown depths. "Who?" he began.

"No, I'm not your dream girl," Mentia said. "I'm better. I'm your dream woman. I have some crazy notions. Let me walk you back to your room where we can have some privacy." She leaned forward, inhaling.

Kandy had to admire Mentia's technique. She had perfected the art of flashing just enough to do the job.

Ease was obviously tempted. If there was one thing better than a distant dream girl, it was a dream woman who was close at hand.

But then the Demoness Fornax caught on. "Begone, bleep!" she called. Actually bleep was not exactly the word she used, though it was close.

"Oh, bloop," Mentia muttered as she disintegrated into smoke. That wasn't exactly the word either, but it was also close. Obviously she could not directly oppose the far more powerful entity.

Ease shook his head as if clearing it of dottle and resumed his march toward the pavilion. However the brief delay had enabled the first of the home party to catch up. Rather, the first three.

"What's this?" Princess Melody inquired, blocking the way ahead.

"Why are you on this fell path?" Princess Harmony continued.

"Leading toward a mysterious pavilion?" Princess Rhythm concluded.

"I have to go somewhere," Ease explained.

"There's nothing there you need," Melody said.

"It's just the Demoness trying to tempt you away from your friends," Harmony continued.

"So she can subvert you," Rhythm concluded.

"Yes," Ease agreed blissfully.

The three princesses frowned in unison. This wasn't working well.

Kandy had an idea. MAYBE MENTIA CAN BE THE DREAM GIRL BACK AT THE CASTLE, she thought to Melody. After all, if her emulated body was to be used subversively, why not use it in a good cause?

Melody nodded. "The demoness Mentia is intrigued by you," she said.

"She is slightly demented," Harmony agreed.

"And sexy as can be," Rhythm concluded.

That got his attention. He started to turn around. Mentia was silhouetted in the window of his room, slowly elaborating her curves.

"Hey!" Fornax cried from the pavilion. "I'm just as intrigued, demented, and sexy as she is!"

"And on the verge of violating your parole," Melody called back.

"You're not supposed to leave the premises or interfere with the Quest," Harmony added.

"And if you do either, we'll Tell," Rhythm finished. Evidently the pavilion counted as an attachment to the castle, so she wasn't in violation yet.

"Oh, bleep it to bleep!" the Demoness swore, though not in exactly those words. The local foliage wilted and there was a smell of scorch.

Meanwhile Astrid and Pewter had come up the path, carrying buckets of sand. "This way," Astrid said. They led the way, with Ease following, and the three princesses bringing up the rear.

Ease was on his way back, but the Demoness wasn't through. She could not interfere directly, but this was her domain and there was plenty she could do indirectly.

A dragon approached the path. It was huge and fiery. It fired a bolt of flame at them, but the bolt became a shower of sparks as it crossed the path. Kandy knew why: the dragon's breath was CT, and when it encountered the terrene air of the path it converted to pure energy. Pewter, Astrid, and Ease walked on past it, Ease pausing only to make a small gesture with one finger that seemed to really annoy the dragon for some reason.

A giant ogre appeared. It opened its horrendous mouth and chomped down on Ease. But its hugely mottled teeth melted into sparks as they came close, victims of the terrene air.

But this ogre was not entirely stupid, which suggested it was a fake, because all true ogres were justifiably proud of their stupidity. It brought around a ham-fist holding a rock that aspired to be a small boulder. The rock was larger than Ease, so could probably annihilate him by merging with his body and exploding both into energy.

Ease lifted his trusty board, ready to whack at the rock. This was foolish; the rock was far too big to knock out of there like a pebble. Also, what would happen to Kandy if she was forcefully smacked into CT stone? Would she explode into energy?

NO!! she thought, two exclamations points strong.

Ease changed his mind and dodged aside instead. The rock just missed him.

Astrid turned and glanced at the ogre. It fell back, stunned, the rock dropping from its paw. It seemed that her glare worked regardless of the polarity of the subject. The group moved on.

Now a sphinx appeared, lumbering forward so that its inertia would carry it across the path even if it got stunned. This looked like bad mischief.

"Sphinx turns tail," Pewter said. And of course the sphinx did. There was no pun virus here in the Fornax Galaxy, so Pewter could use his magic. This, too, seemed unaffected by CT.

"Oh for bleep's sake," a voice muttered. It was Fornax, invisibly watching.

"Now if we had any hint that the CT Demoness was behind any of this, we'd report it," Melody remarked.

"But we don't actually have proof," Harmony continued.

"Yet," Rhythm concluded.

"Beware the stampede," the Demoness' voice said in a conversational tone.

They heard a sound like distant but rapidly approaching thunder, and felt the ground shudder. Then they saw it: a herd of giant rhino-potta-phants charging toward the path. Astrid could not look at all of them at once, and Pewter would have trouble changing all their dull minds.

But they were up to the challenge. Each person dipped out a handful of sand and as the vanguard of the stampede came, flung the sand at it. There was a spectacular display of energy as the sand struck skin and converted it to energy.

The phants, blinded and burning, reared back, colliding with the ones behind them. Soon there was a phenomenal pileup of groaning behemoths.

And the little group of people walked calmly on to the castle, unscathed.

"Curses, foiled again!" But it wasn't Fornax speaking, it was the princesses, each saying one of the words, mockingly. Kandy would have laughed, if she hadn't been a board.

They entered the castle, where they were met by Metria. "You made it!" she said. "I couldn't help, because the Demoness banned all my alters from the path."

Pewter looked at her. "If Mentia's posing in the window, and you're here, who's with Mitch and Tiara?"

"Oops," Metria said. "I must have fissioned into all three alters, and forgot this situation."

"Situation?" Astrid asked.

"My third form is the child Woe Betide, captive of the Adult Conspiracy."

"And she's with Mitch and Tiara?" Pewter asked sharply.

"I must rescue her!"

Then they heard a childish scream resounding throughout the castle.

"Too late," Pewter said.

Metria vanished. The scream stopped in mid syllable.

"What happened?" Astrid asked.

"Metria went to merge with Woe Betide, eliminating her childish aspect," Pewter said. "But be not concerned; the child remains to be evoked again at a more convenient time. Metria will erase her memory of the dread Conspiracy violation and she will be her sweet innocent self again."

"That's a relief," Astrid said. "I wouldn't want a child hurt."

Kandy liked that about Astrid: she was one of the most deadly creatures of Xanth, yet she had human sensitivities. Maybe they came with the body, but Kandy thought there was a core of decency that evoked them.

Meanwhile Ease had lost interest in the dialogue, if he had ever had any, and resumed his forging toward his room. The others let him be, knowing that Mentia might give him an insanely great experience but would not corrupt him to serve Fornax.

Kandy, however, could not go elsewhere and tune it out. She was always with Ease, day and night. That was normally okay, but what about when a demoness seduced him? Kandy knew herself for a jealous female, but there it was: she couldn't stand the notion. If anyone was going to seduce Ease, it should be her.

Ease reached his room and slammed the door behind him. There was D. Mentia, looking every bit as seductive as she had in the window. "Well, now," she said, floating across the floor and into his embrace. "How it is that you and I have not met before?"

"I didn't know you existed," Ease said, enfolding her lush torso. He was still holding the board, but that didn't seem to matter.

"I am D. Mentia, the slightly crazy alter ego of D. Metria. I have no speech impediment, but I can be downright weird at times." As she spoke she was running her hands over his body. "Have you ever done it upside down?"

And Kandy couldn't even complain, because the demoness was doing exactly what they had asked her to: distract Ease from the seduction of Demoness Fornax. She couldn't renege now, lest he go back to Fornax. Kandy herself had suggested it. So what variety of lady dog was she being, resenting it?

Now Ease was grabbing enthusiastic handfuls of Mentia's all-too-willing body while she unbuttoned his shirt, kissing all the while. She was literally floating, making it a bit crazy already. Kandy gritted her wooden teeth, knowing she was stuck for it.

"Well, now."

Ease and Mentia paused to look, startled. So did Kandy.

It was the Demoness Fornax, using the likeness of Kandy's body, nude. The welt on her backside still showed.

"Uh-oh," Mentia murmured.

"Begone, again," Fornax said. Mentia disappeared, her expression of regret lingering a quarter of a moment after.

"I thought you couldn't come in here," Ease said, disgruntled, though his eyes were locked on the body. "So you lured me to the pavilion."

"This is my domain, my galaxy, my planet, and my castle," Fornax said evenly. "I can be anywhere I want to be. I used the pavilion to separate you from your companions, so we would not be disturbed. But we can do it here readily enough."

"But what about the CT? I don't want to get blasted into energy."

"I made this castle and its environs terrene," Fornax said. "For your comfort. It was an effort I hope you appreciate. I am using a flexible superficial shield to prevent my substance from directly contacting the terrene substance. You will

not be able to tell the difference." She smiled. "As you can verify. Stroke me."
She proffered a marvelous breast.

But Ease was belatedly learning caution. "You called me an oaf, before."

"Lout," she corrected him. "I was annoyed at being denied the pleasure of
your company."

"My company? I just wanted to get into your panties."

"Whatever. Panties would just get in the way."

"What do you want of me? Apart from whatever?"

"We'll get to that soon. Right now, let's just enjoy the moment." She took
his hand, making it stroke her upper section. "See? No matter detonation."

He was obviously sorely tempted. But he struggled on. "I think I'd better
know before whatever, because I won't be able to think straight then."

"You can't think straight now," Fornax pointed out as she slid his hand
down and around her body until it stroked the welt. That was, Kandy saw,
absolutely no turn-off for him.

"Just tell me," he said desperately.

She sighed, making her whole body quiver voluptuously. "If you insist. I
want to recruit you to be my agent in the terrene realm. I have trouble interacting
with creatures there, because of my CT nature. It's complicated developing a
CT shield every time. This makes bargaining for points awkward."

"Points?" His hand, guided by hers, was exploring points at the moment.

"Demon points. They are the focus of Demon interactions. All else is dross."

"But I'm no Demon! I can't—"

"Nor do you need to be, sweet man. I merely need a terrene representative
who will relay my messages to the others. That way I won't have to armor
myself against lethal contact. When I am forced to be so defensive, my powers
are diminished until I'm hardly better than a little-d demon like your Mentia.
I don't like that, so prefer to remain here, where my powers are complete, and
send word to you."

How would she send word, Kandy wondered.

Ease picked up on that as his own thought. "But how would you tell me
the messages?"

"You will have a special high-power magic mirror equipped for intergalactic
transmissions, tuned to you alone. To all others it will seem to be only inert
glass. You won't need to touch it, merely watch and listen to it."

"Watch and listen?"

"I will appear to you like this," she said, inhaling against him. "You alone
will see and hear me. Such transmissions don't evoke the CT detonation,

fortunately. I can be extremely naughty in such a private show." She rubbed suggestively against him.

He was being persuaded. "Well—"

"We can discuss the details anon." She led him toward the bed.

Kandy knew she had to act before all was lost. But how? She couldn't do anything, just think to him, and he would not be amenable to any No notion now. He *wanted* to believe, thanks to Fornax's suggestive campaign.

Then she got an idea. Could it possibly work? She had never tried it before, never even thought to try it. But maybe, just maybe...

Fornax had Ease down on the bed, lying on his back, and was working on his trousers. He was completely taken with her. Kandy could hardly blame him. The Demoness's seduction almost made *her* want it, and it had to be ten times as effective on a man. She had to act.

SLEEP! Kandy thought.

And Ease, lying down, slept, put down before he had a chance to question it. Her ploy had worked! Now the Demoness could not seduce him.

"Now that is interesting," Fornax said.

Belatedly Kandy remembered the flaw in her plan. When Ease slept, Kandy reverted to her natural form. She was now exposed before the Demoness, with the man's hand on her ankle. She couldn't even try to escape, because the moment she lost contact she would be the inert board. She would have to brave it through, somehow.

"Uh, hello," she said. Would Fornax smite her to smithereens?

"I thought his dream girl was all in his imagination," Fornax said. "But you're real, aren't you? In fact you are the board."

"I am the board," Kandy agreed. "I wished for adventure, excitement, and romance, and got transformed. I animate only when he sleeps."

"And I am animating a real woman." Fornax reached out to touch her bottom, feeling the welt. "I thought I was sharing the scar with his imagination, so he could appreciate his mark on me." Her mouth quirked. "I will remove it if you wish."

"That's all right," Kandy said. "It doesn't hurt."

"Those occasional flashes of common sense he evinced—they were from you, sending him thoughts without his knowledge."

"Yes. He does not know about me. He thinks I come at night just to tease him." Kandy grimaced, cursing herself for talking too much, but unable to stop. "It's really myself I am teasing. I can't *do* anything with him."

Fornax gazed thoughtfully at her. "It occurs to me that I may have sought the wrong person to recruit."

"Oh, please don't go after Mitch! He doesn't deserve that."

Fornax laughed musically. "I am thinking of you, Kandy. You have more sense than Ease does."

"Me!"

"You know that I was seducing Ease merely to cement his allegiance to me. I can get plenty of boy-toys elsewhere; I don't need him for that. I would not have to seduce you, merely persuade you. That's less fuss. You would not be fascinated by every passing young pretty woman. You would not freak out when she flashed her panties. You would make a better representative."

Kandy could not get her mind around this astonishing notion. "But I'm a dream!"

"And talking to your exact image. I shall be happy to give that back to you. Any anything else you might want. I can be generous, in return for loyalty."

"I'm not making any deal with you!"

"Why not?"

Kandy spluttered. "You're the enemy!"

Fornax shook her head. "I am no one's enemy, merely a Demoness seeking to score points against others of my ilk. My concerns hardly overlap yours. All I want is a representative in your area of the universe. In return for this simple thing, that will harm no one you know, I can give you everything you ever wanted in your life. Will you not at least consider it?"

"No!"

"Proffer me a sensible rather than an emotional reason, and I will let you be."

Kandy scrounged mentally for a moment, then had it. "The centaurs! You treated them abominably."

"I did not. I merely took over their colony planet, as a ploy to interfere with Xanth."

"They were starving!"

"They refused to work when I took over, though I did not interfere in any way with their society. I merely cut off their communication with Xanth so that their hostage status would become evident. When they ran out of food, I provided replacements magically, but they refused to touch them. They were staging a de facto hunger strike. They could have prospered, but were amazingly obstinate about their freedom. Which they knew they would recover, once Xanth paid their ransom. I'm glad to be rid of them."

"They were chained!"

"Not until the rescue ship arrived. Then I had to keep them under tighter control, for appearances."

Kandy disliked admitting that this was persuasive. "But when the rescue party landed, you said you would torture them all."

"A threat without substance. I was merely trying to cow them into submission."

"Then when Arnolde Centaur stood up to you, you developed fangs and claws and dragon wings."

"My warrior persona. I manifested it before I joined the centaurs, as you may remember. You will remember also that you had just walloped my backside, leaving a welt. There are protocols."

"I—I—" Kandy realized that the Demoness had a case. It was after all a valid offer. "How much time can I have to consider it?"

"Shall we say a year? You can consult with your friends, and with the Demon Xanth. This can be an open public deal if you wish, though that might mark you among mortals in a way you would not like."

"I—I think I would prefer a private deal," Kandy said. She had already had more than enough experience being marked for attention. "If I make it at all. Meanwhile I would rather have you entirely out of my life."

"Done," Fornax said, and vanished.

Kandy shook her head, bemused. Just like that! But what had she agreed to?

CHAPTER 9:

PYRAMID

The demoness Mentia reappeared. "She banished me, but only from this chamber; now she's gone, and I can resume my diversion." She glanced down. "But now he's asleep, and you're in your ghost form. I doubt you want to do it with me, though that would indeed be crazy for you."

"She wants to recruit me to be her representative in the terrene realm," Kandy said. "Not to harm anyone. To relay her messages to terrenes, because it's hard for her to handle our kind of matter personally. Does that make sense?"

"Yes, it does to me. She doesn't want to explode into total conversion. But I'm not quite sane. Better check with the others."

Yet this demoness seemed more sensible than her alter ego. "I need to think," Kandy said. "Wake Ease and do what he wants."

"As you wish." Mentia snapped her toes—she was indeed a little crazy— and Ease woke as if coming out of a freak. Kandy was the board again. She tuned out the activity, suppressing her jealousy as well as she could, and pondered. The last thing she had expected was a reasonable offer to her from Fornax. She would have to discuss it with the others, as Mentia recommended, and trust their judgment. But she already knew one thing: if this stopped Fornax from seducing Ease, now or in the future, she had to take it seriously. His wandering eye for other women bothered her for more than one reason, but most terrene women would not corrupt him the way Fornax would.

She couldn't help tuning in to what was going on. She had to face it: she wanted Ease's wandering eye to fix on her alone, and she wanted to be doing what Mentia was doing with him. She couldn't blame him for being with other women, since he didn't even know about Kandy. She just had to hope that in due course she would get past the enchantment and be able to freak him out and seduce him herself. At least she could be honest with herself about that.

Meanwhile she had discovered one useful thing: that she could not only wake Ease, she could put him to sleep. That meant she could talk with the others at any time she really needed to.

Some time later, she did just that, putting Ease to sleep so she could talk with the others. She had a lot to discuss with them.

To her surprise, they agreed with Mentia. "There may be advantages to having regular contact with a Demon or Demoness," Pewter said. "You can gain a great deal of power in your bailiwick."

"I don't want power," Kandy protested. "I just want Ease." She glanced at the man's sleeping form.

"Then take him, when you can," Tiara said. "He'll be worth it," She glanced obliquely at Mitch.

"Take him," Mitch echoed. "He'll be glad of it."

Kandy looked at Astrid. "I agree," the basilisk said. "If I had the right man, I would take him."

"I wonder what the three princesses would say," Kandy mused.

The three appeared. "It seems fair," Melody said seriously.

"Provided you insist that she not use you to do anyone harm," Harmony continued thoughtfully.

"But naughty is okay," Rhythm concluded with a giggle. The three vanished.

Yet Kandy wasn't quite satisfied. "You're all saying that my connection with the Demoness Fornax could enable me to win the man I want, because I could simply ask her for that. I'm not sure that's the way I would want to do it."

Tiara's hair wavered. "You're crazier than my alter!"

That gave Kandy an idea. "Maybe a child could be more objective. May I ask Woe Betide?"

And there among them stood a cute little girl with a sad face. She looked at Kandy. "Hi, ghost," she said shyly.

"Woe Betide," Kandy said. "I'm not really a ghost, just a woman in the form of a board."

The child found that hilarious. "You can whack folk!"

"Suppose I had the chance to win the man of my dreams, but only if I made a deal with a Demoness?" Kandy asked.

The child was confused. "Men are icky. Why would you want one?"

She had to get down to the child's level. "So I could freak him out with my panties."

"Yes!"

"Even if I had to make a deal with a Demoness?"

Woe Betide considered. "She could give you all the candy you wanted, hee hee!" That was evidently the definitive answer, apart from being a pun on her name.

Kandy sighed inwardly. She would have to make up her own mind, in due course. "Thank you, Woe Betide."

"Can I whack something with you? When you're a board?"

"I'm sorry, no. Only Ease can whack things with me."

The child's eyes welled up with tears. "Oh, fudge!"

"But maybe your alters will let you watch when Ease whacks something."

The tears evaporated, literally. "Say yes!" Then Woe Betide vanished.

"Now we should get on with our mission," Pewter said. "Whatever part of it we are supposed to accomplish here."

"I think we have done that," Astrid said. "It was the Demoness's offer to Kandy, that could enable her to accomplish our mission immediately."

"But she's not yet accepting it," Pewter grumped.

"Oh, shut up, or I'll kiss you," Astrid told him.

Pewter shut up. He had no fear of her deadly power; it had to be because he didn't want her kiss. Was he afraid it would corrupt him?

"Kandy is the one person among us who has some ethical conscience," Astrid said to the others. "She wants to do the right thing, and is taking her time to figure it out. We want to complete our Quest successfully, yes, but we need to have a care how we do it."

Kandy stared at her, amazed. How could there be such sensitivity in a basilisk?

"You're right," Tiara said, nodding.

"I am embarrassed for not seeing it before," Mitch said.

"Conscience is fine in its place," Pewter said. "But our first priority must be the accomplishment of the quest."

"I think that is a debate for another time," Astrid said. "Shall we move on to our next Event?"

"In the morning," Mitch said. "We have had a fair day here, and need to rest."

"Yes," Tiara agreed, coloring slightly.

They settled down for the night. Kandy found herself no closer to a decision than she had been before the dialogue.

In the morning Tiara removed a sequin from Astrid's dress. The men's eyes started to glaze. She replaced the sequin.

They were in space falling toward the weirdest planet Kandy might have imagined. For one thing, it was not round but sharply angular. "What is that?" Mitch asked.

"That is Pyramid," Pewter said. "One of the worlds of Ida."

"I don't think I understand," Tiara said.

"The planet Ptero orbits the head of Princess Ida," Pewter explained. "It appears to be very small, and it was once thought that folk of Xanth could visit it only by leaving their bodies behind and condensing their souls to assume their forms on it. That later turned out to be a misapprehension; Ptero merely seems small because it is distant, a victim of the magic of perspective. It is where all the characters who might have made it to Xanth proper exist. There is another Princess Ida thereon, and about her head orbits the planet of Pyramid, appearing much smaller yet, but it too is a full size world. It seems that this is the setting for our next event."

"But we'll crash and go splat!" Mitch protested.

"No, there is a protocol for approaching these worlds," Pewter said. "We'll land safely. Merely focus on slowing your descent."

They tried it, and it worked; they moved more slowly. Relieved, they viewed the approaching planet. It was indeed a pyramid, grandly rotating. Each face of it was triangular, colored blue red, green, and gray below. They saw each side in turn as it turned, covered with mountains, lakes, forests and plains, all of the same color. They would be landing on one of the triangles, but which one? The steady rotation made it difficult to tell.

How could they breathe, out here in space? Kandy wondered. Apparently that was just part of the magic of this realm.

Then they dipped as if about to fly under the planet. They were going toward the shadowy nether face, the gray one, where it seemed the sun never shone directly. Assuming there was a sun; Kandy saw the light but did not see any orb.

"One other thing," Pewter remarked. "Each world has its own laws of magic. Pyramid connects magnitude to generosity. Neither a giver nor a receiver be, unless you wish to change your size, because the giver gains in physical stature while the receiver diminishes."

"Then how can people interact?" Mitch asked. "Are they constantly changing size?"

"Yes. But mostly they arrange for even trades."

They came under the gray face and re-oriented, their heads pointing away from it. Now it seemed to be below them, and they were dropping. Tiara's hair flared, acting like a magic parachute. The others spread their arms. They all landed reasonably gently.

They were on a gray hill with gray trees, foliage, and ground. Except that the ground looked level.

"This is weird," Tiara said. "My eyes say I'm on level ground, but my body says it's a slope."

"We are near the edge of the gray face," Pewter said. "Although the ground is flat, it is angling away from the center, so it has the effect of a slope."

"I would not be able to make sense of that," she said, "if I had not seen the planet as we came in. The edges and points of the faces do rise, in effect."

"That should straighten out as we move toward the center," Mitch said.

"I don't think so," Astrid said.

"No?"

"We are standing not far from the Good Magician's Castle. That must be where our Event takes place."

The others looked. It was true: there, in naturalistic shades of gray, was a stone castle surrounded by a moat. A pennant flying from a turret bore the letters GMC. The Good Magician's Castle.

"But that can't be here," Tiara said. "It's on Xanth."

"The worlds can duplicate any feature of Xanth," Pewter said. "Also any people. Including the Good Magician and his demesnes."

"But what do we want with the Good Magician?" Mitch asked. "He charges a year's service or the equivalent for his Answer to a Question. We're already on a Quest; we can't complicate that."

"Obviously we need to ask where the pun virus antidote is," Pewter said. "The Good Magician of Xanth was unable to give us specific directions, but perhaps the one here will be able to. He may not charge us a further service, since we are already on a mission for him. It may be that the Magician here did not get his Book of Answers messed up."

That seemed to make sense. "We certainly aren't making much progress on our own," Astrid said. "We have been to all manner of places while gleaning only small hints."

"Alpha Centauri, Fornax, Pyramid," Mitch agreed. "As well as some unusual settings in Xanth."

"So let's brave the challenges," Ease said. "I got through them once; it should be easier the second time."

"You are assuming the challenges will be the same as the ones you encountered before," Pewter said. "That is unlikely."

"Oh." Obviously that hadn't occurred to Ease.

"Next question," Mitch said. "Do we select a member of our party to approach the castle, or do we go as a group?"

"Just so long as I'm with you," Tiara said.

Mitch looked around. "Any volunteers to try it alone?"

"Sure," Ease said. "I'll go."

A glance circled around the others. "We are a group," Astrid said. "I believe we should remain a group. We can't be sure what would happen if we separated." She was being diplomatic. The others were not fully confident that Ease was equipped to tackle it alone, even with the board.

Ease shrugged. "Group, then."

"Assuming the Good Magician accepts us as a group," Pewter said.

"He'd better, or we'll bypass him," Mitch said.

The others smiled; that obviously was not much of a threat. The Good Magician normally did his best to discourage visitors of any kind.

They walked toward the castle. But as they moved, groups of soldiers converged from the left and right sides, emerging from the cover of trees. Some were dark gray, the others light gray, and all were brandishing weapons. It seemed they were about to stage a battle. The Quest party was caught right where the two armies would meet.

"Too many for me to dissuade," Pewter said.

"I could lay them waste," Astrid said. "But I'd rather not."

"Maybe you should take off your clothes and freak them all out," Ease suggested.

"And you too?"

"I'll close my eyes," he said insincerely.

"Wouldn't work anyway," Tiara said. "Some of them are women."

"I note that there is a tea tree in the center," Pewter said. "There must be a reason."

"It's growing the wrong way," Astrid said. "See, the teacups and saucers are all upside down."

"But that's reversed," Tiara said. "The tea will all pour out."

"Who cares about a fouled up tea tree?" Ease demanded. "We're about to get sliced and diced by two fighting armies!"

"It's a pun!" Mitch said, a gray bulb flashing over his head. "A reversed tea tree is a tree tea. A treaty!"

The tree became a table with a scroll and pen on it, as well as two steaming cups of tea. The two armies halted just shy of combat. Two leaders came to the table and signed the treaty. Then they drank the tea. Then they and their armies vanished.

"It seems we navigated the first challenge," Pewter said dryly. Maybe he could have used a cup of tea himself.

"All because Mitch got the pun," Tiara said adoringly.

"Well, my village did suffer from the Great Pundemic," Mitch said. "I'm sort of attuned."

They started forward again, but of course there was another Challenge. A huge flock of parrots flew up, filling the air. "Go away!" they cried. "This is our territory. You shall not pass."

Just so. "They don't look as bad as harpies," Mitch said. "But I doubt we can get through them without getting seriously scratched."

"Or pooped," Astrid said.

"I could whack a path clear," Ease said.

"No!" Tiara cried, horrified. "Don't hit parrots!"

"Again, too many for me to dissuade," Pewter said.

"And again, I don't want to hurt what I'm sure are nice birds," Astrid said.

"We need to find a peaceful way to pass them," Tiara said.

"There has to be a way, if we can just figure it out," Mitch said, looking around. "But all I see is that mounted camera."

"Set up to take pictures of them," Tiara agreed. "Some of them do have very pretty feathers."

They considered the camera. A plaque said PARA SHOOT. That confirmed what it was for. But how could taking pictures clear the way?

Then Kandy got a notion. She sent it to Ease.

"In Mundania there's something called a parachute," he said. "It's a sort of cloth cone with strings attached. It is used for floating safely down when folk jump off high places. Maybe this relates."

"It is a pun," Mitch agreed. "But how can it help us?"

"Let's find out," Ease said. He went to the camera, pointed it at the birds, and clicked the button.

A parrot squawked and changed into a little gray parachute. "I'm polly-ester," it said. It floated slowly to the ground.

"Well, now," Ease said. He clicked again, and another bird became a parachute. He kept clicking, and more of them changed. Soon the ground was littered with fallen cloth.

When the last parrot was gone, they walked on to the moat. Once they were through, the scattered swatches of material dissipated into mist and floated away.

They stood at the edge of the moat. There was a drawbridge, but it was up, and evidently not coming down for them. This was the third challenge.

"I don't suppose we can swim across?" Ease asked doubtfully.

As if in answer, a giant gray reptilian head rose out of the water and surveyed them. A muscular gray tongue slurped across massive sharp gray teeth. Gray saliva dripped. As if? That was no coincidence. The moat monster had heard and answered.

"I suppose I could stare at it," Astrid said.

Dark glasses, similar to hers, appeared, covering the monster's eyes.

"I might persuade it to ignore us," Pewter said.

A second, more feminine monster's head rose, evidently its mate.

"But two would be difficult," Astrid said.

"I might send them thoughts of going to the other side of the castle," Mitch said.

Five smaller heads broke the water: their cubs.

"But I am limited to one thought at a time, to one creature," Mitch said.

"I think the Good Magician saw us coming," Tiara said. "I'm pretty sure I couldn't float high enough to avoid them, and that wouldn't help the rest of you anyway."

All seven monster heads nodded agreement.

"We will need a boat," Pewter concluded. "A covered boat, perhaps an armored one. That means we probably can't paddle or row it ourselves."

"As it happens," Mitch said. "I see a metal boat. That must be what we need."

"And it must have something wrong with it," Astrid said.

"Which we'll figure out how to fix," Ease said. The other didn't comment. Kandy knew why: Ease tended to have more confidence than was justified, because of his talent of making tasks easy. What they faced was bound to be beyond his talent.

They examined the boat. Not only was it metal, it had its own pilot, a robot, seated at the rear. Actually, the robot was bolted on. In fact the whole boat was a waterborne robot. "This is one of the steam robots that once threatened Xanth," Pewter said. "Until Magician Trent defeated them in battle. Thereafter they became reasonably good citizens, and one even interbred with a human woman."

"You mean they summoned the stork together?" Tiara asked. "I didn't think that was possible."

"Virtually anything is possible, with sufficient magic. Their son was Cyrus Cyborg, who will marry Princess Rhythm in due course, having romanced her when she was twelve."

"She did say she was the naughtiest," Tiara said appreciatively.

"She did use a spell that aged her a decade for the occasion. But yes, she was phenomenally naughty. At any rate, I see this robot, or more correctly row-bot, is fully equipped for the transit, with seating for our party. But it is not clear why it is inanimate. I see that it has a supply of wood for fuel, and its parts look operative."

"Maybe I can ask it," Tiara said. She seemed to have a certain sensitivity for people and things, especially those in trouble. She got into the boat and faced the face of the robot head. "Can you see me? Can you hear me? Can you understand me?"

There was no response, but she didn't give up. "I'm going to kiss you. If you are aware of me, kiss me back."

Kandy found herself admiring the young woman's technique. If anything could melt the metal heart of a machine, that would be it. She must have had a good deal of recent practice in kissing.

Tiara kissed the robot's faceplate where its mouth should be. Then she drew back a bit. "You did!" she said. "You kissed me back!"

Kandy realized that only a stone could have been unmoved by the pretty girl's kiss. But was she imagining that the metal had responded?

Now the robot made a sound. "Sssss."

"Yes," she translated. "Can you tell us why you're not moving?"

"Ddddd."

"Dry," she said. "But you're floating on water."

"Ooooo."

"Oil!" she exclaimed. "You're out of oil!"

"And so froze up," Pewter said. "Of course. I'm a machine. I should have thought of that." He considered half a moment. "But I'm not the same sort of machine. I'm electronic, while you're mechanical. I don't have your kind of oil."

"There is our challenge," Mitch said. "To find oil for the row-bot, so it can propel us safely across the moat."

"There's our challenge," Ease agreed. "There must be oil somewhere close by. Maybe some oilcloth, oil paint, or cooking oil."

They looked around. There was nothing nearby but a barrel of monkeys. No oil.

"Still, there may be some devious connection," Pewter said.

Ease went to the barrel. The monkeys decamped, leaving it empty. No help there.

Then Kandy saw something squished in the very bottom of the barrel. WHAT IS THAT?

Ease picked up her thought. He reached down inside with the board and pulled up—a mass of gray grease. In a moment it animated and jumped to the rim. It was alive, or at least sentient. What was it?

IT'S A GREASE MONKEY! Kandy thought with sudden revelation.

"A grease monkey," Ease echoed.

"Marginalized by her companions," Tiara said. Somehow she knew the gender. "No friends." She of course understood that sort of experience. "We need to find her a friend."

"A friend," Astrid echoed. She too understood.

"Who would want the company of a blob of grease?" Ease asked.

"A dry robot," Pewter answered.

And there it was. Tiara did the honors. "Grease Monkey, there is someone who desperately needs you," she told her. "Because grease is similar to oil, and he's out of oil. Let me take you to him." She put out her arm.

The monkey considered briefly, then jumped to her arm. She carried her to the row-bot. "Row-bot, I have brought you a friend. A grease monkey."

"Ooooo."

"Yes, similar to oil. Stay close together and both of you should do well." She set the monkey down before the robot form. "Climb all over him," she told the monkey. "He will love being close to you."

The monkey did, embracing the metalwork. Soon the row-bot began to move, at first creakily, then with greater authority. "Thank you, human friend," he said. "You have brought me the girl of my dreams."

Kandy felt Ease start at that. He knew about dream girls.

"Now we'd like to ask a favor," Tiara said.

"Yes, I will take your party across the moat," the row-bot said with increasingly smooth enunciation. "I overheard your prior dialog. By all means board."

They boarded, taking the five available seats. The robot grasped the oars and rowed out into the moat. The moat monsters didn't even try to block it; the challenge had been handled.

In no more than four long moments they were at the inner bank. They disembarked. "Thank you, Row-bot," Tiara said.

"You are more than welcome," the robot answered. Then he and his new friend rowed back across the moat.

They stood before the main gate of the castle. It was open, and a gray woman stood there. Kandy recognized her from before: Wira, the Good Magician's daughter in law, with her baby. "Hello a third time," Ease said.

"That's right, we met in Xanth," Wira agreed. "But this is not quite the same. Please come this way, all of you."

They followed her into the castle. "Not the same?" Ease asked. "Apart from being gray?"

"Apart from that, yes. Here some of the rules are different, such as those for marriage. Magician Humfrey has all five and a half wives attendant."

"All five or six!" Astrid exclaimed. "Doesn't that become quarrelsome?"

"Not at all. They are all old friends, and support each other. It is Humfrey they can get annoyed at."

"Annoyed?" Tiara asked. "Why?"

Wira paused in the hall. "I suppose it is better that you know. MareAnn signaled the stork for a baby, and Humfrey, caught by surprise, made the stork handle three Challenges. It was unable to get through, so the baby has not been delivered. MareAnn is distraught."

"Well of course she is!" Tiara said. "We helped with a similar case in Xanth."

"You did? Oh, maybe you will be able to help us here. Except—"

"Except that such assistance would represent a gift," Pewter said. "And gifts cause changes in size."

"Yes. That is why nobody else has been able to help. It would be invaluable, and MareAnn can't afford to gain that much size."

"Gain?" Tiara asked. "Don't you mean lose?"

"No. MareAnn is the most generous of the Wives. She has done favors for all the others, and given freely of herself throughout. That's why she can't come out herself to get her baby: in the castle we are protected from the give/size equation, but the moment any of us step outside it, those equations will take effect. MareAnn would become a giantess, unable to get back inside."

"The poor woman," Astrid said. "Her own generosity is depriving her of what she wants most. She's that way in Xanth, too: she enabled me to assume this form and join the Quest. Had she done that here, she would grow and I would shrink."

"That is true," Wira said. "Pyramid is a very nice planet, but there are some disadvantages."

"We have to help her, somehow," Astrid said.

"But if we are constrained by the magic of this planet," Mitch said, "we can't."

But Pewter had the logical answer. "We have come to ask the Good Magician a Question. That baby is his too, isn't it? We can exchange this service for our Answer. It should be about even."

"Why yes, it should be," Wira agreed, surprised.

"Which suggests that our arrival here at this time is not entirely random," Mitch said. "The Sequins of Events know what they are doing. We have had relevant experience on a prior Event, so are competent to handle this one."

"Not entirely random," Tiara agreed. "I know how to do it now."

"Let's get on with it," Pewter said.

They resumed their walk down the hall. Soon they came to the main room. There was a strange veiled woman awaiting them. "Hello, Quest members," she said. "I am the Gorgon, Wife of the Hour."

"The Gorgon?" Tiara asked. "We expected MareAnn."

"I see you do not appreciate our system," the Gorgon said. "We prefer not to get in each other's way, so we designate one Wife for each hour of the day while the others relax. The Designated Wife handles whatever business occurs in her hour."

"Oh, I have admired you for so long!" Astrid said. "You have the death stare."

The veil oriented on her. "Do I know you?"

"No. I'm not a person. I'm a transformed basilisk. But we all esteem your qualities."

"A basilisk!" the Gorgon said. "Then your appreciation is genuine."

"Oh, yes. We basilisks can only kill with our looks. You transform folk to stone. That's superior magic."

"We must get better acquainted," the Gorgon said. "Seldom do I encounter a cousin of the trade."

"Oh yes! But may we go see MareAnn now?" Astrid asked. "At least Tiara and I, to see about assisting her with her difficult delivery?"

140

"Why yes, I suppose that would be in order," the Gordon said. "Meanwhile I will feed you males some refreshments. I just curdled some milk; it's my specialty."

"You curdle milk?" Ease asked.

"By staring at it through my veil," the Gorgon explained. "My filtered stare has diluted effect. Even so I have to be careful; if I overdo it, it can crystallize into monster cheese."

"Wira told us how the Good Magician made the stork go through the Challenges," Mitch said. "That's an outrage."

"No, it's one of his Senior Moments. He last track, and didn't realize the stork was on business. But it is true that he can be annoying in his application of the rules. Long ago I came to ask him if he would marry me, and not only did I have to handle the Challenges, he made me perform a year's service before he gave me his answer."

"He did that?" Mitch asked amazed. "What a lout!"

"No, as it turned out it gave me a year working closely with him before the commitment. In that time I learned how grouchy he tends to be, but also how thoughtful."

"Thoughtful?"

"I had the opportunity to change my mind before marrying him. I knew exactly what I was getting into. That was thoughtful of him."

"He has a mechanical kind of thoughtfulness," Pewter said.

"Which, from you, is a compliment," the Gorgon said. Evidently she knew Pewter as of old.

"What about the four or five other wives?" Ease asked.

"That wasn't his fault. A lot can happen in the course of a century or so. They had married him, in due course left him or faded out, and then wound up in Hell for safekeeping. He came there in a hand-basket to rescue me after I died, and wound up getting more than he had expected. So we worked it out. Actually it's better this way; no one of us could stand him continuously, and the others are all nice people. We get along."

Another woman appeared. "Your hour is done," she said.

The Gorgon glanced at her watch, whose crystal Kandy saw was cracked; being constantly looked at by her, even through a veil, must be hard on it. "So it is! I got distracted. I haven't even served those refreshments I promised." She gestured to the newcomer. "This is Sofia, Wife of the next hour."

"I will take care of it," Sofia said as the Gorgon departed. Then she introduced herself more fully. "I am Sofia Socksorter, Humfrey's fourth wife, from Mundania." She fetched a plate of cookies and two mugs of boot rear. Kandy knew the men would get a kick out of that, having endured pun-free meals for a while.

"Socksorter?" Mitch asked. "That's an odd name."

"Not at all. It's an accurate description of my talent, which I developed after a few years in Xanth. Humfrey uses many socks, but has no sense about caring for them. They wind up in crannies, nooks, and lost. He never had a matching pair of clean ones. So he married me to handle his socks."

"To handle his socks?" Mitch asked, seeming to have difficulty assimilating that.

"It was his biggest problem. But they are in proper order now, as is the rest of the household." Sofia was obviously proud of her accomplishment.

Astrid and Tiara returned, escorted by Wira, who had evidently acquainted them with the change in Wives. "It's arranged," Tiara said. "I have MareAnn's written authorization for the baby. I'll go out now, before the stork gets tired of waiting."

"We'll help," Astrid said. "That means all of us." She sent the men a look that crackled even through her dark glasses. "Because we're making a deal to exchange services, our group with the Good Magician, and we're all included even if we play different roles."

The others nodded. It was a valid point.

"We'll help too," Sofia said. Sure enough, the remaining Wives showed up and were duly introduced: The Gorgon, Rose of Roogna, the Maiden Taiwan, Dara Demoness, and of course MareAnn. Astrid hugged MareAnn briefly; they were friends.

The Wives led them along a path that wended its way safely around assorted Challenges in the making, across the lowered drawbridge, under the nose of the moat monster who knew better than to threaten them, and to the verge of the castle environs. There was the stork, standing with its bundle just outside that limit, looking frustrated. In fact a wisp of steam was rising from its beak. "This is an outrage!" it said. "I will file a complaint."

Tiara stepped up to it. "We are so sorry," she said. "It was a misunderstanding. I will take the baby and give it to MareAnn."

The stork did a double take. "Haven't I seen you before? You're colored! You stand out like a sick finger in this shades-of-gray environment."

"Yes, we are from Xanth proper," Tiara said. "Just visiting Pyramid, so we retain our original colors. We met you at the Centaur demesnes, where there was a similar problem of delivery."

"Indeed there was," the stork agreed hotly. Its feathers were ruffled. "I'm just trying to do my job, but do I get any cooperation? Nooo, folk find every idiotic pretext to interfere with a normal delivery."

"We apologize," Tiara said.

"It takes more than an apology to fix such an irregular interference! This puts me behind my schedule."

"A gourd style apology," she clarified. Then she kissed the stork on the beak.

"Oh for wailing loudly!" the stork exclaimed. "Not that. We can't stand the gourd. I accept your apology, confound it. Take the ever-loving baby and be done with it. I have to move on anyway."

"Thank you," Tiara said sweetly. She had clearly figured out how to use what she had learned about the gourd, knowing the stork would not want any such demonstration. She had lived a sheltered life, but she had potential and was a quick study. She carefully picked up the bundle and carried it across to MareAnn, who hugged it joyfully.

"An outrage," the stork repeated as it spread its wings and took off. It had accepted the apology under duress and was hardly mollified.

There was a smattering of applause from the assembled Wives. They understood perfectly what Tiara had done. Then they led the way back into the castle.

"The Good Magician will see you now," Wira said, and showed them up the cramped winding stairway to the cramped office. Somehow the five of them plus Wira managed to fit into it.

"The members of the Quest are here for their Answer, Magician," Wira said. "Per the deal."

The Good Magician looked exactly as he had before, except he was in shades of gray. "Ask," he grumped.

"Where is the pun virus antidote?" Ease asked.

"That's the wrong question."

"Well, answer it anyway," Ease said.

"It's on another world of Ida, impossibly far away, where the sea is made of it. It even has tides. Puns flourish there. Princess Ida can direct you to it. But it is pointless to go there, because the radiation of space between planets, and the differing magic of other worlds, denatures it and it won't work on Xanth."

They digested that. "So what's the right question?" Mitch asked.

"Where in Xanth is the portal that accesses Planet Antidote directly?"

And of course he wouldn't answer that, because his Answer had been expended. Even though they were on a Quest he had sent them on.

"Thank you," Ease said tightly.

They turned around and squeezed out of the study, disgruntled. "There is a reason," Humfrey muttered after them.

"There's always a reason," Pewter muttered back.

Had the situation not been so perversely serious, Kandy would have been amused to see the largely emotionless Pewter reacting exactly like a living person. They all knew how grumpy and perverse the Good Magician could be. But it was true: usually in the end there turned out to be good reason for the way he did things.

"I'm sorry," Wira murmured as they reached the ground floor. "At least now you know the right Question. Maybe you can visit another Humfrey on another world and get the Answer."

"And serve a year for it?" Astrid asked. "We don't have the time. The puns of Xanth are being decimated even as we search."

"We're all sorry," Sofia said. "We truly appreciate what you did for MareAnn, and would help you if we could, but—"

"But you can't do us a favor that will impact our size when we depart," Astrid said. "We understand. But tell me: is advice a favor?"

"That depends on its usefulness," Sofia said. "Useless advice is free."

"Then maybe you could offer us some useless advice."

The Wives nodded, appreciating the logic. "Here's some useless advice," Dara Demoness said. "Go see Princess Ida on the Blue Face. She may be able to show you the Antidote planet. That won't do you any good, but might help you orient."

"But wouldn't any favor Princess Ida does us affect our stature?" Tiara asked.

"No, she's necessarily immune, because it is her job to facilitate travel between the worlds. As long as you keep it to that business, there's no problem."

"Thank you."

The Wives packed them box lunches, the assorted boxes being made of different pastries and crackers, and they were on their way. They followed an enchanted path so that no nasty predators could bother them, and there was a stream with cool gray water to drink. Not only was the path safe, the Wives assured them, it would get them there much faster than otherwise. They would not have to struggle with the formidable geography of this world.

"Why take the trouble to get to the blue face if there's really nothing there for us?" Ease asked.

"Because there will be something there for us," Mitch answered. "It was coded as useless advice to avoid the planetary effect for a favor."

"I don't see how," Ease said.

"That's just as well. If we all understood it perfectly, there would be an effect."

"You're so smart," Tiara said. "I don't see it either."

"Don't argue, or I'll kiss you."

"Argue," she said, smiling.

He kissed her, then paused startled. "You're taller!"

The others checked. Tiara was indeed slightly taller than she had been. That meant that the exchange of favors had not quite balanced. The others were unchanged, which simply meant that Tiara, as the active party, had been affected more. The difference was slight and hardly made a difference, fortunately.

There was a path leading to the sharply defined edge of the gray face. As they followed it, their tilt increased, until they seemed to be climbing a steep slope. They had to be sure of their footing.

Then they came to the edge. Beyond it was the blue face, like the other side of a mountain ridge. They straddled it carefully, for a moment looking at both landscapes, then started down the blue.

As they went the slope decreased, though the terrain was flat, and they walked increasingly upright. That made progress easier. Actually there were hills and valleys, but it was the underlying orientation that counted. Meanwhile they passed fields of blue plants with blue flowers, a blue stream, and saw blue birds of all types. The most common were in the shape of a J: blue J's.

A blue dusk approached as the path led them to a way station where they could spend the night.

A man was there, poring over a kind of blue paper with whitish lines. "Oh, hello foreign travelers," he said. "I am the Blue Prince, checking the specifications for this shelter. It seems to be in order." He rolled up the paper. "It is important that these things be constructed correctly."

Blue prince, Kandy thought. Blue prints. The puns remained in good order, here on Pyramid.

They ate their boxes and settled down for the night. Mitch and Tiara were in one corner, Pewter was by himself, and that left Ease and Astrid. "I don't want to sleep in this dress," she said. "I might knock off a sequin."

"Take it off," Ease said. "I won't mind."

"It's not dark enough. You'll freak out."

"Maybe I won't. Maybe we could—" She had drawn up her skirt to show her panties, and he had freaked out. He was sound asleep.

"You really don't need to worry about being bothered by men when you sleep," Kandy said, amused.

"True," Astrid agreed. "Yet there are times when I wish I could turn it off. So I could..." She trailed off, frustrated.

"So you could love a man," Kandy finished for her. "Darkness would take care of the freakout, and your dark glasses would stop your death stare, but your ambiance would still take him out."

"Yes. I wish I could find a man who was satisfied to look at me and talk to me at a distance, without wanting me to look back at him, so we could know and appreciate each other for reasons other than my appearance. Who might touch me for no longer than he could hold his breath, and be satisfied with that. But that doesn't seem to be the way men are made."

"It doesn't," Kandy agreed. "Yet MareAnn would not have let you join the Quest if she hadn't thought there could be a way."

"I fear she was too optimistic."

Kandy feared the same. Yet her own situation was hardly better. She was with Ease, and could touch him freely, but never have him respond. "We have to believe that things will work out for all of us, somehow."

"Somehow," Astrid agreed, as she moved a bit apart and lay down on the blue hay. "But it's good to have you as a friend, regardless."

"The feeling is mutual." And it was. "When this Quest is done, however it works out, will we have to separate?"

Astrid didn't answer. Kandy was faintly annoyed. Then she heard a muffled sound, and realized that Astrid was crying. That brought her own tears.

"Come here a moment," she called. "I think in my present form I can hug you." She stood up, leaving Ease's hand on her ankle.

Astrid came, and they hugged. It was true: Kandy was somewhat ghostlike, and the basilisk fumes did not affect her much. But they had to break it off soon, because the fumes could harm Ease. Still, it was worth doing. They would continue as friends after the Quest, regardless how it turned out. That was important to them both.

In the morning they resumed their walk, and in due course approached a blue stone house on a ridge of blue mountains. And there, tending a garden of blue gentians, was a woman wearing a small crown. A little ball orbited her head. No, it looked more like a doughnut.

"That is Torus, the next in the procession of worlds," Pewter said.

Tiara approached her while the others hung back. "Princess Ida, I presume?"

"Why yes," the blue woman agreed. "Have we met before? I see you are from Xanth."

"We have not met before," Tiara said. "I am Tiara, an ordinary girl. I am a member of a Quest, and we thought you might be able to help us."

"Yes we have athletic competition," Tiara's hair said.

"We have what?"

"Contested, rivaled, acquainted—"

"Met?"

"Whatever," the hair agreed crossly.

Ida laughed. "Hello Demoness Metria! Indeed we have interacted before. What are you doing in Tiara's hair?"

"Keeping it neat. Otherwise it looks like this." Suddenly the hair went wild.

"You are doing good work," Ida agreed. She gestured to the others. "Come in, all of you. I want to learn about this Quest." She led the way into her house, the doughnut keeping the pace.

They entered her house and explained about the Quest. "So we thought you might be able to tell us about the anti-pun virus antidote," Tiara concluded. "We are baffled about how to find it, or even the portal to it."

"I can show it to you," Ida agreed. "But I'm afraid that won't help you. The planet is a number of levels beyond this one." Her eyes flicked to the orbiting Torus, which quickly retreated to the other side of her head, as if shy. "I have no idea where the portal might be." She got up and touched the inner wall. It illuminated, and the picture of a watery planet appeared. Purple waves crashed against a yellow beach at dawn. Kandy could almost smell the tang of the water. "It's always dawn on Antidote Planet. The elixir carries the odor. So when you smell purple waves at dawn, you'll know you're close."

"Dawn has a smell?" Ease asked.

"Purple has a smell?" Mitch asked.

"This is not logical," Pewter said.

"No, it's magic," Ida reminded them.

And Kandy realized that this was what they had come to Pyramid to learn: about the smell of the antidote. That would let them know when they were close. It seemed crazy, but surely had its own logic.

"Thank you," Tiara said. "We will keep that in mind."

It was time to move on to their next Event. "We won't burden you further, Princess," Tiara said.

"Oh, do you have to go so soon? I would like to catch up on the latest news from Xanth. I am married there, but not here, and it does get lonely. I would like to know more about all of you, as I see you are unusual folk." She glanced at Mitch, evidently recognizing his talent of sending ideas, and Kandy realized she had an idea about that, her talent being the idea, albeit on a much larger scale. "I have plenty of room for guests."

Tiara glanced at the others. "We can go tomorrow," she said.

Kandy knew they were in for a very nice evening. That was just as well, because they had no real idea what their next event would be.

CHAPTER 10:

TROLL

They found themselves back in Xanth—they could tell by the colors—but in a thick fog. Really thick. It was uncomfortable even to breathe the dense air.

"What is this?" Mitch asked.

"A pea-soup fog," Pewter answered. "So we know that puns remain viable here."

"Yuck!" Tiara said. "It's making my dress stick to me."

"Mine too," Astrid said. "I prefer eating pea soup to bathing in it."

"We shall simply have to walk until we are out of it," Pewter said.

"Walk where?" Mitch asked. "I see no path."

"I don't see much of anything," Ease said, rubbing his eyes.

"Downhill," Tiara said. "Where maybe there's a river or pond. We'll need to wash it off."

"I'm outa here," Tiara's hair said. "I hate pea soup." But if her departure freed Tiara's hair, there was no sign of it in the thick fog.

They made their way cautiously downhill, able to see only an arms-reach ahead. They seemed to be in a trackless jungle, the vegetation filling every crevice. They kept having to back off and try for another avenue through the tangle, getting dirtier as they went.

This wasn't getting them anywhere. Kandy thought of an unlikely way to

149

handle it. She sent the thought to Ease.

"How about an idea, Mitch," Ease suggested.

"Idea?"

"Send it to the fog: it's got business elsewhere."

Mitch paused, considering. "It's inanimate, but if it is messing us up on purpose, it's got a mind. I'll try." He concentrated.

The fog abruptly lifted and floated off for parts unknown.

"It worked!" Tiara exclaimed.

"It did, didn't it," Mitch agreed. "You're a genius, Ease." But of course he knew the real origin of the thought.

Now, able to see farther than they could reach, they made better progress. Soon they found a stream meandering through the thicket. It paused when it saw them, then resumed its flow.

"Don't touch it until we know it's safe," Mitch warned.

A young rabbit hopped up. "Hi, folk!" it called. "I'm a bun—the lowest form of rabbit." Then it hopped into the water with a splash, and out the other side.

"The water's safe," Tiara said. "It didn't hurt that bunny."

"True," Mitch agreed. Then he saw something else. "What is that?"

The others looked. It was a dead tree, with clothing piled at its base. "A deceased fur tree," Pewter said. "It shed its furs when it died."

"Isn't that a pun? A fur tree with furs?"

"True. Probably an Aqua Fur, considering where it is growing." Then Pewter paused. "The virus!"

"Set up your firewall!"

Pewter did, and there was the faint crackling as it got established.

"But the virus didn't take out the punny rabbit," Tiara said.

"This tree is evidence that the virus is in the vicinity, however," Mitch said. "It may be thin as yet, catching some things and not others. Pewter has to maintain the firewall."

"Meanwhile we need to wash off the dirt and caked pea soup," Tiara said. "But how can we separate, if we have to stay within the firewall?"

"I suggest that we declare an Adult Conspiracy truce," Astrid said. "We're all adults anyway. We will ignore each other's exposed bodies until we can get clothed again."

"But if I see—" Ease began.

"Someone will snap her fingers to bring you out of it," Astrid said.

"Seems reasonable," Mitch said.

"Truce." Then Ease stripped, set his clothes and the board beside the stream, and waded into the water.

The others followed suit, or rather unsuit, and in less than a moment apiece they were all in the water scrubbing off the soup. Mitch unbound his hair shirt and dipped his long hair into the water, rinsing out the soup.

"I don't need this," Tiara's hair said. "I'm taking a break. See you later, alligator." A puff of smoke floated out of the hair, then vanished. The demoness was gone. Tiara's hair immediately went wild, but she grabbed it and plunged it into the water for the rinse.

Theoretically the men were busy getting clean, but Mitch and Ease's eyes were inspecting the two women as they washed. Mitch had by now seen every part of Tiara, but sneak peeks were different. The girls were pretending not to notice. Only Pewter was properly tending to business. Kandy was able to watch them all without seeming to. She realized that the wandering eyes that had bothered her before the Quest were lurking in all men, especially when unclothed women were in sight.

Then something happened that only Kandy was in a position to see. The water of the stream surged over the bank and swept up their clothing and the board. Suddenly Kandy was floating downstream along with the two dresses and the men's outfits. *HELP!* she thought to them all in capital bold italics.

"Oh, bleep!" Astrid swore. "The sequins!"

They splashed after the lost clothing, but they were bare bodied and bare footed, and there were evidently nettles close by the water and sharp stones beneath it. They could not keep up with the flow. Kandy knew that Pewter might have changed reality in that spot, but he had to maintain the firewall instead. They were in trouble.

"We can't keep up by trying to wade," Mitch said. "We'll have to swim."

They started swimming, but even so they were not gaining on the clothing, only keeping it in sight.

The stream was growing, becoming wider and deeper. There were other things floating in it, such as a belt that seemed to be made of fragments of stone that banged into Kandy's board in the current. "Watch where you're going, splinter face!" the belt exclaimed angrily.

YOU'RE AN ASS! she thought back at it.

"I'm more that than that. I'm an ass-teroid belt, wood-for-brains."

Kandy realized that it wasn't worth arguing with an arrogant pun.

They floated through a section with water lilies. No, these were made of paper, with attached pencils. They were lily pads. But some were spoiled, no longer any good for writing on; they were hardly more than goo. They must have been caught by the pun virus and destroyed. That meant that Pewter was right to maintain his firewall; he would not survive long without it.

Then the water swirled into a cave, carrying them both along. Kandy glimpsed the words CAVE CANEM printed over it. What kind of a cave was a canem?

A huge male dog stood inside the cave. Oh—it was a dog cave.

The dog plunged his head down and snapped the board out of the water. Then, discovering that it wasn't edible, he dropped it and went after Tiara's dress.

At which point Tiara herself arrived in the cave. "Hey, that's mine!" she cried angrily.

The dog dropped the dress, slavering. "I'll byte you!" he said as he plunged into the water, jaws gaping.

Just in time for Mitch to arrive. He was not normally a violent man, but the threat to Tiara galvanized him. "First you'll have to byte me!" He whipped off his shirt, formed his hair into a loop, and flung it over the dog's head. The loop tightened about the burly neck.

That got the dog's attention. He turned on Mitch, but Mitch was already tightening the lasso into a hangman's knot and the dog was gasping. Meanwhile Tiara escaped, carried on by the current.

Pewter and Astrid arrived. "Do you need help?" Astrid called.

"No, just get on out of the cave," Mitch called back. "I'll let him go when you're safe, so he can't byte you."

"That's not byte, it's bite," Pewter said.

"Whatever. Get out of here!"

They looked uncertain, but the current was bearing them on.

Ease arrived. "There's my board!" he exclaimed, swimming toward it. Then he saw Mitch struggling with the dog just beyond it.

The dog's efforts caused both him and Mitch to fall into the water. "I'd better let him go," Mitch said. "I don't want to drown him."

Kandy realized that not only was Mitch courageous in combat, he was decent. He didn't want to hurt the dog whose cave they had invaded, he just wanted to restrain him until the others got past.

Ease got his hand on the board. "Okay, let him go," he said. "I'll whack him if he comes after us."

"Oops, I can't," Mitch said. "My hair's hopelessly tangled."

"I can fix that," Ease said. He dropped the board, put his hands on the tangle of hair and in two thirds of a moment had untangled it. That was his talent at work, making a difficult task easy.

The dog, freed was about to turn on them both. But Kandy, back in the water, sent him a thought: HUGE DOG BONE IN WATER!

The dog immediately splashed after the bone. That was actually the asteroid belt. Mitch and Ease swam away as the dog and belt argued about bytes and asses.

Their group was back in the stream, following the clothing, while Kandy floated behind them. There was a grove of man-shaped trees whose roots were interlaced above and below the water. Kandy recognized them: mangroves.

The people were understandably wary of the complicated roots, and slowed despite allowing the clothes to drift farther ahead. Kandy had no choice, and was caught by a swift little current that zipped her right through the grove and to the clothes. At least they were reunited to that extent.

Then the stream coursed into another cave. Kandy was wary of that, after the business with the cave dog, but what could she do? At least it couldn't be worse than the big dog. The water circled and sucked down, entering below the surface.

But it was worse. Kandy's board floated into the cave first. A big hand came down and grabbed her, lifting her well clear of the water. It was a troll. A big shaggy male.

"Oh, a board," he said, and tossed it up into a high alcove. "Maybe good for firewood."

Firewood! Kandy had to avoid that. But how? She was stuck up here with a bunch of junk the troll had evidently saved for some future use. She had landed with her head section just on the ledge, so she could see down, but she could not take any action.

The clothing floated in. The troll reached down with both hands and swept up Tiara's and Astrid's dresses. "Say, people clothes," he said. "The cave hound must have eaten the people and left the dresses empty." He studied the one with the sequins. "Pretty! Maybe I can use it to lure in a tasty girl." He tossed both dresses up into the alcove.

Next came the men's clothing. "The hound must really have been hungry! But he left me slim trolling." He tossed them up also.

A troll trolling for things in the stream. That made sense, Kandy realized. Probably it was a setup, with the stream stealing whatever it could and carrying it down for the dog and troll to get. And they had neatly fallen into that trap.

Worse, the other members of the Quest would be along soon. Pewter had to maintain the firewall, so couldn't change reality in the troll's cave. Ease was without his weapon. This did not look good.

But maybe she could help. BEWARE! TROLL IN CAVE! she thought warningly to Ease. Did she reach him? She had not tried distance thought sending before. But even if the thought got through, so they knew, the current was swift as it entered the cave and might carry them into it regardless.

There was a pause as the troll waited for the next stream offerings. Kandy was tense, wishing she could do something, anything. But she had already done what little she could.

Then a bare female person floated in. Astrid! Kandy knew her by her long dark hair and her extremely shapely body. Also by her dark glasses, which she still wore.

The troll pounced, catching her in both hands and lifting her well up out of the water. "A delicious girl!" he exclaimed, baring his big yellow teeth. Trolls of course ate people; that was their nature. They didn't seem to understand why that made them unpopular with people.

"Hold on half a moment, big boy," Astrid said. "You don't want to eat me."

"I don't?" Trolls were not as stupid as ogres, but were hardly known for their intellect. "You look awful succulent."

"At least, not yet," Astrid said. "First you will want to play with me for a while."

Play with her? If the troll stayed close to her more than a few minutes he would be drunk or dead, depending on whether he sniffed her perfume or took off her glasses and let her gaze at him. Her perfume would not be strong at the moment, because she had been soaking in the water, but it would regenerate soon enough.

Then it dawned: that was the plan! They had sent in Astrid to nullify the troll!

"But mother told me not to play with my food," the troll protested.

"Do you do everything your mother tells you?"

"No. I do what I want and lie to her."

"So you can play with me a while before eating me," Astrid said. "She'll never know, will she?"

"I guess not," he said, surprised. "What kind of game do you have in mind?"

He didn't know? Kandy would have laughed had she been able.

"I'll tell you in a moment. Right now let's introduce each other. I am Astrid Basilisk. Who are you?"

The troll, perhaps fascinated by the lusciousness of her bare body, did not seem to pick up on the significance of her name. She had given him fair warning. "I'm Tromp Troll."

"Hello, Tromp." She waited half a moment, then added "Say 'hello Astrid.'"

"Hello Astrid. What's the game?"

"First, take me to the dry part of the cave," Astrid said. "Lay me down on the hay. Then put your arms around me and tickle me a little."

"Tickle?"

"Like this," She reached forward and tickled his ribs.

"Ho ho ho!" he laughed. Then he put her on the hay and started tickling her, but he was too clumsy to stick to her ribs. His big hands wandered all over her body. "Say, you feel nice."

"Very nice," she agreed. "Now you can kiss me there."

"Kiss?"

"It's like biting, only no teeth."

"Oh." It was obviously tricky for him to put his mouth to flesh without chomping it, and Astrid's flesh was very soft in front. But he managed, and once he learned how, he seemed to like it.

Kandy had to admire Astrid's technique. She was seducing the troll without his knowing it. She was also keeping his face right up against her body, where her recovering perfume would be strongest.

Sure enough, in three and a half moments he was drunk and unconscious. Astrid kept him close for another moment and a half, to be sure. Evidently five full moments made it certain. It would be hours before he woke.

Astrid carefully disengaged herself. "I was told that men are fools about women, especially bare women," she said. "Thank you for proving it, Tromp. It was almost (not not quite) fun."

Kandy knew that Astrid had never had amorous experience with a man, and wanted to. This at least gave her a kind of practice. Tiara, who had recently learned all about it, must have given her detailed instructions.

Astrid put her hands to her mouth, making a funnel, and called toward the entrance where the water boiled up. "Halloo! It's safe!"

In about four fifths of a moment, give or take a third, there came a faint answer: "Coming through!"

Soon Mitch's head bobbed to the surface. "I see you put him down," he said, spying the prostrate troll as he climbed out of the water. "Is he alive or dead?"

"Alive. I don't like killing. That's one reason I appealed to the Good Magician to find me a new venue. But I'm only halfway where I want to be."

"The Quest is far from over. There is still time."

"I hope so." She glanced at the troll. "His name's Tromp."

"Tromp Troll," Mitch agreed. "I'm glad Ease caught on, so we were warned. It could have been ugly."

"It means the board is here."

He nodded, understanding. "We owe a lot to the board."

Kandy appreciated that. The others never referred to her as other than the board, by day, honoring her preference. She appreciated that too.

Now Mitch turned and called. "I'm in. Next!"

"Coming!" and in a generous moment Tiara's hair appeared, followed by her head. The demoness Metria had not returned, so the hair was wild again, even when wet. Mitch clearly didn't mind. He reached down, caught her under the elbows, drew her up out of the water, kissed her, and set her on the rock of the cave floor to stand beside Astrid. Kandy hadn't realized how nymphly slender she was until seeing her. Astrid, in contrast, was statuesque, well filled and rounded in every portion.

"Astrid put Tromp Troll to sleep," Mitch said.

Tiara shuddered. "I couldn't have done that."

Next came Pewter, and finally Ease. "Where's my board?" Ease asked.

They looked around. There was no sign of any clothing or the board.

LOOK ON THE LEDGE Kandy thought to Ease.

"There it is!" he exclaimed, pointing. "The troll must have tossed it there. I bet the other clothing is there too."

They all looked. "That ledge is way out of reach," Astrid said.

"Maybe if Tiara stands on my shoulders, she can reach it," Mitch said.

"I'll make myself light," Tiara said. Her hair lifted and radiated out, pulling up her head. She put her foot in his linked hands, stepped up, then climbed to his shoulders. That brought her head to the level of the ledge. She peered into the alcove. "It's all here!" she called.

The clothing was still wet, but she dropped it down to them, then dropped the board to Ease. "I'm glad to have you back!" he said as he grasped Kandy's ankles. That thrilled her, though she knew it was merely that he liked the useful tool and weapon. Should she ask the others to tell him her real nature? No, as always she concluded that it was best that he find out for himself, or never know. At least until the spell ended.

"See if there's a magic match or lighter knot," Astrid said. "So we can make a fire and dry our clothes." Kandy knew she wanted to get dressed, because Ease's eyes were starting to wander. Ease knew there was no future for him with Astrid, but her bare body compelled his eyes. Kandy reminded herself for the umpteenth time that men were like that; Mitch was only moderately better.

Tiara looked. "There's half a slew of things up here, but—" She paused, reaching. "A match box! Two match boxes!" She tossed them down, then climbed back down Mitch to the cave floor.

Matching matches, Kandy thought. So the virus had not yet invaded the cave.

They foraged for bits of wood that lay in crevices to make a small pile, buttressed it with dry hay, then touched the matching boxes together. A spark jumped, and the hay caught fire. They held the clothing near to the fire, getting it dry.

Soon they we able to dress again, everything clean. But there was a problem. The moment Astrid put on her dress, she discovered that it was translucent. They had not noticed while it was sopping wet, but now it was flashing her panties. That set off both men in a way her complete nudity had not.

"A sequin is missing," Pewter said. "It must be in the vicinity."

Astrid removed her clothing, and the men relaxed somewhat, though not enough to satisfy either Kandy or Tiara. "We need to find that sequin," Astrid said. "I don't care to risk the Event we might encounter if we tried it with a missing sequin."

"Sensible caution," Pewter agreed.

First they checked the floor. No sequin. Then Mitch boosted Tiara and she got in the high alcove and made a thorough search. She found a single old worn boot, a Mundanian style gas mask, a wet suit, several air bags, some strata gems of the kind that warrior women liked, several kind of pens such as Deep, Hap, O, and Ri, sheets, a musical head band, boxes of hard tacks, water logs, and a battered chair. No sequin.

"It must have fallen in the water," Astrid concluded reluctantly.

They looked at the swirling water that coursed through the cave. Its depths were lost in surging shadow. "Well, we can swim," Mitch said.

The men stripped and dived down, running their hands across the smooth bottom channel of the stream. There was no sequin.

"I hate to say this," Tiara said. "But could it have come off before we got here?"

"No," Pewter said.

"Why not?"

"Because we were pursuing the floating clothing, and the dress had color."

Kandy realized it was true. She had been floating alongside the dress much of the way, and it had been opaque.

"So the sequin must have fallen into the water when the troll hauled the dress out and flung it into the alcove," Mitch said.

"And the current carried it on to join the bones," Pewter said.

"Bones?"

"There are no bones here," Pewter said.

"True. But—" Then Mitch got the point. "Trolls eat people, but not their bones. Ogres crunch bones, not trolls. He must have thrown them into the water to be carried away."

"Convenient housekeeping," Tiara said with a grimace.

They looked downriver. The water boiled up to a slanting wall, and dived under it. That was where the sequin had to have gone. With the bones.

"We don't dare risk swimming there," Mitch said. "We don't know how long it flows before coming up for air."

"We need a boat," Ease said.

"I saw no boat," Tiara said.

"That depends," Pewter said. "I once assimilated a Mundane data file by accident. A compendium of terms. It made my circuits ill, but I do have the information. 'boot' in a certain Mundanian language means 'boat.'"

"No, the words printed on it were plainly Boot," Tiara said "Das Boot."

"Exactly. Anything that strays into Xanth is at risk of getting pun infected. That could be a boat."

"I know a boot when I see one," Tiara said. "That's a boot."

"Humor him," Mitch murmured. "Toss it down."

Tiara went up again, found the boot, and tossed it down. It was definitely an old boot, its leather faded, its laces ragged.

"Das Boot," Pewter said.

The boot expanded, filling out into a huge cylindrical form, its leather turning to metal. They had to jump back to avoid getting shoved.

"Boat," Pewter repeated. "As I suspected."

"That's the weirdest boat I ever saw," Mitch said.

"Otherwise known as a submarine. A boat that goes underwater." Pewter walked to its swollen midsection and opened what turned out to be a hatch. He climbed inside. In three moments he reappeared. "Room for five."

"But it's so tight!" Tiara protested. "We'd be squeezed in like—"

"Sardines," Pewter said. "Subs are tight. But it will convey us where we need to go." He studied the craft. "But we need to be sure we know how to revert it to the boot, so we don't do it accidentally while we're inside."

"Inside!" Tiara repeated, looking faintly ill.

"Every spell has a counterspell," Pewter said. "Usually something obvious."

It did? Kandy was extremely interested. Was there a counter to her being a board? What could it be?

"Sometimes it's just a matter of reversing it," Pewter continued. "Das Boot spelled backwards would be Toob Sad."

The boat quickly shrank back into the boot.

"Good enough," Pewter said. "We shall not utter those words while we are using it."

There was scant danger of that," Kandy thought, because the words were nonsense.

Pewter invoked the boat again. "Das Boot." It swelled back into full form.

"There remains a host of problems," Mitch protested. "How do we propel this craft forward? What do we eat or drink or for that matter breathe if the journey is longer than we expect? And Astrid—"

"I can't go with you," Astrid said. "My perfume would suffuse the craft."

"We're not leaving you here," Tiara said.

"You said you saw a wet suit in the alcove," Pewter said.

"Well, all our clothing was wet."

"A wet suit can be something else. Bring that down, and the gas mask."

Tiara went up and tossed them down. "And the air bags," Pewter called. "And the hard tacks."

The other kept quiet, uncertain what Pewter had in mind. Kandy was glad again for the machine's data bank knowledge.

"Put on the wet suit," Pewter told Astrid.

She did, since she couldn't wear her dress anyway. The suit fit her curvaceous body perfectly; she looked nude but with an extra layer. It covered her from head to foot; only her face was clear. "This is tight!" she exclaimed. "It will hold in my perfume!"

"Yes. A wet suit normally keeps water out and heat in, but this will keep your deadly ambiance confined. Now put on the gas mask."

She put on the mask, which made her look like a humanoid monster with a trunk-like nose. "Mmm-mmmph?" she asked, her voice muffled.

"Exactly," Pewter said. "A gas mask normally keeps poisonous gases out, but in your case it will keep them in."

"Mmmph?"

"Yes. Have an air bag. Everyone needs an air bag, to refresh the local air."

"You're quite a machine for answers," Mitch remarked.

"Thank you. It is my nature."

"But what about water, when we're locked inside?" Tiara asked.

"You saw water logs."

"I did," she agreed, and fetched them. The logs looked solid, but were actually made of water; when the ends were bitten off, they became liquid in the mouth.

"What about food?" Ease asked.

"Hard tacks."

Again they didn't argue. Tiara fetched these down too, and passed them out. They turned out to be edible.

The troll stirred. "I'd better give him another dose," Astrid said.

"Needless," Pewter said. "We'll be gone by the time he wakes fully."

They piled into the boat. It was, it turned out, propelled by pedals connected to external paddle wheels. The steering was up front; it looked complicated, but Ease took that spot and made it easy. The others took the other spots, nestled close together; there was room, barely, for all of them. Astrid folded the sequins dress and put it in an external pocket of her wet suit, then got in, last. They were arranged roughly lengthwise along the tubular boat: Ease in the narrow pilot's compartment, then Mitch and Tiara in the thicker middle, then Pewter and Astrid in the thinning tail section. The pedals connected to rods that poked through the hull to the paddles outside, somewhat like four big rotating legs.

Tromp Troll got dazedly to his feet. "Hey!" he exclaimed. "That's mine!"

"Not any more," Ease said. "Be glad we didn't kill you, you cannibal." He closed the hatch and steered the boat down into the water as the others pedaled. They were on their way.

The boat had portholes along the sides, so they could see out between the paddles. There was a faint glow of fungus on the underwater walls, so it was not entirely dark. Ease steered the craft down, following the current, until he found the hole the stream used to get out of the troll's cave.

Now the boat fairly zipped along the tunnel. Kandy, beside Ease, could see everything. The tunnel evidently knew where it was going.

It continued for some time. They no longer had to peddle; the current handled that. They chewed on their hard tacks, which were surprisingly tasty. Astrid was unable to eat with her gas mask on, but she didn't complain. At least the air remained fresh, replenished by the air bags; all they had to do was open them just enough to let a little air waft out. All except Astrid, whose gas mask prevented her from eating or drinking or even talking.

Kandy thought about that. Astrid had risked herself to enter the troll's cave first, and then undertaken the unpleasant chore of seducing him, without ever hesitating or complaining. Now she was bundled up in suit and mask, surely severely cramped, going hungry and thirsty, and still making no protest. She was doing whatever she could to help the quest move along, making no demands on others. Kandy probably would never have picked up on this had she not been a board with little to do but observe. Astrid was a genuinely good person, regardless of her underlying nature, and yes, Kandy wanted to be her friend always.

"Oh, bleep!" Mitch muttered.

"What is it?" Tiara asked. They were side by side, almost touching, with portholes on either side.

"I've never been below water like this before, in such a confined space, with no control over where I'm going. I'm getting claustrophobic."

"Oops!"

"What?"

"Now that you describe it, so am I. I lived most of my life in a tower well above ground; I couldn't get out, but I could see wide and far. But this—all there is is the boat, and outside, the tunnel. I feel stifled."

"Stifled," he agreed. "I've got to get out!"

"Me too!"

The two started struggling, banging into each other. But there was no way out, at the moment. All they could do was drive themselves into a useless frenzy and maybe hurt themselves. Something had to be done. But what?

Ease was busy steering the craft, making sure it did not bang into the tunnel walls. Pewter was maintaining the firewall, a necessary precaution. Astrid was too bundled up to even talk. That left only—Kandy.

TIARA! Kandy thought.

The young woman paused in her frenzy. "I hear you," she said.

REACH UP AND GRAB ME.

Tiara obeyed. Her hand caught the bottom of the board. "Now what?"

Just relax, Kandy thought, no longer having to shout. She spread a mental blanket of comfort and peace.

"Oh, it's working," Tiara said, relaxing. "What a relief!"

Just hang on to me, and you'll be fine.

"I will," Tiara agreed.

But meanwhile Mitch's frenzy was unabated. He needed to be calmed too, but how? It was all Kandy could do to keep Tiara calm; if she tackled Mitch as well, he'd just drag her into his madness and they'd all lose.

Tiara picked up on the thought. "Maybe Astrid. She's used to confined places. Maybe she can make him appreciate them. Can you reach her?"

Good idea. *I'll try.*

Kandy focused on the basilisk. ASTRID!

I hear you, friend. How can I help?

Grab Mitch's ankle. Mind connect with him if you can. Calm him if you can.

I'll try. She reached up and caught his thrashing foot. *I'm not connecting.*

Bleep! Kandy thought.

"Maybe Pewter can help," Tiara suggested.

PEWTER!

"I hear you," the machine replied grumpily.

CAN YOU SPARE ENOUGH MAGIC TO ENABLE ASTRID TO MIND-CONTACT MITCH? WE NEED TO CALM HIM.

Oh! Hello Mitch!

Mitch paused in his frenzy. "What's this?"

Astrid here. You know I'm a basilisk. Imagine you are a cockatrice, the male of the species. Let's wander the barren rocks together.

"Why?"

To escape the claustrophobia.

Now Mitch got the point. "I'll try."

Then Kandy and Tiara were treated to the mental scene wherein Astrid guided Mitch into the form of a cockatrice in a wonderfully desolate scene. The sun glared down on stones and sand punctuated by dead shrubs: the home of the basilisks and cockatrices, where everything else died. Yet it was beautiful in its fashion, for their kind. Astrid led him on a tour through the dry gullies and stark ravines of her homeland.

"It's great!" he said, surprised. "Why did you leave it?"

Here she could talk. "I was not a happy basilisk. I wanted living interaction and companionship. So I went to the Good Magician and he used a spell to transform me to human for a year, after which I could revert if I wanted to. Then his half-wife MareAnn arranged for me to become a Companion on this Quest to save the puns. With luck I will find a feasible situation."

"But you remain poisonous."

"Yes. The spell could change my form but not my nature."

"What Service did you have to do for the Good Magician?"

"This is it: to facilitate the success of the Quest to the best of my ability. I am really a bodyguard."

"But you don't like killing things."

"True. That's why I was a discontented basilisk. But I will kill if I have to."

"I hope you never have to."

There was a jolt as the boat abruptly came ashore. They were through the tunnel and into a larger cave.

"I'm out of the bind!" Mitch exclaimed. "I never felt it once I became a cockatrice! Thank you, Astrid."

Astrid made her mmmm sound, unable to speak in this environment.

"And thank *you*, Kandy," Tiara said, letting go of the board. "That was educational."

The boat was on a beach of bones. The smallest ones were like sand, with slightly larger ones like twigs, and skulls like rocks. It seemed that the troll had eaten a good many folk.

They got out and stood on this subterranean shore. The fungal glow on the walls illuminated the region like sunlight through a cloud-bank. "Well, we're here," Ease said. "Now we just need to find the sequin."

"It's like looking for a noodle in a haystack," Mitch said.

"We can spread out, each closely checking a section," Astrid said as she drew herself out of the clinging wetsuit. The accumulated cloud of perfume was almost visible. She did not put on the dress, as it remained translucent. "It's bound to be here somewhere."

"Somewhere," Mitch agreed, looking at her.

Tiara glanced at him, then at Astrid. She didn't say anything, but Kandy could guess what she was thinking: the two had made a connection, in that basilisk daydream, and Astrid in her human form was a remarkably well formed figure, now thoroughly exposed. Had Astrid inadvertently become competition? Yet it had been by Tiara's suggestion, to save Mitch from possibly harming himself. The fault was not with Astrid.

They spread out, checking sections. But Kandy wondered whether she had done the right thing in getting Astrid to help Mitch through the crisis. What mischief lay ahead?

"What's this?" Mitch asked, picking something up.

"A bone comb," Tiara said.

"You can have it," Mitch said, presenting it to her.

"Thank you." Tiara ran it through her wild hair. The hair remained floating, but was now neatly so. "This is a good comb. It must be magic."

"Try it on a real challenge," Mitch said, hauling off his shirt.

Tiara stroked the comb through his tangled mass of hair, and it left a swatch of perfectly even texture. She stroked it again, and there was another neat section. In two and a half moments she had his entire mass in smooth order. "It doesn't even snag on tangles," Tiara said, impressed. "It really is magic."

"It is as if we were fated to find it," Mitch said.

"When we were looking for the sequin."

They smiled at each other. Whatever social crisis there might have been had dissolved. Kandy was relieved.

But then Astrid spoke up. "I found the sequin!" she held it high.

"It seems we had to find the comb first, then the sequin," Pewter said. "That may be the point of this Event."

"The comb is wonderful," Mitch said. "But what relevance does it have to the Quest?"

"Merge the hair," Astrid said. "The comb may facilitate that."

The others nodded. It could indeed be relevant.

"So do we rest here, or move on via the sequin?" Ease asked.

They looked around the cave. There was no obvious exit. The water seemed to filter through the piled bones, finding its continuation beneath and beyond them. They would have to do considerable digging to make a navigable channel.

"It's not as if this is a great vacation site," Mitch said. The others nodded.

"The sequin," Tiara said.

Astrid donned the dress, and Tiara fastened the sequin to it.

CHAPTER 11:
PRISON

They were in a pun-clear region. There were no puns in sight, just festering goo where they had been. The virus was surely all around them. Fortunately Pewter had maintained his firewall throughout; he could do it in his sleep now, if he ever slept.

Ahead was a pleasant-looking village. Evidently the people here had learned to get along without puns. It was probably a good place to go and rest before they tackled whatever the event had in mind for them.

But Mitch was dubious. "My talent is ideas, not premonition, but I have a bad feeling about this. We might be better off to bypass this village and forage in the countryside."

"But without puns there are bound to be fewer resources," Ease said. "No milkweed bottles, boot rear, beefsteak tomatoes. We would not eat well."

"But there should be pie plants," Tiara said. "Those are magic, not plants, and the virus doesn't destroy magic."

"True. But I don't see any pie plants."

"They may all have been harvested," Astrid said. "Because without pun foods, the non-pun resources have heavier use."

"So we may go hungry after all," Tiara said. "I'm tired and would like to sleep in a bed, rather than risking nickelpedes in the forest.

"No nickelpedes," Astrid said. "They're puns, or at least half-puns."

"But there are other nasties." Tiara turned to Mitch. "Are you sure you don't want to go to the village?"

"Not at all sure," Mitch said. "Just wary. We can go there, but let's be on our guard."

They walked on to the village. This one didn't seem to have a mare, unsurprisingly, as she would have been wiped out by the virus, but a head man came out to meet them. "Greeting, strangers!" he said jovially. "I am Giles, the mayor of PLO village. What is your interest here?"

"We're on a Quest to save the puns," Mitch said.

Giles seemed taken aback. "To do what?"

"A virus is destroying the puns. We need to find the anti-virus to nullify it and save the remaining puns."

"We need to talk about this," Giles said. "Come to the tavern for a good meal, and we'll discuss it."

"Thank you," Mitch said. "What can we do for you in return for your hospitality?"

"Don't worry about it; we'll think of something." Giles led the way to the tavern.

There, eating a very nice meal, they talked. "We don't actually want to save the puns," Giles said. "We regard them as a curse on Xanth, and are satisfied to see them gone. Why not give up your Quest and let the virus do its job? Xanth will be better for it."

"No way," Mitch said. "The virus wiped out the puns of my village and the people are desolate. We have to find that antidote."

Giles looked around the table. "Do the rest of you feel that way?"

One by one they nodded. Kandy noted that Pewter was silent; if this village hated puns, he preferred to be anonymous.

"We have been on this Quest for some time," Astrid said. "We wouldn't care to give it up after all the effort we have put into it."

"And the rest of you agree with that?" Giles asked the others.

Again they nodded.

"Then I am sorry," the mayor said. "Enjoy your repast." He got up and left the table.

"I don't trust that guy," Mitch said. "He's got something on his mind."

"Can you read it?" Tiara asked.

"No, my talent doesn't work that way. I can draw a thought from one mind and send it to another, but it has to be a specific thought, put up for consideration. All that's in the mayor's mind is his hatred of puns, and he made no secret of that."

"Well, we can move on in the morning," Ease said. "Right now I'm sleepy."

"So am I," Tiara said.

It turned out they were all sleepy, except Pewter. He neither ate nor slept, but emulated both so as to merge with the company. "I fear your misgiving was well placed," Pewter said in a low tone. "I believe the food is drugged."

"Oh, bleep!" Astrid said as she fell asleep. She was deadly, but she was alive, and therefore vulnerable to drugged food.

"I can't change that reality," Pewter said, "without interrupting my firewall and instantly perishing. But I will watch what happens."

"Do that," Mitch said as he slumped unconscious. The others were not far behind him. Soon they were all sleeping, Pewter faking it.

Now the mayor returned. "Too bad," he said. "Those are really pretty girls. It would have been nice to have them in our village. But we can't tolerate puns."

Other men came, and a woman. "That's one beautiful dress with the sequins, she said. "May I take it?"

"No. It might have dangerous magic. We won't touch their clothing or their bodies. You know our policy."

He had just saved himself and his village considerable trouble, Kandy thought. The dress might have embarrassed the woman before putting her into a new Event, and Astrid's perfume could have killed the man despite her being comatose.

"Too bad," a man said. "I'd like to have at that one while she's unconscious."

"And I'd like to have that dress," the woman said.

Just so.

"No," Giles said firmly. "Now put them in the oubliette. We'll hold their trial two days hence."

"Why have a trial?" a man asked. "We know they're guilty. Everyone heard them defending puns."

"The forms must be followed," Giles said. "We don't want to make a mistake."

"Like feeding a princess to the dragon," the woman said, laughing.

"It's no laughing matter. Princesses have power. Some are Sorceresses."

A dragon? This did not look good. But if they were awake for the trial they would have a chance to step into the next Event, leaving this dangerous village behind.

The villagers lifted the Quest members one by one and put them on a wagon. Then they hauled the wagon across the village to what looked like the ruins of an ancient castle. Kandy realized that Xanth must have had quite a history before the current day, because this was not the first evocative ruin they had encountered.

They rolled down a ramp and into a subterranean dungeon. There they put Mitch on a pallet suspended by a rope and pulley and lowered him into a dark hole in the floor. They played out a considerable length of rope; that was one deep hole. But eventually there was the sound of the pallet touching the bottom. They waited a moment, then reversed the pulley and hauled the pallet back up, empty.

They put Pewter on next, and levered him down into the deep hole. At least he would be able to help Mitch, out of sight of the villagers.

The third one was Astrid. "Are you sure I can't—" the man started.

"No! She's probably infected with puns."

Again, Giles had save them mischief. The man was not without honor, meager as it was.

They lowered Astrid down. Then Tiara. Then Ease. "That's a pretty feeble club he carries," the man said. "It's just a dumb board."

And how would he like to have that board smack him upside the head? Kandy was indeed dumb, in the sense that she could not speak, but she was hardly stupid.

They descended into the hole. Kandy began to see the outline of a huge nether chamber: the oubliette, with that faintly glowing moss on its rounded wall.

Hands took hold of Ease and lifted him off the pallet. "This is the last one, I think," a male voice said. "I heard them talking, above."

"Yes," a female voice said. "Too bad for them."

The pallet was pulled up, and the bright disk of the hole went dark: the access had been covered over. They were locked in the oubliette.

"Let them be," the man said. "They will revive soon. That dope they put in the food doesn't last long." He was modestly handsome, with curly black hair, wearing traveling clothes. Obviously another visitor to the village.

"Long enough to do the job," the woman said. "It got us down here." She was modestly pretty, also with curly black hair, probably his sister.

"We're doomed, but at least we can make these other victims more comfortable, and answer their questions," the man said.

Mitch stirred, the first to recover. Kandy knew why: he had distrusted the

Mayor, as it turned out with good reason, and had not eaten heavily.

The man and woman went to him and helped him sit up. "Easy, stranger," the man said. "You're among friends, though we can't help you much."

"We were drugged," Mitch said groggily.

"Yes. And lowered into the oubliette for safekeeping until the kangaroo trial."

"Kangaroo?" Mitch asked. "Isn't that a pun?"

"Not here," the man said. "It means a mock trial whose outcome is fixed, done only for show. They want the semblance of legality, in case there are questions later."

Pewter stirred, playing the role. He of course had picked up on everything Kandy had, but pretended ignorance. The man and woman went to him and helped him similarly. Then Astrid, Tiara, and Ease, who had eaten most heartily.

"We are all victims of PLO," the man said. "That's Pun Liberation Organization, dedicated to liberating Xanth from puns. They welcome the virus. They dispose of anybody they don't like or trust."

"We're on a Quest to save the puns," Mitch said. "And it seems they truly hate puns."

"They truly do," the man agreed. "Let's introduce ourselves. I'm Pastor, and this is my twin sister Futura. Our names relate to our talents, and those are what got us into trouble."

The Quest members introduced themselves candidly, as deception seemed pointless here. "I am Mitch, and my talent is fetching and sending ideas."

"I am Tiara, and my talent is my wild hair, which actually floats."

"I am Com Pewter, a machine. My talent is changing reality in my immediate vicinity, but I can't practice it now because I am busy maintaining a firewall to keep the pun virus from destroying me."

"I am Ease. My talent is to make complicated things easy."

"I am Astrid Basilisk-Cockatrice, transformed to human form. My talent is killing folk with my stare, which is why I wear these dark glasses. But I do not mean you any harm."

"And you hope to save the puns?" Pastor asked. "That's a curious Quest."

"Xanth is largely made of puns," Mitch said. "Without puns, this would be a bleak land. That's apart from folk like Pewter, who deserve to retain their existence. Now you two: what are your talents? We may need to pool our assorted talents to manage to escape this unkind confinement."

Kandy knew what was on his mind: they could escape at any time by using a sequin. But other folk would not necessarily understand, or care to find themselves in a complete shift of venue, a new event. It might be that such a shift would do them more harm than good.

"If you wish," Pastor said. "Our two talents complement each other. Mine is to reinvent the past, though it operates indirectly. Hence my name, Pastor. I can't just change the past by fiat. But I can describe it to others, and the more people who believe it, the more real it is. So I am a storyteller, in a way, because what is a story but His Story? Whatever most people accept becomes official."

"I don't follow that," Mitch said. "Many folk believe lies, but that doesn't make the lies truth."

"If it is a lie I spread, it can become the truth," Pastor said. "That's my magic."

Mitch nodded. "That is potent magic! But can you use it to get the two of you and the five of us to have avoided being drugged and imprisoned?"

"No, because it's not our belief that lends force to our plight," Pastor said. "It's the belief of the villagers. If I were with them, and able to spread a story that there had been no drugging or imprisonment, and enough of them came to believe it, then it would become reality. But as it is, the most who could unbelieve our captivity are seven, while there are dozens of villagers who believe it. Only if I could escape, and talk to them, without their realizing who I am, could I change it. And of course if I could escape, I would not need to change it."

Mitch nodded. "So it's like stepping in a hole you can't step out of."

"Pretty much," Pastor agreed. "Now my sister's talent is to reinvent the future, hence her name, Futura. We named ourselves once we discovered our talents. She can dream and tell stories of far off lands and kingdoms and fair princesses in danger by ugly trolls and fire breathing dragons, and before you know it there will be a far-off kingdom with exactly those things. Provided enough people believe it."

"So can she tell a tale of our miraculous escape from this dungeon and make it come true?"

"Again, no," Futura replied. "You know the nature of her talent, and that what she says is just a story. If you did not know, then it could happen."

"Like Princess Ida," Mitch said. "She can make something true by agreeing with a person who believes it."

"Yes," Futura agreed. "She is my idol. But my agreement alone isn't effective. My whole audience has to believe. So Pastor and I could not free ourselves, in the past or the future, and neither could you. But if I told a persuasive story to the villagers, and enough of them came to believe, then it could be true."

"Again, you need to get free in order to accomplish your freedom," Mitch said.

"It's a paradox," she agreed sadly.

"But if there were a way for you to get out of here, into the village, unrecognized, then the two of you could tell stories of the past and future that would eliminate this whole captivity."

"And we would no longer need to," she said. "That's another aspect of the paradox."

"Not necessarily," Mitch said. "We just might have a way out. But it has its own paradox, in that we would probably be nowhere near the village."

"Is there any other way out?" Astrid asked, not eager to discuss the mechanism of her dress.

"No, the oubliette is completely walled in," Pastor said. "The only access is via the hole in the top. Every few hours they lower food and drink so we won't starve. There's a bit of a trench at the edge that we use for refuse."

Meanwhile a wasp flew up and landed on Kandy's board. It seemed to sniff the wood, then took a bite.

OFF! Kandy thought at it.

Startled, the wasp flew off. But it was joined in another moment by several more wasps, all quite interested in the wood.

Now Astrid noticed them. "Paper wasps," she said. Then she reconsidered. "Except they can't be, because that's a pun."

Mitch smiled. "You're used to wasps made of folded paper," he said. "Those are a pun. But there are also real wasps who make paper from wood. These are that type. No pun."

"They come and go," Pastor said. "They leave us alone and we leave them alone. They mostly feed on the lichen on the wall. But they do seem attracted to that wooden board."

"Do they live here?" Tiara asked.

"No, we have not seen any hive. They just feed here."

"Then they must have an access."

"I suppose so. But it would be a wasp-sized hole. Nothing we could use."

"I wonder," Mitch said. "The air here is reasonably fresh. There may be more of an access than we see."

"We have had nothing to do for two days," Futura said. "We inspected every stone of the wall. None are missing."

"I wonder," Mitch repeated. "Let's track the wasps."

Pastor shrugged. "Why not."

They watched the wasps as they flew toward and away from the enticing board. Meanwhile other wasps lifted from the wall and flew to a particular stone, where they disappeared.

"Look at that," Mitch said. "They fly right into the stone without crashing. It's illusion!"

"Illusion!" Astrid repeated. "And big enough for a person to fit through."

Now they were all really interested. But the stone was too high for any of them to reach.

"Maybe I can do it," Tiara said. "Boost me up, Mitch."

Mitch lifted her up to his shoulders. Then her hair flared out and drew on up into the air. She was floating! She managed to reach the wall and put her hand to the key stone. And her hand passed through it to the elbow.

Tiara put her other hand to the stone, and through it. She caught on to something beyond it. "There's a passage!" she gasped. "I can feel its rough walls, and the air coming down through it." Then she lost her grip and fell slowly until Mitch caught her.

"Well, now," Mitch said.

"This is amazing," Pastor said. "We never thought of this, and certainly did not invent it. It was there all along."

"All along," Futura agreed. "Maybe we can escape after all."

"Maybe we can," Astrid agreed.

"But now I am wondering whether we really should escape," Mitch said.

The others looked at him. "You prefer to be fed to the dragon?" Pastor asked.

"No, it's more complicated. Our quest had taken us to a number of odd aspects of Xanth, and in each there turns out to have been some reason for it. At first it was to recruit the remaining members of the party. Then it was to glean information that should help us when we come to the finale. We have not yet discovered the point of this imprisonment. It may be that we need to go through their trial in order to discover it."

Pastor shook his head. "You have rare dedication. I would be extremely wary of the risk."

"Well, I'm thinking that you and Futura can escape, and talk to the villagers anonymously, and perhaps persuade them that they are not against puns or strangers. Then we would not face much risk."

"We could try," Pastor said. "But it can take time for a consensus to develop. With only two days remaining before the trial, its chancy."

"Focus on just one thing," Mitch said. "That puns are not enemies but friends, and should be preserved. If they accept that, the case against us will fade."

"It may," Pastor said. "But probably not all the way, in that brief time. We can't guarantee your acquittal."

"Well, we have other means, if necessary," Mitch said, glancing at Astrid.

"Oh, the basilisk," Pastor said. "Who can kill with a stare. But that would be ugly."

Kandy suspected that Mitch had been thinking of the dress and sequins Astrid wore. But he handled it with aplomb. "Yes, so we prefer an amicable settlement. Let's help you on your way, so that you will have as much time as possible to change village history."

"I should check it first," Astrid said. "To be sure there are no dangers in the tunnel."

"Thank you," Futura said. "I never thought I would say that to a basilisk."

"She's a nice person," Tiara said. "She'll make some man an excellent wife, someday."

Pastor's sentiment seemed mixed. "I can see that she has a very nice form. But how could there be love, if she can't directly look at any man eye to eye without killing him?"

"There's a way," Tiara said. "We will find it."

Pastor did not argue the case, but it was evident that he was not persuaded.

They made a human pyramid with Mitch and Ease at the base with the board resting on their shoulders. Then Tiara stood on it, her hair making her light and stabilizing her. Then Astrid joined her on the board. She put her foot in Tiara's linked hands and reached up to the invisible hole. She found it, got a hold, and drew herself up, in the process showing a good deal of her legs. Then she disappeared into the hole, first her head and upper section, then her mid-section, then her legs.

They dismantled the pyramid, carefully. "She should not be long," Mitch said. "We're not that deep underground."

Pastor made no response. He stood there looking up, unmoving.

"Oh!" Futura exclaimed, alarmed. "Something's happened to him!"

"Don't be concerned," Tiara said. "He just saw Astrid's panties and freaked out."

"But she's a basilisk!"

"In human form," Tiara said. "Men don't much care about a woman's real nature, just her form, and Astrid was given the best. Her panties are potent. Mitch and Ease have learned not to look." She snapped her fingers.

Pastor recovered. "Did something happen?"

"A passing indisposition," Mitch said smoothly. "Astrid is on her way."

Before long an arm appeared in the stone. "I'm back," Astrid called.

They quickly reformed their pyramid and helped her safely out and down.

"Any danger?" Mitch asked.

"No. Just some harmless centipedes."

"Centipedes! That's a pun."

"No, nickelpedes is the pun. Centipedes are just multi-legged bugs. The passage leads up to an old covered stone well. Whoever built the oubliette must have made it deliberately and hidden the exit so others wouldn't know. There are even steps in the steepest part of it."

"That's ideal," Pastor said. "Thank you, Astrid."

"You're welcome." She glanced at him a fraction of a moment longer than necessary, as if assessing him as a potential companion. But he was shying away from her, so she knew he was not a prospect.

They formed the pyramid once again, this time helping Pastor and then Futura up into the hole. Ease started to freak as Futura's legs swung over his head, but Kandy snapped him out of it with a curt thought. He had learned not to look at Astrid's legs, but not, it seemed, at others.

"Thank you!" Futura's voice called down. "We'll do our best!"

"Welcome!" they chorused after her.

They were about to settle down to wait and rest, when there was activity at the entrance hole. The disk of light appeared as it was uncovered, and the pallet slowly descended. It was an unconscious woman. They lifted her off and put her on the hay, as Pastor and Futura had done for them, and let the pallet swing back up. Then it came down again, with another woman.

"They certainly don't care about the safety of the distaff," Mitch muttered. "We could attack them while they are unconscious and do anything."

"Don't you dare!" Tiara snapped.

"He has a valid point," Pewter said. "Unconscious women are often considered fair game. The villagers seem not to care."

In due course the first woman recovered consciousness. "What happened?" she asked dizzily.

Tiara did the honors. "You were drugged and lowered into the oubliette for safekeeping until the trial. I am Tiara, one of several others here."

"But I didn't do anything!" the woman protested.

"Neither did we," Tiara said. "We merely stated that we are on a Quest to save the puns of Xanth, and it seems they don't like puns, and here we are."

"Oh. I am Tani. My talent is to make a pet of any nonhuman creature."

"I don't see why that would bother the villagers," Tiara said. "Is there anything else?"

"Well, I didn't know what to do with myself, because I don't need countless temporary pets. One remains a pet until I tame another, then the first reverts, so it's really not all that useful. So I went to see the Good Magician, and he assigned me to a Quest, but it didn't work out. For one thing he didn't tell me that I was supposed to be the leader, not a follower. By the time I realized, I was the only one left. So I was on my way home, a sadder and not much wiser girl, when I passed though PLO Village. The last I remember is explaining about being the leader."

"They thought you might take over the village!" Tiara said. "So they dumped you in here."

"They are paranoid," Mitch said.

Then Tiara introduced the others, and explained about their own Quest.

"Well, at least now I know what happened, and maybe why," Tani said.

The other woman stirred. Tiara went immediately to help and reassure her. It was evident that Tiara had deep sympathy for people in trouble or imprisoned, having lived as a prisoner so much of her life.

The other turned out to be Terri, whose talent was to jump forward in time to the next morning, to escape sadness on any given day. She had passed through the village, and they had given her a free meal and inquired about her talent—and suddenly here she was in a dungeon.

The others introduced themselves. Then they considered Terri's case.

"You must have said something that made them suspicious of you," Tiara said. "Just how did you describe your talent?"

"Well, it's a little like a pun. To escape mourning, I go to the next morning. I have no memory of the intervening time, though nobody else ever seems to notice my absence. It does save me much grief, literally."

"Mourning, morning," Tiara said. "That does sound like a kind of pun. That explains it."

"Explains what?"

"They hate puns. That's why we're down here. They thought you made a pun, so they drugged you and dropped you in the hole. But don't worry; we have found a way out."

"I do worry. This whole business is very depressing. So I think I'll just jump to tomorrow morning. Bye."

"Don't jump yet!" Tiara said. But she was too late; Terri had already slumped to the hay.

But then she spoke again. "Hello, folk. I am Tammi, Terri's alter-ego. Maybe I can explain some things."

"Alter ego?" Tiara asked. "You mean like a different personality in the same body?" Kandy knew she was thinking of Demoness Metria, with her two alter egos.

"Yes. I was actually the original personality, but my talent spooked so many folk that they banished me and put Terri in my place. But they didn't realize that her talent of jumping to the next morning would leave her body unattended, and so I take it back for those hours. Don't tell."

"But isn't that something Terri should know about?" Tiara asked.

"She doesn't want to know. She jumps ahead to leave her sadness behind; that would just bring it back. It would also require her to report that I'm not entirely gone. That could be more mischief. What other spirit might take over her body in her absence if I couldn't?"

Tiara shrugged. "It's not our business, I suppose."

"Your name is Tammi?" Tani asked. "Mine is Tani. I hope we don't confuse each other."

"Maybe we'll be friends," Tammi said, laughing. "Then we'll confuse others, but not ourselves."

Tani laughed too. "I am short of friends at the moment."

Tammi returned to Tiara. "Meanwhile I may be able to do your Quest some good, because of my talent."

"You said it spooked others," Tiara said. "What's so bad about it?"

"I see through conspiracies."

"Well, that seems helpful, not dangerous."

"Including the dread Adult Conspiracy, when I was a child."

"That would have been awkward," Tiara agreed. "But really, what would be so bad about a child knowing what she will learn when she grows up anyway?"

"It's a power issue," Tammi said. "If children learned how to signal the stork, they might do it and cut the adults out of the picture. Who would need adults anymore? They could be dispensed with. So the adults conspire to make sure they retain their power base. They couldn't afford to let me blab the truth, so they got rid of me, they thought."

"But we wouldn't do anything like that," Tiara protested.

"You were never oppressed as a child? Punished for being different?"

It was as if she had struck Tiara with a solid pillow, rocking her back. Of course Tiara *had* been punished for having different hair.

Astrid came forward. "Perhaps we should introduce the rest of us."

"No need," Tammi said. "Terri's experience is in my memory. You exchanged routine introductions with her. You are the basilisk."

"Yes," Astrid said, taken aback. "You said you might be able to help us. What did you mean?"

"You are here not entirely because you support puns," Tammi said seriously. "You are here because you represent a perceived threat to four conspirators in the village. The puns were only the pretext."

"How can you know this?" Astrid asked. "Terri never got to know the villagers before she was drugged and brought here."

"Terri's a nice girl. That's her problem. She had no suspicions. But checking her memory, I recognize the pattern. Had I been in control I never would have been deceived. As it is, it's a bit late."

"You never met the villagers," Astrid said. "Only the Mayor. Yet you say you know of four conspirators. Mayor Giles and who else?"

"No, Giles is not a conspirator. He honestly believes in what he is doing. In fact he's an honest man. But he is a figurehead, doing the conspirator's work. Once they achieve sufficient power, they'll dispose of him."

"How can you know this? You have no basis."

"It's part of my talent, the same way as your death-stare is part of yours. When I enter a situation, I know its nature, if it's a conspiracy. That's how I fathomed the Adult Conspiracy; no one told me its details."

Astrid looked at the others. "We may be in trouble. How can Pastor and Futura change things if it's not just innocent belief, but a planned conspiracy?"

"I doubt they can," Tammi said. "They may change the villagers' attitude toward puns, but that won't address the real problem."

"Then it must be up to us," Mitch said. "We can use the escape tunnel and avoid the whole issue, or we can tackle it directly."

"You have a plan?" Astrid asked.

"Yes, if you're willing."

"I can stun or kill folk, but I can't change their minds."

"I'm thinking of the way you took out the troll."

"He was an inhuman beast. I didn't mind putting him down. But I don't want to hurt a village full of largely innocent people."

"How about just four conspirators?"

"Now I begin to get your drift. But still, getting to them without setting off a riot could be a challenge."

"With Tammi's help you can do that."

"I'm glad to help," Tammi said. "I can see through conspiracies, but that doesn't mean I like them."

Mitch glanced at Tani. "We can use your help too. In fact it's critical. Are you in?"

"Of course I'm in," Tani said. "I couldn't save my own Quest, but I'll be glad to help save yours."

"Ours might even be the Quest you were destined to help, by a devious route," Mitch said.

Tani looked surprised. "I wonder!"

"Then let's work out our Plan. Here's what I have in mind."

He presented it to them, and the others found it worthy. It had key roles for Tammi, Tani, and Astrid. They rehearsed them, getting the details right.

The disk of light appeared above. "Hey!" a man called. "If you want food, send up the doll with the sequins, only without them." The pallet started descending.

"The flies are walking right into the spider's web," Mitch murmured. "If you are willing, Astrid."

"I'm willing," she said. "This makes it easy." She doffed her dress, then her bra and panties. "I don't want to freak him out, I want to get close to him, long enough."

"Understood," Mitch said. Then he called up "She's on her way."

The pallet descended. Astrid got on it, and it cranked its way upward. In due course it reached the hole, and passed through it.

"Well, now," they heard the man say. "You look even better naked."

"There's nothing else quite like me," Astrid said. "But first send down the food. You promised.

"No, first you take care of me. You know how."

"I do."

"Men are such fools," Tiara murmured. "Present company excepted."

"No, we're fools too," Mitch said. "But you women have us under control."

There was a brief silence. Then Astrid called down. "He's asleep. I'm winding down the pallet." They saw the pallet start down.

"That is some woman," Mitch said.

"And if you try to touch her, you'll be unconscious too," Tiara warned him.

"My admiration is limited to her effectiveness for the Quest."

"All the same, I'll go up next."

"Of course," Mitch agreed.

The pallet arrived and Tiara got on, using Astrid's dress and underclothing to lie on. After she was up, it descended again, and Mitch got on. The others followed, including Tammi and Tani, with Pewter the last.

There was the man, naked, unconscious on the stone floor. He was the one who had wanted to have Astrid before, but Mayer Giles had prevented it. Now, thanks to his sneakiness, he had gotten his wish, and been literally intoxicated by her perfume. "He didn't even get to the point," Astrid said, seeing them looking. She had dressed while waiting for them, not having to crank the pulley once another person joined her. "He was so busy kissing my body, and I haven't had a bath recently." She sounded almost disappointed. Kandy realized that she would have liked to have the experience, even though her purpose had been to do exactly what she did: put him to sleep for the duration. It would not have been romantic, any more than with the troll, but she was unlikely to have that particular experience any other way.

"Good for you," Tiara said. But both Tani and Tammi looked thoughtful, perhaps appreciating the frustration that lay in that success. The basilisk could do it only with a man she didn't mind putting down.

They ate the food the man had brought and tried to charge them for. It was good enough, considering how little the villagers cared about their welfare.

"He's not even one of the conspirators," Tammi said. "Just a foolish man who's not much on discipline."

"Next stage," Mitch said briskly. "We will dawdle here while Astrid and Tammi search out the four real conspirators and seduce them similarly. Meanwhile we will question this man when he wakes."

"This way," Tammi said. "I will know them when I see them, but we'll have to look; my talent does not give direction."

"But if other villagers see you, they may spread the alarm," Ease protested.

"That should not be a problem," Astrid said, removing her dress again, to stand in bra and panties. Those were her other weapons: men who saw her would freak out. She gave the dress to Tiara for safekeeping.

"Good idea," Tammi said, removing her own outer clothing. Her figure was not as robust as Astrid's, but she was young and healthy. "But how do we deal with the women?"

"I am trusting that they won't recognize us in this state," Astrid said. "They may not have seen us at all, as we never went around the village, and it was men who hauled us to the oubliette. We'll be just two somewhat exposed girls."

"We can say we lost our clothing," Tammi agreed. "As we have, though not accidentally."

The two departed. Mitch checked the unconscious man. "He's coming around," he said. He squatted beside the man. "Quick, where is the dragon?" he asked before the man opened his eyes.

"Other side of the castle," the man said. "One side's the oubliette; other side's the dragon cave. We lower them down the same way."

"Thank you," Mitch said. Then they departed before the man recovered further. He might wonder what had happened, but he would not talk about it, knowing better than to incriminate himself.

They posted Pewter by the castle entrance to intercept and guide Astrid and Tammi when they returned, and walked around the castle. Sure enough, there was another chamber, with another hole in the floor, and a pulley apparatus with a pallet. It was a pretty simple operation, really.

"My turn," Tani said. "Lower me down."

"Are you sure you can do this?" Tiara asked, concerned.

"Oh, yes. I have tamed many creatures, some of them dragons. I will have it eating out of my hand, literally."

Tani got on the pallet and Ease cranked her slowly down. They heard a muffled roar as the dragon winded her and charged over to gobble her up. But then there was silence.

"Safe," Tani called.

"My turn," Mitch said, a trifle grimly. He got on the pallet and Ease cranked him down. Then after two and a half moments, he called back "Safe!"

The others followed. There was the dragon, a huge fire breather now lying with its head on the floor gazing soulfully at Tani. She had indeed tamed it.

"Next stage," Mitch said. "Making sure the dragon knows each of us, so it won't eat us when we haul the conspirators here. And to explain exactly what we want done with the conspirators."

They performed the unusual introductions and explanation. The dragon listened passively. "Do you understand?" Tani asked it at the end.

"Of course I understand," the dragon said, startling them all.

"You talk!" Tiara said.

"No less surprising, so do you, damsel."

"But you look like a monster!"

"And you look good enough to eat."

"Druce is an educated dragon," Tani explained. "He doesn't even like the taste of humans. So he herds them down into the catacombs for the cats to deal with. The cats don't like their taste either, so they generally pass them along to the goblins. We're not sure what happens to them then; goblins vary."

"But Druce will keep the four conspirators with him, cleaning out his stables," Mitch said. "They will not be harmed unless they try to escape. That way we can draw on their expertise later, if we need to."

That made sense, Kandy thought. But it also avoided bloodshed, as they had agreed. Tani had made a worthwhile contribution to the effort.

They returned to the upper chamber. Soon Astrid and Tammi appeared, dragging the body of a conspirator. Ease worked the winch and lowered the man down into the dragon's lair.

In due course they had processed all four conspirators. The last one, to their surprise, was a woman.

"Now we tackle the Mayor," Mitch said, satisfied.

"Do we really need to?" Astrid asked. She was back in her dress, her undercover mission done. "With the conspirators gone, and the pun animus being ameliorated by Pastor and Futura, won't the village revert to normal soon enough?"

"You're right," Mitch said, surprised. "Our job here is done: we have dealt with a local crisis, and eliminated a bastion of anti-pun sentiment. That was surely the reason for this event. We can be on our way."

"And so can we," Tani said. "Tammi, why don't you and I walk on to the next village together, and get to know each other, since we almost share a name? Then in the morning I can get to know your alter ego too, without saying more than I need to about our adventure today."

"I'd like that," Tammi agreed. "It will give my existence better continuity."

The two bid farewell to the five, and set out for the next village.

Then Tiara removed a sequin from Astrid's dress. "I hope we don't land in another dungeon with a dragon." Then she replaced it.

CHAPTER 12:
CLOUD

It was not a dungeon. It was a wide open plain with wind gusting across it. Clouds floated low in the sky, scudding rapidly here and there.

"That's odd," Mitch remarked.

"Odd?" Tiara asked.

"Those clouds are not going all in the same direction."

Now Kandy saw it: the clouds were small, as clouds went, at different levels and colors, and they were scudding different ways. That was odd indeed.

It got worse. Two clouds collided and fell apart, the red mist mixing with the green vapor to form a weird brownish fog that turned upside down and floated upward like a dead fish. It was as if it had expired and given up the ghost. It did not rise far before other clouds converged, blowing it back and forth, shaking loose vapors that they then sucked in.

"Cannibalism!" Tiara exclaimed, shocked.

"And to think I thought Fracto was bad," Mitch said.

"Fracto?" Astrid asked.

"Fracto Cumulo Nimbus, the king of clouds. Remember him? He likes to rain on parades."

"But I gather he didn't eat other clouds," Astrid said.

"Not that I know of. But these are obviously a different breed of cloud.

How can they move opposite to the wind?"

"And what does any of this have to do with our Quest?" Ease asked.

"There must be some relevance," Astrid said. "There always has been, so far."

"What's happening with that yellow cloud?" Tiara asked.

They looked. The yellow cloud was floating very low and looked lumpy, as if having some internal complication. Then it rained a shower of yellow drops.

"I think it's pooping," Astrid said.

"That's called raining," Tiara said. "Clouds don't poop."

"Those pellets look solid to me."

"Maybe it's sleet, or hail."

"We'll find out soon," Ease said. "It's coming toward us."

Indeed it was, with yellow pellets dropping and bouncing on the ground. "Duck!" Mitch said.

They ducked down, hunching against the threatened hail. It came at them fiercely, bouncing off their backs. Ease put the board up as a shield, and the pellets bounced off it with a loud rapping sound.

Then the cloud was past. They straightened up cautiously, shedding snagged pellets.

"That's the funniest hail I ever saw," Ease said. "It's like alphabet soup."

"Letters!" Tiara said, picking up a handful. "Different letters of the alphabet. How can they be raining from a cloud?"

"This is curious," Pewter said. "There was once a virus in the OuterNet that infected machines like me, causing the letters of a printed page to drop down and pile up on the floor. It was impossible to maintain a complete document."

"A virus," Mitch said. "Can they do other things than melt puns?"

"Indubitably. There are many different viruses on the OuterNet. That's why I learned to make a firewall, that is standing me in good stead now. It keeps the viruses out."

"Could a virus infect a cloud?"

"I doubt it could mess up a regular cloud, as they are little more than floating vapor. But there is another kind of cloud that could be devastated."

"These are not regular clouds," Mitch pointed out.

"True. These just may be animations of OuterNet clouds. That would explain the special effects."

"And what is an OuterNet cloud?"

"It is an electronic database of enormous capacity that stores data for third parties."

"Can you repeat that in plain talk?"

"It's like a huge storage bin for information for anyone."

"Thank you. So there could be letters of the alphabet in one of those?"

"There would be data files containing records of many types. To assimilate them a person would summon them and read their words."

"Which are now falling out of the cloud as loose letters."

"Well, after a while the letters would become too heavy for the cloud floor," Tiara said. "So they would drop to the ground."

Mitch nodded. "I'd say that's the virus Pewter described."

"It could be like the pun virus," Astrid said. "Or another of a host of viruses, none of them doing anyone any good."

"So we need to get rid of them," Tiara said. "That must be why we're here."

"And how to we do that?" Ease asked.

"That it seems is our challenge," Pewter said. "But we can't even get into a cloud, let alone clear out a virus."

"I am not sure of that," Astrid said.

"You think we can get into a cloud?"

"I fear we can't avoid it. That gray one is coming for us."

So it was. Kandy saw that it was so close to the ground that bits of its fluff were scraping off as it scudded over irregularities on the terrain. They had nowhere to go. They just had to stand and let it smite them.

It loomed rapidly closer, its surface roiling. Then suddenly it was upon them, and the world was gray.

Slowly the dense fog thinned, and they were able to see again. They were standing in a cubic gray room with several doors in the walls. The doors were labeled with words like FILE, EDIT, VIEW, FORMAT, TOOLS, and HELP.

"What is this?" Mitch asked.

"It is a dialogue box," Pewter said. "It offers a number of options, as represented by the doors. The user clicks on the option he wants."

"Clicks?"

"Touches."

"And what happens when he selects an option?"

"He normally gets a new series of options."

"New?"

"Like this." Pewter rapped on the door marked FILE. It opened, and they filed through to another chamber girt by more doors. These had the words NEW, OPEN, CLOSE, RELOAD, PROPERTIES, and PRINT.

"What good is it?" Mitch asked.

"Good is irrelevant. This is the Cloud."

"Yes, the cloud swallowed us. I meant, what good are all these options?"

"The Cloud is a huge database, part of the OuterNet. It always offers myriad options."

"Is there one that will let us out of here?"

"Somewhere there should be a QUIT door. But that will accomplish nothing. We must be here for a reason. We need to tackle that reason."

"Is there an option that will clarify that reason?"

"Of course not. Net options never offer you the one you really need."

"One door says HELP," Astrid said. "Could we open that one to find what we need?"

Pewter seemed amused. "You can try."

Astrid went to the HELP door and opened it. It showed a chamber with doors marked MENUS, TOOLBARS, SHORTCUTS, MACROS, SPREADSHEETS, and COMMON HELP TOPICS.

"I have no idea what these are about," she muttered. She opened the COMMON door.

That one's chamber had doors marked GENERAL, WIZARDS, LINKS, GUIDES, INTERFACE, and CONFIGURING.

"I'll try one more," she said grimly. She opened GENERAL.

Those doors said SHORTCUTS, ACCESSIBILITY, GLOSSARY, VERSIONS, LAYOUT, and MENU.

Astrid reversed course, closing the doors behind her. "You're right. HELP is no help."

"Actually they all make sense on their own terms," Pewter said. "They simply are not intended for real folk."

"Such as those who actually need help?"

"Exactly. Only when you need no help do the HELP menus help you."

"That's insane."

"Welcome to the OuterNet."

"I don't think we need help to figure out our problem," Mitch said. "We knew there are viruses infecting the clouds of the Net, just as the pun virus infects Xanth. If we figure out how to nullify the viruses here, we may have a clue to dealing with the pun virus. That may be our purpose in this Event."

"That does make sense," Astrid agreed.

"You're so smart, dear," Tiara said, kissing his ear.

"What's this door?" Ease asked. "It says DO NOT OPEN. That makes me curious."

"Don't open it!" Pewter warned.

But as usual, with Ease, the warning was too late. Ease put his hand on the knob and opened it.

A torrent of little metal bugs swarmed out. Some were scuttling along the floor. Some were crawling across the wall. Some were flying.

"What are these?" Ease asked, taken aback.

"Those are bots," Pewter said. "They normally are used to crawl through the OuterNet and collect any new information they can find, so the big Search Engines can use it."

"Search engines? Are they like trains looking for scenery?"

"No. They have names like Goggle and Binge, and they can find anything in the Cloud. But I don't think these are legitimate info gathering bots; I fear they are virus bots, probably sent by Stuck Net. That's why they were walled out, but opening that door gave them access. Now we're in trouble."

"How can you tell?"

"Because my firewall is holding them at bay. It stops viruses. These are viruses masquerading as bots, and they are up to no good."

Now they saw that the bots had formed a circle, or rather a sphere, around them, and those that tried to get closer were burning and crashing to the floor. They could not quite reach the members of the Quest. They were viruses all right.

"Sorry," Ease muttered.

"Oh, we would have had to go out among them anyway," Pewter said. "Because if what we need could be found in the Cloud, someone would have found it already and exterminated the viruses. We need to locate their source and get rid of it. Meanwhile, let's hope the Cloud has a secondary firewall."

There was the snap, crackle, and pop of viruses hitting a nearby barrier. It seemed there was another firewall. The Cloud had not depended on just one.

"How come there was a door to let the bots in?" Mitch asked.

"A hacker probably made it," Pewter said.

"A hacker?"

"If you listen, you can hear them hammering, sawing and hacking, trying to make new portals. They don't like being shut out of anything."

They listened, and did hear the faint sounds of demolition. So it seemed that a hacker had made a door that could be opened only from the inside, and Ease had opened it, letting the bots in.

"What now?" Mitch asked.

"We deal with the rogue bot plague."

"How?"

"That is for us to figure out."

"Are you sure there's anything to figure out?" Tiara asked. "That there really is a way to handle this menace?"

"Oh, yes," Pewter said. "There's always a way. But it is seldom simple or obvious."

"We can't just use Goggle or Binge to find it?"

"It won't be listed in their data banks. The first thing a virus does is protect itself from discovery, because discovery dooms it. It is high-tech."

"So why don't we go through this labyrinth and open every door?" Tiara asked. "The answer must be somewhere."

"Because there are thousands of doors. MacroHard alone has more doors than you can wave a Mouse at."

"Do you have a better way?" she asked evenly.

Pewter sighed. "No."

"But maybe I do," Astrid said. "If these bots are from Stuck Net, won't they try to conceal their source so nobody can destroy it?"

"They should," Pewter agreed guardedly. "Protecting their source from discovery, as I said." The machine obviously felt she was asking a stupid question.

"So if we open doors and they ignore us, we're on the wrong track. But if they start paying attention, and trying to stop us, we're on the right track."

"That's just foolish enough that it might be true," Pewter said.

"So let's get moving, low-tech. Maybe they don't expect this, and can't stop us from blundering into the key chamber."

Pewter spread his hands. "*I* did not expect this, so probably they did not either."

"Then we will organize," Mitch said, clearly glad to support his girlfriend. "We shall have to act as a group, staying close to Pewter, so as to remain within his firewall. But we should be able to open many doors at once, speeding up our search."

"But each door leads to a different chamber," Astrid said. "Unless we go beyond the firewall, we won't be much better than a single person."

"Apt point," Mitch agreed. "Which of us can most safely go beyond the firewall?"

"That depends on what the bots try to do to us," Astrid said. "I don't think I can glare them off, because they aren't alive. But maybe they can't hurt me either."

"Maybe we should test this," Mitch said. "We can take turns stopping outside the firewall, and see whether the bots can hurt us. If they threaten to overwhelm one of us, the others can quickly rescue the one at risk. Does that make sense?"

"It does to me," Astrid said. "I'll go first."

"Wait!" Tiara cried. "Suppose they pull the sequins off your dress?"

"Oh, my," Astrid said. "They could, and that would be disaster."

"Unless you go naked again," Ease said.

"I could do that," she agreed. "If it didn't disrupt you and Mitch."

Mitch shook his head. Those panties are almost as deadly as your perfume, and a lot faster. We're bound to freak out." He glanced at Tiara. "No offense. I love you, but panties are magic."

"I know," Tiara said.

"I said naked," Ease said. "No panties or bra."

"I could do that. I could give my clothing and underclothing to Pewter for safekeeping and go nude. That wouldn't really bother me, because in my natural state I wear no clothing."

"Let's do it," Tiara said.

Astrid removed her clothing and gave it to Pewter, who stored it carefully in a knapsack. Then she stepped beyond the firewall.

The bots converged, grabbing at her with their little hands. "Ooo, that tickles!" she exclaimed. But that was all; it seemed they couldn't actually hurt her. They were designed to mess up machinery, not living flesh.

Astrid strode to a door and opened it. The bots showed no special alarm. She entered the adjacent chamber and they heard her opening other doors. Still no alarm. "This can't be the right route," she called, returning.

"The test was whether the bots could hurt you," Mitch said. "We are reassured. It would be unfortunate if such a lovely body—" He broke off as Tiara pinched him, then resumed. "Of information were blocked off."

Then Ease tried it. When the bots converged, he lifted the board and batted them out of the way. Soon they gave up pestering him.

Mitch tried it, with similar success, though they did tug at his long hair. Then Tiara, who swatted them away as they poked her too personally. But she was unhurt.

"We can do it," Mitch concluded. "We don't have to stay within the firewall. That's a relief."

"That's a relief," Astrid agreed. "Still, we probably should work in pairs, in case of the unexpected."

"I do not require a second," Pewter said. "I will give you some of my cells, so we can remain in constant touch."

"Cells?" Mitch asked.

"Living folk have tiny cells that make up their bodies," Pewter explained. "My android body is made up of similarly small inanimate cells. They will serve as cell phones for communication." He chipped off bits of his artificial hair and passed them out. The others put them in their own hair, where they clung invisibly.

"I don't see how this works," Ease said.

"You will when the time comes," Pewter's voice in his hair said.

"Oh!" Tiara said. "Talking hair! Like the demoness Metria."

"Exactly," they heard Tiara's hair respond.

"Can we also talk to each other?" Astrid asked.

"Say the name and I will relay your call," Pewter's voice told her.

"Tiara," Astrid said. "Can you hear me?"

"Yes, Astrid," Tiara responded. "These cell phones are fun."

"Let's get to work," Pewter said impatiently.

"I will work with Tiara, of course," Mitch said.

Astrid turned to Ease, "Then it seems it will be the two of us together."

"Yeah," he agreed, eying her splendidly nude body.

FOCUS ON BUSINESS! Kandy thought to him.

"But I will focus on business," he concluded.

A faint smile played about Astrid's lips. "Of course." She not only agreed, she understood where that thought had come from. Astrid had no designs on Ease, knowing about Kandy, apart from the lethal nature of her closeness. Kandy admired the way she handled his occasionally wandering eyes. At such time as Kandy recovered her natural form she would try to emulate that herself. Being eyed was really not such a bad thing; she had surely over-reacted before.

Meanwhile the myriad little bots hovered nearby, watching them but not trying to interfere. It seemed that the bots simply didn't know how to mess up living folk in the works.

They took the TOOLS door. It led to a chamber with doors marked SPELLING, OUTLINE, UPDATE, MACROS, CUSTOMIZE, and OPTIONS. The first led to obscure doors that did not seem relevant to anything they needed, so they tried the second. The doors there were numbered, and again seemed irrelevant. The third had several doors whose words were grayed out, and they would not open. The fourth, MACROS, had doors marked RECORD, RUN, and ORGANIZE. The first door opened onto just two doors RECORDING and STOP RECORDING. There was a sort of quivering as if something was happening.

"Recording what?" Ease asked.

"I don't know, but it seems to be running," Astrid said. "I think we'd better push the other button." She did.

The quivering stopped. Suddenly new doors appeared in the wall. The first said MACRO NAME and the second said PLAY.

Astrid shrugged. She opened the first door and said "Whatever." Then she opened the second, and paused, amazed.

There were images of nude Astrid and clothed Ease, with a small cloud of bots surrounding them. "Recording what?" Ease asked.

"I don't know, but it seems to be running," Astrid answered. Then she pushed a button and the scene vanished.

Astrid hastily shut the door. "It recorded *us!*" she said.

"You look great," Ease agreed.

She did look great, Kandy thought. But she wished that someone other than Ease was looking at her.

"Let's see what else is here." Astrid opened the third door, which was labeled MY MACROS. Inside was a chamber with several doors, the first of which was STANDARD. Inside that was one marked MODULE 1. "This isn't getting us anywhere," she complained.

They backed off a few doors and tried CUSTOMIZE. That led to a bewildering assortment of doors that left them thoroughly confused. They backed off again and tried OPTIONS. Again there was a huge number of doors, none of them comprehensible.

"Pewter," Astrid said.

"I hear you," the machine's voice responded immediately.

"We're not getting anywhere. Do you have any suggestions?"

"Yes. Hide."

"Hide?"

"Big bots are coming."

"Big bots?"

"Big enough to hurt us. The small ones evidently summoned aid."

"But there's no place to hide!"

"Consider it a challenge."

Now they heard the thudding of heavy robotic feet. The big bots were coming for them, guided by the spying little bots.

Ease got an idea. "That door where we're recorded—hide behind that."

"And they'll think the recording is us," Astrid agreed.

They hurried back to the MACROS door and opened the PLAY door. That now had a door saying WHATEVER, the name she had given the recording. She opened that and dived though, followed by Ease. They stood behind the door, out of sight.

The recorded scene was playing. It came to the end and started over. "Recording what?" the image Ease asked.

"I don't know," the image Astrid replied.

The first big bot burst through the door. It spied Ease and grabbed him. Except that its metal hands passed right through the image.

A second big bot entered. This one grabbed Astrid, with no better success.

Both bots paused uncertainly. But then the hovering mini-bots buzzed. The big bots turned and spied the real Ease and Astrid.

"Oh, bleep!" Ease swore, and lurched to and through the door. But the big bot was too fast for him. It caught him and heaved him up onto its metal shoulder. Meanwhile the second bot caught Astrid and heaved her similarly. Kandy, dangling down the back of the first Bot, saw Astrid's bare legs and posterior against the back of the bot. It was just as well that Ease was not in a position to see that, because he would have freaked instantly despite the lack of panties.

Where were the bots taking them? Soon they joined two other big bots carrying Mitch and Tiara, and then another carrying Pewter. The five tramped down an obscure hall to a new door. Kandy saw the label XUNIL, then EDK, then CLOSED END. What could those possibly mean? Finally there was a door labeled NET HELL. She saw Pewter tossed through it, then Mitch and Tiara, then Astrid. Finally Ease.

They landed on a slide that descended steeply through dark chambers until finally it dumped them on a pile of sawdust in what seemed to be a dungeon. The five climbed to their feet, dusting themselves off. None were hurt, and there were no bots of any size here. But where were they?

"I believe I recognize this place," Pewter said. "It is the Discard Dungeon for old discarded software that will never be used again."

"They wanted to get rid of us," Mitch said. "So they tossed us on the discard pile. So can we climb out?"

"Doubtful," Pewter said. "They will have the way guarded. Note how the entry is a one way slide. We will not be able to climb back."

"Oh?" Ease said. "Let's see about that." He went to the chute and tried to walk up it. But his feet slipped and he landed back on the sawdust.

"Magically slippery," Pewter said. "No access there."

"But there must be a way out somewhere," Tiara said. "We just need to find it, as we did before."

"A sequin," Astrid said. She remained beautifully bare. There did not seem to be any bots here, but it wasn't worth risking.

"But have we done or discovered what we were sent here to do?" Mitch asked.

"We have not eliminated the bots or the virus," Astrid said.

"So we're not done here," Mitch concluded. "But even if we find a way back upstairs, it won't do us much good as long as the big bots are there. We'll just get thrown away again."

"So we need to find a way to neutralize them. Then we need to find the Answer we were looking for before."

"I wonder," Tiara said.

Sometimes she came up with good ideas. Mitch, aware of that, was careful not to discourage her. "You have a notion?"

"It's foolish, but—"

"Tell us and let us judge."

"The doors were generally leading down, as if the important things are kept on the lower levels."

"Yes. A building rests on its foundations."

"Now we're really low. Could what we want be down here?"

"Could it?" Mitch asked Pewter.

The machine considered. "Software is not like hardware. The new generally replaces the old. But conceptually it is based on the old."

"Isn't it a concept we want?" Tiara asked. "To learn how to get rid of the virus?"

"This is uncertain."

"And if the new software is built upon the old, could the new virus derive from an old virus?"

"This is possible."

"So maybe the secret to stopping the new virus could be found in an old virus?"

"This is possible," Pewter agreed.

"So maybe we need to find an old virus and take it apart to find its weakness."

"Which might carry through to the new virus," Mitch said. "But be so old that it has been long forgotten, like the discarded software. That could be our answer."

"That could be," Pewter agreed.

"So how can we find an old virus?"

Pewter considered. "One of the old-timers might know. Someone like CPM or QDOS or Xinu."

"Who?"

"CPM was an early operating system," Pewter said. "It was later displaced by QDOS, which stood for Quick and Dirty Operating System. It then evolved into MSDOS, and thence to MACROHARD DOORS. An early and continuing rival was Peach. Meanwhile there was Xinu, the best of them all, but it was held captive and wasn't allowed to compete. So finally they made a reverse-engineered copy called Xunil. Now there is also Automaton for hand-held units. It's a long history."

"I saw a door labeled XUNIL," Mitch said.

"Yes, it is now a leading operating system, and fundamental in the larger system."

"Captain M, Ms. Dos, Peach, Xinu, and Tomato," Tiara said. "Got it. So are they down here?"

"Tomato?"

"Automaton is too complicated for me to remember, so I'm cutting off the ends. That leaves Tomato."

Pewter didn't argue further with her terminology. "They may be down here, yes."

"So let's go find them."

Pewter looked somewhat helplessly at the others. He clearly was not used to dealing with female logic.

"Have we anything better to do at the moment?" Astrid asked.

That decided it. They set out to find Captain M, Ms. Dos, Xinu, or Tomato.

The dungeon was a desolate place, with piles of refuse scattered around. Their substance seemed mainly to be 0's and 1's. Kandy could not begin to guess how such repeated numbers could relate to sophisticated programs.

In the dreary distance they spied a squat roughly cubic building. It had no windows, just a big M painted on the side. "That would be Captain M's residence," Pewter said. "He has fifteen floors plus a basement for the heavy machinery. Once you are inside, you simply call out a number to move instantly to that floor, where there will be a complete array of the files you normally use. Each floor can be different, so that many folk can be in that building without interfering with each other."

"That seems comfortable," Mitch said. "Why didn't it last?"

"The Captain is old and crusty. When someone wanted a new array of programs from him, he ignored them. So they went to Ms. Dos instead. That doomed him."

"Too bad," Mitch said.

"It looks dusty," Tiara said, wrinkling her nose.

"Everything here is dusty," Astrid said. "Because this is the Discard Dungeon where nobody who is anybody comes. But we don't have to go to that ugly building."

"Look! A garden!" Tiara exclaimed.

There was a section of the plain that had not been trashed. A path wound through a pleasant culture of grass, flowers, and shrubs.

"That would be one of Ms. Dos' paths," Pewter said. "She likes to have scenes for her paths to tour."

Then they heard a scrabbling sound. "That sounds like insects," Tiara said nervously.

"Those would be Bugs," Pewter agreed. "They get into programs and mess them up."

Now they saw the Bugs. Most were small, but some were medium and a few were large. They were black papery things, running on the ground and buzzing their wings. They were orienting on the group of people.

"I don't want them near me," Tiara said.

"There's no avoiding them," Pewter said. "They can pop up anywhere."

"Unless we hide in the Captain's building," Mitch said.

They hurried to the building and knocked on its main door. It opened, and a gruff old sailor stood there. "Who are you?" he demanded, seeming unpleased by the intrusion.

"Hello, CPM," Pewter said. "May I call you Captain? We are refugees from the Bugs."

"What do I care about that? I keep them out of my domain."

VAMP HIM Kandy thought to Astrid.

Astrid, still nude, presented a marvelous smile. "We'd really like to see your building, Captain. We have heard so much about it." She took an amazing breath. "Please."

"Then come in before the Bugs do," the Captain said, mollified. Like Pewter he did not freak out, but it would have required eyeballs of ice and a heart of glaciated stone to resist Astrid's charm.

Soon they were inside, where it was nice enough. "We should explain that we're actually from the software future," Mitch said. "Bots tossed us here, and we want to escape."

"I can't help you. I have been confined here for generations."

"In the future," Pewter said, "Bots and viruses galore are wreaking havoc. I must maintain a constant firewall to keep them from getting me. We are searching for some way to abolish them."

"I wouldn't know about that," the Captain said. "They aren't part of the good old way."

Kandy was able to see why the Captain hadn't gotten anywhere. He lacked ambition.

"Would Ms. Dos possibly know a way?" Mitch asked.

"I want nothing to do with that harridan! She stole my business."

"Fortunately she was replaced, and no longer holds sway," Mitch said. "She might like to restore the old way too."

"That so? Maybe she's not so bad." The Captain took a deep breath. "I'll tell you the only way I know to fix things when everything is hopelessly messed up: hit the reset button."

Pewter nodded. "That might do it. Where is it?"

"I have no idea. Ms. Dos might know. Follow her paths and you might find her. Tell her to pay me a call someday."

"We certainly will," Astrid said earnestly. Kandy realized that the basilisk liked using the power of her appearance in a good cause. It was a new kind of magic to her.

"But the Bugs are out there," Tiara said.

"The paths are enchanted to keep the Bugs off. You'll be safe as long as you stay on them."

"Ah. Thank you, Captain," Mitch said.

"Thank you so very much," Astrid echoed, favoring the Captain with another phenomenal bare-bodied smile. "You have been most helpful."

"Just so," he agreed gruffly.

They exited and hurried to the nearest path before the Bugs could catch them. "That was remarkable," Mitch told Astrid.

"My pleasure."

"If only there were a way to nullify your ambiance."

"But then I would not be me."

There was the problem. A basilisk without deadliness would not be a basilisk.

They walked the path through the garden. The Bugs paced them but could not approach them. That was just as well, because they looked hungry and some of them were big enough to bite off a leg or two.

Then a monstrous bat flew down to land on the path before them. A frowzy middle-aged woman sat on its back. "What are you doing on my path?" she demanded.

"My turn," Mitch muttered. Then he put on an enormous smile. "Ms. Dos, I presume? You are looking wonderful today. Captain M sends his regards and hopes you will call on him."

"That old lecher? I wouldn't go near him or his dusky old house."

This wasn't working. "That's a marvelously trained bat," Astrid said.

"This is Auto Exec Bat," Ms. Dos said proudly. "I programmed him myself. He takes me anywhere in a flash."

Astrid favored the Bat with another beguiling smile, one animal to another. "And maybe you even know where the Reset Button is."

"Don't mess with that button!" Ms. Dos snapped. "It's dangerous."

"We are from a kind of future," Mitch said. "Where bots and viruses wreak havoc. We desperately need to abolish them."

"Ah. Resetting would do it. It would also wipe out any recent special projects. You would have some rebuilding to do."

"But perhaps it would be worth it," Mitch said.

"You say M wants me to call on him?"

"He is desperate for your company," Mitch said. "He is extremely lonely and surely most apologetic for whatever wrongs he may have done you in the past."

"It does get dull here. Very well, follow Exec. He will lead you to the Button." Ms. Dos dismounted from the Bat and walked toward the M building.

They didn't argue. The Bat took off and flew in a straight line. Unfortunately that cut across the Paths. That meant they would have to plow through the Bugs.

"I don't think my glare will work here," Astrid said.

"But my board will," Ease said. He led the way, bashing Bugs with enthusiasm. Kandy cooperated, glad to enhance the blows. The others followed in the path cleared for the moment.

"You did not say anything to Ms. Dos," Mitch said to Pewter. "Was there a reason?"

"Yes. She might be considered my grandmother. She would not have taken anything I said seriously."

The Bat hovered over what looked like an ancient outhouse. "There?" Tiara asked with dismay.

"No wonder it hasn't been found before," Mitch said.

But it was guarded by several huge bugs with horny carapaces and giant pincers. Ease raised the board. The biggest Bug opened its mouth to reveal monstrous teeth. It was ready to chew the board to bits. That made Kandy nervous. "I don't think we can handle this one," Ease said.

"I can't change its mind without letting down the firewall," Pewter said.

"I'll try," Astrid said. She faced the Bug and removed her dark glasses. They exchanged gazes and the Bug didn't blanch. "It's not alive," she said. "So I can't kill it."

"I can't put an idea into a dead thing," Mitch said.

"Maybe I could float over it," Tiara said uncertainly.

"You'd have to come down to touch the Button," Mitch said. "Then they'd get you."

They stood there. Were they to be balked after all?

A man strode up to them. He wore a colorful costume with a cape. "What seems to be the problem here?" he asked.

This time Pewter spoke. "I recognize you. You are Xinu."

"Yes. I have a lot of power I am not allowed to use. I see you have a firewall. Who are you?"

"We are a party from the virtual future," Pewter said. "There is much mischief there from myriad bots and viruses. The only way we can clear them out is to press the Reset Button. But we can't get to it."

"My geis prevents me from doing anything heroic," Xinu said. "But I could clear out local Bugs. Why should I?"

"Because the most significant operating system of our future time is Xunil," Pewter said. "Who is in a sense your offspring. You will want to help him succeed, rather than leaving the field to the offspring of Ms. Dos. You will not want him to be hampered by rogue bots and viruses."

Xinu nodded. "You are correct. I am constrained, but my stepson is not. I will help clear the field for him." He faced the big Bugs, who had remained quite still since his appearance. "Begone!"

The Bugs fled.

"My work here is done," Xinu said, and faded out.

They went to the outhouse. There inside it was a simple square with a big red button. The Button.

"Who does the honors?" Mitch asked.

"Pewter," Tiara said. "He cleared the way."

Pewter went to the Button. He put a hand on it and pressed down. The Button depressed, flashed, and snapped back into place.

They paused, alert for the Happening. But nothing changed.

"It didn't work," Tiara said, disappointed.

"Not necessarily," Pewter said. "Its effect will be in the future software. We must return to the future to verify its action."

"I suppose," she said dubiously.

They returned to the chute that had deposited them in the dungeon. It remained as slippery as ever.

"I am familiar with things of the earth," Astrid said. "I recognize a stickum plant." She fetched a fruit and broke it open to reveal a gooey interior. Then she smeared the two halves on the slide. Its brightness turned dull. She put a foot on it, and it held. She put the other foot on it and stood without sliding off. She smeared more goo on the slide, stepped up, and spread still more. She was making it navigable.

"Good enough," Mitch said, eying Astrid's bent bottom until Tiara kicked his ankle. Then Ease eyed it, until Kandy ordered him off.

Could they really go back to the future this simply? Just by climbing a few stories up a slide? Actually, they could, because they had not really traveled to the past, just to the dungeon of discarded old programs that represented part of the history of the machinery of the OuterNet. Kandy found it interesting.

They followed Astrid up the slide, never slipping. Progress was slow but certain. In due course they reached the door through which they had been thrown. They opened it and got out into the hall.

There were no bots of any size.

"And no viruses!" Pewter said. "My firewall is clear."

"Better maintain it anyway," Mitch said. "Just in case."

They walked back along the hall, and through doors at intervals, until finally they stood where they had first entered the Cloud. Everything seemed to be operating smoothly. There was no evidence of any disruption.

"I think the Reset Button worked after all," Astrid said, finally putting her underwear and dress back on. Kandy knew that Tiara was as relieved as she was. The men both knew that Astrid's body was not for them, but their eyes didn't.

"It restored the system to its defaults," Pewter agreed. "Eliminating the corruption of the bots and viruses."

"We have accomplished our mission here," Mitch agreed. "Shall we move on?"

"Let's rest first," Tiara said. The others agreed. They had had a tiring session.

CHAPTER 13:
ZOO

In the morning, rested, they invoked another sequin. And found themselves in a maze formed of avenues through tall stalks.

There was a crackling noise, and flames flickered near. "Firewall," Pewter said tersely. "We eliminated the bots and OuterNet viruses, but the pun virus remains. It is of a different type."

"Too bad," Mitch said. "So the Quest continues."

"And if this Event is typical, we'll soon be in trouble," Astrid said.

"So we had better get a fair notion of the setting," Mitch agreed. "Which seems to be one big puzzle."

"I wonder," Tiara said. "Could these plants be corn?"

"They do look like corn," Mitch said. "Why do you ask?"

"Well, when I was in the tower I had a lot of time to read. I read how there's a type of corn called maize. But there's also maze, a labyrinth. If this was a field of that kind of corn, could the pun virus have wiped out the pun and left it as a puzzle?"

"A maze made of maize," Mitch said. "Amazing!"

"So now it's neither maize nor maze, but just a puzzle made of corn, no pun," Astrid said. "But that doesn't explain why we were brought here."

"Unless the pun virus antidote is here to find," Pewter said.

"So let's solve the puzzle," Ease said, striding forward.

Kandy saw the others circulate a glance of resignation. Ease tended to plunge into things without proper caution. Then they followed.

The passages between the stalks were intricately convoluted, and they were soon lost in their confusing depths and not getting anywhere. "I hate to suggest this," Astrid said, "but maybe we should split up again, each following a passage, and whoever finds the end can call to the others."

"That might save time," Mitch agreed. "We still have Pewter's cell phones, so we can stay in touch."

They did it. Astrid diverged along the next intersection, and Pewter went the opposite way. The remaining three continued straight ahead. When the way forked, Ease took the left fork and Mitch and Tiara took the right fork.

Ease's passage led to a kind of chamber, a square with a metal plate set in the center. Curious, Ease used the board to pry up the plate. Below was a dark hole, a seeming passage of another kind. Kandy realized that it might be an access to the middle of the maze, so that the farmer would not have to navigate the convolutions in order to bring in fertilizer or water for the corn. The curious thing about it was that the depth of it was a smooth slope, similar to the slide they had found themselves on when they were dumped in the Discard Dungeon of the Cloud. But the surface was not slippery.

Ease dropped the plate back, losing interest, and went on.

"Found something interesting," Astrid's voice came, using the cell phone. "A large gate to what looks like a zoo. At least there are animals there."

"What kind of animals?" Mitch asked.

"Pink elephants."

Pink elephants? Kandy wondered about that. Elephants of any color were Mundanian animals. That must be a really exotic zoo.

"We do not want to be in a zoo," Pewter said.

"Because the animals may be unfriendly?"

"Because we could get locked in with them."

"Oh."

"But we should at least see it," Mitch said. "There may be a reason we are near it."

"I will Halloo," Astrid said. "So you can find me by sound."

That was smart of her. Their cell phones did not indicate direction.

HALLOOOO! Astrid called.

The others worked their way to the gate, orienting on that sound. The way seemed almost to open out before Ease, facilitating his progress.

"And it didn't even spook the animals," Astrid said, pleased.

Kandy saw words printed on the ground. IF YOU BUILD IT, THEY WILL COME. Why would such a message be on a corn field? She could make no sense of it.

They gathered before the gate. "Those are not animals," Pewter said. "They are pictures. Propped up cardboard pictures."

"Why so they are," Astrid said, surprised. "That's why they didn't spook."

"Who would such a show be for?" Mitch asked.

"Us," Pewter said. "We need to get away from here."

They turned to retreat from the gate. But as they did, two things happened: the gate swung open, and there was a huge crashing in the cornfield.

"Bleep!" Pewter swore.

"What's the matter?" Tiara asked.

"I recognize the pattern. It's what I use to bring quarry into my cave. An invisible giant herds them there. That is the sound of an invisible giant. This is a trap."

"But there's no smell," Mitch said.

"Some giants are cleaner than others."

There was another crash, closer. They saw corn stalks fly outward as from a crushing impact. The giant was approaching.

"Scatter!" Pewter said. "It's the only way."

Ease ran to the left and Astrid ran to the right. Pewter, Mitch, and Tiara spread out between them, radiating into the corn field.

But they were too late. There was a crash before Ease, and a foot-shaped section of corn went flat. He had to stop.

The others were being herded similarly. It seemed there was more than one invisible giant. They all had to retreat toward the open gate.

"We don't want to go in there," Pewter said.

Then an unseen foot stomped down right behind them, barely missing them. As one, they bolted through the gate.

The gate swung closed behind them.

"Bleep," Pewter repeated.

"What is going on?" Tiara asked.

"It seems that we have just become zoo specimens," Mitch answered grimly.

Then Mitch rose into the air, flailing. "Something's picking me up!" he cried. "And removing my clothes." Indeed, his clothes detached themselves and floated away.

Then Tiara rose up, screaming. Her clothing too came off and moved away.

"It seems there are several invisible giants processing us," Pewter said as he too rose up. "They want us to be in what they deem our natural state."

Astrid and Ease followed. Kandy could see nothing, but at one point felt the surface of a giant invisible hand as it stripped Ease. He automatically gripped the board, and was allowed to keep it. That was a relief; Kandy didn't want to be separated from the Quest.

Soon all five were standing on the ground again, mutually naked. The giants departed. They could tell by the sounds of their feet, which were no longer crashing down but could not move completely silently.

Tiara was sobbing into Mitch's shoulder. "What now?" he asked.

"There will be facilities," Pewter said. "Zoo specimens are normally well treated."

"But they can't leave the zoo," Astrid said.

"Exactly."

"Aren't zoo animals for people to look at?" Mitch asked. "I don't see anyone looking."

"This is evidently the capture area," Pewter said. "The display area will be elsewhere."

"Maybe we can avoid it," Ease said.

"I doubt it. These appear to be experienced collectors."

"What now?" Mitch repeated.

"There is a path," Astrid said. "We should follow it before we get driven along it."

They followed the path. It led to a simple open house. It was well appointed with a living room, kitchen, bedrooms, and a bathroom. There was food in the pantry, and water in the tap. There were closets, and their clothes were neatly displayed there. It was a serviceable house, except for two things: the closets were locked, and all the rooms had a transparent glass wall in front.

"So not only are we naked," Astrid said. "We are exposed in the house too. Anything we do here can be seen from outside."

"That is the nature of a display," Pewter agreed.

"Display for whom?"

"For them."

They looked out. Another glass wall had appeared, parallel to the glass face of the house. Behind it was a family of large purple snails with intricately coiled green shells. Their yellow eye stalks were eagerly perusing the all-too-visible contents of the house.

"I have seen nothing like that in Xanth," Mitch murmured.

"My guess is that they are alien visitors from another planet," Pewter said.

"You mean we're an exhibit in an interplanetary zoo?" Tiara asked, horrified anew.

"So it seems," Pewter said.

"We have to get out of here!"

"I suspect we will have trouble finding food or alternate clothing," Astrid said. "Let alone escaping the zoo compound."

"We should at least try," Tiara said.

Astrid shrugged. "We can explore."

They left the house. The eye stalks of the snails followed them, curious as to what the exhibits were up to. They followed a path continuing beyond the house. It wound through a copse of neatly kept trees that served as a kind of barrier between exhibits but not between exhibits and the alien viewers.

And there, beyond a formidable wire fence, was a family of dragons. One of them saw the humans and sent a blast of fire-breath their way, but it bounced off the fence. It seemed that one exhibit could not interfere with another.

Meanwhile the snail family lost interest in them and gazed at the dragons, surely a more exciting exhibit. Beyond the dragons they could see another fence, beyond which were centaurs.

"This is one comprehensive zoo," Mitch remarked.

"And we were fed into it," Astrid said. "There must be a reason."

They walked on. The path curved around, leading to a transparent goblin mound where the goblins could be seen wherever they were. "Fresh meat!" one called, and waved one finger at them. They were typically rude goblins, happy to insult anyone in the vicinity. The far side had another glass wall, with insect-like aliens gawking, marveling at the gestures of the local life forms.

The path moved on to an exhibit of harpies perching in a spreading tree. "Go away, you skug rats!" one screeched at their party.

"What is a skug rat?" Tiara asked.

"Anyone they don't like," Mitch said.

"But harpies don't like anyone."

"There are many skug rats in Xanth," Astrid said, smiling.

"Also in the universe," Mitch agreed, glancing at the glass wall beyond the harpy tree, where tentacular aliens gawked.

Ease paused, glancing at a square tile similar to the one he had seen in the maze, then moved on without commenting, because Kandy squelched it. That was another service access, she realized. Now she understood its slide surface beneath: the caretakers might be snails.

The path finally led back to their own house. Their spot tour was complete. "Dragons, goblins, harpies, people: one wing of the zoo," Mitch said, summing it up. "Each of similar interest."

"So how do we escape?"

"There may be a way," Astrid said. "We can discuss it when we have some semblance of privacy."

They entered the house and made use of its facilities. Tiara was skittish about using the glass toilet in plain view, but had no choice, so closed her eyes. She was in luck: no aliens were watching at the moment.

As night came they chose rooms and beds. Even the blankets were transparent. Kandy was not surprised to see that Tiara chose to sleep separate from Mitch; she simply could not stand to have any interaction between them visible to the universe. Pewter took another bedroom. Astrid chose to share a room with Ease.

Ease, encouraged by Kandy, promptly slept. Kandy appeared.

"If you do not move they should not see you," Astrid said without looking at her. "They're not expecting ghosts."

"Or hear me, I hope," Kandy said.

"I saw Ease looking at that square manhole cover. That was you?"

"Yes. We saw a similar one in the corn maze. I think they are service accesses. This zoo doesn't just maintain itself."

"Would a person fit in one?"

"Yes. But he would have to crawl. It's designed for snails or something similar."

"I could do it. I'm used to crawling."

"You would leave your dress behind?"

"Oh, bleep! I can't do that. You know why."

"Yes. Maybe have just one person slip out, and he can find a way to free the others."

"You are thinking of Ease."

"Yes. Neither Mitch nor Tiara would go without the other."

"You have thought it through."

"I do have time for thinking," Kandy agreed ruefully.

"Okay, let's try it. I'll wake Ease and explain it to him."

"Do that," Kandy agreed.

Astrid crossed to the bed and touched Ease's shoulder. "Wake," she said quietly.

He woke. "Huh? What do you want?"

"Fear not. I am not getting romantic. I think you should go to that access hole and crawl through it to escape the zoo and find some way to rescue the rest of us. Can you do that?"

"Sure I can do it," he agreed. "That's the kind of thing that's easy for me. I don't like being in a zoo."

"Move quietly in the dark so as not to attract attention. With luck they won't even miss you until morning."

He nodded, gazing at her faint outline in the dark. "You're sure it's not romantic?"

"Ease, I can't stay close to you without putting you to sleep, and worse beyond that. You know that."

"Yeah," he agreed regretfully. "I'll be on my way, then."

"Good luck."

Kandy really appreciated that not only did Astrid politely deflect Ease's interest, she did it without mentioning her underlying reason: that she was reserving him for Kandy, at such time as Kandy could claim him. Astrid was a true friend.

Ease made his way out of the house and walked to the access panel. He used the board to pry at the square. He lifted it up, then got down into it, sitting on the slide below. There was enough room to sit up, but not enough to stand. He lowered the lid above him. There was a bit of a glow that sowed only when the passage was closed. He put his hands down and scooted into the depths, not at all claustrophobic, keeping the board on his lap.

The surface was not slippery, but neither was it abrasive. Ease was able to move along at a fair clip, considering his position. He continued until he saw another access above. He stopped beneath it, put up his hands, and pushed the lid up and clear. He climbed out and stood on the ground, looking around in the gloom.

"Where am I?" he murmured rhetorically.

There was a high-pitched roar. Something charged toward him.

DRAGON! Kandy thought. That was the sound of the young one.

Ease dived back into the hole and pulled the cover back in place just before the dragon got there. The creature growled in frustration, but did not understand the mechanism of the access hole. It stood on the panel, searching for the prey.

So they had gone from one section of the zoo to another. WE NEED TO GET ALL THE WAY OUT OF THE ZOO, Kandy thought.

"All the way out," Ease echoed. He scrambled along the tunnel, following it wherever it went. But when he tried another access, it was the goblin section.

Then they heard a sinister sound. Something was moving in the tunnel, sounding like a metal cable scraping through it. The aliens must have realized that something was in there, and were sending a hook or something to fish it out.

GET OUT AT NEXT ACCESS!

Ease obeyed, scooting along at top speed. But the scraping sound was gaining. Then they came to an access. Ease pushed up and jumped out just as something like a metal snake shoved through. He dropped the panel back in place and stood on it, preventing the thing below from emerging.

After a moment and a half the scraping stopped. The thing was retreating whence it came. But that did not mean they were safe. It might mean the aliens were satisfied that they had located the intruder.

RUN!

Ease hardly needed the urging. He ran into the brush, pushing aside stalks. Stalks? They were in the corn field! That was outside the zoo!

STOP RUNNING. FOLLOW THE MAZE PATHS. HIDE.

Ease, taking this for his own sensible thinking, did so. He found a nook and paused, listening.

Before long something came to the access. Kandy could not see it, but heard it. She recognized the sound. A GIANT.

The giant checked the access. There was a loud stiff. The giant smelled Ease! But couldn't locate him. Soon it went away. They had escaped!

What now? LET'S FIND A SAFE PLACE AND REST, Kandy thought, knowing it was probably safer to remain still than to move around. Moving made noise, and noise could be tracked.

"This is safe enough," Ease decided, and settled on the ground where he was. "I wish I had my dream girl here with me."

He wanted the dream girl. How sweet. Kandy was touched. SHE IS ALWAYS NEAR YOU, she projected. SOMEDAY YOU WILL FIND HER.

"Someday I'll find her," he said, and drifted off to sleep.

Kandy animated. She made herself comfortable lying beside him. "I like you, Ease," she told him. "Someday I'll be with you, and let you do this." She took his hand and set it on her bottom. "And this." She kissed him.

In his sleep, he smiled. He was definitely dreaming of her.

But what were they to do now? Ease was out of the zoo, but the invisible giant knew he was near. That meant that the alien proprietors knew too. That was dangerous. Regardless, how was Ease to free the others? The simple plan seemed less feasible now that it was in process.

Ease woke before dawn, hungry. He got up and looked around. "Maybe some corn," he said. He checked the nearby stalks, and found some ears of ripe corn. They were not shaped like human or animal ears, because they had been de-punned, but they were edible in their fashion. He chewed on them carefully. It wasn't enough, but it took the edge off.

They watched dawn come to the zoo. The other members of the quest got up in the transparent house as if accustomed to this existence. They were pretending, knowing that Ease was out, giving him time to do whatever he could. The alien proprietors had to know he had escaped, and how; those service accesses would no longer be safe to approach.

A giant came, carrying something. He set it down outside the gate and walked away. Ease peered at it from the cover of the corn stalks.

It was a table set with a sumptuous meal. There was an array of fruits, breads, pastries, main courses, and beverages.

IT'S A TRAP! Kandy thought. DON'T GO THERE!

"It's a trap," Ease muttered. "Bleep, I'm still hungry."

GET AWAY FROM HERE. DON'T LET THEM TEMPT YOU.

Ease reluctantly walked away from the table, his stomach growling. Kandy felt for him. How long would he be able to hold out eating raw corn?

Ease hesitated, turning back toward the table. DON'T DO IT!

He paused in place, warring with what he thought were his own thoughts. He stood in the shadow of the tall stalks, peering out, unable to move until he got his thoughts settled.

Meanwhile Kandy looked around. She saw that beside the big swinging gate was a small shed, the gatehouse, where the mechanism was to crank it open or closed. An invisible giant must have been cranking it when the gate opened before, and when it closed, shutting them into the zoo. The shed was open on the side away from the gate, where the giant could put in a hand to turn the crank. Too bad they hadn't caught on to that mechanism before it was too late.

There was the sound of tramping giant feet. The table lifted up and floated away, carried by the invisible giant. It tilted slightly and a loaf of fruitcake fell off. It bounced on the ground and lay there as the table retreated into the distance. The giant had not seen it.

Ease launched himself forward before Kandy could stop him. He swept up the cake and ran back to the cover of the corn.

DON'T EAT IT! Kandy warned. IT'LL BE SPIKED. She was sure that the loss of the cake had been no accident. Even if it was, probably all the food was spiked. But again she was too late; Ease was already biting off chunks and gobbling them.

What could she do? There might be only seconds before he lost consciousness. Then they would sniff him out and recapture him. They knew he would not be far away.

Kandy got an inspiration. THE GATE HOUSE! GO THERE!

Ease walked toward the gate house, still cramming in fruitcake. He never questioned the source of the thought, distracted by the joy of the eating. He stumbled as he approached it, caught himself, and stumbled again. The knockout medicine was taking effect.

LIE UNDER THE CRANK HANDLE.

Ease fell, but reached the shed on hands and knees. He crawled under the man-sized handle, and went to sleep, one foot sticking out of the shed.

Kandy assumed her human form. She reached for his leg and pulled it in so that he was curled up entirely within the shed. Then she spread herself on top of him, facing up. There was barely room for her under the handle. The beauty of this was that the group of them including Ease had already been through the gate, so the smell was already here; the giant would not find it remarkable. She waited.

The tramping resumed. The giant was coming back. He knew the cake would be taken and eaten, and that the body would be close by. The corn stalks swished as the invisible hand brushed them aside, but of course there was no human body to be found.

The tramping proceeded across the area as the giant searched, frustrated. He knew the quarry had to be here, but where? Then he came to the shed. He lifted up the roof and peered down.

Oops. They were exposed. It had not occurred to her that the roof would be hinged, though it made sense for servicing. But Kandy was ready. She waved a hand up toward the invisible face. "Hi there, big boy! Can't a nymph have some privacy when she sleeps?" She moved her hands as if to try to cover her nakedness. She knew she was giving him a nice eyeful, but of course there was nothing he could do with such a tiny girl.

"Sorry," the giant boomed, and lowered the lid. Soon the tramping departed.

She had done it! She had covered Ease's body with her own, and fooled the giant, who might have seen Ease beneath her had he not been distracted by her bareness. Men were pretty similar in this respect, whatever their size; she was actually coming to appreciate their wandering eyes. She had, on the spur of the moment, found the perfect hiding place, right where no one would ever suspect: right by the gate itself. The irony was that it never would have worked had Ease been conscious. Or if the giant had been female.

Ease slept for an hour: time enough to be found and captured, had the zoo-keepers' plan worked. But now she needed to get him out of here, lest the gate be re-checked.

BACK TO THE CORN FOREST, she thought. AND WATCH.

Ease obeyed. Soon he was hiding again at the fringe, watching the gate and its vicinity. Fortunately the solid fruitcake had fed him so that he was no longer hungry. That incident had worked out better than they might have expected.

The giant came again, carrying a cage. He set it down before the gate and departed. A cage? Did they think Ease would get into such an obvious trap?

Then they saw what was inside the cage. It was a live person. A girl. In fact it was Tiara.

Once again Ease was moving before Kandy thought to stop him. He ran to the cage. "Tiara! What are you doing here?"

"Ease!" she exclaimed. "Don't come close. It's a trap. The cage is sticky. If you touch it you'll be caught."

Ease halted without touching the cage. "But you're inside it!"

"They put me in as bait." She blushed. "I think they think I'm your girlfriend."

"So I'd have to save you," he agreed. "But Tiara, I don't want you stuck in there like that. What can I do?"

"Do nothing," she said. "I'll be all right. They'll just put me back in the zoo. They don't want to hurt me; they just want to recover you. Don't let them do it."

"Well, if that's the way you want it."

"That's the way it has to be." She paused, then added. "And Pewter says maybe if you have time on your hands, you can check the other exhibits to see if they want to be rescued."

"But the aliens will see me."

"Pewter says they are keeping things clear until they recapture you. They don't want you to spook. So the way is clear right now, for a while. Go."

"I'll do that," Ease said, walking away from the cage.

He walked around the zoo to the dragon section. Kandy saw that the alien walk was a channel that was closed off from the regular landscape as well as the zoo exhibits. Maybe the aliens didn't even breathe local air; it might be pressured with their kind of air. It was really a big tube that Ease could get under in dips in the ground.

Ease came to the fence. "Hey, dragon!" he called to the nearest one. "You want to escape?"

The dragon whirled and shot out a jet of fire. The flame glanced off the fence and dissipated.

"I'll take that as a no," Ease said, halfway amused. Some dragons were smart, and some could even talk. These were evidently not that type.

Next was the centaur section. "Do you want to be rescued?" Ease called.

A splendidly endowed lady centaur oriented on him. "If you had asked a week ago, we would have been interested. But now we realize that this is actually a pretty good life. There's a phenomenal library of books, and the food is good. So thank you for your interest, but no."

They didn't want to be rescued? Pewter must have suspected.

Ease walked on around to the goblin section. "Hey, goblins!" he called. "Want to get out?"

"Go poke your finger in your right ear," the nearest goblin called back. "And pull it out your left ear."

That was another negative. Ease walked on around to the harpies. "Hey, you're from the fresh-meat section," a harpy called. She had messy hair, a dirty torso, and greasy wings: a good specimen of her kind. "Whatcha doing outside, bleep for brains?"

"I guess you're not interested in getting out," Ease said.

She answered with a stream of invective that wilted the local shrubbery. That completed her description: a fowl temper.

Ease completed the circuit. The cage remained, but the occupant had been replaced. Now it was Astrid. "Different bait, same trap," she called. "Don't fall for it. They figure that if Tiara is not your girlfriend, I must be."

"I'd like you to be," Ease admitted. "If only we could stay close."

"Someday you'll find your dream girl. Now clear out before the giant returns."

"But I was out in the open all the time," Ease said. "No giant came after me."

"They knew you'd scoot for cover the moment one approached you," she said. "It's hard for giants to catch creatures our size if they don't want to hurt them. They want you in good condition for the alien visitors. So they're trying gentle methods."

"And if they don't catch me today?"

"It may be less nice tomorrow," she said. "So if you have a rescue plan in mind, best implement it tonight."

"I'll try," Ease said.

She eyed him. "You have no idea what to do."

"Right," he agreed ruefully.

"Commune with your inner self. Maybe you'll come up with something." This was actually an appeal to Kandy to figure out a plan if she could.

"Maybe," he agreed without conviction, and walked away.

Before long the giant came to take away the cage. This time he left another cage in its place. This one was of lighter construction, wickerwork, with large holes between the crisscrossing slats. And it held a different girl. This one was nicely clothed, and quite pretty overall.

When the giant left, Ease approached. "Who are you?"

"Hello!" she said cheerily. "I am Timothea, and my talent is conjuring clothing. Any kind." She eyed his nakedness appraisingly. "Would you like some? I could make you a very nice outfit."

"I've got clothing. Just not here."

She made a gesture with her hands, and a pair of trousers appeared. "Maybe start with these. Cover up your awkward hardware."

Ease was tempted, but Kandy nixed it. I DON'T TRUST HER. SHE'S TOO SMOOTH.

"I don't trust you," Ease said, echoing the thought.

Timothea's face clouded up. "You don't like me!" she sobbed.

Ease took a step toward her, but this time Kandy was ready and stopped him literally in his tracks. TEARS ARE A STANDARD FEMALE PLOY. DON'T FALL FOR IT.

"I—didn't say that," Ease said. His feelings were not merely mixed, but homogenized.

The cloud dissipated. "Really? I am reassured. Hold my hand." She reached out through the cage.

DON'T TOUCH HER!

Ease froze in mid reach. "Sorry," he muttered.

"Oh, bleep!" she swore, and dissipated into smoke. So did the cage.

She was a demoness! The zookeepers had really pulled out all the stops this time.

Ease retreated to the corn, shaken. He knew he had had a close call. Only his common sense had saved him.

Kandy was annoyed. *His* common sense?

So they had avoided the several traps the keepers had set. But the problem remained: how could they free the others? They now knew that the other exhibits weren't interested in escaping, which simplified things, but that wasn't enough. They had to recover their clothing, notably the dress with sequins, and invoke one to enter the next Event. How could they do that from out here?

Then Kandy got an inspiration so bright that it made a bulb flash over Ease's head. Suddenly she knew how to do it.

WAIT TILL NIGHT, she thought to Ease. REST, SLEEP UNTIL THEN.

Ease, trusting his common sense, settled down in the corn and soon slept. Kandy reviewed her plan, looking for flaws and finding none. It should be feasible.

When night came, Ease returned to the gate, alert for any sound of a giant. There was none. Evidently the giants preferred to work by day.

He went to the gatehouse and took hold of the winch handle. He threw his full weight into it, shoving it slowly around until the gate cranked open by a sliver. Then he squeezed through it, reached back from inside, and shoved the handle back the way it had come. The gate nudged shut again.

The zoo keepers had never thought that anyone would try to break *into* the zoo. They had set no alarm on the gate, and the little bit it had opened had not been enough to attract any attention. They were safely inside.

Still, Kandy was not completely reassured. This had been a bit too easy. Yet how could it be another trap, since the keepers wanted Ease where he was: in the zoo?

Ease went to the glass house. "Pssst!" he whispered.

The others joined him immediately and silently. Then he went to the closed glass closet. "In case of emergency," he said, "Break Glass."

Ease swung the board hard against the glass. Kandy enhanced its impact as it struck. The glass shattered. The clothing was exposed.

They pulled out their clothing and quickly donned it. But the sound had attracted attention. The girl, Timothea appeared before them, glowing to illuminate the house. "What are you up to?" Then she spied Ease. "And what are you doing inside? If you had taken my hand, I'd have clamped it with a grip of steel and held you for admittance." She was no longer making any secret of her nature or her loyalty: she worked for the keepers.

"I guess I missed my friends," Ease said.

"You broke the glass. You got your clothing." Then Timothea's eyes fixed on the board. "With that board! That thing is dangerous. Well, I'll just take that now, and keep you out of future mischief." She reached out her hand, the one that could make a grip of steel.

Astrid stepped in between them. "Leave him alone."

"Get out of my way, girl, or I'll throw you out."

Astrid removed her glasses and stared Timothea in the face.

Timothea rocked back. "Oh, my! You're a basilisk! Good thing I'm not alive, or I'd be dead by now."

"Even demons are affected to a degree," Astrid said. "Now get out of here and leave us alone." Then, to Tiara: "Take a sequin."

Tiara looked stricken. "I just realized: Sequins of Events is a pun! And this dress has been out of Pewter's range. The pun will have melted."

Now they all looked stricken. She was right. They could no longer use the sequins to jump to new Events.

"What's this about a sequin?" Timothea demanded.

They ignored her. "We'll have to find another way," Mitch said.

"What about the troll?" Ease asked.

"What troll?" Timothea asked.

"Ease, the troll is past history," Mitch said. "We need to deal with the present crisis."

"The dress," Ease said. "It floated down the stream, and the troll got it. Then we used the sequins to go to the next three Events. Why didn't the virus get it then?"

There was a significant pause.

"Virus?" Timothea asked. "You specimens don't need to care about that any more."

"You're right," Pewter said. "The dress and sequins were outside my firewall for some time. Yet we used them thereafter. How can that be?"

"Somehow the dress and sequins pun avoided being destroyed," Mitch said. "Could they have their own firewall?"

"No," Pewter said. "I would have recognized it."

"Then how?"

"I think I know," Astrid said. "Something may be de-punned and still work, like the maze maize. Sequins of Events is a pun, but the sequins are real regardless where they are or how they are named. Putting a sequin on the dress is the signal to bring the next Event, no pun required. So it worked after the troll, and should still work now."

"Then let's do it!" Mitch said.

"I think I'd better take that dress," Timothea said.

"Touch it and I'll claw you into confetti," Astrid said.

The demoness was not frightened but angered. She leaped on Astrid, her own claws forming. Astrid hugged her and breathed into her face, setting her back. "Invoke a sequin!" Astrid snapped to the others.

Tiara came to her as the others drew close. Tiara quickly removed then replaced a sequin.

Timothea's mouth expanded, forming giant pointed teeth. She opened it, ready to bite off Astrid's face. Astrid grabbed her ears and twisted the head until the neck was a tight knot of fibers and the face was pointed backwards. "Give over, idiot!" she hissed. "You lost. You're not in the zoo anymore."

Timothea looked. "Oh, bleep! Where are we?"

"I have no idea," Astrid said, letting her go. "But I'm sure you can find your way home if you try."

The demoness's head spun about until the neck untwisted. "No. I'll stay and fetch you exhibits back to the zoo. That's my job."

"We need to get rid of her," Tiara muttered. "She's a nuisance." She was well aware of the way both men were covertly eying the shapely demoness, whose body remained spectacular.

Kandy prompted Ease. "You'll stay?" Ease asked. "That'll be fun. Come here, you luscious creature. I've got great ideas for you." He reached for Timothea.

"Oh for pity's sake," the demoness said. "As if I'd ever touch a lout like you except to push your silly face in the mud." She dissipated into smoke and blew away on the wind.

"Good job, Ease," Astrid said. "You bluffed her off."

"Bluff? Shucks, I'd have liked to have her," Ease said. "At least for five minutes. She's pretty." And of course that was his whole definition of a woman: her appearance, however come by. Kandy was disgusted, but also intrigued: she had the necessary looks herself, when she wasn't a board. Also, she had to recognize that what attracted her to Ease was that he was handsome, goodhearted and manageable. So she wasn't much better in her own definitions.

"Same thing as a bluff," Astrid said. "She'd be as bad for you as I am, in a different way. You need a better woman."

"I need my dream woman," Ease agreed. "But I see her only in my dreams."

"Someday she'll come to you when you're awake. Have faith."

"I hope so."

Kandy wished she could reassure him that she would indeed come to him when she could. But that was the rub: how long would she be stuck with the curse of being a stiff board? So far there had been no hint of any way to escape that.

"Did we accomplish our Event?" Tiara asked. "We didn't rescue any other exhibits."

"They weren't interested," Ease said. "I queried them. They're satisfied to be zoo specimens."

"There must have been something," Mitch said.

"There was," Pewter said. "We realized that the Sequins are not pun-powered. That means we can wade into virus territory without all of you staying within the firewall. That could make a difference."

"It could indeed," Astrid said. "I am relieved."

Now they paused to see where they were. It was of course a completely different scene.

CHAPTER 14:

STORM

Actually it was not a bad scene. It was night, but there was good moonlight so that they could see. They stood in a meadow beside a lake bordered by flowering trees. Above the lake hovered a lone cloud. It seemed quite peaceful.

"Let's sleep," Mitch suggested. "We don't know what the morrow may bring, but I don't trust it. I want to be fully rested before I tackle it."

"Sleep," Pewter said. "I still need to maintain my firewall, though the virus does not seem to be here yet, but I can keep watch."

"Good enough." Mitch and Tiara settled down together, while Ease and Astrid lay down a modest distance apart.

Soon Ease slept; he was a quick sleeper. Kandy reverted. "Hello again, friend," Astrid called softly.

"You handled that demoness well," Kandy said as she sat up, moving the man's hand to her leg.

"I'm supposed to be the Quest bodyguard. It was Ease who really got rid of her."

Kandy laughed. "By threatening to smooch her! That's ironic. He couldn't get rid of *me* that way."

"Or me," Astrid said sadly. "No offense. I'd like to safely kiss any man, even if all he wanted was my body."

"And a beautiful body it is."

"Yours too."

"We remain sisters in spirit," Kandy said. "Neither of us can touch Ease or any man. Not in any way that counts."

"Let's kiss him," Astrid said. "Me fleetingly, you lingeringly. So we can pretend."

"Let's," Kandy agreed.

Astrid got up and walked across to them. She took a breath, held it, got down beside Ease, and kissed him momentarily on the mouth. Then she got quickly away before her ambiance could poison him.

Kandy hugged Ease, then kissed him so passionately that he started to wake. She quickly broke it off lest he discover he was kissing a board. She knew that Astrid had made the suggestion not only to tease herself, but to give Kandy reason to do what she wanted to. They truly were friends.

"We just have to hope that the Quest will solve our problems as well as save the puns," Astrid said.

"We do."

Pewter came over. "Ready for chess?"

"Always." Chess was her salvation from boredom.

When morning came, Ease stretched and looked around. When he saw Astrid he paused. "I dreamed you kissed me," he said.

"Things are possible in dreams that may not be done awake, as we know," Astrid said. "You may dream what you wish."

"Then my dream girl kissed me." He shook his head. "Bleep! I wish she'd come to me in daylight."

"Then she wouldn't be your dream girl."

"She'll always be my dream girl! I love her."

Kandy loved hearing that, frustrating as it was.

"I'm sure she loves you too, in her fashion. But it seems she is limited to your dreams."

Mitch and Tiara, who had no such problems, joined them. "I see there are pie plants and milkweeds here. The virus hasn't found this spot yet."

"But it inevitably will, in time," Pewter said. "If we don't find the antidote."

They feasted on pun foods, then considered. "There seems to be nothing threatening here," Mitch said. "That makes me suspicious."

"Justified," Pewter said. "It probably means that we are not seeing the threat, and therefore not taking proper steps to deal with it."

"Like some dragon sneaking up on us?"

"Astrid would have smelled it and backed it off."

"I would," Astrid agreed. "There is no animal threat nearby, and I think no plant threat either."

"And it seems no virus threat," Tiara said.

"So why are we here?" Ease asked. "There's been a reason for each Event so far. Did we draw a blank?"

"That cloud," Mitch said. "It is floating over the lake, not moving. That's not normal. This is not the OuterNet Cloud Event."

Pewter scrutinized the cloud. "Let me check my data banks. Yes—that is no ordinary cloud. That is Fracto."

"Who?" Tiara asked. "I saw clouds from my tower, but they were not named."

"Fracto Cumulo Nimbus, the self-styled king of clouds," Pewter said. "Otherwise known as a developing thunderstorm. This must be where he sleeps when not raining on parades."

"We've run afoul of him before," Mitch said.

"Oh, yes," Tiara said. "At Centaur Island. I had forgotten. But that was far from here, I think."

"Distance doesn't matter," Pewter said. "He goes where he wishes."

"He's puffing up," Tiara said. "It's almost as if he can hear us."

"He *can* hear us," Pewter said. "He's a form of demon. But our Quest is no business of his. Ignore him and he'll float away."

"He's not floating away, he's expanding. His top is coming to look like an anvil, and his bottom is getting dark gray."

"Oh, bleep," Pewter swore. "I forgot that I have to maintain the firewall, and can't simply make Fracto change his vaporous mind. I was speaking dismissively of him, and he doesn't like that. Now he'll rain on us."

"So who cares about a little rain?" Ease asked. He faced the cloud. "Hey, fog-for-brains! You think a little rain will bother us?"

"That was not wise," Pewter said.

Not wise at all, Kandy knew. Clouds could get violent when worked up.

"Oh, pooh!" Ease said. "Take that, Fracture!" He made a gesture with one hand.

"Best to ease off, no pun," Mitch said. "Rain can get heavy."

"So we'll take shelter under a tree for half an hour until he blows himself out."

"I think we had better get away from the lake," Pewter said.

"Because of a blob of mist?" Ease demanded. "What kind of pantywaists are we?"

This was going too far. Kandy sent a DESIST thought to Ease.

But it was too late. The cloud had burgeoned to cover the whole lake and was now expanding to include the meadow. Swirls of fog formed to make baleful eyes. A cruel crack of a mouth formed. Wind blew out.

It caught them, perfectly aimed. It was a hard, icy blast that almost swept them off their feet. In fact it did catch the dresses of the two women and carried them a short distance back. Mitch quickly caught Tiara's arm, while Astrid ducked down to make a smaller target.

Kandy's knothole eyes were not bothered by the wind or rain. She saw that things were falling from the cloud. Animals. It was raining cats and dogs!

No, these were different creatures. They were deer who plainly loved water. She groaned inwardly. Rain Deer. More proof that the pun virus had not reached this area.

"Get under cover," Pewter said.

"What cover?" Mitch asked. His shirt was coming apart, his hair severely tugged by the wind.

"Or a hole in the ground," Pewter said. "Anything to get us out of the direct blast."

They found a depression and huddled down in it, letting the wind pass over them. "But won't this flood?" Tiara asked.

As if in answer, a sluice of water blasted down on them. Water puddled immediately. Their lower portions were soon soaked.

"But if we try to run elsewhere," Mitch said, "We'll be exposed to the full force of the wind."

"Indeed," Pewter agreed. "That is why it is better not to aggravate demon clouds."

"We need shelter of some sort," Mitch said. "Ah—I see a canopy. That may do it."

"A what?" Tiara asked.

"It's a pun," he said, picking up a sealed can. "Fortunately they still exist here. I will invoke it." He held the can up before him. "Manifest!"

The can expanded explosively, becoming huge. Kandy could now read lettering on its side. CAN O' PEA. It was a pun all right.

The top of the can popped up, and green paste welled out. The can was filled with pea mash.

"But what good will this do us in this deluge?" Tiara asked. She was now standing beside Mitch in the lee of the huge can, her dress plastered to her slender torso.

"We can get in it and be sheltered from the wind and rain," Mitch said. "See, the lid is the canopy."

"But it's full of pea! It's as bad as the pea soup fog!"

"Yes, we won't go hungry during the storm. Then we'll wash off when it's over."

There did not seem to be much choice, because the wind and rain were fierce and the water on the ground was rising, overflowing the depression.

Mitch boosted Tiara up and over the rim of the can. The others followed. There was just room around the edge, their lower bodies surrounded by pea.

The rain continued to torrent down. The canopy-lid shielded them from it, but it was an almost solid wall just beyond the can.

"What are those shapes out there?" Tiara asked.

Kandy prompted Ease. "Rain Deer," he said.

Tiara grimaced. "Sometimes I wonder if the pun virus is such a bad thing."

"I don't," Pewter said tersely.

And that was the thing: puns could be annoying, but Xanth without them simply would not be the same.

The deluge did not let up. It seemed that Fracto was really angry. The water was now causing the lake to overflow its boundary and flood the meadow.

"This can't continue much longer," Mitch said. "There's simply not that much water in the air."

"You forget that Fracto is a magic cloud," Pewter said. "He can conjure whatever water he needs or wants."

"All because Ease disrespected him?"

"Some folk are very sensitive to respect."

"Some stupid folk," Ease said.

The downpour intensified into a drenchpour. "Stop talking," Pewter said.

Because Fracto was still listening, Kandy realized. But they were already in for it. This would be a long siege.

"This pea mash isn't bad," Astrid said, chewing on it. She too was plastered, her dress becoming almost a second skin with sequins attached.

The others tried the pea mash, and pronounced it good. They would not go hungry, no matter how long the rain lasted.

The level of the lake rose until the meadow disappeared entirely and the few trees were spot islands. The water surged around the base of the pea can, until, with a lurch, it rose off the ground and floated. They clung to the rim as the can wee-wawed in the tide.

"I am feeling sea-sick," Tiara said, and vomited into the storm.

"Oh, bleep!" Mitch muttered, and followed suit.

Now that the can o' pea was loose, the wind caught it and drove it along like a raft. "I fear Fracto is taking us somewhere," Pewter said.

"It's an inland lake," Astrid said. "Where is there to go?"

"It is now more like an inland sea," Pewter said. "Wherever we are headed, I'm sure we will not like it."

"And we thought there was no Event here," Ease said.

"There wasn't, until you started ragging Fracto," Tiara said, showing a flash of ill temper. Her face was greenish, her hair was a spiky mess, and her plastered body was shivering; there was a suspicion she wasn't feeling well.

"Sorry about that," Ease said. "Can't fix it now."

"You could apologize to Fracto."

"Apologize to an idiotic cloud?"

The rain seemed to intensify even further.

"Yes," Tiara said. "It couldn't hurt."

"Maybe a gourd-style apology?" Ease asked sarcastically.

"Oh, you're impossible!"

"I wonder," Mitch said. "I doubt Fracto would care for Ease's apology, but maybe if a pretty girl did it..."

"Never!" Tiara snapped. She wasn't actually very pretty at the moment.

"A pretty face has been known to pacify savagery," Pewter said.

"Let me try," Astrid said. She adjusted her sopping dress to uncover a bit more cleavage, and adjusted her sodden hair to frame her face appealingly. She leaned out over the rim so that raindrops splatted on her bosom. "Fracto!" she called. "We know we insulted you, and we're sorry."

The rain eased up in her vicinity. The cloud was listening.

Astrid took a deep breath that made both men sway dizzily, on the verge of freaking out. She was really learning to use her body. But could it impress an angry cloud? "We know that we were entirely out of line. We should not have disturbed you in your private retreat. We behaved wretchedly. We beg you to have mercy on us and let us resume our Quest to save Xanth from the pun virus."

The rain diminished further. Fracto was paying attention.

"Oh, that? The Good Magician sent us to find the anti-virus that will stop the pun virus from wiping out all the remaining puns of Xanth."

A mini-gust of wind toyed with her hair.

"Me? Why am I not looking directly at you? I'm actually a basilisk with a deadly gaze and poisonous ambiance. The Good Magician transformed me so

I could assist the Quest. So I am sparing you my gaze."

There was a roll of thunder.

"If you insist," Astrid said. She removed her dark glasses and stared into the cloud.

The rain halted entirely. The cloud dissolved. The sunlight reappeared.

"Thank you!" Astrid called, putting her glasses back on. Then, to the others: "Fracto understands, now that he knows I'm telling the truth. He will let us be now."

"Or maybe your direct gaze blasted him," Ease said.

"No, he's a demon, and he was ready for it. I didn't hurt him. But it showed him that I *am* a basilisk, so he believed the rest."

"Except that we're floating on a trackless sea," Mitch said.

"There has to be a reason for us being here," Pewter said.

A wind came up and blew the can onward.

"I don't trust this," Mitch said. "Maybe Fracto is leaving us alone and maybe he isn't. He may be sending us somewhere we don't want to go."

"An island!" Astrid said. Her sharp vision was the first to spy it.

"That is not necessarily good news," Mitch said.

"Hello." It was a voice from the water.

They looked. There was a mermaid with a pretty face and extremely well formed breasts. "Well hello to you, miss," Ease said, looking down with interest.

"Are you going to the Doctor's island?" the mermaid asked. "If so, I'll like to hitch a ride with you. The storm washed me out to sea and I'm not a good swimmer."

A mermaid not a good swimmer? Kandy was suspicious.

"Welcome aboard, miss!" Ease said, reaching out to her.

"Thank you." She clasped him about the shoulders so that her bosom pressed against him and flipped her tail over the rim. Ease, delighted by the clasp, was clearly thrilled. But the others could see her tail. It was badly misshapen, as if her body had not made up its mind whether to form the tail or legs.

"Let's introduce ourselves," Astrid said, and quickly named the members of the Quest.

"I am Mexine," the mermaid said. "As you can see I am congenitally malformed."

"Not that I noticed," Ease said.

"Neither did I," Mitch said.

The mermaid smiled. "You have to look lower. We merfolk tend to be well endowed, to pad our upper portions so we don't get cold."

"This is true," Pewter said. "Mermaids inhabit rivers and lakes. Merwomen inhabit the sea, and are even better endowed, for similar reason."

The men forced their reluctant eyes down. "Oh."

"Healing elixir doesn't help, because it's not exactly an injury," Mexine said. "I can swim, but not well, and I tire easily. I will surely fall victim to some predator, or die of hunger when the next fish famine occurs. Meanwhile I make do as well as I can. So I thank you for the lift to the island, though I am surprised you are going there."

"Surprised? Why?" Astrid asked. It was apparent that the men were no good for this interview, as their eyes kept straying upward.

"Well, it's the infamous Island of Dr. Moribund. No one goes there voluntarily. They say he does weird experiments on people."

"What kind of experiments?"

"I'm not sure. I can't go on land, of course, so remain in the rocky surf. The Doctor looks but leaves us alone; I think he's more of a leg man." She grimaced, evidently resenting the advantage legged women had with men. "But every so often I see him. He's halfway cute. Yet he has a terrible reputation. Something about putting pieces of people into animals, or vice versa. His assistant, Frank, looks sort of assembled, actually."

The wind continued to blow them toward the island. "I think Fracto has not forgiven us," Mitch muttered. "Astrid's apology persuaded him to let us drift to the island instead of shipwrecking on it, is all."

"I fear you are correct," Pewter said. "Our reckoning is still to come."

"This is good pea paste," the mermaid said. "It was smart of you to come provisioned for the storm."

"Eat all you want," Ease said.

"I will, thank you." Mexine was clearly hungry.

"Are there many of you?" Mitch inquired.

"Merfolk? Yes, we are everywhere, but we generally hide from men, because they get funny ideas."

"We do, when we see girls like you," Mitch agreed. "Do you have talents, as people do?"

"People?" she asked sharply. "We *are* people."

Tiara cut in. "Of course you are. He didn't mean anything disparaging. He's just—distracted." Her eyes flicked to the mermaid's bosom.

"Oh. Of course." Mexine considered. "Actually we do have talents, but they aren't as well defined as those of landlubber people."

Kandy saw Mitch wince. The mermaid was getting back at him.

"Talents," Tiara prompted her.

"Mine is to see the future, vaguely. It's really not much use."

"That depends," Astrid said. "What do you see for us?"

Mexine focused. "We will meet again, and it will change my life. But that doesn't necessarily mean anything. My life changes minute by minute. This encounter changed it, by getting me back to the island and feeding me, which I really appreciate. As for you people, I see danger. But of course just setting foot on the Island is dangerous, so that's no help."

The wind bore them on until the dread island loomed. They had no choice but to land on it.

"I'm sorry you are stranded here," Mexine said. She seemed contrite about her sharpness on the "people" issue. "I really do appreciate the ride; it saved me an awful swim I might not have survived. If there's anything I can do for you in return, go to the shore and call my name and I'll come to you." She hauled herself up and over the rim.

"We will!" Ease called after her.

The man was hopelessly optimistic. What could a lame mermaid do for them on land, however willing she might be? But all Ease could see was her breasts. Kandy found herself increasingly annoyed. There had been a time when *her* breasts had caught the wandering eyes.

The can crashed into a rock at the shore and tilted, dumping them out. They splashed in the water, then made their way to land. Like it or not, they would visit Dr. Moribund.

They dragged themselves out of the surf and stood shivering on the fragmented bit of beach. "I've had more than enough of getting soaked," Mitch said. "The prospects here do not look appealing. I wonder whether it would not be better to cut this short and move on via a sequin."

"I wonder too," Tiara said. "Maybe we should vote on it."

"Yet there is likely to be reason for this event," Pewter said. "I would hesitate to cut it short."

"Vote," Mitch said. "All in favor—"

"Vell now."

They turned, startled. There was what could only be Frank, the doctor's assistant. He did indeed look assembled, with rather different limbs attached to a gross central torso and a child's head.

"We're just passing through," Mitch said.

"No. Dr. M needs bodies. He vill velcome you. You come to mansion."

"Needs bodies?" Tiara asked nervously.

"For exchanges. Come now."

"I think not," Mitch said, and Ease lifted the board menacingly.

"Then me make you come," Frank said. He raised a small wand.

"That's a knockout wand," Pewter said. "Its range will be limited. Scatter!"

But before they could do that, the wand flashed blue. The four people dropped to the ground, unconscious, and Pewter did too, faking it.

Kandy started to manifest, but as Ease fell the board was knocked loose and landed beside him, not touching. Kandy was helpless.

Frank had a wagon. He methodically piled the people on it, two on the bottom, two more crosswise over them, and the last, Pewter, on top. But as he was being lifted, Pewter's hand swung out and caught the board. "We need you," he murmured, speaking to Kandy. "If there is serious risk to the party, I will abate the firewall and change spot reality to fix it. But I prefer not to chance my own extinction without compelling reason."

Kandy understood. Until they learned exactly what the good doctor had in mind for them, it was better to play along.

Frank seemed strong enough, despite his patchwork body. He hauled the laden wagon along a bumpy path up to the grim mansion.

"I don't know of Dr. Moribund," Pewter murmured to Kandy. "But there are precedents in mundane literature. This may not be pleasant."

They were trundled into the mansion, and on into a laboratory where a professorish man was reading a manual. "What did you find, Frankenstein?" he asked. "Heh. Was there anything on the floating can?"

"Who cares about a can?" a female voice demanded. Kandy saw that it came from a wild-haired, wild-eyed woman in an adjacent cell. She was not at all pretty except for her legs, which were marvels of symmetry and tone.

"Me find five bodies, Dr. M," Frank replied.

"Who cares about five bodies?" the woman demanded.

"Wonderful! I am in dire need of bodies. Heh. Put them in the cell and lay them out so I can examine them."

Frank dutifully unloaded the bodies and lay them on the floor of a barred prison cell, face up.

"More meat for the grinder," the woman said. "They'll be sooory!"

"Be quiet, Maddy, or I'll tell Frank to kiss you."

Maddy instantly shut up. Apparently it was an effective threat.

"They're sopping wet," Dr. M said. "This won't do. Heh. Strip them clean so I can see their details."

Frank did that. Soon five bodies lay naked, their clothing piled haphazardly between them. Kandy's board lay between Pewter and Tiara.

"Wonderful!" Dr. M repeated. "These will be ideal. Heh. Put the buxom woman in Slot 1 and the handsome man in Slot 2."

Frank obeyed. Soon Astrid was standing in a waist-high cavity in a counter and Ease was standing in another cavity beside her, both their heads lolling.

"Now we must wake them," Dr. M said. "Heh. the experiment is no good if they don't know what is expected of them. Reverse the wand."

Frank lifted the wand. It flashed red.

The members of the Quest revived. Evidently Dr. M and Frank were immune to the wand's effect. Mitch and Tiara and Pewter sat up, looking confused. Astrid and Ease straightened out, similarly confused.

"Let's give them time to recover," Dr. M said to Frank. "Heh. They need to be fully alert for the finale. We'll go fetch a bite to eat."

"Very vell, boss," Frank agreed.

The two of them departed the laboratory, leaving the captives alone. Was this a ruse, Kandy wondered, or were they simply quite nonchalant about their activities? The captives seemed to be securely confined.

"You'll be sooory!" Maddy repeated, now that there was no threat of a kiss.

The recovering captives looked around. "Where are we?" Mitch asked.

"We are in the laboratory of Doctor Moribund," Pewter said.

"You bet you are, you straggling creeps," Maddy said.

"And who are you?" Pewter asked her.

"I am Maddy, so called because I'm absolutely mad. I hate this place, I hate Doctor Heh, I hate Frankenstein Monster, I hate all of you, and most of all I hate myself." She paused. "But I will hate you slightly less if you pass me that board."

"What do you want with the board?" Pewter asked.

"I want it to knock my head until my crazy brains fall out my ears and I'll be dead. Then at last I'll be at peace."

"Perhaps some healing elixir would help you."

"Grossly obese fortune! Doctor poop-for-brains already tried that on me. It didn't work, because crazy is my fundamental nature. Nothing can give me peace except death, and that is what I shall seek the moment I get out of this cell." She grabbed the metal bars and rattled them.

"How did you get here?" Pewter asked. "You don't seem to be much use to Dr. Moribund."

"So-called friends shipped me here," Maddy said. "Since nothing else worked, they thought maybe Dr. Crazy Experiment could fix me. But he's not into mind exchanges, just physical ones."

"Physical exchanges?"

"Didn't you see Frank? He's assembled from all the left-over parts of prior experiments. An arm here, a foot there."

"How is it you were not recruited for one of those exchanges?"

Maddy paused. "Now that I don't know. I'm sure nothing worth salvaging."

"I suspect he likes your legs," Pewter said. "I saw him look at them."

So had Kandy, now that she thought about it. While Frank was undressing the bodies, Dr. M was gazing not at them but at Maddy's legs. That was curious.

"Well, if he ever got close to me, I'd wrap them around his head and crack it wide open. Then I'd bite off his nose and stuff it in the crack."

"That might account for his caution," Pewter agreed.

"Now will you pass me that board?"

"To literally beat out your brains? I think not. A member of our party is adverse to displays of that nature."

"I certainly am," Tiara said. "And I think the board wouldn't like it either."

Kandy agreed emphatically.

"Cretin! Crapface! Sadist!"

Pewter ignored her, as Dr. M and Frank had before. "We seem to be in a situation," he said to the others.

"How can we get out of it?" Mitch demanded, pulling his eyes away from Maddy's legs.

"It occurs to me that Dr. Moribund does not realize the nature of either Astrid or the board," Pewter said. "Would you be able to throw it accurately?"

Mitch nodded, beginning to understand. "The good Doctor it seems is not turned on by unconscious legs, but can be quite taken with animate ones."

"Just let him try!" Maddy said. "I'll jam my foot down his gullet!"

But Kandy knew they were not talking about Maddy's legs. Could it actually work?

"I believe I could stun the Doctor," Astrid said from her pedestal. "But I'm not sure about Frank, whose head seems to be underage. We could be caught locked into our present confinement with no one to free us."

"I am thinking of Kandy," Pewter said, confirming Kandy's suspicion.

"Who?" Ease asked.

"A mutual acquaintance. Don't be concerned."

Astrid nodded. "She does have legs."

The Doctor and Frank returned. The show was about to begin.

"Your attention, please, subjects," Dr. M said. "I am Doctor Moribund and this is my assistant Frankenstein Monster. Heh. You may call us M and Frank. Do you understand me?"

Astrid was fast on the uptake. "All too well," she said. "What mischief are you up to, Dr. M?"

"Ah, you're a saucy one! Heh. You are about to have the honor to be part of my first portion gender exchange. Do you understand?"

"No. It sounds like gibberish to me."

Dr. M smiled. Kandy realized that he really liked having an audience beyond the dull Frank. He was surely a lonely man. "You will note that you are a healthy woman ensconced beside a healthy man. That is important, because unhealthy people might not survive the exchange well."

"What exchange?"

"Ah, that is the sheer beauty of it. Heh. The mechanism you are in is the exchanger. When I pull the switch, what is in the left compartment will be exchanged with what is in the right compartment."

Astrid looked down. "All that's in this compartment is my lower half."

"And my lower half is in mine," Ease said.

Then both paused. "Oh, no!" Astrid said.

"It will be my finest experiment yet," Dr. M said enthusiastically. "The top of a woman merged with the bottom of a man, and vice versa. You must both be sure to tell me in detail how you feel. I am so glad that you volunteered for this remarkable mergence."

"There is something you don't know," Astrid said. "I am not human. My bottom half would kill my friend, and my top half would kill his bottom half, and we both would surely die."

The Doctor squinted at her. "You certainly look human to me."

"I am a transformed basilisk. If you doubt, meet my gaze." Astrid removed her dark glasses, which had clung to her despite the loss of her clothing.

"I do doubt," Dr. M said. "I will meet your challenge." He stared into her face. And froze. "Oh, my!"

"Be glad that I have closed one eye," Astrid said. "So that you are not dead. Now have Frank release us."

But the canny Doctor fought back. He put his hands over his face, blocking off the basilisk glare. "Don't do it, Frank! All we need to do is switch out this female for the other and the experiment can continue."

"No!" Tiara cried.

Meanwhile, during the distraction, Mitch picked up the board and went to the bars. "Ease!" he called, hefting the board. When he had Ease's attention, he threw it, carefully, between the bars. It sailed up and right to Ease, who caught it with one hand.

"Thanks," Ease said. "Now if I can just bash my way out of this box." He swung the board at the metal counter.

He had the wrong idea. Kandy sent a thought that put him to sleep. She transformed, becoming her full naked self. She tucked one arm behind Ease's arm, sat on the counter facing the Doctor, crossed her legs, and called out to him. "Dr. Moribund!"

"Now isn't that something!" Maddy exclaimed. "Or am I even crazier than I thought I was?"

But the Doctor's eyes were covered. He didn't realize there was something new to look at. Meanwhile Frank's hand was on the switch, awaiting his master's order.

Kandy oriented on Frank. "Frank! Look at me."

Frank obeyed the voice of command, as he normally did. "Gee, you're pretty!" But his gaze did not linger.

Pretty, but not pretty enough, it seemed. His head was too young to get the full impact of her nudity, even with her legs crossed in his direction.

Then Tiara called. "Kandy! Catch!" she threw a wadded up something.

Kandy caught it. It turned out to be Tiara's wet bra and panties, which she had removed under her dress. They would not have carried across the chamber had they not been water-logged.

"Thank you!" Kandy quickly put them on. They were clammy, and tight on her, because her figure was more ample than Tiara's. But comfort was not the point.

Now, more effectively armed, or bodied, Kandy called out again. "Frank!"

Frank looked again. Kandy recrossed her legs to flash her panties, and inhaled. If he was even close to teenagism...

"Vov!" Frank's eyes were glued to her torso. "Me never see that before."

Vov? Then she remembered his problem pronouncing W. He was saying Wow.

"Frank, release these two from the exchanger," Kandy commanded, continuing to breathe deeply.

Frank, now dazzled by underwear, stepped forward.

"What's going on?" Dr. M demanded, uncovering his eyes. But Astrid immediately glared at him with one eye, forcing him back.

Under Kandy's direction, Frank unlatched side panels and freed Astrid and Ease. Then he opened the cell gates, except for Maddy's. Astrid quickly recovered her dress, while Mitch went to dress Ease, who was still asleep. Then they gathered around Ease, and Astrid snapped her fingers.

Ease woke. "Huh? What happened?"

"It's a complicated story," Pewter said. "We are moving on before things complicate further."

Frank, freed from the vision of Kandy's underwear, and without the Doctor's direction, stood dazed.

Kandy, as the board, lay on the floor. Ease picked it up. "What's this on my board?"

For Tiara's bra and panties were hanging loosely on it. She quickly went to recover them. "Must've gotten tangled up together when they stripped our clothing," she said, quickly sliding them on under her dress.

Tiara squatted to remove a sequin from Astrid's dress, while Astrid continued to hold the Doctor off. But when she tried to replace it, it would not attach. She tried several times, but it determinedly balked.

"What are you idiots doing now?" Maddy demanded from her cell.

"It won't go," Tiara said, perplexed.

"I'll do it," Pewter said. He took the sequin and tried. And failed. "This is magically resisting," he said, surprised. "I could change its attitude, but—"

"Don't risk it," Astrid said. "This simply means that we are not finished here. We have not done or learned what we came to the Event to do."

"So it seems," Pewter agreed.

"But what could it be?" Mitch asked. "We face a dire threat, and need to escape it."

"You morons can't figure out your own mission," Maddy called.

Pewter looked at her. "I wonder."

Astrid nodded. "Once we go, Dr. M will continue messing up people. We should stop that."

"How?" Mitch asked. "He won't behave without someone to keep constant tabs on him."

"What he needs is a wife," Tiara said.

"True. But there is no one." Then he looked at her. "Are you thinking what I'm thinking?"

"Mexine. She thinks he's cute."

"With Maddy's legs, which he already likes," Mitch agreed.

"You characters sound as if you're plotting something truly devious," Maddy called almost admiringly.

"We are," Mitch agreed. "And you are part of it."

"Me!"

Mitch walked to stand just outside her cell. "We are going to give you the chance to commit suicide, if that's what you really want."

"Of course that's what I want, imbecile! I have nothing to live for."

"Then we will put you in Dr. M's machine, and Mexine Mermaid in the other. She has a broken tail and can't swim well, a horror for a mermaid. She will get your legs, you will get her tail. She'll take over Dr. M, keeping him fascinated with your legs, and Frank will give you a wagon ride to the sea, where you will be free to drown yourself if you still feel that way. Okay?"

"Okay!" she agreed in a flash.

"Dr. M," Astrid said. "We propose to assemble a good wife for you. She will have a nice personality, a splendid bosom, and Maddy's legs. Are you amenable?" She narrowed her gaze to a squint so that he could answer.

"A wife? No woman wants me."

"This one might. She thinks you're cute."

"Maddy's legs," he repeated thoughtfully.

Maddy lifted a lovely bare leg toward him. "I won't be needing them anymore. You want them, you got them."

"I—want them," he said. "But I don't want you to bite my nose off."

"Frank, take your wagon and fetch Mexine Mermaid here," Mitch said.

"She no like me," he protested.

"I'll go with you," Mitch said. "I will explain to her."

Frank and Mitch departed with the wagon, while Astrid continued to watch the Doctor, just in case.

"Ah, death," Maddy said. "I feel your glorious approach."

Before long the wagon returned, bearing the mermaid. "Is this true?" she asked them. "I can have legs?"

"These legs, doll," Maddy said, flexing them.

"But there's a price," Mitch reminded her. "You'll have to marry Dr. Moribund."

Mexine looked at the Doctor. "I could handle him, if I had legs."

"Then let's get on it."

With Frank's assistance they put the woman and the mermaid in the two compartments. Then Frank pulled the switch. Nothing happened.

"Was it all a bluff?" Astrid asked. "I was terrified."

Frank opened the panels. There was Maddy with a malformed tail. And there was Mexine with phenomenal legs. "Oooo!" she exclaimed, loving them.

Then she walked somewhat unsteadily across to the Doctor and kissed him. Little hearts flew up. "Will you marry me?"

"Oh, yes," he breathed. "Heh."

"But you're not going to do any more nasty experiments."

He hesitated. She lifted a knee, showing off a fine thigh. "Yes dear," he agreed quickly.

It was plain that Mexine had things under control. She knew about men and women; it was land she had to get used to.

Mitch turned to Frank. "Pick Miss Maddy up and put her on the wagon," he said. "Take her down to the sea and let her go."

Frank just stood there, staring at Maddy.

"What's the matter, jerk?" she asked. "Can't stand to let me go?"

"Me—me vant to kiss you," he said. "But me don't know hov."

"Hov" meant "how," Kandy thought.

Maddy was astonished. "You find me attractive? I'm nothing but misshapen leftovers with a bad attitude!"

"Yeah," he agreed blissfully. "Just like me."

"And so is Frank," Tiara said, catching on. "To him, you are beautiful."

"I'll be bleeped," Maddy said. "Well, then, let's try it. I've got nothing better to do at the moment. Come here, Frankenstein."

Frank went to her where she remained propped in the exchange compartment. She caught his head in her hands and pulled him in for a solid kiss. Little hearts flew up.

"I'll be bleeped," Mitch echoed. "They're a match."

"I think I'll postpone suicide for a while," Maddy said. "No one ever liked me before, except for maybe my legs." She shot a briefly venomous glance at the Doctor. "And I don't have those any more. So I guess it's real." She faced Frank again. "Understand, I've got a sharp tongue." She stuck it out momentarily so he could see the point on it. "You're going to have to keep me in a tub of water or something, or the lake, except when we're—" She broke off, for Frank was blushing. He understood her well enough.

"I think now we can replace that sequin," Mitch said.

"One more moment," Pewter said. "Mexine, you were correct about our interacting again, and I think it is changing your life more significantly than you anticipated. Your insight into the future facilitated your cooperation with us, which required considerable trust. Your talent may seem vague, but it is genuine. Do you see anything else in our future?"

The former mermaid focused, then nodded. "One of you will be in deadly danger, and another will make a significant sacrifice to save her. But it will end well, I think, maybe."

"Thank you, Mexine." Pewter turned to the others. "That is our warning. We must be prepared for danger and sacrifice."

"As usual," Mitch muttered.

Then Tiara took the sequin and pinned it to Astrid's dress.

CHAPTER 15:

SACRIFICE

They were standing at the brink of a monstrous gulf. "This would be the Gap Chasm," Pewter said. "For centuries it was forgotten, because of a powerful forget spell, but now it is known and in my data bank. It is approximately one mundane mile deep and from three to ten miles across. The dread six legged Gap Dragon dwells in it, steaming prey and consuming it, so we would not care to descend into it." The machine inspected the area closely. "This would be where the invisible bridge crosses it. Our appearance here can hardly be coincidental; we are meant to cross on that bridge. But we must be careful, because it is also a one way bridge."

"One way?" Tiara asked.

"It is invisible but solid for a single passage only," Pewter explained. "It dematerializes behind the last member of a party. So once we start across, we must continue; there will be no turning back."

"This makes me nervous," Mitch said.

"Me too," Tiara said. "Do we really have to tackle it now? All I want is a chance to rest and dry out thoroughly, and hold someone close for a few hours."

"Oh, yes," Mitch breathed.

Ease and Astrid exchanged a glance, both clearly wishing they could do the same, but knowing they couldn't. Kandy understood completely. She would have let them do it, had it been possible, knowing that Astrid did not have any long-term designs on Ease. They simply needed a pleasant break.

"Our schedule is our own," Pewter said. "We can explore the jungle opposite the chasm, and perhaps find a suitable place to stay the night."

But the jungle was densely forbidding. "I'll go first," Astrid said. She led the way between the trees, peering around and sniffing the air. There turned out to be a winding avenue, not quite aspiring to the status of a path. They followed her, single file.

The avenue widened, becoming a full aisle. But Astrid halted. "Not this one."

"But it's pleasant," Ease protested. "We can follow it readily."

"It leads to a tangle tree. I can smell it."

Both Ease and Mitch froze in place, recognizing the danger. But Tiara, who has spent much of her life in an isolated tower, didn't. "What is a tangle tree? Something that messes up hair?"

Astrid smiled somewhat grimly. "Perhaps I should show you."

"Caution," Pewter said.

"I can handle a tangler," she reminded him. "But do stay clear." She touched her dark glasses.

Astrid and Tiara followed the nice path, and the others followed at a moderately reasonable distance. It led to handsome tree with hanging green tentacles instead of branches with leaves. The tentacles fell to either side, allowing admittance to a cozy glenlet beside the gnarled trunk of the tree. There were fresh red applets, twin yellow pairs, and other luscious looking fruits on the ground, there for the eating.

"Oh, that's lovely!" Tiara said. "A perfect place to relax! I'm so tired and hungry!"

As were they all, Kandy thought, except for herself. The last meal they had had had been pea mash, and they had not gorged on that.

"Appearances can be deceptive," Astrid said. "Stand back, and I will walk under the tangle tree." She removed her glasses and tucked them into a pocket, careful not to look at Tiara.

Tiara stood back, watching curiously, while Astrid walked to the trunk. She picked up one of the pairs.

And the tentacles came to life. They wrapped around Astrid, hauling her into the air. The trunk cracked open a huge wooden mouth with splinter teeth.

Tiara screamed and fell back. Mitch caught her, reassuringly. "Just watch," he said. "She knows what's she's doing."

Astrid glared around. Wherever her gaze touched, the green tentacles withered and blistered. The ones holding her were reddening where they touched her flesh. When she looked at the trunk, the wood scorched.

The tangle tree was not stupid. It immediately dropped her and whipped its tentacles clear. It knew a basilisk when it encountered one. It wanted no part of her, literally.

Kandy had tended to forget exactly how deadly Astrid was, because of their friendship and the basilisk's normal niceness. How would she ever find a man to love her?

Astrid stood for a moment beside the trunk. "Nothing personal, Tangler," she said. "It is just a demonstration for my friend. No hard feelings?"

The tentacles shivered. Then one dropped to the ground, picked up the remaining pair, and proffered it to her.

Astrid smiled as she replaced her glasses. "Why thank you," she said, accepting it. "I will be on my way now. With luck we shall not meet again." She walked away. Not a tentacle moved to stop her.

She rejoined the others and presented the second pair to Tiara. It was of course a pear-shaped fruit, ripe and tasty. "Courtesy of the tangle tree, who is happy to see us on our way."

"Now I understand," Tiara said. She waved nervously to the tree. "Thank you, Tangle Tree," she called.

Several tentacles twitched in response.

"Tangle trees are best avoided," Mitch said.

"Yes," Tiara agreed, shuddering. "I won't forget."

They backtracked, the girls eating the juicy pairs. Astrid found another almost-path, which led to a small abandoned cemetery. Several plants grew on the graves, their vines curling around the weathered headstones. It was rather peaceful and pretty, in its unkempt way. Kandy wondered who had died there, and been forgotten.

"We'll bypass this too," Astrid said. The others were glad to agree.

The jungle thinned into a mixed forest, where trees, brush, turf and rocks had been mixed together like a tossed salad. Then they came to a goblin mound. The goblins were busy going about their business. They were about half normal human height, but made up for it in numbers.

They halted. "Now that is odd," Pewter said. "The goblins should have been harassing us long since. How could we just walk up to their mound unchallenged?"

"I will inquire," Astrid said. Again the others waited while she went ahead. Yet again Kandy appreciated the woman's readiness to risk herself for the benefit of the Quest, though of course for her the risk was small.

Astrid approached a goblin woman who was scrubbing laundry in a tub. Like most female goblins she was lovely, while the males were ugly, with big heads, big feet, and nasty expressions. Their personalities, Kandy knew, matched their appearance: men were brutes, woman were nice. How goblins ever cooperated long enough to make families was a mystery.

"Excuse me," Astrid said. Kandy could hear her clearly enough. "I am a member of a party passing by in peace. We don't understand why we are being ignored."

The gobliness looked up. "It is your good fortune to happen by on election day. My brutish husband is running for chief of the Good Riddance Goblins and can't be bothered by routine activities such as capturing, cooking, and eating passing strangers."

"That is good to know," Astrid said. "We shall try to be gone before the election ends. I am Astrid Basilisk, intending no harm to you. I wonder whether we might make a deal for some food and a place to rest?"

"That is doubtful," the woman said, glancing around at the working goblins. "I am Glinda Goblin. I was expecting you." She smiled briefly. "I will have my daughter Glenna sneak you some food, but I think that is all we can safely do at present."

So it had not been sheer coincidence that put her out here at this time, Kandy realized. But why had she expected them, when they themselves had not known they were coming here?

"We prefer to earn our keep," Astrid said. "What can we do in return for the food?"

Glinda looked up, not quite meeting Astrid's gaze. "You're a basilisk? There might be something. Glenna has a little herb garden she very much values, but she is missing one rare plant, and I won't let her go into the jungle alone to look for it. It is dangerous out there."

Astrid nodded understandingly. "What is it?"

"It is called Grave Expectations. One sniff of its bloom and you're dead. I don't know why she wants such a nasty plant, but she does."

"I am familiar with it," Astrid said. "In fact I know where one is. But I must caution you that despite its deadliness, this is a delicate plant. If we transplant it to your child's garden it will require a poisonous ambiance for several hours until it safely roots. I would have to stay with it for that period."

"Do that, and you will have my eternal gratitude," Glinda said. "I so much want my little girl to be happy, and happiness is not common among goblins. I see that my talent guided me correctly. Take her to the plant."

"You would trust me with your child? Remember, I'm a—"

"I am a fair judge of character."

Astrid looked gratified. "Let me meet your child."

Glinda put two fingers to her mouth and made a piercing whistle. Soon a cute little girl goblet appeared. "Yes, mother dear?" she asked sweetly.

"Hide some good food in your knapsack and go with these folk," Glinda said. "This is Astrid. She knows where your flower grows."

"Oooo!" Glenna exclaimed, clapping her hands gleefully. She ran back into the mound.

"Oh, I envy you." Astrid said.

"You want a human child?"

"Yes, challenging as that may be. I am tired of skulking under rocks and dealing death in my natural form."

"I wish you well," Glinda said. It was plain she did not believe Astrid would be able to get a human child.

Glenna returned, wearing her backpack. "This way," Astrid said. "I can't take your hand, but stay reasonably close."

"Why not?"

"Because I am a basilisk. My touch would poison you."

"Oh. Cool."

Glinda smiled obscurely as she focused on her washing.

Astrid led Glenna back to the others. "We must return to the graveyard."

They did not question this. They walked back the way they had come, Glenna skipping along beside them.

"Mommy says this food's for you," the child said, taking off her knapsack. It turned out to be filled with cheese & jelly sandwiches, evidently Glenna's favorite. They thanked her and ate them with gusto.

They came to the grave yard. "Oooo!" Glenna cried, spying the twining plants. She recognized the one she wanted.

Astrid located a pot pie plant and harvested a small metal pot. Then she used her hands to dig out a little Grave Expectations plant and put it in the pot. It seemed a bit unhappy, so she breathed on it and it perked up. Basilisks and grave plants had a long association, and neither hurt the other.

They accompanied Glenna back to the goblin mound. A ferociously ugly goblin came out to meet them. "Election's over," he announced. "I won. We'll bury the losers later. Now how would you intruders like to be cooked?"

"Oh, Daddy," Glenna said. "You can't eat these folk. They're my friends."

The male swelled up like an inflating balloon. "Yeah, well—"

Glinda came over. "Stifle it, Glower," she snapped. "I told them they could come. They're helping Glenna with her garden."

Glower glowered. He was good at it. "Yeah? Well—"

"And one of them's a basilisk."

"I don't believe it."

Astrid held the pot in one hand and lifted her glasses with the other. She delivered a glancing glance.

Glower turned green around the edges. "Uh, yeah," he said, backing off.

"This way," Glinda said, leading them around the mound to a sheltered area beyond.

There was the little garden. Kandy verified that it was indeed a rare one. She saw an all-purpose flower she knew was harvested to make fruit, grain, greens, and the roots made boot rear. There was an E S Pea that would produce mind-reading vegetables, and a G Pea S that would one day give directions. Also a Pup-Pea that would one day make a pet. An Al-Pine and a Su-Pine tree. Several Butter Fingers growing around the edge.

"Is that an Egg Plant?" Pewter asked, surprised.

"Yes!" Glenna said proudly. "There are very few of those."

"What's unusual about an egg plant?" Ease asked. "They're all around. We love the eggs."

"This is not an egg plant," Pewter explained. "It's an Egg Plant. It's like the difference between a demon and a Demon. Its eggs will hatch into a number of different creatures, including even a harpy without a mother. There are only three or four of those plants in all Xanth." He looked at the child. "How did you obtain such a rare specimen?"

"It's my talent," Glenna said proudly. "I can find the rarest type of an ordinary thing."

"I believe it," Pewter said. "You are a remarkable child who will no doubt grow up to be an extraordinary adult."

"That's what mommy says. That's why she encourages me. Her talent is knowing who can help with something, and when to expect that person."

That explained a lot, Kandy thought.

And now the garden also had a Grave Expectations plant, that would surely protect it and the goblin mound when it matured. Astrid made a hole in the ground where the child indicated and carefully placed the plant there, breathing on it again. "Remember, I must be close to it for several hours," she said. "Overnight would be better. Once it roots firmly it will make its own ambiance."

"Stay," Glinda said. "All of you. The men will not bother you." She shot a glance toward Glower that was reminiscent of Astrid's bare-eyed look. No, the new chief would not be bothering them. He might be ugly, fierce, and tough, but he knew better than to really annoy either his wife or his child.

Seeing the way of it, and buoyed by his political victory, Glower accepted the situation and became almost affable. He brought a keg of hard cider, really hard cider, and they broke off chunks of it to chew. Soon the men and Tiara were happily drunk.

But Pewter and Astrid were not. There would be no funny business, or even moderately humorous business, during the night. Not that anyone was accusing anyone of any such intention. The experience at PLO Village had made them wary.

"In the old days we dropped travelers into the Chasm just to hear them scream," Glower said. "But then we realized that this was a waste of perfectly good food, so we had to stop. Some folk didn't want to stop, and unrest was brewing, so the chief of that time, Goodrid Goblin, made a deal with three human Magicians to change things without violence."

"How'd they do that?" Ease asked, interested. "I mean, I thought goblins didn't approve of nonviolence." He bit off another chunk of cider.

"He was a cunning one," Glower said. "Sometimes cunning is almost as good as violence. First he had to buy the favor of the Magicians. Fortunately our womenfolk can be persuasive. That's how Glinda and Glenna come by their magic talents: there's a Magician in their ancestry."

"Of course," Tiara said, aware how a lovely gobliness could be persuasive with the help of an accommodation spell.

"The first Magician sent the steamer dragon to clean out the orcs," Glower continued. "But that didn't work too well, because then it was the dragon who ate the travelers, instead of the orcs. Meat was still being wasted. The second Magician changed the name of the chasm from Orc to Gap. That still didn't do it; the gulf was just too tempting. So the third Magician invoked the Forget Spell. That did it. After that no one wanted to admit that they had ever had an Orc Chasm."

Mitch and Ease laughed. Tiara blushed. The goblin chief had had his little joke.

Glinda hustled Glenna off to bed, and the others settled down near the garden. Astrid lay down next to the Grave plant and slept. This was as good a place to spend the night as any, as no one would be bothering them.

In the morning Pewter tried to educate Glower about the coming menace of the pun virus. "Many of the plants of this garden, and the things you harvest and use, like shoe trees, are likely to be eradicated by the virus. You need to take what precautions you can to store food for the famine."

"Ah, we're too busy for that," Glower said.

"Not necessarily," Glinda said. "I have heard of this pun virus. Glenna has not worked so hard to plant her garden only to have it wiped out. How can we protect it?"

"We are on a Quest to locate the antidote to the virus," Pewter said. "But we do not know where it is. We have been wandering, searching for hints."

"An antidote," she said thoughtfully. "Could the answer lie in the science of chemistry?"

"You believe in science?" Pewter asked, startled.

"It's a form of magic, less reliable but useful in its place. But mainly, we know where there is a chemistree, that fruits potion bottles. The Random Factor messed with it a while back, so now they are random potions, but with correct identification they can be used. For example, if a love potion is mixed with a hate elixir, they will neutralize each other and the result is pure neutral water."

"There is a reference in my data bank. But its location is unknown."

"Unadvertised," Glinda said, smiling. "I suspect it is one of the secret resources of the Good Magician. But for this purpose, it might be better to use it. Do you think a mixture of those potions would stop the virus?"

"They might," Pewter said. "It would not be the same as the anti-virus, but it might protect your garden. A mixture of healing elixir and firewater might mess up the virus." He looked at the others.

"That's a valuable garden," Mitch said. "Saving it might be our purpose in this Event."

"And it might mean we would not have to cross the Gap Chasm," Tiara said.

"The tree is too big to move here," Glinda said. "But we can harvest the bottles, and we might find seeds."

"Let's do it," Ease said.

"Glenna and I will show you the way," Glinda said.

"But dear—" Glower protested.

"You have your chief-ship to consolidate," Glinda said firmly. "This will get us out of your way for a day."

Glower considered, recognizing the convenience of that, and let it be.

They set off, following the woman and the girl. The woman was the size of a human girl, and the girl was half that, but they were sturdy and knew where they were going. It seemed that the chemistree was not far distant.

"And here it is," Glinda said with a flourish.

They gazed at the tree. It looked like an ordinary fur, with holiday decorations. The glossy pendants were little colored bottles of potions.

"We need to ascertain whether the colors are consistent," Pewter said. "That is, does red mean love and white mean lethe, or do they vary? I suspect we shall need to check every bottle as we harvest it."

"I will open and sniff; you classify and record," Astrid said.

The two of them walked to the tree.

"That leaves the rest of us," Mitch said. "This promises to be a tedious wait. We can make camp."

"There is a very nice campsite close by," Glinda said. "But for some reason no one uses it."

"Then we'll be the first," Ease said. "Where is it?"

"This way." Glinda walked around the chemistree, Ease, Mitch, and Tiara following. Kandy realized with a start that the men were eying the gobliness' shapely little form from behind. Every time she thought she was used to the superficiality of men, there was something else.

"Here," Glinda said. "It is even marked. The Grong Grong." Indeed, there was a sign saying GRONG GRONG.

"What does that mean, Mommy?" Glenna asked.

"We don't know, dear. Folklore has it that a passing visitor from Mundania, an Austra-Alien, named it. He did not stay long enough to explain."

"This seems ideal," Mitch said. "It is close, there's a shelter, a river, and pie trees. What more could we ask?"

"We could ask why no one uses it," Tiara said.

"They probably just don't know of it," Ease said. "If the tree is secret, maybe this campsite it secret too."

"Perhaps," Glinda said. "But probably it is best to be careful. Stay close to me, Glenna."

"Awww," the child said.

Ease went to a fruit tree. "Cherries," he said, picking several bright red ones.

"Cherry bombs!" Glenna said, delighted.

Ease paused with a cherry at his mouth. He had been about to bite into it. He looked at it more carefully. Then he threw it away. It exploded when it hit the ground, making a puffball of fiery smoke.

"And pineapples!" Glenna said, delighted again. Sure enough, several were growing there, far more explosive than the cherry bombs.

"I am beginning to appreciate why this campsite is not more popular," Mitch said grimly.

"But the rest looks good," Ease said, shrugging off his close call with the cherry. "Let's check out the shelter."

They went to the pavilion. It offered nice refuge from the elements, and there were piles of hay to rest on. Ease plumped down on a pile. "This is great."

Something stirred in the hay. Shapes boiled out of it. Kandy was alarmed.

"Nickelpedes!" Glenna exclaimed, delighted a third time.

Ease launched out of the hay, shedding the vicious insects, which were already tangling with his pants, trying to gouge out nickel sized chunks of flesh. He grabbed the board and whacked himself repeatedly, smashing more bugs.

Tiara shuddered. "If I had sat there—"

"Maybe we had better look elsewhere," Mitch said.

"Let's check the river," Ease said determinedly.

They went to the passing river, which obligingly meandered close. Ease dipped a cupped hand into the water to fetch out water to drink.

"Ow!" For two small fish were biting his fingers.

"Piranha fish!" Glenna cried, delighted once more.

"That does it," Ease said. "This is a bad camping place."

"A very bad camping place," Tiara agreed with another shudder.

"Now I remember," Glinda said. "That's what Grong Grong means."

"It's not an invitation but a warning," Mitch said. "That's why others avoid it."

"We shall vacate the premises," Glinda said. "I'm sorry I suggested it. I didn't remember. I should have."

There was a pie tree growing beside the river, laden with ripe pies. Ease eyed them, then shook his head, deciding not to risk it.

They started to walk back out of it. "Wait," Glenna said. "There's something in the grass."

"It's just a little lizard," Ease said.

"No. It's a salamander."

"Uh-oh," Mitch said.

The salamander scooted across the path in front of them. Fire blazed in its trail. It paused a moment as if searching, then started spreading toward them.

They backed up, but the river was close by. They were caught between the fire and the water.

"Why does this smell like a trap?" Ease asked.

"The fire's not big yet," Mitch said. "Use your board to beat out a section so we can cross it."

Ease did that, smashing the flat of the board down on the blaze. Kandy was concerned, but did manage to beat the fire out before it burned her wood. They made a gap and they quickly stepped through it.

"I love my board," Ease said. "I once longed for a sword, but really this is better. More versatile."

Kandy saw Mitch and Tiara exchange a quick glance. Ease did not know the half of it.

They crossed a cleared court they had not noticed before. At one end was a pole supporting a metal rim. Below it was a big ball. Ease picked up the ball and bounced it on the ground.

Suddenly a huge dog ran out on the court, growling. He was the size of a small horse. Surprised, Ease hurled the ball at him. The dog caught the ball on his nose, flipped his head, and sent it sailing up in a high arc. It passed through the hoop with a swish. Satisfied, the dog departed.

"Big puppy," Glenna said, pleased.

Mitch grimaced. "The Hound of the Basketballs," he said. "You messed with his ball."

Glenna glanced at the sky. "Dragons," she said.

"And we can be pretty sure they are more mischief," Mitch said. "We need to hide."

They hurried to the side where there was a cluster of cacti. "Careful," Glinda said. "I recognize that type. Needle cactus."

"I have heard of it," Mitch said. "We don't want to get close."

But they were hemmed in by the fire, which had reversed course to follow them, the basketball court, and the cactus. Only the spot where they stood seemed safe—until the dragons arrived.

"I can help, maybe," Glenna said.

"Stay out of it," Glinda snapped protectively.

"Awww." Then the child brightened. "But maybe you could do it, Ease. Mommy can't tell you no."

"Do what?" Ease asked, eying the approaching dragons.

"Get the ball. Throw it at a cactus. Duck. Everybody duck."

Ease considered, then nodded. He fetched the ball. The Hound came out again, pursuing the ball as the first dragon swooped in for a strafing run.

"Duck!" Ease cried, and hurled the ball at the cactus. The Hound bounded after it. The ball struck the cactus as the five of them dropped to the ground.

The cactus, enraged, fired off a volley of needles. They passed over the people, but caught the Hound in the rump and the dragon on the snoot. They also popped the ball, which exploded into tatters. The Hound whirled to bite his own needled rear, and the dragon's stifled fire shot out of its nose, ears, and tail.

It was hard to see the detail from the ground, but Kandy saw enough to get a notion. The Hound thought the dragon had done it, and the dragon thought the Hound had done it. They pounced on each other, chomping tails.

"Now we flee," Glenna said. "The cactus is out of quills."

They scrambled up and charged past the cactus. It quivered, but had no more ammunition. They managed to escape the Grong Grong at last.

"That was fun," Glenna said. Her mother rolled her eyes.

They made their way back to the chemistree. Pewter and Astrid were concluding their survey of potions, and had a bag of bottles. "We can't be sure these will be effective," Pewter said. "But if you make a channel around the garden and pour some of each into it, the mixture may discourage the virus."

"And we found a chemistree seed," Astrid said, presenting it to Glenna.

"Oooo, cool!"

"It is good that the rest of you got to relax while we worked," Pewter said.
No one commented.

"I think we don't want to linger near Grong Grong at night," Glinda said.

"We don't!" Tiara agreed.

They returned to the mound by evening. "You will stay the night again," Glinda said. "Our hospitality may not be much, but I think it is better than the Grong Grong."

"You were there?" Glower asked. "I thought no one stayed there."

"Daddy, it was great!" Glenna said. "There was this big dog, and a dragon, and nickelpedes and piranha fish and a salamander and a needle cactus! And we got potions to maybe protect the garden, and a seed from the chemistree. Maybe I'll get real science in my garden!"

"That does sound like fun," Glower agreed. It was clear that his daughter took after him, and he was proud of that.

"So is our business in this Event done?" Pewter asked.

"I will try a sequin," Tiara said. She did, but it wouldn't take. "No, not yet."

Mitch sighed. "So it seems we must brave the Chasm after all."

In the morning they trekked back to the Gap Chasm. It looked as formidable as before, a yawning gulf they would have to cross without apparent support.

Tiara was distinctly anxious. "I wonder if anything down there will look up and see under our skirts."

"We've all been naked more than once," Mitch reminded her.

"That's not the same. Sneak peeks are worse than nudity."

Actually, Kandy knew, Tiara was just nervous about venturing out into seeming space unprotected. Kandy would have felt the same way, before she became an almost invulnerable board.

"Worse," Astrid said. "I see a cloud on the horizon, coming this way, and it looks like Fracto."

"How could he know we would be here?" Mitch asked.

"He's a demon," Pewter said. "He knows things. Obviously he feels there remains a score to settle."

"That could be the danger Mexine predicted," Tiara said. "If we have to cross, we should do it quickly, before the cloud arrives."

"Unless it is better to wait until he passes," Mitch said. "Maybe he'll make such a deluge that it will fill the Chasm and we can sail across." He smiled, hinting that this was possibly humor.

There was a sound behind them. "That is the growl of a hungry dragon," Pewter said. "Coming this way. It will not be safe here for long enough."

"The sequins are putting us through their paces," Mitch said. "So it seems we'd better cross now. How do we find the bridge?"

"We feel for it," Pewter said. He walked along the brink of the gulf, touching the edge with his toe. "Here." He stepped out over the edge.

The others stared. Pewter was walking in mid air. The bridge was truly invisible.

"So be it," Mitch said, following. He, too, stood seemingly unsupported. "Ah, there's a hand rail. That helps."

"Yes," Pewter said. "The bridge is safe, provided there is not an external problem."

Tiara came next. The slight wind tugged at her dress, as if to make sure something below could see under it. "This is weird."

Ease stepped out. "But fun."

Finally Astrid followed. Her dress also flexed in the breeze, flashing her legs. "Just so long as a sequin doesn't fall off."

"Don't scare us!" Mitch said.

They moved along, a procession of five people in seeming space. The cloud rumbled angrily; Fracto saw them, and knew he would not be able to reach them before they completed their crossing.

"Something else," Astrid said. "Dragons. Three of them, approaching swiftly."

"Oh, no!" Mitch said. "Fracto enlisted help!"

"I will deal with them," Astrid said, removing her dark glasses. "Keep moving."

The dragons rapidly loomed larger, definitely orienting on the exposed party. "Can you tell what type they are?" Mitch asked nervously.

"A fire breather. A steamer. A smoker. All are dangerous. But all I have to do is meet their gaze."

"I do not like this at all," Mitch said.

"Just keep moving," Pewter said. "We can't retreat."

They kept moving. The dragons kept coming. They were flying in a line, aiming for the crossing party.

Kandy saw Astrid turn her head as she walked, focusing.

The first dragon emitted a jet of fire, then veered crazily and plunged into the void below. Soon they heard the crash and explosion as it struck the ground. A plume of debris flew up and spread. Astrid had scored.

The second dragon swelled like a blimp, then popped like a punctured balloon, its steam forming a swirling cloud as it too dropped below. Two down.

The third dragon shook in the air, but was too close; it collided with Astrid as smoke burgeoned explosively. It was done for, but like a suicide bomber, it had taken out its object.

Astrid screamed as she dropped out of the expanding ball of smoke and plummeted toward the ground.

Kandy was not conscious of even thinking about it before she acted. FORNAX!

The scene froze, the four people in mid stride, the ball of smoke in mid expansion, and Astrid below it, all in a fixed tableau. *Yes, Kandy.*

SAVE ASTRID AND I WILL BE YOUR REPRESENTATIVE IN XANTH.

Done.

Then the action resumed. Astrid continued to fall, but now there was a new figure in the air. A giant roc bird appeared. It swooped down, caught Astrid with a talon, circled, climbing, and deposited her back on the invisible bridge.

"Oh!" she said. "Thank you, Roxanne."

The bird squawked and departed. The line halted as the others stared. This rescue had been yea close to unbelievable.

"Roxanne?" Mitch asked.

"She mind talked to me as we flew," Astrid said. "She is Roxanne Roc, who was and may still be the guardian of Sim Bird, the son of the Simurgh.

It is his duty to learn everything in the universe, and he's working on it, with Che Centaur tutoring him; he's a very smart bird. Roxanne protects him and ferries him from place to place. She spent five hundred years egg-sitting for the Simurgh until Sim hatched, so she's experienced. She was flying past on routine business when she spied me falling. She recognized me as a land monster and rescued me, as she is a winged monster herself. It was a courtesy call, really. I am fortunate that Roxanne was in the vicinity; otherwise I would not have fared well."

"Fortunate is not the applicable term," Pewter said. "That was beyond coincidence."

"Actually I saw the roc and sent her a thought," Ease said. "That Mitch relayed. She was glad to oblige."

Had they done that? Kandy had been too distracted to prompt him.

"Still beyond coincidence," Pewter said. "Roxanne is a busy bird; she does not have slack time."

"She saved Astrid," Tiara said. "Why should we question it?"

"Because if there is magic involvement, we could be in trouble."

"What trouble?"

"Demon trouble."

"What are you talking about?" Ease asked. "There's no Demon here."

Then the tableau froze again. A donkey-headed dragon appeared, floating in the air beside the bridge. "What happened here?"

"Demon Xanth," Pewter said. "We hope we can explain."

"I smell an alien," Xanth said. "Fornax. She intervened here."

Uh-oh. She *had* intervened, and that was a Demon no-no here in Xanth's territory.

Kandy sent a signal the put Ease to sleep. He sagged between the rails. Kandy manifested. "I did it," she said.

The donkey head oriented on her. "You?"

"My friend Astrid was falling to her likely death. I had to save her. I appealed to Fornax. I agreed to be her emissary here in Xanth if she saved Astrid."

Astrid looked at her, startled. "You did that?"

"I had to. You're my friend, Astrid. I love you. I couldn't let you die."

"But Kandy, you put yourself in peril!"

"I had to," she repeated.

"Clarify," the donkey said.

"Fornax is contra-terrene, CT, antimatter, whatever. She has trouble interacting with terrene Demons," Kandy said. "And she needs to, to contest for Points. So she needs an interface, someone who won't go up in total conversion of matter to energy the moment she touches anything terrene. So she asked me to be her representative here in Xanth, to receive her thoughts and relay them to you when the occasion requires it. Nothing to harm the Land of Xanth or anyone or anything in it. Merely to be a mode of communication. I told her I would think about it. But then when Astrid was falling I had no time to consider. I called Fornax and told her I would do it if she saved my friend. And she saved her. I was the one at fault; Fornax did not come until I called her, and she did only what I asked her to do. She did not interfere in Xanth in any other way."

"This is interesting."

"Now, as my first act of representation, I am pleading with you to accept this role for me. I believe it is a necessary thing that someone has to do, if not me, than someone else. You may not care about me or Fornax, but this is a convenience you should have. For one thing, it will keep Fornax from messing with Xanth just to get your attention. You will not have to deal directly with her at all, just me. That should simplify things for you."

"Done," Xanth said, and vanished.

But then he reappeared. "My mortal wife says I need to do you a small favor or two in return for your sacrifice and service. She must be humored. Accordingly, I will." He vanished again.

A small favor? Or two? For a Demon that could be anything from a matchstick to a world, immediately or in a century. "Thank you," Kandy said, relieved mainly that her role had been accepted, and that Fornax was not in trouble for her part.

"Well done," Pewter said. "Now please let us complete our crossing before the rogue cloud gets here."

Kandy sent a wake-up thought to Ease. He woke, and she became the board. The group resumed the crossing without further comment, and reached the other side just before Fracto got there. The cloud raged, but then blew over.

"You know, I had the funniest daydream," Ease said.

"It was real," Astrid said. "Roxanne Roc rescued me after you sent her a thought."

"That, too. It was weird. I think Fornax sent me the notion, so Mitch could send it on. But I also dreamed that my dream girl was here. She—"

"We know nothing about that," Pewter said gruffly. "If she's a nymph, she can visit your dreams at any time."

Ease let it go, satisfied that the others didn't believe him.

But that night, when Ease's sleep was natural, Astrid came to Kandy. "What you did—"

"What else could I do? I'm your friend."

"You certainly are! Hold your breath; I'm going to kiss you."

Kandy dutifully held her breath, and Astrid kissed her. Then the ordinary routine of the night commenced.

CHAPTER 16:
HAIR

In the morning they tried a sequin again, sure that it would work. It didn't. It connected to the dress, but nothing happened.

"We *can't* be incomplete on the Event," Tiara wailed.

"There must be something else," Mitch said. "This is a different kind of balk from before. Before, the sequins would not connect at all."

"Let's think of reasons," Astrid said. "Maybe we can figure it out."

"Maybe the dress is tired of having the same person do the sequins," Tiara said, looking guilty.

"Then let me try," Ease said. He squatted and removed a sequin. The dress became translucent, showing panties, and he promptly freaked out.

Pewter took the sequin from his hand and connected it. The dress went opaque, but the scene did not change. "It does not seem to be that."

Astrid snapped her fingers, and Ease revived. "Nothing happened," he said.

"What reason do you suggest?" Pewter asked him.

"Maybe they got wet too often and shorted out."

"They worked after the Troll cave and the Island."

Ease shrugged. "Not that, then."

"Could there have been a time limit, and we are now past it?" Astrid asked.

"Possibly, but there has been no indication of such a limit," Pewter said.

"How many sequins are there on the dress?" Mitch asked.

"Fourteen," Astrid answered.

"And how many Events have we triggered?"

They considered and came up with the answer: fourteen.

"So maybe we have used up all the Events."

"But we have not completed our Quest!" Astrid protested.

"I am thinking of something," Pewter said. "But it is unkind."

"Out with it, machine," Astrid said.

"It is that our last event related in the end to the Demoness Fornax. Is it possible that she provided the dress and sequins to the Good Magician for the purpose of locating a representative, and once that was accomplished, she let the magic fade?"

Astrid looked stricken. "It certainly is possible! The dress got in the pile by accident, we thought, but I was strangely attracted to it and insisted on wearing it. Then it took us to Alpha Centuri where Fornax was, and to Galaxy Fornax itself. Then it put me in such danger that—somebody—had to intercede by giving the Demoness what she wanted."

"What are you talking about?" Ease asked.

Astrid smiled. "Your dream girl."

Ease shut up, thinking he was being mocked.

"And, its purpose completed, it turned off," Pewter said. "Does this make sense to the rest of you?"

The others nodded. "It is the way Demons work, it seems," Astrid said. "All that is left is the translucence magic, which may be a property of the dress rather than the sequins."

"So now, it seems, we are on our own," Mitch said. "We thought the sequins were helping us with our Quest, but they had another agenda. But we still do have our mission, and should pursue it to the end. So what now?"

"Look," Ease said. "I don't know or care about this business of someone making a deal with Fornax. All we know is that we have to merge the hair, and that the man who made the Virus has descendants. So why doesn't Pewter key in his data banks and figure out where they are? We can maybe get what we need from them."

"I lack that information," Pewter said.

"Well, look anyway."

Pewter looked, humoring him. "Amazing! I found an overlooked data file that has the information. Those descendants live in the South Village."

"Maybe a Demon added it," Tiara said. "So we'll stop being a nuisance."

"That is possible," Pewter agreed.

"So now we trek to the South Village," Ease said. "There'll be an enchanted path."

"Connecting to the invisible bridge," Mitch agreed. "In fact we are on it now."

They started walking. There were road signs at each intersection of paths, identifying where they went, and South Village was one destination. They were on their way.

That night they camped at a legitimate campsite, one guaranteed to have no untoward elements. The girls went to one section of the local pond, suddenly shy about exposure, and the men went to another. There was a hot furnace bush to dry their washed clothing, and plenty of pies and drinks. Then they retired, Mitch and Tiara taking one cabin, the others taking another. All of them seemed far more relaxed than they had been before.

Before the three settled down, another person arrived. This was a gruffly handsome young man with red hair and a ruddy complexion, who wore dark glasses similar to Astrid's. "Excuse me—is there room for one more?"

"Sure," Ease said. "Who are you?"

"I go by the nickname Art, because I am an aspiring artist. I like to paint pretty women. Unfortunately I tend to fall in love with them, and they don't like that, so I can't keep a good model long. My talent is not useful to others."

Ease, Pewter, and Astrid introduced themselves. "We are on a quest to save the puns," Ease said.

"I don't care about puns one way or the other," Art said. His covered gaze fixed on Astrid. "Perhaps I misheard. Did you say you were a basilisk? You certainly don't look like one."

"I am one," Astrid said. "As you would know if you got close to me. I exude poison."

"Oh, my!"

"Yes, it does make social relations awkward," she said sadly.

"Not at all. I got a sudden mysterious notion to come here at this time. That must have been the finger of fate, because it is highly appropriate."

"I don't understand."

"You are the most beautiful woman I have seen. The kind I would love to paint."

Astrid shook her head. "But you wouldn't want to fall in love with me."

"Ah, but I would."

"Would?"

"You see, my talent is to be immune to poison."

Astrid seemed to glow. "Including basilisk poison?"

"Yes." Then he reconsidered. "Actually I would not care to exchange gazes with a basilisk. That's not poison, that's death, and my gaze would not do you any good either. My talent seems to concentrate in my eyes; they are cyan colored. So I am cyan eyed."

"Cyanide," Pewter said, getting it.

"Others tend to become suicidal when they see my eyes, so I keep them covered. But I don't need my model to look at me while I'm painting her; I merely need to look at her. But the rest of your ambiance would not affect me."

"I find this difficult to believe."

"I will be delighted to prove it. Leave your glasses on, and I will leave mine; I understand why you wear them. Come embrace me and kiss me."

Astrid stood, but hesitated. "I do this cautiously, because my ambiance first intoxicates, then kills. It is merely somewhat slower than my glance."

Art crossed to her, enfolded her in his arms, and kissed her passionately. A heart floated up.

He broke the kiss but not the embrace. "I can do this as long as you can."

"You are not suffering?"

"I am suffering the pang of dawning love."

She was not convinced. "I will breathe. Smell my breath."

"Gladly."

She breathed. He inhaled her breath. "I love your perfume."

"Let me think about this. Paint me." Astrid disengaged, then shrugged out of her dress. She removed her bra and panties and sat cross-legged on a cushion. Kandy was struck again by how shapely she was.

Art produced an easel they had not noticed before, set up a canvas—ditto—and a palette with paint. He took a brush and started painting. "I am a slow worker. Let me know when you tire of the pose, lovely creature."

"I think I will never tire of this," Astrid said seriously.

Ease walked behind Art to look at the forming painting. That enabled Kandy to see it too. It was hardly started, but looked competent. The man really was an artist, and he really was immune to Astrid's ambiance. What a coincidence that he should appear here like this.

Then it hit her. It was no coincidence. It was Demon Xanth's gift! Or one of them.

Her thought was so strong that Astrid picked it up. "The gift!" she echoed. "But this is to me, not—"

Pewter caught on. "The gift is to your friend, whose second fondest wish is for you to achieve your ambition. Possibly that is half of it, and the other half will be for herself. I sense that only one gift has been activated."

"What friend?" Ease asked.

"Astrid has an anonymous friend," Pewter said. "She is being rewarded for a favor she did the Demon Xanth."

"I know nothing about this," Ease said.

"True. But I do."

Art, painting, paused. "I am as baffled as Ease is. But I presume it is not my business."

"That depends," Pewter said. "You will need to accompany us, because Astrid will not leave her friend. This will not interfere with your life or your painting."

"What friend?" Ease repeated.

"I think I would be glad to accompany Astrid anywhere," Art said. "In fact—"

"I have thought about it," Astrid said. "There is one more thing I need to know before I can make an informed decision. Please, men, may I be alone with Art for a while?"

"What's going on?" Ease asked querulously.

Pewter took him by the arm. "I will explain it as we explore the premises." They left the pavilion.

"I still don't get it," Ease said outside.

"She wants to make love to him," Pewter said. "If he survives that, literally, she will marry him."

"Oh. But marriage—that's pretty sudden."

"Sudden happens, in Xanth, as it did with Mexine Mermaid and Dr. Moribund, and with Frank and Maddy. Didn't you see that heart when they kissed?"

"Yeah," Ease agreed. "I wish I could find someone like that."

"I suspect that once the quest is complete, you will. She will manifest and you will love her instantly."

"Yeah, sure."

Again Kandy wondered. Pewter was good at analyzing things, but so far they had found no way to nullify the spell on her. What was Pewter thinking of?

They circled the premises in a leisurely manner and returned. "May we come in?" Pewter called.

"Come in!" Astrid called back. She was sitting, still nude and almost glowing.

But Art was lying on the floor, unconscious, still with his dark glasses on and not much else. Oh, no!

Astrid laughed. "Do not be concerned. I did not poison him. I put him to sleep the conventional way, as a woman does with a man. It was wonderful! We will keep company for a suitable time, then marry."

"The conventional way?" Ease asked.

"You will discover that in due course," Pewter said.

Kandy understood. After a couple made love, the man typically rolled over and went to sleep. Some women could put their men down in minutes, even seconds. Astrid had verified that she could do that without hurting her lover.

Art woke. "Oh, sorry. I must have nodded off."

Astrid leaned down and kissed him. "It happens, dear."

Kandy was thoroughly gratified. Xanth had come through, giving her the gift she most wanted. Except for her own situation: to recover her own body while Ease remained awake. Pewter evidently believed that this would happen when the quest was complete. Yet again she wondered: how could he be sure? They still did not know how merging anyone's hair would evoke the pun virus antidote. All she could do was hope that it happened.

Soon.

Art and Astrid spent the night together, of course; their love was instant and complete. That left Pewter, who hardly cared, and Ease, who was vaguely frustrated. Soon Kandy put him out of his misery, making him sleep. She regretted that she couldn't do it the conventional way.

She manifested, and Pewter came over to play chess. "That was a nice thing you did for Astrid," he said.

"You helped. You took Ease for a walk so Astrid and Art could explore their love unimpeded."

"I have been learning how to be human. It does not come naturally, but observing humans in action helps. But I referred to the deal you made with Fornax to save Astrid. You had not yet made up your mind about Fornax, but the moment Astrid was in trouble, you committed. That is something I have not understood, but I think I am beginning to."

"Friendship," she said. "When a friend needs you, you don't think about it, you do what you can to help."

"Is that a form of love?"

"Yes."

"I would like to kiss you."

Kandy was so startled she knocked over a chess piece. "What?"

"I see I am still too much the machine. I mean that the nuances of friendship and love are foreign to me, but I will not regard my participation in this mission as complete until I have at least a partial comprehension of them. That is one reason I elected to join the Quest."

"To observe live people in action?"

"Yes. My significant other companion is Com Passion, who resembles me but with far more feeling. She tells me that if we are to have a truly satisfactory relationship I must learn some feeling too, because as a pure machine I am simply too dull. So I have been observing and trying to understand. But it is not enough. I have seen the hearts when men and women kiss, and I have seen what friends will do for friends. I doubt the others would understand, but I hope you do. I would like to experience a kiss."

Kandy considered, touched. "You know there will never be anything romantic between the two of us, but friendship is possible. I appreciate the way you caught up my board on the Island so that I would not be lost."

"I believed that Ease would need you to enable him to escape captivity. You are an effective weapon."

She gazed at him evenly. "Is that all?"

His gaze dropped. "No. I have observed the friendship between you and Astrid. I would like to have a similar friendship between the two of us. That would bring me one step closer to humanity."

"If my board were thrown into a fire and no one else could help, what would you do?"

"I would temporarily freeze the fire so I could fetch you out of it."

"But what of the virus? You can't change spot reality without interrupting the firewall."

"I would have to risk it."

"You would risk your own extinction to save me?"

Pewter looked embarrassed. "I would hope you do not bruit that about. I know it is not logical."

"It is not logical," Kandy agreed. "It is friendship."

Pewter gazed at her. "I appreciate that insight. Perhaps I am learning it."

Kandy set Ease's hand on her ankle and stood. "Now I will kiss you."

"I do not see the logic in that at this point. You have already clarified the nature of friendship."

"The kiss will establish that we are not romantic but are friends." She opened her arms.

Pewter did not argue further. He came to her and stood somewhat awkwardly. "Should I embrace you?"

"Yes."

He put his arms about her body.

"Now bring your face close to mine."

He did so, still awkward.

She took his head in her hands and brought his face to hers. "Firm your lips." She kissed him as passionately as it was possible for a non-lover to do. She felt his android body softening in some respects and hardening in others as the kiss impacted him. Then she lifted his face away from hers. "Are there any hearts?"

"I see none. Merely a fleeting planet or two."

"So we are not lovers. But we are friends."

He looked confused. "Yet there is such power in your kiss that I suspect that if you wished it, you could—" He broke off, shaking his head.

"Seduce you?"

"Yes. I know it is not logical."

"Logic is not part of this particular interaction. I will not seduce you because you are my friend."

He nodded. "The way Astrid does not use her death gaze on the other members of the Quest. Because they are her friends."

"Exactly. Friends use their powers *for* friends, not *on* them."

"That is logical," he agreed, brightening.

"Now let's return to our chess game."

"Yes. But thank you."

"You're welcome, friend."

"One other thing," Pewter said as they played. "It is in the nature of spells involving a person sleeping or being transformed that they are best resolved by an interested party who does not know their nature."

"You are saying that Ease needs to catch on to my nature for himself, and not be prompted by anyone else, including me?"

"Yes. Interference tends to foul them up, leading to unfortunate outcomes."

"And Ease is clueless in this respect."

"Yet if he should catch on, he should be able to abate the spell."

"I will be patient," Kandy said. "Miserable, but patient." Actually she had been proceeding on this assumption all along.

Before the game was finished, Astrid and Art appeared. "Between bouts of whatever, I have been telling Art about my friend," Astrid said. "I want him to meet you, Kandy."

Art stared. "It is hard to tell in the gloom, but you look almost as pretty as Astrid."

"Almost," Kandy agreed with a smile.

"I would like to paint you."

"Why not? Astrid and I will be traveling together, after the quest is done, one way or another."

"There are different ways?"

"By day I am a board," Kandy said. "If I remain so, Astrid and I will associate mostly by night. If I find a way to break the spell on me, then I will revert to normal, and we will associate by day. Either way, you may paint me if you wish, by night or day, provided Astrid agrees."

"Oh yes!" Astrid said.

"But I will not fall in love with you," he said. "Astrid governs my heart."

"Of course," Kandy agreed. "I will pose for you as a friend."

"A friend," Pewter echoed, appreciating the distinction.

"Astrid tells me that you are her best friend," Art said.

Kandy smiled. "And she is mine."

"Do you play chess?" Pewter asked Art.

"I do."

"Then we shall get along."

Art and Astrid departed. "Friendship seems as complicated to fathom as chess," Pewter said, "but I believe I am getting it."

"As I am getting chess," Kandy agreed.

In the morning the group resumed the walk, with one added member. They harvested sugar canes from the camp garden and used them to steady their walking, knowing they could be eaten later. Tiara also found a honey comb and used it to fasten down her floating hair. So Mitch took another for his hair.

"You folk have interesting hair," Art remarked.

"The only thing we know about the resolution of our Quest is to merge the hair," Mitch said. "So we are ready to do that when we understand how."

They came to a fork in the path, but there was no sign. "How do know which one leads to the South Village?" Ease asked.

A pair of donkeys was grazing nearby. One lifted his head and spoke. "Take the right one, of course."

"What are you?" Ease demanded.

"I'm a smart ass. What did you think, board wielder?"

"I should have known," Ease said. "What about your friend here. Does he know?"

The other donkey lifted a front leg and pointed to the right fork. "He's the dumb ass," the smart ass explained. "He knows things but can't talk, so he pantomimes."

"And he is pointing to the right path," Ease said.

"Obviously not the left path," the smart ass agreed.

Kandy was sure she was not the only one annoyed by the donkey.

They took the right fork, hoping that it was indeed the correct one.

Soon they came to a pasture with several cows grazing. There was an elaborate bow formed of a vine hanging on the fence. Nearby were several curved sticks.

"I get it," Mitch said. "That's a bow vine, in case we go in for archery."

"Obviously the pun virus has not struck here yet," Tiara said.

Then the bow shriveled and fell writhing to the ground. "It just did," Mitch said grimly.

"Then why aren't my eyes hurting?" Art asked. "They're a pun."

"Our friend Pewter maintains a firewall that prevents the virus from reaching us," Astrid said. "Now you will have to stay close, at least until we manage to nullify the virus."

"And thereafter," Art said, squeezing her hand. "But I admit this helps; I was afraid that when the pun virus caught me I would go blind."

"I would love you anyway. But I would give my own eyesight rather than have you lose your ability to paint."

"I would not take it."

"But if you could not paint—"

"Last night painting became my second love."

Then they saw a sign: SOUTH VILLAGE EXIT.

"It was the right path!" Tiara exclaimed, gratified. "So the asses weren't so asinine after all."

"Now all we need to do is find the Magician's grandchildren," Mitch said.

They paused to survey the South Village. It seemed quite typical, consisting of a cluster of thatched cottages with a street meandering from one to another, somehow managing to connect all of them without recrossing itself. But the pun virus had passed, leaving rotten puns in the surrounding fields.

"This does not look promising for the source of the anti pun virus," Mitch muttered.

"It is not the source, merely the access to the portal that will access the antidote," Pewter reminded him.

"Ah, yes. But even when we find them, how will we know them?"

"They are five maidens with wonderful hair," Ease said. "Fornax told me."

"Fornax! Can that be trusted?"

YES Kandy thought. Because she had agreed to represent the Demoness, she was sure she would not be given false information.

"Yes," Ease said.

"How can you be sure?"

"Fornax took the form of my dream girl. My dream girl would never lie to me."

A look circled, avoiding Ease. But it died out unclaimed. No one cared to challenge that reasoning openly. For one thing it would likely lead to the violation of their tacit agreement to let Kandy remain unknown until she chose to reveal herself, or somehow broke the board spell.

"Five maidens," Mitch said. "And of course the hair counts."

"What's this about coffeemaking?" a voice inquired.

"About what?" Mitch asked.

"Java, beverage, drink, potable, hairy—"

"Coiffure?"

"Whatever," the voice said crossly as Tiara's wild hair smoothed out. "Since when did hair start counting?"

"Welcome back, Metria," Mitch said dryly. "We missed you."

"Well, you folk were getting dull, and I didn't like the pea soup fog. But then I got caught by the virus, and my two alter egos are gone. I miss them. D Mentia's got most of our common sense, and Woe Betide has our beguiling innocence. So I thought I'd better come goose you loafers into completing your Quest."

"It's so nice to have a benign motive."

"Thank you."

"You can help," Astrid said. "We are looking for five maidens with wonderful hair."

"I will appraisal."

"You will what?" Tiara asked.

"Bill of exchange, assay, draft, certified—"

"Check?"

"Whatever." Tiara's hair floated as the demoness departed.

"I'm sorry about Mentia," Ease said. "She was nice."

Kandy knew that what he meant was sexy.

"We'll just have to hope that she and Woe Betide return once we nullify the virus," Mitch said. "They're really partial puns, so may not have been destroyed completely."

Metria returned. "They're in a big old house on a private estate south of the village, quarreling as usual."

"Quarreling?" Mitch asked.

"Seems they have five different personalities. They don't get along well."

"Show the way," Mitch said.

Tiara's hair pointed to the village.

They walked that way, ignored by the populace. The recent arrival of the virus evidently preempted the villagers' attention.

There was an intersection in the center of the village. Tiara's hair pointed south. They walked south. There was the estate, which surely had been attractive before the virus wiped out many of its ornamental plants. They went to the front door of the ancient mansion. Mitch knocked.

The door opened. "Well look at that!" a brown-haired girl exclaimed. "A man with hair!"

Four other girls quickly clustered at the door. Their hair was black, red, yellow, and light blue, all of it tightly braided and tied back. That seemed a shame to Kandy, because loose it would be waist length and beautiful. "OoOoo!" they chorused. "Which one of us gets him first?"

"Be practical," the black haired girl snapped. "He obviously has some other purpose, because there are already two pretty girls in his party."

"Awwww," the others moaned.

Black was evidently the practical one. She eyed Mitch in a seductively challenging manner. "What can we do for you, handsome?"

"My name is Mitch. My companions and I are looking for the grandchildren of a long-ago Magician who—"

"That's us," Black said. "Come in, all of you."

Soon they were ensconced in the capacious family room of the mansion, with the five young women spaced evenly around, as if each needed her own personal space. "So that's why we're here," Mitch concluded. "Do you have the access to the antidote?"

"We know nothing about it," Black said. She wore a black outfit, matching her hair. "We know the story, of course, but it's just a story. Whatever secret our Sorceress grandmother had is long since lost."

"It has to be here, somewhere," Mitch said. "The Good Magician would not be wrong about that."

Brown made an expansive gesture. "You are welcome to explore the mansion. It has half a myriad rooms we don't even use." She wore a warm brown fur dress, matching her hair. "But I don't think you will find it there." She smiled. "On the other hand, if you are looking for friendly companionship with benefits, we have plenty." She took a deep breath, and the top brown edge of her décolletage parted to reveal nice double curvature.

"He's taken," Tiara snapped.

"You have a temper," Red said. "I like that." Her dress was the same shade of red as her hair. Apart from that she looked very similar to her sisters. In fact, Kandy realized, if the five were to dress the same and cover their hair, they would be almost indistinguishable.

"We have a prediction of our own," Blue said. "It is that someday a Quest will happen by and solve our problem. But it has never happened, and you folk do not seem to relate. We are disappointed."

"We have only one hint," Pewter said. "That is 'Merge the hair.' Does that make sense to you?"

"Horrible sense," Blue said glumly. Her mood evidently matched her blue dress. "But it's disaster."

"Disaster?"

"Our hair is constantly trying to merge. It gets all tangled and is awful to get free. That's why we stay clear of each other."

"Why haven't you separated and gone out to make your individual ways in Xanth?" Mitch asked. "You are all attractive young women; you could surely interest men."

"Oh, we couldn't leave each other!" Yellow said. "We fight constantly, but we're sisters. We hurt when we're too far apart. We have to be together." She seemed to be the shy one, but this was important to her.

"And men are not interested in the company of several women at once," Blue said. "Not in any polite way. It's depressing."

"I would be," Ease said.

Red looked at him. "For more than ten minutes?"

"Well, no. Then I'd want to sleep."

"And only one woman would be satisfied."

Mitch did not argue that case. "May we see a sample of how your hair behaves? Because it seems to tie in with our clue."

"Why not," Black said, unbinding her dark hair. It was indeed waist length. "We'll show you just enough." She glanced around. "Any volunteers?"

"Oh, I'll do it, you bleep," Red said combatively. She stood and approached Black, who stood to meet her. As she walked she undid her own hair.

As they approached, their hair seemed to take on a life of its own. It crossed their shoulders and reached forward. They stopped, facing each other, but their hair didn't; it extended like pseudopods, the black meeting the red and twining around it. In a moment their hair was thoroughly tangled together.

The two women drew apart, slowly. Their hair did not let go. Their heads were tied together by the locked locks. "See?" Black asked. "This happens whenever any two of us come within range. It's been that way since childhood. We have learned to keep our hair bound, and to stay clear of each other."

"So we can't be together, and we can't be apart," Red said. "It is infuriating."

The two women brought up their hands and started pulling strands of hair clear, carefully. It did not want to come, but they knew what they were doing, and got it free, strand by strand. In due course they had it clear, and quickly rebound their hair to keep it under control.

"It does seem to want to merge," Mitch said. "I wonder: could I stand with one of you? I have very long hair."

"Why not," Brown said. "I haven't had a good hair-pulling encounter in a while." She stood and unbound her hair.

Tiara looked as if she wanted to protest, but Astrid signaled her to stifle it. They needed to know just how far the hair magic went.

Mitch pulled off his shirt and shook his hair into a large mass. When he trained it straight down his back it fell to his knees.

"Oh, lovely," Brown breathed warmly. "I'd adore tangling with that."

Tiara opened her mouth, but Astrid cautioned her again.

Brown and Mitch went to stand before each other. The hair on both their heads remained quiescent. Mitch caught a hank and brought it toward Brown's tresses. Still no reaction. He caught a lock of hers and laid it across a lock of his. Nothing.

"Apparently not," he said. But of course my hair is not magic, merely long and voluminous." He glanced at Tiara. "Dear? Your hair is magic."

Tiara jumped up. "This should be interesting," her hair said.

Brown stared. "It talks!"

Tiara smiled. "No. There's a demoness nesting it in, keeping it straight. Metria, can you vacate for a moment? We need to see if magic hair attracts magic hair."

"Very well," the hair said sulkily. Mist emerged from it, forming a small cloud that floated away.

Now Tiara's hair strained upward, trying to float off her head. She approached Brown as Mitch retreated from her. But her hair showed no interest in Brown's hair, or vice versa. Magic wasn't the answer either, at least not in this manner.

"Thank you," Mitch said, quickly weaving his hair back into a shirt. "Now we know that your hair seeks only the hair of your sisters. It could be a broader aspect of that magic that prevents you from separating and seeking lives apart. It is definitely related to hair, but we don't know exactly how."

Black shook her head. "How can our tangling hair relate to your Search for the anti-pun elixir? I can't make sense of that."

"We are having difficulty seeing how our presence can solve your problem of hair and isolation," Pewter said. "Yet it does seem likely that there is a connection."

"So you suspect that we have been brought together for mutual reason?" Brown asked. "That the solution to one problem may also be the solution to the other?"

"In magical situations, which this is, that could well be the case," Pewter agreed.

"If only we could think of it," Blue said glumly.

Hair. Merging. Magic. The thoughts circled each other in Kandy's mind, threatening to collide. Then they did. MERGE THE HAIR! she thought.

"Merge the hair!" Ease echoed.

The five sisters were taken aback. "All of it? That would be an awful tangle."

Astrid looked at the board, knowing the source of Ease's notion. "Have you ever tried to do it all together?"

"Of course not!" Red snapped. "It would take us hours to get it all untangled, and we would be largely helpless until we did."

"Perhaps not," Pewter said. "There must be some reason that the hair seeks hair. But if the tangle is bad, we will be here to help you get it free."

"You are a Quest," Black said thoughtfully. "We do have a prophecy. We may regret it, but perhaps we should try it, if only to eliminate it from consideration in the future."

The others nodded. "What do we have to lose?" Brown asked rhetorically. "It was after all suggested by a handsome man."

So they had designs on Ease. That griped Kandy, but she was not in a position to protest.

The five sisters stood in a circle, safely distanced from each other. They unbound their hair. Then they stepped slowly toward the center of the circle.

Their hair came alive: black, brown, red, yellow, blue. It circled their heads, reaching forward in bands of color. The tips met in the center and intertwined, pulling the sisters forward. A big colorful knot formed, still drawing the women in. Their faces touched.

And merged.

Kandy was as shocked as the others. The five heads were merging into one, pulled by the hair. Then the necks, and the rest of their bodies. They were being drawn into a kind of hungry vortex, a globular mass of hair.

Had the sisters been thrown into some destructive storm? A black hole, from which there was no escape? Kandy and the others watched, appalled, as the bodies fed into the globular maw, leaving their dresses behind, until only their legs and feet remained. Then the feet disappeared too, leaving their shoes behind.

For a moment the ball of hair hung there, pulsing, emitting coruscations of color. Then it dissolved.

A woman stood there, nudely perfect, holding an urn. She looked much like any one of the sisters, except for her hair, which was a glittering array of colors. She was absolutely beautiful. The men, of course were mesmerized.

"Oh, I must paint that!" Art murmured.

"What, are you jilting me so soon?" Astrid asked.

"Never! You are my love. But a perfect woman must be painted."

Astrid nodded, satisfied. It was his nature to paint, and women were his prime subjects.

The phenomenal woman looked around. "I am whole at last," she said. "Thank you, Ease, for giving me the clue."

Ease was as amazed as the rest of them. "You are—all of them?"

"All of them," she agreed. "They were but fragments of me, condemned to living apart. You may call me Merge."

"But what of the pun virus antidote?" Astrid asked. "That is what we came for."

"Yes," Merge agreed. "This is the portal." She tilted the urn, and shining fluid poured out. It vaporized as it dropped, not striking the floor. "There is a planetful more where this is coming from. It will safely neutralize the virus."

"Just like that," Pewter said. "Our Quest is complete."

"All this time we thought the key hair might be mine or Tiara's," Mitch said ruefully. "We were wasting the time and effort of the Quest."

"But we value your support and companionship," Astrid said. "That is never a waste."

"I will travel Xanth, pouring out elixir wherever required," Merge said. "But I do not wish to do it alone. My former parts have never been away from the South Village. I would be eaten by the first hungry dragon I encountered. I need company and protection." She looked at Ease again. "You gave me the key. I owe my completion to you. Let me be your woman as we travel."

Oh, no! Kandy thought, horrified.

"Well," Ease said, interested. "I guess me and my board could protect you."

What irony! Kandy would wind up protecting the woman who took Ease from her. She couldn't even blame Merge, whose assessment made perfect sense and who didn't know about Kandy. Or Ease, who was a sucker for any pretty face and form, and Merge's were the prettiest; she would make him a wonderful wife. If only Kandy weren't stuck with being a board!

"You carry a board. I carry an urn. These are like male and female symbols."

Now she was a male symbol! Kandy felt humiliated.

"Yeah, I guess." But Ease's gaze remained locked on something other than the urn. If only Merge would put on some clothing!

The other members of the party stood silent, letting this play out as it would.

"Perhaps I can persuade you," Merge said. She held her urn carefully to the side and stepped into him. She kissed him. It was immediately apparent that however inexperienced she might be as a traveler, she was thoroughly competent in this respect. Kandy felt Ease's whole body responding to her touch. His knees weakened and he might have fallen had the firmness of the woman's contact not supported him.

Yet there was no orbiting heart. The kiss was perfect, but true passion was missing. Kandy clung to that faint hope. Would Ease know the difference?

Merge finished the kiss and stepped back, looking at him expectantly.

Ease steadied himself, recovering equilibrium. Then he spoke. "Merge, I can see that you are the perfect woman. You would make any man a fine wife, including me. The most sensible thing I could do would be to marry you and stay with you always." He took a breath and shook his head. "But you are not my dream girl. She is the only one I could ever love. So I can't be with you. I mean, I'll help you spread the anti-virus, because that's our mission, but I can't love you. I know this is crazy, because I can't even find my dream girl; maybe she doesn't exist except in my imagination. But that's the way it is."

"You are dumping me for an imaginary woman?" Merge demanded, her eyes flashing little multi-colored sparks.

"I guess so. I'm sorry."

"Well, I hope you find real satisfaction with your board," Merge said acidly.

"Yeah. My board's my best companion. It's always there when I need it."

He paused. "Except when my dream girl comes."

Nobody said a word.

"What happens to it when she comes?" he asked himself. "Why is it always there when she goes? Why have I never seen them together, even in my dreams?"

Silence.

Ease lifted the board before his face. He stared at it. "It's like it has two knothole eyes, and a crack for a mouth," he said, really looking at the board for the first time. "And there's sap at an eye, like a tear."

Oh yes, there was a tear. Would he catch on, or was she doomed?

He stood a moment more. "I think I've been a fool. I love you, board."

Then he brought the board to his face and kissed it on that mouth.

And the spell dissolved. Kandy manifested, in the midst of an ardent kiss. The spell had been broken. Like a sleeping beauty, she had been roused by the kiss of the right man, who truly desired her. At last.

After an eternal moment Kandy broke the kiss. She saw that their heads were surrounded by orbiting hearts. No more needed to be said. She realized that the wishing well had granted her wish for adventure and romance in perhaps the only way it could. And along the way she had gained so much more she had never even thought to wish for! Such as true friends, and—

The scene froze. One of the hearts assumed the form of Fornax's face, which was Kandy's own face, as the Demons assumed any form they chose. "And the position of liaison between Demons," Fornax said. "My communications to you will be of a preemptive nature; you will stop whatever you are doing at the moment and attend to them. In return for this occasional inconvenience, you will be safeguarded from all threats to your person, and will be granted a long and healthy life, in addition to Xanth's little gift."

"I understand," Kandy said. "Thank you, Demoness."

The scene unfroze. The hearts resumed their orbiting. Kandy remained in her clinch with Ease. Fornax was gone.

In the background Pewter spoke. "Ease is taken, Merge, as you can see. But your mission will still be facilitated, for it is also ours. You do not require a boyfriend at this stage; you need a protector. In your presence, with the pun virus antidote elixir, I will be able to relax my firewall and practice my normal magic. I can protect you from virtually any threat simply by changing local reality. I can make a hostile dragon friendly, or change vicious nickelpedes into half as many innocuous dimeopedes, or render a dangerous river placid, at least in our immediate vicinity. It will be good to exercise my powers again. agreed.

"We'll travel together, as a group, as friends," Astrid said. "Completing our mission. I will help protect you from any unkind monsters."

"And I will have four lovely ladies to paint," Art said. "Tiara, Astrid, Merge, and Kandy."

"Five," Tiara's hair said. The demoness Metria formed, assuming the likeness of a splendidly buxom creature. "This promises to be interesting."

"Five," he agreed, thrilled.

Ease finally spoke. "But I sort of liked my board. It served me well. I wish I could have it too."

Then Kandy felt her power. It was the other part of Xanth's gift. "You will have both. Now I can change at will. That will enable me to rest while you carry me on long dull hikes. But I'll always be your dream girl when you want me, by night or day." She paused, considering. "And if you annoy me, I will do this." She kissed him again, and in the middle of it became the board.

The others laughed. It was bound to be a pleasant tour.

AUTHOR'S NOTE

Every novel I write is a personal adventure as well as a fictive one, and each has its own special identity, like a person. This one is special in that it completes the alphabet in Xanth novels, from *Air Apparent* to *Zombie Lover*, with some duplications along the way. The first Xanth novel was *A Spell for Chameleon*, published in 1977, which I thought would be a singleton. I had no idea then that the Xanth series would make me halfway famous as a writer, and put me on the bestseller lists. The fifth one, *Ogre, Ogre,* published in OctOgre 1982, may have been the first original paperback fantasy novel by any author to make the NEW YORK TIMES bestseller list. Have I mentioned the story behind that? I was accused of being an ogre at fan conventions, when I had never even attended a convention. One of my problems with fandom is that it is not too concerned about truth. So I made an ogre the hero of the next Xanth novel I wrote. Stupid, no? But ogres are justifiably proud of their stupidity. And that one put me on the map. Now they can call me an ogre if they like; ogres are not bad folk when you get to know them. At this writing I am 78 years old; I think I have earned the right to be ogrish on occasion, though I have attended many conventions since and never been that way there. Visit my website if you wish, at www.HiPiers.com, where I do a monthly blog-type column and maintain an ongoing survey of electronic publishers for the benefit of aspiring writers. I was one of those myself, once upon a time; I know how rough it can be.

I wrote this novel in the months of SapTimber, OctOgre, and NoRemember, 2012. Those are ogre months, of course, reflecting the legendary violence and mental weakness of the species. As it happened, I got a new computer system and moved to it the first of OctOgre, which required some adjustment, because things didn't happen quite the same way. You can't fix a balky computer by bashing it into smithereens. Com Pewter is of course a parody of the mundane computer, often unfeeling and perverse. Getting along with a computer is like getting along with the opposite gender: can't live with it, can't live without it. I use a free open-source Linux system, which is why I can get away with parodying MacroHard Doors, with Fedora, KDE and LibreOffice. They're not perfect, and they do glitch on occasion, but I like them very well. Then along came Hurricane Sandy, which devastated northeastern America. Then came the Presidential election. I live in Florida, so naturally the fouled up Florida election tally was not complete until four days after the election. Xanth is based on Florida, only with magic added; you can see that it is needed. You can see it in the place names: the friendly Kiss Mee River, which feeds into Lake Ogre-Chobee. The Ogre-fen-Ogre Fen to the north. I live near the With-a-Cookee River in the central area, by Lake Tsoda Popka. No, Lake Tsala Apopka in Florida does not have soft drink water, and cookies do not grow beside the Withlacoochee River, alas.

Sometimes the local news inspires episodes. For example, in this period there was a macaque monkey loose in the city of St. Petersburg, Florida that the natives, that is, people, were hiding and feeding. He was pretty well making a monkey out of the wildlife authorities. Then one day he bit a woman, apparently because she was sunning herself instead of offering him food, and the resulting commotion located his position for the authorities. But how to catch him without hurting him? They tried putting food in cages, but he was too smart to fall for that. Then they put another monkey in a cage, and when he came close, they got him with an anesthetic dart. And I thought, suppose it was a man escaping an alien zoo, too savvy to fall for their tricks, and then they put out a cage with a young woman in it? That became the chapter "Zoo."

I had many suggestions for puns, character, and stories, and used what I could. I try to use a suggestion by a new fan before using a second one by an old fan.

I also try to maintain some balance. Would you believe, there are some readers who don't much like puns and ask me to use less of them—while making their own pun suggestions. I even lose some readers because they get pundigestion. So every Xanth novel is a compromise, and there are always puns left over. As it is, a number of notions I could make much more of have to be given incidental treatment; I simply can't do full justice to them all, to my regret. But some fans hardly know when to stop. Tim Bruening sent so many puns that I had to make a separate section for him in my list; that section is 1,500 words long. I told him that if I tried to use all his puns, I'd have to say that the novel was merely attached. Andrew Fine sent notions that became the bases for two chapters; in the credits I list only the basic notions, but he also filled in considerable detail, such as the centaur economic model, and the complete roster for the space voyage to Alpha. The most frustrating one was the idea that formed the original basis of this novel: that a virus destroy the puns of Xanth, so that they have to be saved, by heroic effort. I agreed it was a good idea, and this novel was born. But because that suggestion came long before I started writing the novel, I did not have it in my record, and was unable to credit it here. You'd think I'd have been smart enough to note the source at the time. Remember what I said about the intelligence of ogres? Sigh. Someone is going to be deservedly mad at me.

I'll start the credits with one so abysmal that it needs an explanation. That is the parachute gun that shoots parrots, in Chapter 9 when they face the challenges of the Pyramid Good Magician's Castle. It was conceived by a six year old boy who had recently immigrated from Europe and perhaps did not yet have the language straight. It is also the oldest suggestion I have processed, as it dates from about 1940. Right: that was me. As you can see, advancing age did not reform me much.

Board Stiff title—Joshua Harrelson. Irrelevant Kandy—Aimee Van den Broeke. Irrelephant—Logan Anonymous. Ease, makes things easy—John Smith, mentioned in *Knot Gneiss*. Absorb magic, then play it back—Brant Tucker. Emulate animalistic ability—Bear Rollins. Talent of taking the shortest distance between two points—Misty Zaebst. Cutless/Cutmore—Harli. Cherry Centaur—Heather Jordan. Navel Orange, Centaur society, dream space voyage, all-purpose flower—Andrew Fine. Sweet Tart, Bully-Proof Vest, Camouflage Panties—Cathy Donaldson. Fire Bed, bi-polar bear, salad bar, Sisters Apopto, Ba, Cri, Ellip, Gene, Neme, Sta—Isle of Flies, Isle of Bats, Isle of Conclusion, Key Board Island, assorted Miss puns, assorted Peas, pun musical instruments, bars, dances, Peace Tree Tea, scram bull, terns, app pill tree, Cough-Fee, the Great Pundemic, stork having 3 challenges, blue J, blue prince, Aqua Fur, Asteroid Belt, Dog Byte, strata gems, assorted Pens, musical head band, PLO, talent of conjuring any type of clothing, E S Pea, Pine trees, G Pea S, Pup-Pea, Butter Fingers, —Tim Bruening

Boot Hill, zombie undead not stupid, sleazeball, De-Ogre-Ant, grease monkey, Cave Canem, —Mary Rashford. A year thwarting other petitioners—

Matt Britt. Assorted Eggs: splore, plain, etc—Jennifer Nichols. In-Car-Nations—Kyle Woodruff. Zom Bees—Darrel Jones. Wira gets a baby—Liz Magnelli. Sequins of Events—Richard Lynch. Bull siblings—Brent Johnson. Messed up puns, Seeing through conspiracies—Caroline McLachian Darling. X-punge—Ken Kuhlman. The Book of Lost Answers, Orc chasm—Laura Kwon Anderson. The Elfabet—Alan Story. Penny for your thoughts—Tyger B Dacosta. Com Peter becomes an android—Alexander Jones. Fatherboard, Motherboard—Olivia Davis. Soul-R-Plexus—Naomi Blose. Rarity of unicorns—Louis Steiner. Tearable/Terrible idea—Anthony Keech. Summoning and sending ideas—Chris Mitchell. Con Template—Bonnie Lind. Ram pages, hand maiden, mangroves, Cyan-eyed—Kyle Bernelle. Porcu-Pine, Blood Hound, Lily Pad—Meredith Lemke. Punhibition—Sara Rodriquez. R U Dunn—Cecily A Dunn. Tea Tree reversed, Bow Vine—Eve Parker. Bunny the lowest form of rabbit—Buffalo Texan. Talent of reinventing the past, and reinventing the future—Nehemiah Lewrel. Talent of making any nonhuman creature a pet—Brittani Tichi. Moving forward a day to avoid sadness, Egg plant with special eggs— Kerry Garrigan. Canopy (can-o'-pea)—Kurtis Steggall. Rain Deer Sugar cane, Honey comb—Nicole Valicia Thompson-Anderson. Chemistree, Grong Grong—Travis Allen. Smart Ass, Dumb Ass—Steve Frazier.

Also a credit of another nature: for my proofreader, Rudy Reyes. As I put it, typos seem to grow on the page after I edit the novel, but he catches them.

There you have it. I suspect the story of this Quest is not yet finished, because there will be a considerable post-virus cleanup effort to be made, and Merge has not yet found a man to nab, um, I mean to love, and who knows what Demoness Fornax will be up to? But we'll see. And those of you who are totally tired of puns, remember that I do write non-Xanth novels where puns are rare. Look up my name on the OuterNet and you will surely find them.